BEST KEPT
SECRETS

BEST KEPT SECRETS

ROCHELLE ALERS

sepia

BET★ BOOKS

BET Publications, LLC
http://www.bet.com

SEPIA BOOKS are published by

BET Publications, LLC
c/o BET BOOKS
One BET Plaza
1900 W Place NE
Washington, DC 20018-1211

All Kensington Titles, Imprints, and Distributed Lines are available at special quantity discounts for bulk purchases for sales promotions, premiums, fund-raising, and educational or institutional use. Special book excerpts or customized printings can also be created to fit specific needs. For details, write or phone the office of the Kensington special sales manager: Kensington Publishing Corp., 850 Third Avenue, New York, NY 10022, attn: Special Sales Department, Phone: 1-800-221-2647.

ISBN 1-58314-670-9

First Trade Paperback Printing: January 2006
10 9 8 7 6 5 4 3 2 1

Printed in the United States of America

I dedicate *Best Kept Secrets* to all who wanted to know what happened before there was *Hideaway* and before there was *Vows*.

A man should fulfill his duty as a husband, and a woman should fulfill her duty as a wife, and each should satisfy the other's needs.

1 Corinthians 7:3
Good News Bible—Today's English Version

PART 1

1924

Marguerite-Josefina Isabel Diaz

The history of every country begins in the heart of a man or a woman

—Willa Cather

1

'Twas mercy brought me from my pagan land; taught my benighted soul to understand.

—Phillis Wheatley

Havana, Cuba—veintiuno de Octubre 1924

At the age of twenty-six, Samuel Claridge Cole was on a Portuguese tanker sailing for Havana harbor, following his heart. All he had was his name, a business proposal, and a bank draft for enough money to buy a sugarcane plantation in Artemisa, Cuba.

Oblivious of the twin smokestacks belching smoke, the minute black particles dotting his white linen suit, oblivious of the tropical sun beating down on his head, he stood calmly at the rail of the prewar ship instead of the sleek cruiser to which he'd been denied passage in Miami because of his race. He was determined that neither prejudice nor racial bigotry would dissuade him from his quest.

His mother had called him a dreamer, but his father's constant ridicule made him an overachiever. Before Charles would compliment him he'd say, *You won't never 'mount to nothin' because yo head is always up yo ass.* Samuel's sole mission was to prove Charles Cole wrong.

But his maternal grandmother believed in him, listened to his tales of grandeur, encouraged him to follow his heart, and depend on nobody but the goodness of the Creator.

His daddy hadn't lived long enough to witness his youngest son's success, but that no longer mattered because he didn't need Charles's approval.

He reached into a pocket of his trousers for the watch attached to a gold fob at his waist. It was after four o'clock—an hour later than his appointed time to meet his guide and interpreter.

Samuel returned the timepiece to his pocket and rested his arms on the railing, his gaze narrowing as the skyline of Havana grew larger. He was certain his guide would wait indefinitely for the *norteamericano* who would pay him more for a week of his services than he would earn in six months as a Havana taxi driver. A cynical smile lifted the corners of Samuel's mouth. Everyone had a price. That was something he'd learned as a soldier during the war.

Before peace had been declared and he found himself on a battleship sailing back to the States, Samuel had witnessed firsthand black marketeers selling everything from cigarettes, tins of food, and medical supplies, to shoes and wine. Some Frenchmen willingly bartered priceless heirloom pieces for a case of quality Bordeaux or Chardonnay.

Samuel learned more from the marketeers in three months than he'd learned in twelve years of instruction in a segregated Tallahassee, Florida, school system. Even though he didn't smoke or drink wine he'd managed to stockpile the much-sought-after products and trade them for a strand of perfectly matched pearls, a gaudy ruby and diamond broach, and a woman's ring with a large, flawless pale pink Australian diamond. After smuggling the jewels into the States, he sold them, using the proceeds to buy land to set up one of the first soybean farms in the South.

He knew he was taking a risk investing in Cuba, but he knew any attempt to set up a plantation within the United States would be viewed unfavorably by both whites and Negroes. His hope was to purchase either the Cuban sugarcane plantation or, if this proved futile, a banana plantation in Costa Rica.

Forty minutes later, Samuel disembarked from the tanker after dock officials had checked the captain's manifest and cargo, and it was another half hour before he was able to clear customs.

Samuel sat in the rear of a Ford Model T staring at the Spanish Colonial buildings as the driver increased his speed to twenty miles an hour along the Malecon, the seawall built in 1901 when the United States government controlled Cuba. Waves crashed over the wall, soaking cars and strollers alike.

"Are there many Americans living here?" Samuel asked.

Hernan Cruz nodded, but did not turn around. "Yes, Senor Cole. Too many," he added, wondering how the *norteamericano* would interpret his response. If Samuel Cole had been other than a Negro he would've lied to him.

"They come here," he continued in accented English, a language he'd learned while working in a Tampa cigar factory, "with their bossy attitudes yelling orders as if we were slaves."

Samuel rested the back of his head against the leather seat. "Although I've seen very little of your very beautiful country, I have no intention of living here."

Hernan glanced up into the rearview mirror. Samuel Cole was a *norteamericano* but could easily pass for a Cubano. His coloring and facial features reflected those of African ancestry throughout the Caribbean and the other Americas, the result of European slaveholders mixing their blood with their slaves.

"I am certain it would be different with you, Senor Cole."

Samuel lifted a thick, black eyebrow. "Why me?"

Hernan's gaze returned to the wet roadway. "You're not Anglo."

How right you are, Senor Morales, I am not Anglo, Samuel mused. He was a citizen of the United States—albeit a second-class citizen who'd risked his life fighting with the 369th Infantry, the first black U.S. combat overseas unit, a regiment that didn't lose a man, trench, or any ground, a regiment known to the Germans as the "Hell Fighters." He'd been one of 171 who'd earned a *croix de guerre* or a Legion of Merit, France's highest military medal. No U.S. medals of honor were awarded to any black troops.

He had been a black soldier, returning from World War I, and he refused to march at the back of a victory parade because a segregated parade seemed contradictory to the principles they'd supposedly fought for.

Closing his eyes, Samuel recalled the first time he'd killed another man—a German boy with peach-fuzz cheeks, a soldier whose uniform collar was too large for his scrawny neck, an enemy soldier who would've killed him if he hadn't bayoneted him first. It took days before he was able to erase the image of his sightless blue eyes staring up at the darkening sky, blood staining the front of his uniform, the distinctive sound of a death rattle. After his first kill, the others no longer mattered to Samuel. It was either kill or be killed, because he'd had no wish to die on foreign soil.

A wry smile twisted his mouth, but he did not open his eyes. He'd killed white men in Europe and had received a medal for his actions. But if he had killed a single white man in Florida he would've forfeited his life—with or without a trial.

A weighted fatigue swept over him as he sank deeper into the leather seat. He didn't know when the car increased its speed or when Hernan left the city of Havana, heading southwest. He slept soundly, waking only when the vehicle stopped in front of a small salmon-colored, two-story building several hundred feet from a plaza filled with an elaborate marble fountain, palm trees, and flowering shrubs. The cloying fragrance of orchids, bougainvillea, and frangipani lingering in the sultry air wafted through the car's open windows.

Straightening, his dark eyes widening, Samuel stared at the small crowd that had gathered around a group of musicians. The sounds filling the air had a distinctive Latin beat infused with rhythms that were unmistakably African. A lithe dark-skinned woman in an ankle-length white dress swayed and twirled in tempo with the hypnotic drumming. Her ruffled hem snapped and fluttered wildly as she danced as if under a powerful spell that made her spin as fast as the hands pounding the skins stretched over drums of various shapes and sizes.

"Senor Cole?" Hernan held the car door open for him.

Samuel blinked as if coming out of his own trance. He didn't know whether it was the music, the flora, the tropical heat, the smells, or the sight of the woman dancing in a sensual, unrestrained abandonment that held him captivated, but there was something about the island country that pulled him in and refused to let him go. Within seconds he had become enthralled with Cuba, its people, and its music.

Ducking his head, he stepped out of the car, smiling. The sounds of spoken Spanish floated all around him, and although he could not understand more than five words of the language it still sounded like music to his ears.

Hernan reached for the bag with *SCC* branded into the supple leather, cradling it in his right hand while his own corrugated luggage sat on the ground beside him. He had thought himself blessed when his Florida cousin asked him to act as Senor Cole's driver and interpreter. The money he would earn coupled with what he'd saved would be enough to buy the house he'd wanted for years. He was tired of living in the little guesthouse behind his in-laws' much larger residence.

He leaned closer, noting his passenger's entrancement. Samuel Cole had fallen in love with Cuba.

Samuel followed Hernan and the proprietor of the converted convent up a staircase to the second story. Despite the heat, the interiors of the stucco building remained cool. The owner unlocked the door to a room facing the plaza and pushed it open.

"This is my best room," he said to Hernan.

Hernan nodded, his expression purposefully serious. "Senor Cole is a very important businessman from the *Estados Unidos*," he said in Spanish, his tone low and mysterious. He would occupy another room—a much smaller room—connecting to Samuel's by a common door.

The innkeeper stepped aside, bowing slightly. "I understand. If there is anything you need, please let me know." He smiled broadly when Hernan handed him a coin. "*Mil gracias.*"

Hernan could afford to be generous because Samuel had been more than generous with him.

Samuel found the furnishings at the hotel provincial, but they would serve his purpose during his stay. All he needed was a clean bed and indoor plumbing with a private bath.

A bed, a mahogany armoire, and a matching rocker were the only furnishings in the space that was no larger than the dressing room in the master bedroom suite of his West Palm Beach home. He sat down on the side of the bed, patting the mattress. At least it was firm—the way he liked it.

Reaching into the pocket of his trousers, he took out a stack of bills and handed several to Hernan. "I'm going to need a Panama hat."

Hernan took the money. "What size?"

Samuel gave him his hat size as he unbuttoned his shirt. "I also need someone to press my clothes." The woman who kept his house had packed his luggage very carefully, but there was no doubt some of the articles would bear wrinkles or creases and he'd always prided himself on his appearance.

He had heard people speak of the seven deadly sins, and he was guilty of committing most of them on one or more occasion. Sloth was the only one he knew he would not commit. Charles Cole was gone, but unconsciously Samuel was still driven to prove his worth to a man who blamed his youngest son for all of his own failures.

He shrugged out of his shirt, leaving it on the rocker, opened the lock on his luggage, and withdrew a case containing his shaving equipment. By the time he'd disappeared into the bathroom, closing the door behind him, Hernan had removed half a dozen shirts and several suits from the calfskin bag.

A woman dressed in a pale pink uniform escorted Samuel and Hernan into a rear courtyard. The sun had moved lower in the heavens, taking with it the intense heat and leaving the fragrant air cooler.

Samuel stared up at a massive acacia tree with its twisted roots spreading out over a lush lawn, shading the rear of a sprawling Spanish Colonial house made of pale pink limestone.

Arturo Moreno rose from where he sat under the shade of fanlike banana leaves to greet his visitors. His gaze swept over the American, cataloguing everything about him within seconds. He was tall, at least six feet or more, slender, and broad-shouldered. The cut of his double-breasted reefer jacket lounge suit was as exquisite as the finely woven Panama hat perched on his head at a jaunty angle. As the man came closer he examined the lean angular face with large deep-set, dark eyes. Samuel Cole presented an imposing figure, radiating confidence and power. And

Arturo had to hide his surprise that the man who wanted to buy his sugarcane plantation wasn't Anglo.

Samuel removed his hat, holding it in his left hand while he extended his right one to his host. "*Buenas noches*, Senor Moreno."

Arturo inclined his head, accepting the proffered hand. "*Buenas noches*, Senor Cole." He gestured to a nearby chair. "Please, sit down," he continued in slow, halting English. He retook his seat, then turned to his servant. "Please see that Senor Cruz is given something to eat." He'd switched fluidly back to Spanish.

Hernan and Samuel exchanged questioning glances. It was apparent Arturo wanted to conduct the meeting without Hernan interpreting his Spanish into English.

The woman bowed her head and made her way toward the house, Hernan following.

Unbuttoning his jacket, sitting, and crossing one leg over the other, Samuel rested his hat on his lap. He gave Arturo a direct stare. He had waited a year to get an appointment with him, and there was something about the man that made him feel uneasy. He was short, barely five feet, slight, with hands and feet that were no larger than a child's. Inky black hair, parted and brushed neatly on the left and off his forehead, enhanced the pallor of his pale skin. His light brown eyes bulged from their sockets like those of the tiny dogs Samuel had seen in Mexico.

He closed his eyes for several seconds, trying to recall the breed. *Chihuahua!* It was the name of the city in Mexico where he and his brothers had transported their soybean crop for processing.

"Are you aware that I hired Senor Cruz to act as my interpreter?"

A slight flicker wrinkled Arturo's forehead. "That may be so, but I believe my English is better than your Spanish."

Although his English was very heavily accented, Samuel was able to understand him. "You're probably right about that."

"I know that I *am* right, Senor Cole. What you and I have to discuss should not be overheard by servants."

Samuel wanted to tell the condescending little man that Hernan wasn't his servant, but decided to hold his tongue.

Arturo glanced at his pocket watch. "I want us to talk before we dine."

"I've come to purchase your sugarcane plantation, Senor Moreno."

Nodding, Arturo laced his fingers together. "That is true."

"Your solicitor quoted me a price that I'm prepared to meet."

"Would you answer a question for me, Senor Cole? Why do you want a Cuban sugarcane plantation when you can purchase one in the United States?"

It was a full minute before Samuel replied. "Even though our countries are separated by ninety miles of ocean I'm certain you're aware of the racial bigotry in my country. I have no doubt my business endeavors would anger certain people."

A cold smile parted the Cuban's thin lips. "Do you think Cuba is exempt from racial bigotry?"

A muscle throbbed noticeably in Samuel's jaw as a sixth sense told him that his attempt to buy the plantation would be thwarted because of his race.

"No, Arturo," he replied, using the man's name for the first time. "Any time a ruling class enslaves another group or race of people, there is always bigotry, and therefore injustice. Cuba will have to pay for its sins just like my country will have to pay for its own."

"How much do you know about our history, Samuel?" It was Arturo's turn to use Samuel's given name.

"Apparently you believe I don't know enough."

The landowner glared at the brash American, hating him and everything he represented. He was young, tall, handsome, healthy, a Negro, and had enough money to meet the asking price for his plantation, while he'd been stricken with an illness that baffled the best medical experts, an illness that made his eyes bulge, affected his breathing, and weakened him so much that getting out of bed and walking more than ten feet was becoming more difficult with each sunrise.

His doctor had recommended he leave Cuba and live in Switzerland. He hadn't wanted to leave the country of his birth, a land where his Spaniard grandfather had worked alongside African slaves in the cane fields to earn enough money to buy a little farm—a farm that in less than one hundred years had become one of the most profitable sugarcane plantations in Artemisa.

"You're quite young to want to embark on such an expansive venture, but if you learn nothing from your trip to Cuba let me leave you with this. Never go to a country to negotiate a business deal without prior knowledge of that country or its people."

Samuel stiffened as though he'd been struck across the face, but recovered quickly. "Point well taken," he said softly.

"Are you familiar with *Los Independientes de Color*?"

There was a pulse beat of silence before Samuel said softly, "No, I'm not. But since you've mentioned color, then I assume it has something to do with Cuba's blacks."

"Yes. In 1909 the Morua law was passed banning political parties based on race or religion, and because of this ban secret societies of black Cubans, known as *independistas*, joined forces to fight this law. Although poorly organized, they managed to gather enough support to make history. In May of 1912 they revolted against the government and their uprising sent a wave of panic across the island.

"U.S. Marines landed in Daiquiri, under the terms of the Platt

Amendment, to protect the lives and property of American citizens. Our President Gomez, who did not want outside intervention, ordered the Cuban army to crush the rebellion. The cavalry, armed with American-made machine guns, was ordered to hunt down a poorly armed political group who were not prepared for a war.

"More than six thousand of them were massacred as they retreated to Oriente Province. *Los Independientes de Color* were armed with old guns and machetes, and by June the leaders of the insurrection were dead and most of their followers killed or disbanded. The fear and resentment left by the episode have hindered black participation in Cuban politics. Those not wishing to share political power celebrated whites killing blacks with a banquet in Parque Central. Officials from your country came to the celebration because they were happy to resolve what they believed would've become a military and economic crisis."

Samuel's eyes narrowed. "Why are you telling me this?"

"I just want to let you know what you may face if I decide to sell you my lands."

"I don't intend to live here permanently. What I'm prepared to do is pay the workers wages comparable to what they would earn in the States."

Arturo's raven-black eyebrows lifted and reminded Samuel of a Vincent van Gogh painting he'd seen where the painter used black hash marks for birds in flight.

"That sounds noble, but it is not a good idea."

"Why is it not?"

"The word will get out that you're paying much more than the other owners, and their workers would demand equal pay for equal work. Your good intentions will only serve to incite another rebellion."

The sun had sunk lower behind the many trees, and the waning daylight cast long and short shadows over the house and surrounding property. Samuel sat motionless, watching Arturo like a predator watching his prey, waiting for a time to strike.

He'd underestimated the tiny man with the bulging eyes. There was no doubt he was used to negotiating business deals that would prove advantageous to him. Arturo Moreno did not want to lose, but neither did Samuel Cole. He'd come to Cuba on a mission to purchase a plantation, but was faced with a situation wherein his race and citizenship, not money, had become an issue.

He wasn't as versed in Cuban history as he should've been, and had just learned of the resentment of the U.S.'s involvement in Cuba's politics, military, and economy.

And it was obvious he had two strikes against him: he was black *and* American.

"Would you not rebel against unfair labor practices and inequality?"

Samuel's voice was low and chastising. "Was that not the reason for the Spanish-American War?"

Blood suffused Arturo's face as his spare mouth thinned into a slash across his face. He reached into a pocket of his jacket and removed his watch. "It's time we go inside and dine. I will give you my decision before the end of the week."

Not waiting for response from his guest, he pushed to his feet and headed toward the large two-story mansion.

2

I've never cared what others thought of me. With me, it was always—just me.

—Ethel Waters

Jose Luis Diaz stopped pacing long enough to glare at the ramrod-straight slender figure perched on the edge of a tapestry-covered settee. "You have shamed not only yourself and me, but also our family's name!"

Marguerite-Josefina Isabel Diaz's expression did not change as she endured her father's tirade. Why, she mused, did he equate shame and family honor with a mortal sin?

"How could you take your clothes off and pose for that *cabron* whose sole intent is to bring disgrace upon my head because I refuse to let him court you?"

Marguerite inhaled and compressed her lips, attractive dimples showing in her flawless cheeks. "I did not take off my clothes, Papa. I wore a dressing gown when Antonio photographed me."

Jose Luis placed a hand over his chest and felt the rapid beating of his heart. His daughter, the sole issue of his loins, was conspiring to kill him. She had blatantly disobeyed him when he told her to stay away from Antonio Santamaria.

"I send you to the *universidad* to get an education because you claim you want to be a modern Cuban woman, but if I'd known you wanted to be a . . . a *puta* . . . or one of those actresses who prance around half naked I could've saved my money."

Pinpoints of red dotted Marguerite-Josefina's cheeks as her large dark eyes glittered wildly. She sprang to her feet. "I am not a *puta*! And don't you dare call me that."

"*Bastante!*" Jose Luis shouted. "You will not go back to the Universidad de La Habana, and you *will* not leave here until I find a suitable husband for you."

Tears filled Marguerite's eyes and she blinked them back before they fell. She refused to let her father see her cry. She had no money of her own, so there was no way she could pursue her studies, but knew she'd never be a willing participant in an arranged marriage.

Her slender hands curled into tight fists. "This is not the nineteenth century where women have no rights. I will kill myself before I become chattel to some stinking old goat!"

"And the man who took pictures of you for all of Cuba to see isn't a *cabron*?" Photographs of Marguerite-Josefina Diaz in a number of provocative poses, her hair flowing down her back or over a revealing décolletage, were currently on display at a Havana gallery.

Jose Luis gave his daughter a steady look, then shook his head. "You do not understand."

"What is there to understand? Antonio is an artist." Her voice was lower, softer.

"He's nothing more than a peasant who will take advantage of you and your innocence. He knows when I die you will stand to inherit everything. All you have to do is tell him that I'm leaving my money and the cigar factory to the Church and he will move on to seduce another woman."

"He doesn't need your money because he has a benefactor."

The elderly man angled his head and lifted his eyebrows. "So I've heard."

There was something in her father's voice that caused a shiver to snake its way down Marguerite-Josefina's spine. She shuddered noticeably despite the late morning tropical heat.

"What do you mean?"

"Did he tell you who supplies him with paints, film, and his expensive cameras? Who gives him money for his rent and his *mojitos*?"

Marguerite-Josefina's right eyebrow froze a fraction. "It's none of my business who supports him."

"Sit down, *querida*," Jose Luis ordered quietly. She complied and he took a matching chair several feet away. "Cristina Perez is Antonio Santamaria's benefactor."

The natural color drained from her tawny brown face, leaving it a sickly sallow shade. "She can't be," she said quickly.

"Why not, *Chica*?"

It had been years since Jose Luis had called her "little girl." What he had to remind himself was that Marguerite-Josefina wasn't a little girl, but a woman.

"Because . . . because . . ." Her voice trailed off. She could not continue; the words were lodged in her throat.

"Because of the rumors that she is also the mistress of Liberal *presidente* candidate General Gerardo Machado's closest confidant?"

Marguerite-Josefina's eyelids fluttered as she nodded. She'd heard the rumors, but refused to believe them. Antonio told Marguerite-Josefina that *she* was his muse, his inspiration for his artistic success, and the day she was ordered back home he'd confessed to being in love with her.

"I'm sorry, *Chica*."

"How do you know this, Papa?" Pain radiated from the depths of her dark, velvety eyes.

"Someone close to Machado contacted me after he saw you with Santamaria."

"You had someone spy on me?"

Jose Luis's patrician features were deceptively composed. At sixty-four he was reprimanding his nineteen-year-old daughter for conduct unbecoming a woman of her station when he should've been spoiling and bouncing grandchildren on his knees.

"No, my child. However, I did entrust you to the protection of my sister, who should've chaperoned you more closely."

"I've never done anything that would bring disgrace to you or Tia Gloria."

Running his hand over a mane of silver-white hair brushed off a high forehead, Jose Luis averted his gaze. "This Santamaria fellow did not . . . he did not touch you?"

Vertical lines marred Marguerite-Josefina's smooth forehead as her eyes narrowed. "I did not share his bed, Papa." She heard the exhalation of breath across the space separating them. "Even though you claim I've dishonored the family's name because I permitted myself to be photographed for all of Cuba to see, I would never defile my body by lying with a man who is not my husband."

Jose Luis slumped against his chair's cushioned softness, smiling. What he feared most was his daughter bearing a child without benefit of marriage. Bringing his hands to his mouth in a prayerful gesture, he studied the feminine face that was an exact replica of his long-deceased wife. To say Marguerite-Josefina was beautiful was an understatement. She was tall for a woman, five-seven, and had a dimpled smile that could melt the coldest heart. She wore her coal-black hair either in a single braid or in a chignon when many women were now affecting shorter hairstyles and hemlines.

"I suggest you take your siesta early because we've been invited to a farewell fiesta for Arturo and Hilda Moreno tonight."

Marguerite-Josefina felt a measure of triumph. Usually her father's tongue-lashing tirades went on for at least half an hour. This one was less than ten minutes. She peered closely at him, wondering whether he was feeling poorly. But nothing in his appearance and manner indicated he was anything but healthy.

"Are they really leaving Cuba to live in Switzerland?"

Jose Luis inclined his head. "Yes. They're scheduled to leave in three weeks."

She'd attempted to befriend the youngest Moreno daughter, but had found her as stimulating as a grain of uncooked rice. She'd even tried coaxing her to attend the *universidad* with her, but Elba was too timid to ask her father for his approval.

Rising to her feet, she leaned over and kissed her father's cheek. "I'll see you later." Straightening, she turned and walked out of the *sala*, up the winding staircase, and down the hallway to a bedroom overlooking a formal garden. Closing the door, she pressed her back against it, gritting her teeth in frustration. It had taken two years for her to convince her father that she should go to college, and two days after photographs of her were exhibited in a Havana art gallery she was ordered to return to Pinar del Rio.

She was angry with her father, but enraged with Antonio. Whenever she asked who supported him while he spent hours painting and photographing people, buildings, and landscapes, his response was always, "I have a generous benefactor who allows me to concentrate on my art."

"*Estupida*," she whispered. How could she have become so vain to believe that she was the only woman in Antonio's life? And there was no way she would be able to compete with Cristina Perez, purportedly one of the most beautiful women in Cuba.

There were rumors that Cristina had paid a *bruja* for a potion wherein no man could resist her. And if the gossip was true, then the man closest to Gerardo Machado, who was certain to become Cuba's next president, had also fallen under her spell.

Well, Antonio would have to find another muse and she would have to formulate a plan that would make her father change his mind about allowing her to return to Havana and the *universidad*.

Her hands went to the buttons on her dress and she released them from their fastenings. Her movements were slow, deliberate as she slipped out of each article of clothing. She loved her father, but felt his attitude of how women were to *behave* belonged in the prior century with their rigid standards and stuffy, hypocritical morals.

Everything and everyone was changing—all except Jose Luis Diaz.

Women were cutting their hair into boyish bobs, higher hemlines showed not only ankles but an expanse of leg, and some were wearing trousers and smoking cigarettes in public places.

M.J., as her classmates referred to her, wasn't rebellious by nature. All she wanted was to determine her own future, but that would not happen as long as she lived in Cuba and under her father's control.

You will not go back to the Universidad de la Habana, and you will not leave here until I find a suitable husband for you. Jose Luis's words were branded not only in her brain but also on her soul.

"No, Papa," she whispered. She would not permit him to select a husband for her from the sons or grandsons of his stuffy friends. If or when she married, the choice of a husband would be hers and hers alone.

"Senor Cole, it's time to get up." Samuel's right arm flailed out and Hernan stepped back. "Senor, you're going to be late for your meeting."

Samuel felt as if he were swimming underwater as the roaring in his ears continued unabated. He'd gotten up earlier that morning and purged his stomach of food and drink until he had dry heaves, but the sound of his runaway heartbeat echoing inside his head had escalated.

He was drunk!

Hernan had introduced him to a popular drink—*fuego liquido*—made with 150-proof rum, pineapple juice, sugar, crushed ice, and a splash of beer. The combination proved lethal, because he rarely drank. Before the enactment of Prohibition in 1919 he'd sampled bourbon and scotch, preferring the latter.

Samuel sat up slowly, blinking against the bright sunlight pouring into the room. Heat swelled in the space through the open shutters; it smothered him like a lead blanket. "What time is it?"

"*Son las cinco y diez.*"

"Speak English," he slurred, cradling his head in both hands.

"It's ten after five."

"Please get me some coffee, Hernan. Lots of it, and make it strong."

"*Sí*, senor."

Samuel knew he had to sober up for Arturo Moreno's dinner party. A printed invitation had been delivered to him at the hotel the morning following their meeting, and he knew before this night ended he'd know whether he would return to the States with or without his sugarcane plantation.

He sat on the edge of the mattress, head lowered, until Hernan returned carrying a chipped enamel coffeepot and a large cup. He reached for the cup with a shaky hand; the strong steaming brew burned his tongue but he managed to down two cups before he was able to get out of bed to shave, shower, and dress for the Moreno social gathering.

*　*　*

Samuel was escorted into the garden at the rear of the Moreno mansion and was met with the scent of blooming flowers, the sound of a small band softly playing a popular American love song with a Latin beat, and dozens of lighted tapers that lit up the night like stars. A warm breeze provided the perfect setting for entertaining alfresco. Arturo stood with a group of men, all in formal dress, and several sipping champagne from tulip-shaped crystal glasses.

A uniformed waiter, with skin the color of polished mahogany, balancing a silver tray with bubbly wine, approached Samuel and stared at him as if he were an apparition. It was the first time since he'd been in Senor Arturo's employ that a black man had been invited to mingle with the Cuban aristocrats.

Bowing reverently, he hid a sly smile. "*Vino*, senor?"

Samuel understood that he was being asked whether he wanted champagne. "No, *gracias*," he answered in his limited Spanish.

The waiter dropped his startled gaze. Senor Arturo's guest was not Cuban, but an American.

"Do you have water . . . *agua*?"

"*Sí*, senor." He caught the attention of a woman and asked her to bring the *Americano un vaso de agua*. She returned and handed the glass to Samuel.

He sipped the cold water and waited for Arturo to acknowledge him. He'd spent the past three days with Hernan, sightseeing and shopping. The items he'd purchased for his mother and sisters-in-law were shipped to Tallahassee. He hadn't bought anything for himself except for half a dozen *guayaberas*—loose-fitting shirts with four pockets and pleated front panels. They were not only comfortable but also practical because they were worn not inside but outside the waistband.

Arturo excused himself and made his way over to Samuel Cole. Again he was impressed with the man's appearance. The tailoring of his white dinner jacket was exceptional, and the color a resplendent contrast to his sun-browned face.

He extended a hand. "Welcome again, Samuel. Come, let me introduce you to my friends."

Samuel shook the tiny hand. "Thank you for inviting me back."

He wanted to ask Arturo if he'd made a decision as to whether he would sell his plantation, but thought better of it. He'd waited three days, and if negotiations were to go in his favor, then he was willing to wait three years.

His two brothers had accused him of being brash, arrogant, and at times too ambitious, yet they hadn't complained when their first soybean harvest yielded an unforeseen profit that changed them from dirt-poor cotton farmers to prosperous businessmen.

Samuel saw a myriad of expressions ranging from shock to bewilderment cross the faces of the men as he approached them. He only had to travel ninety miles from his homeland to be reminded of the stigma attached to those of African descent.

Arturo made the introductions in Spanish, and Samuel wasn't certain whether his host had done this deliberately, or because the men weren't familiar with English. Three of the six nodded, two turned their backs, and one smiled and offered his hand.

"Welcome to Cuba, Senor Cole." His English was only slightly accented.

Samuel smiled and accepted the firm handshake. "Gracias, Senor Diaz." He nodded politely to the other five. "Senor Velez, Avila, Pacheco, Gonzalez, Torres."

The ones who'd deliberately snubbed him turned, astonishment freezing their features. Samuel Claridge Cole had a secret weapon—the ability of total recall. This mental gift had served him well in school when he graduated at the top of his class. His dream of attending college was dashed after his brothers, Thomas and Mark, married and left home, leaving Samuel to help Charles run the family farm.

The sounds of feminine laughter punctuated the night as four young women walked into the garden. Samuel felt as if he'd been poleaxed when he saw a tall, willowy figure in white seemingly float over the slate path leading to an area where a long table had been set with gleaming silver and delicate crystal stemware. There was still enough daylight to discern high color in her lightly tanned cheeks as she wielded a delicate white lace fan inches from her face. She turned and met his curious gaze with one of her own. He was enchanted with her loosely braided dark hair, entwined with tiny white flowers, that touched her waist.

She appeared ethereal and virginal in a knee-length dress of a wispy fabric with a low, hip-length waistband. A single strand of pearls, knotted at the base of her throat, touched the dress's hemline. His gaze inched lower to her shapely legs in white silk stockings, and lower still to a pair of tiny feet pushed into silk-covered shoes with a low heel. He knew it was impolite to stare, but Samuel was unable to look away.

Jose Luis saw the object of Samuel Cole's entrancement. His reaction was similar to those of other men who'd found themselves temporarily dazzled by his daughter's beauty. However, their fascination was usually short-lived because of her outspokenness. Upper-class Cuban women saw to the needs of their husbands and children, while maintaining a well-run household. They did not discuss politics, the world's economy, or the Catholic Church's influence in Latin America.

He knew Marguerite-Josefina wasn't entirely to blame for her freethinking stance. If he'd remarried after his beloved Carlotta died from a riding accident, then perhaps having a woman in his daughter's life probably would've softened her. His unmarried sister had tried, but Gloria was dealing with her own eccentric lifestyle.

There was no doubt the American was attracted to his daughter, but before the night ended Samuel Cole would discover that her beauty was a foil for a sharp mind and an even sharper tongue.

3

Manners are made up of trivialities of deportment, which can be easily learned if one does not happen to know them.

—Emily Post

Marguerite-Josefina watched the man seated across from her through a fringe of lashes, noting his hesitation in choosing a fork. Although he was as elegantly attired as the other men at the table and his beautifully formed slender hands well groomed, she knew he was ill at ease with a formal dinner party table setting.

She traced the handles of the sterling pieces at her place setting with a fingertip before tapping the fork for the seafood cocktail. He gave her a direct stare, then picked up the fork and acknowledged her assistance with a barely perceptible nod.

Arturo Moreno had waited until everyone was seated to announce that Senor Cole was an American businessman interested in doing business in Cuba. The reaction of those seated around the table was surprise and overt revulsion.

Marguerite-Josefina almost laughed aloud when one of her father's pompous business associates who usually went on incessantly about being a direct descendant of a Spanish king clutched his throat and had to be led inside the house to recover from the shock that a *norteamericano* Negro would attempt to cross the threshold into a world and lifestyle that favored a privileged few—Cuba's social elite.

"You like him, don't you?" Elba Moreno asked Marguerite-Josefina, sotto voce.

She put down her fork and dabbed the corners of her mouth with a cloth napkin without looking at her friend. "How can I like him? I don't even know him," she whispered. The petite young woman who'd inherited her father's small stature and dark eyes and her mother's shimmering blond hair picked up a water goblet and held it to her pale mouth.

"If you don't like him, then stop staring at him."

"I like looking at him."

"Why?"

"His face is interesting."

Samuel's lean face, dark slanting eyes, high cheekbones, strong nose, and firm mouth reminded Marguerite-Josefina of the tiny African masks Antonio concealed in all of his paintings. Samuel's coloring reminded her of cured golden tobacco leaves. She liked his face *and* his hair. It was close-cropped and brushed back off his forehead. She wanted to touch his hair, to discover if the tightly curling strands were soft or as stiff as Antonio's whenever he applied pomade and water to keep his wiry hair in place.

Elba took a sip of water. "But, Marguerite-Josefina, he's not one of *us*."

"Us? Who the hell are we? And I told you to call me M.J."

Bright color suffused Elba's pale face. There was no need for M.J., as she wanted to be called since she'd enrolled in the *universidad*, to use foul language with her. "You know what I mean."

"No, I don't know what you mean."

Burnished eyebrows lifted several inches. "Did you forget our promise that we would only marry for love?"

M.J. shifted her gaze from Samuel Cole to Elba, frowning. "We made that promise when we were thirteen. It's different now."

Elba stared at M.J. as if she'd grown another head. Although M.J. looked the same, Elba did not recognize her childhood friend. So much about her had changed since she'd gone to Havana to further her studies. And when the rumors about M.J. becoming a model for a popular Cuban artist swept over the island, her father had raised his fist in triumph, saying that was why he hadn't wanted her to go to the *universidad*.

She waited for a waiter to remove a plate for the next course, then asked softly, "Why is that so?"

"Because as modern women we now have more choices."

"You're not a woman."

Vertical lines appeared between M.J.'s large dark eyes. "I am not a girl."

The color drained from Elba's face as her jaw dropped. "You . . . you did it?"

M.J.'s frown deepened. "Did what?"

A becoming flush replaced Elba's former pallor. "You know. Did you and your artist do *it*?"

Heat stole its way into M.J.'s cheeks. Elba and probably everyone in

Cuba wanted to know if she'd shared the artist's bed. "Of course not! And his name is Antonio."

"Has he kissed you?"

There was a pause before M.J. said, "Yes. But it's not the kind of kiss you think it is."

"And what kind of kiss is that?"

"*No hay pasion, no fuego.*"

"If there's no passion or fire, then why do you continue to see him?"

"I was his muse, Elba."

"Was?"

"I'll tell you later."

She did not want to relive the confrontation she'd had with her father earlier that morning. Sitting for Antonio had given her a sense of worldliness and independence much like her tia Gloria. Never married, middle-aged Gloria Luz-Maria Diaz lived a Bohemian lifestyle most repressed Cuban women fantasized about. She wore trousers, smoked cigars and cigarettes, never retired for bed until dawn, and took lovers whenever the mood hit her. She had become much sought after for her soirees where her guests included university intellectuals, artists, writers, poets, and political dissidents.

M.J.'s gaze met that of the American as she picked up a wineglass. A mysterious smile parted her lips seconds before she took a swallow. Something in Samuel Cole's gaze communicated that he was as interested in her as she was in him. A thought flashed through her mind, but she banished it quickly. She would not contemplate that possibility until she learned more about the foreign businessman.

She looked at her father, noting his tortured expression. There was no doubt he saw her staring at the stranger. Lifting her chin in a haughty gesture, she turned back to Samuel and flashed her enticing smile.

Samuel was bored and impatient. Bored because he couldn't understand any of the conversations floating around him, and impatient because Arturo continued to play cat and mouse with him when he could've given him his decision the moment he arrived.

He would return to Florida if Arturo sold him the plantation. If not— he would then book passage on a freighter to Costa Rica.

Staring across the table, he met the demure gaze of Jose Diaz's daughter, seeing curiosity in her dark eyes. His pulse quickened and the flaccid flesh between his thighs stirred, and he knew there was something about the beautiful woman with the dimpled smile that had affected him as no other had.

Samuel wasn't a novice when it came to women—in or out of bed— but felt something he did not want to feel: lust. He'd come to Cuba for

business, not to become besotted with a woman—albeit the most exquisite woman he'd ever encountered in all of his travels.

Samuel waved away a waiter poised to fill his wineglass. His head had
stopped pounding and his stomach settled enough for him to eat sparingly. He'd had three days to get used to the delicious spicy cuisine of
which he could not get enough. Pork and chicken served with *mojo
criollo*—a potent garlic sauce—had become his favorite.

Dinner concluded three hours after it had begun, and Samuel sat in a
solarium with his host and other male guests. Sherry and cigars were
passed around, Samuel declining the wine and accepting a cigar.

Fragrant, tightly rolled tobacco leaves wafted in his nostrils as he
moistened the cigar with his tongue. He clipped the end, lit it, and inhaled a mouthful of sweet, flavorful smoke.

Arturo, watching Samuel's expression, smiled. "Your first Cuban cigar,
Samuel?"

He nodded, blowing out a cloud of smoke. "Yes."

"Do you like it?" Samuel nodded again. "Good."

Arturo placed his cigar in a large ceramic ashtray. "As soon as you finish your cigar we'll go for a walk."

Samuel followed Arturo away from the light showing through the
many windows in the pink structure that resembled a frothy confection,
beyond the sputtering, flickering candles in the garden, away from the
Moreno household staff cleaning up the remains of dinner, and along a
footpath leading to an overgrowth of trees and flowering shrubs.

The light from a full moon, the flower-scented breeze, and the sounds
of nocturnal wildlife provided a magical setting for Samuel and his host.

Arturo stopped, hands clasped behind his back. Tilting his head, he
stared up at Samuel. "I don't know how to say it."

Samuel's expression was impassive. "Just say it, Arturo."

"I want so very much to sell you my land, but I cannot." He held up a
hand when Samuel opened his mouth. "Let me explain. *Por favor*, Senor
Cole."

Samuel nodded. It was apparent Arturo sought to make his declination more palatable with formality. "Okay."

"I cannot sell you my lands because you are American—"

"And not because I am black?" he asked, interrupting Arturo.

"No, Samuel, it is not because you are black. If you knew anything
about our history you'd know why. Cuba has traded one oppressor for
another—the United States. In 1905 an estimated thirteen thousand
American colonists bought about fifty million dollars' worth of land on
our island. They own our lands, meddle in our politics, and pay us pen-

nies to keep their military base at Guantanamo Bay. Your country's so-called Platt Amendment has made my country a protectorate. Do you know what a protectorate is?"

Nodding again, Samuel said, "I am familiar with the word."

Arturo affected a weak smile. "Therein lies the reason why I cannot sell you my lands. Now, if you will excuse me I must get back to my guests."

Samuel closed his eyes, listening to the fading footfalls as Arturo made his way back to his house. He didn't know why, but he would've preferred that his race had become a factor rather than his nationality. He'd become accustomed to rejection because of his color, not because he was an American.

He opened his eyes and slipped his hands into the pockets of his dress trousers. His disappointment in not securing the sugarcane plantation was softened by Arturo Moreno's truthfulness. However, he would take the man's suggestion and learn all he could about Costa Rica before meeting with a representative from the United Fruit Company.

Turning, Samuel retraced his steps. He'd forgotten his manners. He wanted to thank Arturo for his hospitality before taking his leave. He hadn't gone more than a hundred feet when he saw a slender figure in white sitting on a stone bench in the moonlight. He stopped, unable to go forward or retreat.

He stared at Jose Luis's daughter as she leaned back on her hands, lifted her chin, and stared up at the alabaster sphere. A breath of cold air swept over the back of his neck despite the eighty-degree nighttime temperature, and the hairs stood up as a warning that had served him well when on the battlefield in Europe. It always foretold of a threat of danger. But what did he have to fear from a woman he'd just met? From someone he would never see again after tonight?

Without warning she turned, staring directly at him. Samuel wasn't able to make out her features in the diffused light, but saw her spine straighten. He hadn't realized he'd been holding his breath until she rose to her feet like a silvery specter, the motion galvanizing him into action, as he exhaled and put one foot in front of the other in a slow, deliberate approach. He eased his hands from his pockets, acknowledging her presence with a nod.

"Good evening, Senorita Diaz."

M.J. smiled, dimples winking attractively. "Good evening, Senor Cole. I'm surprised you remembered my name."

A slow smile softened the angles in Samuel's face. There was no way he could forget anything about the stunningly beautiful young woman who spoke English with barely an accent. And she had a wonderful low voice, soft and clear.

"You speak English very well."

"It was one of my favorite subjects."

"Did you learn it in school?"

"Yes." She'd excelled in languages at the convent under the tutelage of Dominican nuns. "Do you usually go for walks in the moonlight, Senor Cole?"

"No, I don't. This is the first time, Senorita Diaz."

She snapped open the fan suspended from a cord around her wrist. "What do you say we dispense with the senor and senorita and call each other by our given names?"

"I would not presume to take such liberties, Senorita . . . Miss Diaz."

Closing the fan, M.J. slapped it against her open palm. "M.J.," she said defiantly. "Please call me M.J."

Samuel knew he was treading on dangerous ground. He was alone with a young woman in a country where he was not only a foreigner but also regarded as an interloper. When he left Cuba he wanted to leave with his head intact.

Those who were familiar with Samuel Cole knew that he'd shunned permanent liaisons because his sole focus was to become a successful businessman. If he saw a woman more than three times, then she was one of the luckier ones.

Samuel wanted to get away from Jose Luis Diaz's daughter because there was something about her that had slipped under the barrier he'd erected to keep all women, regardless of their age or looks, at a distance until he achieved his goal.

He inclined his head politely. "Good night, Miss Diaz." His attempt to move past her was thwarted when she tapped his shoulder with the fan.

"Please don't leave."

Samuel stopped and glared at her. "What is it you want with me?"

M.J. saw the frown settle into his features, heard his chilly tone, but refused to back down. "I want to talk to you."

"What about?"

"Your country."

"What about my country?"

She gestured toward the stone bench facing the one she'd just vacated. "Please sit down."

Samuel wondered if she was part of a conspiracy to lure him into a situation from which there was no escape. His suspicions were short-lived when he heard Jose Luis calling his daughter's name.

"I'm over here, Papa."

Jose Luis came closer, slowing when he saw his daughter with the American. His eyelids fluttered at the same time he swallowed a moan. First Antonio Santamaria and now Samuel Cole. He had to see Marguerite-Josefina married without delay.

M.J. looped an arm through her father's. "Are you leaving now?"

Jose Luis stared at Samuel Cole. The man hadn't bothered to give him a glance. There was no doubt the American was as entranced with his daughter as she was with him.

Marguerite-Josefina had accused Jose Luis of clinging to the old ways, and she was right because he'd believed she would agree to an arranged marriage. He gritted his teeth in frustration. How could he have been so wrong, so blind as to what she wanted? He knew she was attracted to black men, but feared she would select one so unworthy of the Diaz name and legacy.

He forced a smile. "No, *Chica.* I just came to see whether you were all right."

M.J. patted his cheek. "Of course I'm all right. Senor Cole was going to tell me about his country."

Jose Luis shook his head. "Let me warn you in advance, Senor Cole, that my daughter can be quite opinionated if she feels strongly about something."

"If that's the case, then whatever we talk about should be quite interesting."

"No doubt," Jose Luis countered. Leaning over, he pressed a kiss to his daughter's raven-black hair. "Do not shame me," he whispered close to her ear. "I'll come back to get you later," he said loud enough for Samuel's ears. "Senor Cole, I trust you to protect my daughter's good name."

Samuel straightened as if coming to attention. "You have my word as an honorable man that she will come to no harm."

He wanted to tell the elder Diaz that there was no need to warn him about M.J., as she'd asked him to call her. She was as safe with him as she would be cloistered in a convent.

"*Gracias*, Senor Cole." Jose Luis turned and walked back the way he'd come, his thoughts tumbling over themselves as he recalled what Arturo had told him about Samuel Cole. He would be the perfect son-in-law if only he weren't American.

M.J. sat down on the stone bench, crossing her legs at the ankles, and waited for Samuel to sit opposite her. She watched his every move as he folded his tall frame down and looped one leg over the opposite knee in one continuous motion, M.J. finding the action masculine, graceful, and as fluid as a dancer's for a man his height. *Very nice*, she thought. Everything about him pleased her.

She unfurled her fan, moving it slowly over her face to offset the heat that rose without warning from between her breasts. "What is it exactly that you do in your country, Senor Cole?"

Samuel angled his head and smiled. M.J. was brutally direct. "I'll answer your question. But first you must answer one for me."

She lifted an eyebrow and stopped fanning. "What do you want to know?"

"What does M.J. stand for?"

"Marguerite-Josefina."

"It's a beautiful name."

"It's too many syllables."

"What if I call you Marguerite?"

She shook her head. "No. You can't call me Marguerite without adding the Josefina because that is my given name. What is your name?"

"Samuel."

"Samuel," she repeated softly. "Do you know what it means?"

He nodded. "It's Hebrew for 'God has heard.' "

The corners of her mouth tilted. "Has God heard you, Samuel?"

"I don't know, because I've never asked him for anything."

Her eyes widened. "You do not pray?"

"I pray."

"For what?"

Samuel stared at M.J. until she dropped her gaze. "Now, that's between God and me," he chastised in a dangerously soft tone.

Her fanning started up again. "I'm sorry, Samuel. Please forgive my impertinence."

"There's nothing to forgive. What do you do, M.J.?"

"I asked you first."

"I'm a farmer."

She went completely still, the hand holding the fan poised in midair. Then she laughed, the husky sound bubbling up from her throat and floating into the warmth of the night.

"You look nothing like a farmer. You do not dress like a farmer, and you do not have the hands of a farmer." His hands were beautiful, fingers long and slender.

"Would you've said the same thing if I told you that I was a murderer?" There wasn't enough light for Samuel to see the flush darken M.J.'s face. "I am a farmer, as was my father, and enslaved grandfather. The only difference is the crop. They planted and picked cotton, while I grew soybeans."

M.J., her cheeks still burning in remembrance of Samuel's cutting remark, said, "You no longer grow them?"

Samuel's mouth curved into an unconscious smile. M.J.'s sharp mind matched her exquisite beauty. "No, I no longer grow soybeans. I sold my share of the company to my brothers."

"And now you're looking to invest in Cuban sugar?"

Samuel wondered how much he should tell M.J. about his failed attempt to purchase Arturo Moreno's plantation. There was no doubt she would hear the news before he departed Havana the following morning.

He told her everything—the conversation he'd had with Arturo when they'd discussed race and politics, concluding with why he would leave Cuba without securing the sugarcane plantation.

M.J. listened intently to Samuel Cole's soft drawling voice, expecting to hear a hint of censure or condemnation. Either he was used to rejection or pride would not permit him to accept it.

She leaned forward. "What are you going to do now?"

"I'm sailing to Costa Rica tomorrow."

A soft gasp escaped her at the same time her heart lurched. She'd hoped he would remain in Cuba a little while longer. Other than her aunt's acquaintances, Samuel was the first man she'd met who did not relate to her as if her only place was in the home caring for a husband or children.

She fanned herself furiously, as if she could eradicate her disappointment. "Do you plan to come back to Cuba?"

"If I come back it will be as a tourist. There is so much more I'd like to see." Samuel regarded M.J. with an intense curiosity that shocked him. He planned to leave Cuba, but did not want to leave M.J.

"If and when you come back I'd like to appoint myself your guide and show you places most Americans don't see."

He blinked once. "I wouldn't want you to trouble yourself. I can always hire Hernan to take me around."

"I'm a student, so whenever I'm not attending classes I can take you around."

"What are you studying?"

"Philosophy and Latin American history."

"That's serious."

"They only sound serious."

"Your father wouldn't object to you being seen with me?"

M.J. closed her fan and tapped it against her open palm. "If my father had any objections he never would've permitted me to be alone with you."

"But he knows nothing about me other than what Arturo Moreno may have told him."

"Are you a murderer, Samuel?"

"No."

"Are you wanted by your American police?"

"No," he repeated, holding back a smile.

"Have you abandoned your wife and children in order to seek your fortune?"

It was Samuel's turn to laugh, the sound deep, rumbling, and infectious. "No and no," he said, still laughing. "I have neither."

M.J., also laughing, stood up, and Samuel rose with her. "Then that does it. All you have to do is let me know when you will return and I'll ask my tia Gloria to accompany us."

"Is she as outspoken as her niece?"

"She's even more so."

Samuel moved closer to M.J., and inhaled her perfume's subtle sensual scent that was a hypnotic combination of flowers and citrus. He was close, close enough to feel her warmth.

"Then I look forward to meeting her. How can I contact you?"

"We have a telephone."

"What's the number?"

She told him and he repeated it. "Aren't you going to write it down?"

Samuel shook his head. "No. I'll remember it." Reaching for her right hand, he held it within his larger grasp, lowered his head, and pressed a kiss to her delicate knuckles. "It's been a pleasure, Senorita Marguerite-Josefina Diaz."

He was there, and then he was gone, leaving M.J. standing in the moonlight with the image of Samuel Cole's long legs, his broad shoulders, his soft drawling voice, and his promise to return to Cuba lingering around the fringes of her mind.

Her earlier confrontation with her father was forgotten as she walked along the path leading away from the garden. Elba met her as she stepped into a room where the women were sitting around talking softly to one another.

"Where were you?"

M.J. fanned herself. "In the garden."

"With the American?"

She stared at Elba until the other woman dropped her gaze. She was past seeking approval—from her father and her so-called friends. Talking to Samuel offered her a respite from her repressive lifestyle.

She did not want think about what else he *could* offer her.

4

Superior achievement, or making the most of one's capabilities, is to a considerable degree a matter of habit.

—Rose Kennedy

Samuel lay on a too-soft mattress, folded arms cradling his head, staring up at a slow-moving overhead fan, waiting for the sudden downpour to stop. He'd closed the shutters to the tall windows to keep out the rain, resulting in a buildup of suffocating heat inside the small room.

He had selected the hotel because of its English-speaking proprietor, onsite restaurant, and proximity to the offices of the United Fruit Company. He could walk there from the hotel.

It had taken the slow-moving freighter four days to sail from Havana to Costa Rica, making ports of call in Jamaica and Mexico's Yucatan before he was able to disembark at Puerto Limon, Costa Rica.

Samuel wasn't scheduled to meet with a United Fruit Company representative for another two days, and planned to spend the time adjusting to a different time zone and researching the history of the Central American country. What had shocked him was the number of dark-skinned people who spoke Spanish as well as English with a distinctive West Indian accent.

The rhythmic sounds of rain beating against the shutters and the whir of the fan's blades lulled him into a state of total relaxation; his eyelids grew heavy and fluttered closed. Heat and exhaustion overtook him, as his chest rose and fell in a measured cadence, and minutes later he succumbed to the comforting arms of Morpheus.

Samuel woke up hours later, left the bed long enough to relieve himself in a communal bathroom, then returned to his room and opened the shutters. He hadn't had a restful night since leaving Cuba. The cabin he'd secured on the freighter was located above the engine room, and the noises and vibrations had taken their toll on him. He was sleep deprived and paranoid. He lay down again and went back to sleep.

He slept on, barely conscious of the noises outside his door: the hotel's laundress arguing with her husband, the lusty moans and groans and squeaking bedsprings coming from the room adjoining his. The few times he was aroused from his deep slumber were to turn over and smother the hardness between his thighs whenever the image of Marguerite-Josefina Diaz entered his dreams.

It had been months since he'd lain with a woman, because he had not wanted any distractions, not even one as lovely as Jose Luis Diaz's daughter. He would only consider a relationship with a woman after he established his own company. Until then he would remain unattached and celibate.

Samuel woke up seventeen hours after he'd gone to bed, dehydrated, ravenous, and in need of a shower. His underwear was pasted to his sweat-drenched body.

Sitting up and swinging his legs over the side of the bed, he pulled on a pair of pants and reached for a towel from a supply he'd been given when he checked in, then gathered a small case with his grooming supplies and a change of clothes. He left the room, locking the door behind him, and walked down the narrow hallway to one of two bathrooms on the floor.

Fortified with a late morning meal of white rice, black beans, steak and onions, and fried sweet bananas, Samuel set off on foot to tour the Caribbean coastal region of Costa Rica.

He could've passed for a native with his Panama hat, sandals, cotton slacks, and *guayabera* if he hadn't stopped to examine fruits and vegetables piled on tables at an open-air market. Barefoot children chased one another as their parents called out to them in various languages and dialects. Two women in neighboring stalls were engaged in a heated argument that had gotten everyone's attention close enough to overhear the virulent words they hurled at each other.

Samuel felt a kinship with the black inhabitants of Puerto Limon that he hadn't felt with those in Cuba. They appeared more relaxed, outwardly friendly, and were quick to engage him in conversation. Once they heard him speak, they were unable to conceal their shock that an American black man had come to their isolated region of Costa Rica.

"What's that?" he asked an elderly woman sitting on a wooden crate and holding an umbrella over her head. He pointed to a large sphere with bumpy yellowish skin.

"Breadfruit."

Samuel smiled. "The same breadfruit Captain Bligh brought from Tahiti to the West Indies?"

She smiled, displaying gold-capped teeth. "Yes, mister."

He pointed to another strange-looking vegetable. "And this one?"

"Yucca, mister." She adjusted her umbrella, peering closely at the tall stranger. "You from America?" Samuel nodded. "Do you want to buy sum-ting from Miss Alva, mister? I have fresh coconuts and pretty bananas. You like bananas?"

Her lilting speech reminded him of music. "Yes, ma'am."

She picked up two large, ripe, blemish-free bananas. "I give you real cheap."

"How cheap?"

"One dollar."

"One dollar?" Samuel repeated. "One dollar for two bananas?"

"Yes, mister." She cradled them gently like one would a newborn baby. "Are they not beautiful?"

A frown appeared between his eyes. "Yes, they are. But not for a dollar."

Alva's broad face creased with a wide smile. "What is a dollar to a rich American?"

"He will be a very poor American if he pays your outrageous prices, Miss Alva," said a deep drawling voice from a neighboring stall. "Why is it you always have one price for Ticos and another for foreigners?"

"Mind your mouth, Lennox, " she hissed, waving at him. "You bad for my business." She shifted her attention to her customer. "You want bananas?"

Never go to a country to negotiate a business deal without prior knowledge of that country or its people. Arturo Moreno's words were branded into his brain and in Samuel's heart, and he knew he had to acquaint himself with the culture and some of the customs of the Central American country before his meeting.

He glared at Miss Alva, hoping to intimidate her. "I'll buy your over-priced fruit, but not before you do something for me."

"What you want, mister?"

"I need to speak to someone who knows about doing business in Puerto Limon."

"You want him to speak English?"

"Yes, ma'am."

"Go down the road to Donovan's," she said, pointing an arthritic finger. "You will find the American there."

"Does the American have a name?"

"No. Just ask anyone for the American."

Reaching into his pocket, Samuel took out a silver dollar and placed it on the tabletop. "I'll be back for my bananas." He winked at Alva, heading in the direction she indicated and wondering who or what Donovan's was.

It turned out that Donovan's was Puerto Limon's local saloon. A lopsided, hand-painted sign hung precariously from a rusted chain in front of a tin structure erected on stilts. A quartet of elderly men, sitting on crates under a sagging wooden porch, were engaged in a vocal game of dominoes.

Samuel walked in and went completely still, struggling to breathe as a wave of heat sucked the air out of his lungs. Moisture beaded up on his forehead and upper lip. How, he wondered, could anyone remain inside for more than a few minutes without passing out from the heat?

Waiting until his eyes adjusted to the dim interior, he made his way to a makeshift bar that had been constructed with a long board resting on two large metal drums. The bartender, a thin, light-skinned man with a scruffy reddish beard, watched his approach, gaze narrowing.

"Good afternoon."

"Yeah, mon."

"Are you Donovan?"

"Yeah, mon. What you drinking?"

"I didn't come to drink."

His gray-green eyes widened. "Why you here asking for Donovan then?"

Samuel reached into a pocket of his trousers and placed a silver dollar on the wooden plank covered with food stains, making certain the man saw the coin before he covered it with his hand. "I need some information."

The bartender smiled, displaying a mouth filled with yellowing teeth. "What you want?"

"Where can I find the American?"

"I'm over here," came a disembodied masculine voice with a distinctive southern drawl. "And who's asking?"

Samuel squinted, unable to make out his features. "Samuel Cole." His own drawling voice carried easily in the stagnant, stifling space.

The shape stirred. "Come closer." The command was strong and uncompromising.

He bristled at the sharp tone because he was used to giving orders, not obeying them. "Who are you?"

"I'll ask the questions, Mr. Cole. After all, you're the one who came looking for me."

Gritting his teeth, Samuel deliberately placed one foot in front of the other as he closed the distance between him and the *arrogant bastard* hiding in the shadows.

It wasn't the dark bearded face, the strong odor of stale liquor floating around him, the long matted hair littered with lint particles, or the rumpled clothes that looked as if they'd been slept in that stopped Samuel in his tracks, but his eyes, a glittering gold brown, the eyes of a madman. What accurate information would he be able to glean from someone who looked as if he belonged in an asylum?

"Sit down. And try not to talk too loud. My head hurts like hell."

"I'd rather talk somewhere else. I can't breathe in here."

"There's nothing wrong with the air in here unless you think you're too good for—"

He never completed his sentence. Samuel Cole had turned on his heel and was heading for the door. The bearded man panicked. "Wait!" Samuel stopped, but did not turn around. Rising to his feet on wobbly knees, the man managed to walk the half dozen steps that left him less than a foot from the stranger who'd sought him out. He stared at the broad shoulders under a white *guayabera*. "Mr. Cole?"

A knowing smile flitted across Samuel's face, but vanished within seconds, replaced with an expression of annoyance. "I need information from you, information I'm willing to pay for. But not here."

"How much are you willing to pay?"

"That depends on you." A deep sigh and a rush of rum-soured breath wafted in the oppressive air behind him. "If you tell me what I need to know, then you can name your price."

"What do you want to know?"

"Are you familiar with the United Fruit Company?"

There was a pulse beat of silence before the man said, "Quite familiar. I worked for them for two years before I was fired."

Samuel turned and stared at the unkempt man. He was tall and thin. No, emaciated was a more appropriate description. "Why did they fire you?"

"I got sick."

Dark eyes regarded a pair of gold ones, glittering with rage and something else. It took less than three seconds for Samuel to identify the something else: revenge.

"What did you come down with?"

"Consumption, also known as pulmonary tuberculosis."

Samuel successfully curbed the urge to take a step backward. "Are you contagious?"

"No. Not now."

"Are you certain?"

"I got a clean bill of health last week."

Praying that he wasn't being lied to, Samuel forced a smile. Tuberculosis had claimed the lives of his father and grandmother. The debilitating disease had laid waste to their bodies with fatigue, weight loss, and a persistent cough with green, yellow, and finally bloody sputum.

"What did you do at United Fruit?"

"I worked in their accounting department."

"Are you an accountant?"

"Yes."

"Did you attend college?"

"Yes."

"How much can you tell me about their financial stability?"

"That all depends."

"On what?"

"On how much you're willing to pay me for the information."

"What do you want?"

"Enough money for a ticket back to the United States."

Samuel blinked once. "What are you going to do, or where are you going once you get back?"

"That is for me to decide."

Samuel felt a strange numbing comfort. There was something in the man's tone that belied his outward appearance. His speech and choice of words revealed that he was educated, and there was a spark of defiance in his eyes that reminded Samuel of himself. The same look he'd given Charles Cole whenever he sought to break his spirit.

"Have you eaten?"

The gold eyes were steady. "Not today."

"Do you have a change of clothes?" Samuel asked, continuing his questioning.

The man shook his head. "I don't have the money right now to pay the woman who does my laundry."

"I don't want to insult you, Mr.—"

"Kirkland. It's Everett Kirkland."

"Mr. Kirkland," Samuel said softly, "you need to wash and change your clothes. I'm going to give you some money so you can clean yourself up. Meet me at the Casa del Caribe in three hours."

He handed him a ten-dollar gold note. It was enough money to feed Everett Kirkland for at least a week, that is, if he didn't squander it on rum, but definitely not enough for a ticket to get him back to the States. And if Everett was serious about wanting to return to the United States, then Samuel knew he would keep their appointment.

If it hadn't been for his voice, Samuel never would've recognized Everett Kirkland. He'd bathed, shaved, and wore a clean shirt and slacks; he'd also gotten a haircut. Without the beard, his thin, angular face was made up of sharp angles that did little to detract from what should've been quite a handsome countenance. And despite the large portions of food on the table in the hotel dining room, Everett ate sparingly.

Samuel listened intently, not interrupting as the accountant talked openly about growing up in Tennessee as an only child of elderly schoolteacher parents. A maiden schoolteacher aunt encouraged him to attend Tennessee State University in Nashville after his mother and father died in the 1918 influenza epidemic. Three months after he'd graduated, he went to work for a Colored insurance company in Richmond, Virginia.

"How did you wind up in Costa Rica?" Samuel asked as Everett paused to take a swallow of a blended drink of rum, mango, pineapple, and guava juices.

Everett stared across the small table at the man who would provide him with the opportunity to return to the United States after a three-year absence, and despite his current financial status he knew instinctively that he and Samuel were more alike than not.

"My aunt made me promise her that after she passed away I'd take time off and travel. I kept her promise, took a leave from the insurance company, went to New Orleans, and boarded a tanker that was scheduled to go through the Panama Canal. I got off in Colombia and met a photographer. The National Geographic Society had sponsored an expedition for her to take pictures of the Amazon River and Brazil's rain forest.

"I became her assistant as she took hundreds of pictures of trees, vines, flowers, snakes, monkeys, birds, and fish. She came down with malaria, so instead of returning to Washington, D.C., she came back here."

"And you came back with her," Samuel said, smiling.

Everett nodded and closed his eyes. "I was twenty-four and in love with a woman ten years my senior." He opened his eyes and met Samuel's amused stare. "I gave up everything for Eladia. My job, my country, and in the end a part of myself."

"What happened to her?"

"I don't know," he said quietly, with no expression on his face. Everett focused on a small lizard that had attached itself to the wall behind where Samuel sat.

"She recovered from her bout of malaria, developed the photographs of the expedition, and then took off again. She wouldn't tell me where she was going, only saying I should stay at her place until she got back. I was running short on money so I got a job with the United Fruit Company and waited. After the first year I stopped waiting, and halfway through the second year I all but forgot what she'd looked like."

"What about her family? Hadn't they known where she'd gone?"

"She wasn't Costa Rican."

"What was she?"

"Panamanian."

"What about the National Geographic Society? Did you contact them as to her whereabouts?"

Resting an elbow on the table, Everett cradled his chin on his hand. "I cabled them, but no one would give me any information because I wasn't a relative."

Samuel leaned forward. "Why didn't you go back home?"

Shrugging a thin shoulder, Everett affected a sad smile. "I was in love, and a part of me wouldn't permit me to believe that she wasn't coming back. The woman who owned the house where she lived told me that Eladia would stay away for years, but whenever she came back she would pay her all of her back rent."

"I can see why you've waited," Samuel said softly.

"I'm through waiting." A muscle twitched in Everett's lean jaw. "Getting sick and not knowing if the next day was going to be my last has made me look at life very differently now."

"How's that?"

A pregnant pause ensued. Samuel thought perhaps he'd asked a question that was too personal in nature. After all, he did not know anything about Everett Kirkland aside from what he'd just revealed. He stared at him, seeing things he hadn't noticed before. The slanting gold-flecked eyes reminded him of some of the Chinese-Cubans he'd seen during his recent trip there. The bridge of his nose was narrow, which made his flaring nostrils more pronounced, and his sun-darkened skin was layered with shades of gold to alizarin. He was only an inch or two shorter than his own six-foot, two-inch height, but Everett's weight loss made him appear taller.

"I will never love someone more than I love myself."

"What do you want, Everett?"

"What do you mean?"

Samuel decided to be straightforward. It was the only way he knew how to be. He abhorred evasiveness and detested innuendoes. That was why he'd respected Arturo Moreno's decision not to sell him his sugar-cane plantation, because he'd not softened his declination with an apology and sugary words layered with a falsity that would leave him angry, bitter, and filled with resentment—emotions that would prove detrimental in future endeavors.

"What do you want for yourself? Where do you see yourself in the next five to ten years?"

"How truthful do you want me to be, Samuel?"

"I'd like complete honesty."

"I don't want to be in the position where I'd have to wait for someone to offer to feed me, or sell myself like a whore for boat fare, and I don't ever want someone to order me about before they will sit down and talk to me."

Samuel recoiled as if he'd been struck across the face. "Don't blame me for your predicament."

"I'm not blaming you," Everett countered, his voice lowering to just above a whisper. "I accept full responsibility for my own fucked-up predicament."

Leaning back in his chair, Samuel crossed his arms over his chest. Flat broke, hungry, and having faced death from a fatal disease, Everett Kirkland had come at him like a rabid coon.

"How old are you, Everett?"

"Why?"

"Just answer my question."

"You like giving orders, don't you, boss man?"

Pushing back his chair, Samuel rose quickly. "I don't have to take your shit."

Half rising, Everett reached out and grasped his wrist. "Sit down. Please," he added when he saw Samuel glaring at the fingers gripping his arm.

Samuel shook off the hand and sat down. "Let's get something straight, right here, right now. I didn't come all this way to waste my time arguing with someone who has messed up his life, and then feels the need to lash out at someone who had nothing to do with it."

"I'm sorry, Mr. Cole," Everett mumbled.

"You've already called me Samuel, so why act remorseful now?"

"I wasn't raised to be disrespectful."

"Neither was I," Samuel countered. "Now, I'm going to ask you again. How old are you, Everett?"

"Twenty-eight."

"When will you be twenty-nine?"

"Next February. Why?"

"I'll tell you after you tell me about the United Fruit Company."

"What do you want to know?"

"Everything."

Everett Kirkland told him things about Costa Rica and the United Fruit Company that he didn't have time to read in a book. He learned that Costa Rica was the first Central American country to export coffee and in 1892 Minor Keith, a New Yorker turned Texas pig farmer, had obtained concessions to build a railroad employing thousands of Jamaicans, Chinese, Europeans, and indigenous Ticos. He displaced local banana growers before securing a monopoly on the production of the fruit. After merging with the Boston Fruit Company in 1899 he expanded his empire and subjected immigrant workers to restrictive systems, such as payment with scrip.

"How much influence does the United States have here?"

"They have their noses everywhere in the Caribbean, Central and South America," Everett said, frowning. "They've intervened in Colombia, Honduras, the Dominican Republic, Cuba, Panama, Puerto Rico, Nicaragua, and Guatemala."

"Who are United Fruit's competitors?"

Everett shook his head. "They don't have any. If your intention is to buy a banana plantation, then I suggest you save your breath and what money you have."

"What do you suggest?"

"Approach them with a plan to ship their bananas throughout the States and the Caribbean."

"Why not offer to buy shares in the company?"

"You don't want to get caught up in the ongoing politics of labor unrest coupled with the unstable governments in this region. A prolonged strike can lead to a loss of profits and eventual bankruptcy." Everett hesitated, frowning. "What experience do you have with crop production?"

Samuel told him about the soybean company he'd established with his brothers. A knowing smile softened the sharp angles in Everett's face. "You're really an ambitious son of a bitch."

Samuel's smile matched his. "No more ambitious than the arrogant son of a bitch talking to me."

Everett touched his glass to the one next to Samuel's right hand. "Touché. Tell me about your soybeans."

Samuel picked up his glass for the first time and drained it, the combination of fruit juices and rum pleasantly intoxicating on his palate. He explained the properties of the soybean to Everett, comparing it to the peanut. "It's a crop of the future on this side of the globe even though it's been a food staple cultivated in Asia for over five thousand years. Richer in protein than most meats, it also contains calcium, vitamins, and many other nutritional minerals. Its oil is extracted for the manufacture of paint, soap, and other nonfood products. A major advantage of planting soybeans is that they don't deplete the soil like tobacco."

"Why don't you concentrate on growing soybeans?"

"I did for four years until I sold my share to my brothers."

"Why?"

"Because I want to control my own company."

Everett squinted, as he appeared deep in thought. "Have you considered becoming an importer *and* exporter?"

"No. How would I do that?"

"Buy your brothers' soybean harvest, sell it abroad, then export produce that's not grown in the States."

Excitement shimmered in Samuel's eyes as he contemplated the accountant's proposal. Everett was young, only two years older than he was, and worldly. "How would you like to become a wealthy man, Everett?"

A hint of a smile touched Everett's mouth. "I'd like that very much."

"I believe it can become a reality if you come work for me." He had the resources to start up another company, but needed Everett's education and business savvy.

He reached into his shirt pocket, pulled out an envelope, and pushed it across the table. "There's enough in there for a ticket to the States, my telephone number, and a little extra to take care of whatever it is you need to get back on your feet. Once you're settled, give me a call."

Samuel stood up and walked away, leaving Everett staring at the envelope. It was a full five minutes before he opened it and counted the contents.

Samuel Cole had just saved his life.

5

I ask no favors for my sex . . . All I ask for your brethrens, that they will take their feet off our necks, and permit us to stand upright on that group which God designed us to occupy.

—Sarah Grimke

I can't believe I've become a prisoner in my own home. M.J. sat with her bare feet resting on a padded footstool, staring at the open book on her lap. She hadn't turned a page in fifteen minutes.

She'd become a prisoner because she refused to bend to her father's will. He had forbidden her to leave the property or accept visitors—except those he approved of. The man whom Jose Luis wanted her to marry was repulsive. He was too old and there was something about him that reminded her of a reptile.

The photographs Antonio had taken of her were duplicated and were now on display from Havana to Santiago de Cuba. She'd sat mute while her father ranted and railed for almost an hour about how could he show his face in polite society now that she'd ruined the Diaz name where no self-respecting man in Cuba would have anything to do with her?

She didn't want a Cuban man—not one who would treat her as chattel, like his lands, servants, and other material possessions. She wanted to be M.J. and not some man's *mi esposa*. She wanted to complete her education and tour Rome, Paris, Barcelona, and London, and do so much more than most Cuban women in her station did; but family honor had to be preserved at any cost. And that meant not marrying out of her class. Pressing her head to the back of the cushioned chair, she closed her eyes, knowing she had to formulate a plan to regain a modicum of independence.

*   *   *

M.J. hadn't realized she'd dozed off until she heard someone calling her name. One of the live-in maids stood in the doorway. "Yes, Hilda?"

"Senorita, you have a telephone call."

The words were barely out of the woman's mouth when M.J. sprang to her feet and raced down the staircase to the first floor. Her heart pounded a runaway rhythm as she neared the small, round table cradling the telephone.

Picking up the receiver, she cleared her voice. "*Hola.*"

"M.J.?"

Her dimples deepened as she grinned from ear to ear. "Hello, Samuel."

"How are you?"

"I'm well. In fact, I'm wonderful." She was wonderful. His soft, drawling voice sent shivers up her spine.

"I'm glad to hear that."

"Are you, Samuel?"

"Am I what?"

"Glad you're talking to me?"

"Of course I am, M.J. Why do you think I'm calling you?"

"Is it because you're planning to come to Cuba?"

"I'm already in Havana."

M.J. couldn't stop her knees from shaking. Groping for a nearby straight-back chair, she sat down. "When did you arrive?"

"A couple of days ago."

"And you're just calling me?"

A deep laugh came through the earpiece. "Your father warned me that you were outspoken."

M.J.'s face was flushed with humiliation and anger at herself. Her quick tongue had gotten her in trouble again. She wanted to get to know Samuel Cole better, not chase him away.

"Please forgive my impertinence, Samuel."

"There's nothing to forgive. I'd like to know if your offer to act as my guide is still available."

Her embarrassment was short-lived. "Yes, it is. When would you like to meet?"

"How's tomorrow?"

"It's good but . . ."

"But what?" Samuel asked when her words trailed off into silence.

"I have to get in touch with my aunt." She actually did not want her aunt to chaperone her and Samuel but knew doing so would alleviate some of her father's anxiety about her being alone with a man. "What are you thinking, Samuel?"

"I could always arrange to see you another time."

"No!" she shouted before clamping her free hand over her mouth. "As soon as I hang up I'll call Tia Gloria and ask her to come."

"What if she has other plans?"

"She'll change them for me." M.J. smiled when Samuel laughed again. "What's so humorous?"

"You," he replied, chuckling. "Do you expect everyone to stop what they're doing because you deem it?"

"No. Is there a telephone where you're staying?"

"Yes. Why?"

"I'll have Tia Gloria call for you and the both of you can come together. Where are you staying?" He gave her the name of a hotel in Habana Vieja. "I'll give her the number and I'll see you tomorrow."

"Okay."

"Samuel?"

"Yes, M.J.?"

"Thank you for coming back."

"I'm glad to be back."

"*Hasta mañana.*"

"What does that mean?"

"Until tomorrow."

"*Hasta mañana*, Senorita Diaz."

M.J. laughed at his bungled attempt to speak Spanish. The words, which should've sounded musical, came out flat and nasal. "You need a Spanish tutor, Senor Cole."

"Are you available to take on a student?"

"Very available."

"Good. Can we begin *mañana*?"

"*Sí*, Senor Cole. *Adios.* That means good-bye."

"*Adios*," he repeated.

M.J. hung up, covered her mouth, and swallowed her giggles. It had taken Samuel Cole a month, but he had kept his promise to return to Cuba. Now all she had to do was tell her father that he was coming to see her, then wait for his reaction.

M.J. found her father in the library, reading glasses perched on the end of his aquiline nose. Rays of late morning sunlight glinted off a full head of silver-gray hair. The crisp crackle of turning newspaper pages competed with the soft twitter of a pair of colorful birds flying around a large wicker cage.

"Papa?"

Jose Luis turned and peered over the top of his rimless eyewear, a slight frown vanishing when he saw who'd interrupted him. Just once he wanted to be able to finish reading the paper in one day.

"*Que tu haces?*"

"Tia is coming tomorrow."

"Good," he said quickly before turning back to the article about Cuba's newly elected president.

"She's coming with Samuel Cole."

"What!" The word exploded from Jose Luis. Rising slowly to his feet, he stared at his daughter as if she were a stranger. "What on earth have you done?" he whispered harshly.

M.J. knew it was too late to retreat or withdraw her invitation to Samuel. "He's going to be our houseguest. I knew this would probably upset you, so I asked Tia if she would act as a chaperone."

"Chaperone! I asked her to chaperone you in Havana, and what did you do? You pose naked for a *cabron* to take pictures of you for all of Cuba to see," he said, answering his own question.

"Samuel Cole is not a *cabron*, Papa. He is decent, respectful. He told me that he felt uncomfortable being alone with me in the garden that night at the Morenos."

"You know nothing about this man. You don't even know if he's married or has children."

"He has neither."

"How do you know?"

"I asked him, Papa. You're afraid I'm going to shame you when it is the last thing I want to do. I want to be able to fall in love and select my own husband, not someone you feel is suitable for me. You married for love. Why shouldn't I?"

Jose Luis gave her a direct stare. "Are you saying you're in love with this American?"

"He has a name, Papa. It's Samuel."

Jose Luis threw up a hand. "Oh, now it's Samuel?"

"Yes, Papa. Samuel Cole."

"You love this Samuel?"

"No, Papa. But I do like him. A lot. But if I'm not permitted to spend time with him, then I'll never know if I can fall in love with him."

"You would actually consider marrying a foreigner when you can choose from any *Cubano*?"

M.J.'s spine straightened as she lifted her chin. The gesture of defiance was not lost on Jose Luis. "If I love him, yes."

"How do you know he likes you?" Jose Luis asked, deciding on another approach. "You are throwing yourself at him when he may be toying with you. Men are known to do that until they get what they want."

Twin dimples kissed her cheeks like thumbprints. "He must like me because he did return to Cuba." Her smile faded, a frown taking its place. "He will not use me, Papa, because I won't let him."

"You let Antonio Santamaria use you."

"He did not use me. I trusted him and he deceived me."

"And you believe you can trust this American?"

Her delicate jaw tightened as she clenched her teeth. A faraway expression in the dark eyes made M.J. appear older, wise beyond her years.

"Right now I don't trust any man. Including you, Papa. You plot behind my back to arrange for me to marry strangers—men whom you believe would be perfect husbands for me." Her angry gaze swung back to her father. "If you force me to marry someone I have not chosen for myself I swear on my mother's grave that I will bring shame on you and this house by taking lovers—as many and as often as I can."

A shocking and paralyzing fear would not permit Jose Luis to utter a sound. Sharp pains knifed his chest as objects became fuzzy. He clutched his chest, praying for the pain to stop as the image of his own father holding his chest at the dinner table before he collapsed, facedown, into the food on his plate came back in vivid clarity. His father died as he and Gloria witnessed the last seconds of his life. Miraculously the tightness eased, his vision cleared, and he drew in a lungful of air.

"You cannot, Marguerite-Josefina," he whispered hoarsely.

"I will, Papa, if you force me to marry someone I do not love."

He knew he had lost the battle. Marguerite-Josefina was too much like her aunt. "What do you want from me, *Chica?*"

M.J. walked over to her father and hugged him. "I want you to trust me, Papa. I want you to see me happy. I do not like the men you want for me. They are boring, weak, and they repulse me."

Jose Luis tightened his hold on her slender body. "Pedro Acevedo comes from one of the best families in Cuba."

"He looks like a frog! And he's old and ugly." Pulling back, she stared up at Jose Luis. "I cannot change who I am or what I want."

Jose Luis buried his face in her fragrant black hair. "I don't want you to change, *Chica.* You've always brought joy to my old heart."

"You're not old, Papa."

"Are you now a *mentirosa?*"

"I'm not lying, Papa. You're only sixty-four."

"Sixty-four is old. I should be a grandfather already."

"That can happen if you stop trying to control my life."

His eyebrows lifted. "You want children?" She nodded, smiling. "But I thought you wanted to be a libertine like your aunt."

"I want to marry and have children, but I also want to control my destiny. I want a husband who thinks of me as his partner and not as his possession. I don't want my children hampered by archaic laws or customs that will limit their success."

Jose Luis kissed her forehead. "You are so young and so very idealistic, *Chica.*" He kissed her again. "We'll talk again later—after you've made preparations for your American houseguest."

"Thank you, Papa. Thank you, thank you, thank you," M.J. crooned as she raced out of the library, then slowed considerably when she spied one of the gardeners. She inclined her head when he stepped aside to let her pass him as she sought out the housekeeper. Unconsciously, she'd slipped smoothly back into her role as mistress of the house.

M.J. stood in the doorway, mixed emotions of anticipation and jealousy gripping her as she watched Samuel Cole with her aunt, who'd rested a hand on his shoulder while smiling adoringly up at him.

She'd spent the past four weeks trying to recall everything about him and failed—miserably. Samuel had changed. He appeared taller, slimmer, his face several shades darker. He reminded her of a well-to-do *Cubano* with his Panama hat, tan lightweight suit, stark-white shirt, brown necktie, and coordinating tan and white shoes.

She held her breath, watching as he came closer and closer until he stood less than three feet away. His warmth, his smell, and the way he'd angled his head while staring at her made her feel things she did not want to feel—at that moment. Her heart fluttered in her chest like the delicate wings of the caged birds in her father's library.

She offered him her right hand. "*Bienvenido,* Senor Cole."

Samuel removed his hat and cradled her hand, kissing the back of it. "*Gracias,* Senorita Diaz."

M.J. gave him her winning smile. "Did you enjoy Costa Rica?"

"*Sí.*"

Her smile widened with his attempt to speak Spanish. "I hope your visit met with success."

"It was *bueno,*" he said, releasing her hand, "and before you ask me anything else, let me tell you that my entire Spanish vocabulary consists of all of ten words."

"Which means you'll still need a tutor."

Samuel found it impossible to look away from the woman who unknowingly had cast a spell over him. Staring at her in the daylight was like a punch to his midsection. He couldn't breathe or swallow without experiencing pain—pleasurable pain. Intelligent, sensual, and ardently feminine, Marguerite-Josefina Diaz possessed all he admired in a woman.

"*Sí,* Senorita Diaz."

Gloria frowned at Samuel. "Do you plan to spend the rest of your life calling my niece Senorita Diaz?"

"*Tía!*"

Fifty-eight-year-old Gloria glared at M.J. "I did not leave Havana to watch you react to him like a convent novice," she chastised in rapid Spanish. Like quicksilver, her mood changed and she smiled sweetly at Samuel. "It's time for siesta," she said, switching fluidly to English. "M.J. will show you to your room. Don't worry about your luggage. Someone will bring it up to you."

M.J. threaded her fingers through Samuel's. "How long can you stay?"

He went completely still, his gaze fusing with hers. "How long do you want me to stay, M.J.?"

"Long enough for us to become friends."

Samuel's solemn expression did not change. "That shouldn't take too long. Three days should do it."

Her delicate jaw dropped. "Three days?"

"Is that too long?"

"No! It's not long enough."

He squeezed her fingers. "If that's the case, then we should spend as much time as we can together."

M.J. gave him a saucy grin. "Isn't that why you're here?"

"*Sí.*, Senorita Diaz." Samuel gave her fingers a final squeeze.

He wanted to tell M.J. that he wanted her, but not as a friend. He knew women, those he'd grown up with or gone to school with, who were his friends.

He'd secured an agreement with the United Fruit Company to export bananas and other tropical produce to the States in exchange for the Cole brothers' soybean crop. His attorney had drawn up the papers required to file for a corporation in the state of Florida.

Seven years.

It had taken a little more than seven years, give or take several weeks, after he'd found himself on a battleship sailing back to the United States with his black market booty—booty he thought of as spoils of war—secreted in bars of soap and in a jar of hair pomade to realize his goal to become an independent businessman.

Confident his Latin American venture would eventually make him a very wealthy man, he was free to concentrate on the person who disturbed his dreams and whose image filled his waking moments.

Gloria Diaz had shown him the photographs of M.J. taken by popular Cuban artist Antonio Santamaria. His camera lens had captured the essence of her youth, her femininity, and her unabashed sensuality for perpetuity.

Samuel had stared at the photographs, trying to connect the scantily clothed Marguerite-Josefina with the prim but outspoken M.J. he'd spent time with in the Moreno garden. She may have looked the same, but the large, dark eyes staring out at the camera in the photograph were mysterious. The slight smile curving her lush mouth made it appear as if she were hiding a secret.

If Marguerite-Josefina hid a secret, then Samuel Claridge Cole also had one. He'd returned to Cuba not to tour the country but to court Jose Luis's daughter, his thirst for wealth temporarily assuaged and replaced by lust and obsession.

Marguerite-Josefina Diaz had become his obsession.

6

A photograph is a secret about a secret.

—Diana Arbus

Samuel spent siesta reclining on a chaise in a spacious, airy room with a view of a formal garden, an orchard with lime and lemon trees, and a lush lawn stretching for acres. He felt relaxed, carefree for the first time in his adult life; a foreign, indescribable joy he'd never experienced before would not permit him to fall asleep, because if he did he feared he would not wake up again.

The room he'd been assigned for his stay was wholly Spanish with stucco walls, terra-cotta floors, massive mahogany furniture, and wrought-iron wall sconces. A dressing room and an adjoining bath provided privacy and convenience.

A soft knock on the door startled him as he sat up and swung his legs over the chaise. He stared at the door. "Yes?"

"It's me, M.J. Open the door, Samuel."

"I can't," he said quickly. "I'm not presentable." He'd removed his shirt and shoes, but had left on his trousers.

"Are you naked?"

Samuel smiled. "No."

"Then open the door."

Crossing the room, he opened the door to find M.J. standing on the other side, smiling up at him. "My father would like to see you in half an hour. He told me to tell you that he'll be in his library."

Samuel couldn't pull his gaze away from the single braid that fell over her right breast, the curling ends secured by a narrow, white satin ribbon. Her simple outfit of a white blouse and navy blue skirt reminded him of the uniforms worn by schoolgirls.

"Let him know I'll be there." Nodding, he closed the door slowly, shutting out the vision of the face and body of the woman with whom he did not trust himself to be alone with.

He closed his eyes, still seeing her photograph with the soft swell of breasts above a lacy décolletage, parted lips, half-closed eyes, and heavy black hair flowing over the edge of a divan. She had the face of an angel and the body of a courtesan. A most winning and tempting combination.

Jose Luis was standing with his back to a wall of floor-to-ceiling bookcases, hands clasped behind his back, when Samuel entered his library. A cynical smile touched his mouth. His daughter had chosen well. Samuel was elegant; he radiated an inherent breeding that could not be purchased like a priceless bauble.

"I'm sorry I was not here to greet you upon your arrival." The foreman at the cigar factory had summoned him because of problems with several of his best workers who were demanding an increase in wages.

"There's no need to apologize. I'd like to thank you for inviting me into your home."

"I did not invite you, Senor Cole. It was my daughter. It's apparent she's quite taken with you."

Samuel stared at the tall, slender man with thick white hair and classically handsome features. He didn't know what M.J. had told her father, but he wouldn't lie to him.

"I've done nothing to mislead your daughter, nor do I plan to take advantage of her."

Jose Luis pointed to a mahogany pull-up chair near a table that held a full-leaded crystal decanter and two matching goblets. The decanter was filled with red-gold liquor.

"Please sit down."

Samuel took three long strides and pulled out the chair closest to the older man. "Please sit, sir."

Jose Luis hesitated, sat, then waited for Samuel to sit in a matching one. "Thank you . . . Samuel." He reached for the decanter. "May I offer you something to drink?"

"No, thank you."

"I know your country has a ban on alcohol, but here in Cuba you are free to enjoy our wines and our excellent rum."

Samuel crossed one leg over the opposite knee. "I don't like wine, and the last time I sampled your Cuban rum I woke up with a hangover."

"What did you drink?"

"*Fuego liquido.*"

Smiling, Jose Luis shook his head. "It is a miracle you woke up at all. You had what we call liquid fire. If you won't drink with me, then I'll wait for dinner." He glanced away, staring at the birds hopping nimbly from one perch to another. "What are your intentions toward Marguerite-Josefina?"

Samuel's eyebrows lifted. "My intentions?"

"*Sí*, Samuel. Your intentions. Why have you returned to Cuba?"

Samuel's eyes widened as he registered M.J.'s father's challenging query. The first time he'd come to the Caribbean country he'd been viewed as an interloper, just another American colonist seeking financial supremacy and domination. This trip was of his own free will where he hoped to capture the heart of a young woman of whom he could not rid his thoughts.

"I've come to court your daughter, Senor Diaz."

Jose Luis inclined his head. "Thank you for being truthful. Now I'm going to be truthful with you. There has been talk—a lot of talk—about photographs of Marguerite-Josefina—"

"I've seen the photographs," Samuel said quietly, interrupting him.

"You were not bothered by them?"

He wanted to laugh at the older man's pained expression. "Not at all. Marguerite-Josefina happens to be an incredibly beautiful young woman."

Clasping his hands in a prayerful gesture, Jose Luis gave Samuel a direct stare. "They are shameful, Samuel. Men who would've considered marrying my daughter now think of her as soiled goods."

"Then those men are fools."

The words came out more harshly than Samuel wanted them to. He did not want to be disrespectful or insult the elder Diaz, not when he was residing under the man's roof while at the same time requesting permission to court his daughter.

"And you would not think of yourself as a fool to want to be seen with her, Samuel?"

Samuel's impassive expression did not change. "No. Not in Cuba or in the United States."

Jose Luis was hard-pressed not to smile when Samuel mentioned the United States. He lowered his hands, resting them on the arms of the chair. "You are thinking of taking Marguerite-Josefina to the United States?"

"I would. But only as Mrs. Samuel Cole."

He sat forward on the chair. "You want to marry her?"

The beginnings of a smile tipped the corners of Samuel's mouth. He had spent the past four weeks thinking about M.J., her outspokenness, delightful laugh, wit, intelligence, and hypnotic beauty. He'd found himself comparing her to the other women in his past, but none had lingered with him beyond their brief encounters.

He knew M.J. was different the moment she sensed his dilemma over which fork he should select for the first course at the Moreno dinner party. And with the wave of anti-American sentiment on the island she could've waited for him to make a social faux pas that would've garnered the ridicule of those at the table.

Samuel angled his head, studying the man sitting less than five feet from him. "It is too soon to speak of marriage. I'm interested in getting to know Marguerite-Josefina. That is why I've returned to Cuba. But in order to propose marriage I would have to find myself in love with her."

"While you are contemplating falling in love with Marguerite-Josefina, I believe it is only fair to apprise you that she is to be promised to another."

A muscle twitched in Samuel's lean jaw as he went completely still. "What do you mean promised?"

"I've arranged for my daughter's betrothal to the son of a business associate."

"What the hell do you mean by arranged?" Samuel's quick temper had gotten the better of him. It was as if he'd learned nothing from his father's daily whippings for talking back.

Jose Luis, seemingly unperturbed by the outburst, said, "I've spoken to Pedro Acevedo about offering my daughter's hand in marriage. They will marry December twenty-seventh."

Samuel felt a roaring in his head. It was the same sensation as being held underwater. "Does she know?" His voice was a whisper.

"She knows I've spoken to Senor Acevedo."

"Does she know about the wedding date?"

Jose Luis shook his head. "Not yet."

"Don't tell her."

"I don't understand."

Samuel's head was filled with a jumble of thoughts and questions to which he had no answers. They were one-fourth into the twentieth century and in the Western Hemisphere, and he couldn't believe women were still being forced into arranged marriages.

He uncrossed his legs and placed both feet firmly on the priceless Persian carpet. His dark eyes burned with a strange, lethal fire. "I said don't tell her."

"But, Senor—"

"Shut up and listen to me," Samuel said between clenched teeth, cutting off Jose Luis's entreaty. "I'll marry your daughter, but only if she will have me as her husband."

Leaning back in his chair, Jose Luis closed his eyes and whispered a silent prayer of thanksgiving. It had worked. He'd gotten Samuel Cole to agree to marry Marguerite-Josefina.

He opened his eyes and stared at the arrogant American. "She will agree."

Shocked by the enormity of what he'd proposed, Samuel took in deep breaths to slow down his pounding heart. He'd just offered to marry a woman he'd seen briefly during one encounter, a woman he didn't know, a woman with a quick tongue who he was certain would challenge him without regard to the consequences, a woman who would be the perfect hostess for their soirees, and a woman who was certain to give him beautiful, intelligent children.

"What makes you so certain she will?"

A knowing smile crinkled the skin around Jose Luis's jet-black eyes. "You are young and you are also not, as she refers to Senor Acevedo, a frog." His smile widened as Samuel lowered his head and forced back a grin. "You are also a Negro."

Samuel's head snapped up. "Why should that matter?"

Jose Luis sobered. "It matters because the blood of Africa also runs in my veins. My grandmother was a black woman—a Cuban slave who gave my grandfather his only child and heir. My mulatto father was educated in Spain, and while there he married a Spanish woman and brought her back to Cuba. She and four of my brothers died from yellow fever in seventy-three, leaving Papa to raise my sister Gloria and me.

"I waited until I was thirty-eight to marry, and Carlotta made me a father at forty. Carlotta was carrying our second child when she was injured in a riding accident. A feral pig frightened her horse and she fell and lay bleeding for several hours until I found her. The doctor couldn't stop the bleeding and she died the next day. The hardest thing I ever had to do was tell my four-year-old daughter that her mother was never coming back. When she was six I sent her to a convent because I felt she needed to be around other girls her own age."

Samuel studied the face of the man who was to become his father-in-law. "You never remarried?"

He shook his head. "No. It took me almost forty years to find a woman like Carlotta, and I wasn't willing to spend the next forty looking for someone to replace her. I love my daughter, even though there are times when I don't show it, because she is so headstrong and rebellious."

Samuel smiled. "She's a modern woman."

"Too modern for Cuba," Jose Luis countered.

"Too modern for Cuba or too modern for you?"

A flush spread over Jose Luis's face as he swallowed a retort. He didn't want to debate with Samuel about how the island's proximity and economic ties to the United States substantially influenced Cuban culture. North American social mores had significantly affected Cuban social mores, especially in urban cities like Havana.

Reaching for the decanter, Samuel poured a small amount of sherry into both glasses, handing one to Jose Luis. They touched glasses. "To family," he said in a quiet voice.

"*La familia*," Jose Luis repeated in Spanish.

Sharing a smile, the two men tossed back their drinks in a single swallow. Samuel felt a wave of warmth settle in his chest as a pleasant nutty flavor lingered on his palate.

"Do you like it?" Jose Luis asked, seeing Samuel's expression.

"Yes. I like it much better than French wine."

Jose Luis snorted. "The French. What do they know? Now, Spanish wine is *magnifico*."

Samuel held out his glass for a refill, and as he stared at the sherry he recalled all that had happened to him within the short span of a month: he'd become an exporter and importer of fruits and vegetables, and he'd promised a man he would marry his daughter before the end of the year.

He'd committed his future to a stranger—a woman whose first language he didn't understand, a convent-educated woman who'd permitted a photographer to capture her sensuality, and a woman he would bring to the United States, his home and country that would become her country *and* her home.

Samuel, seated opposite Gloria Diaz at a table in the smaller of the two dining rooms in the exquisitely decorated home, watched M.J. as she nodded to a serving girl that she was ready for the next course. The gesture was only discernible to those staring at her, and despite what Gloria had told him about her niece's unorthodox views into which the class she'd been born; the result was that Marguerite-Josefina was undeniably a product of her upbringing.

Gloria, sporting a stylish salt-and-pepper bob hairdo, touched the corners of her mouth with a napkin. She'd exchanged her man's shirt and trousers for a simple shirtwaist dress.

"I just received a call from a friend who's only going to be in Havana for a few days, so I've decided to drive back early tomorrow to spend some time with her."

An expression of distress furrowed M.J.'s smooth forehead. "Tia, you promised—"

"It's okay, *Chica*," Jose Luis, said. "She can go back to Havana."

M.J.'s eyebrows lifted. "But, Papa. Who is going to chaperone me and Samuel?"

Jose Luis stared at her, then Samuel. "You won't need a chaperone if Samuel treats you like the lady you've been raised to be."

Samuel stared back at Jose Luis. "You have my word as a gentleman that no harm will come to your daughter." It was a repeat of what he'd promised him in the Moreno garden.

There was a pregnant pause before Jose Luis spoke again. "Okay."

M.J. forced herself to remain seated when she wanted to jump up and throw her arms around her father's neck and kiss him. She would note this day in her diary as the first day of her emancipation.

Gloria's hazel eyes twinkled mischievously behind the lenses of her glasses. Her brother had revealed the details of his conversation with Samuel Cole and his decision to withdraw the offer of his daughter's hand in marriage to Pedro Acevedo in favor of her marrying the *americano*.

She'd told her older brother that the attraction between M.J. and Samuel would progress more quickly without her presence.

Gloria was grateful that her mother hadn't lived long enough to witness her only daughter's unconventional lifestyle. Jose Luis complained about Marguerite-Josefina shaming the Diaz name when all she'd done was pose for a photographer wearing a revealing dressing gown.

When she'd traveled throughout Europe and Africa she'd done things so wicked that once she returned to Cuba she sought out a priest for absolution.

Gloria smiled. She was proud of her niece. M.J. had challenged her father's archaic way of thinking, and won. Gloria stole a glance at Samuel Cole, and her smile widened. Marguerite-Josefina Isabel Diaz had chosen well. And there was something about the American that indicated he was destined for greatness. She just hoped she would live long enough to witness it.

Banana leaves obscured Samuel's face as he leaned against the tree, puffing leisurely on a Cuban cigar. He'd grown quite fond of the taste of the smooth, fragrant tobacco. A near-full moon provided the only light in the darkened area as he inhaled the cloying scent of flowers and damp earth. He was still attempting to come to terms with conspiring with his future father-in-law.

He wanted M.J. to come to him of her own free will and not because she wanted him to rescue her. He was certain he could love M.J. After all, she was perfect in every way.

A rustling, followed by a soft crunching sound, brought him from his leaning position. Peering into the blackness he made out a flash of white; then a figure wearing a flowing white dress came into his line of vision.

"You shouldn't be out here with me."

"And why not?"

"It's not proper, M.J."

He froze, his breath catching in his throat when he saw her face. She'd let her hair down. He wanted her; he wanted to touch her, kiss her. He wanted her in his bed, her hair fanning out over his pillow, his flesh buried so deeply in hers that they would become one with each other.

"Did not my father give permission for us to be alone together?"

Samuel nodded, wondering how he hadn't noticed the low, sensual timbre of her voice. It was soft, soothing, intoxicating.

"Then what is the problem, Samuel?"

He wanted to tell M.J. she was the problem. She'd bewitched and taunted him until there were times when he couldn't think straight. "The problem is that you can't come to my room again when I'm not presentable." She moved closer and he felt her warm breath brush his throat.

"It's not that I haven't seen a man's bare chest before. What's not proper is my sharing your bed. That I would only do with my husband."

"If that's the case, then why don't you wait until I'm your husband before you see my chest again?"

M.J.'s soft gasp was followed by a swollen silence, then the sound of her breathing in a hiccupping, offbeat cadence. She recovered first. "What makes you so certain that I'll become your wife?"

Samuel put out the cigar against the bark of the tree, the ashes falling to the earth in shimmering red-orange sparks. "You didn't invite me back to Cuba because you enjoy talking to me."

"Why do you think I asked you to come back?"

He smiled. "Curiosity."

Her eyebrows flickered. "Why else?"

He lowered his head, his mouth inches from her ear. "Because you want something from me you can't get from the men in your country."

M.J. felt trapped, and it was too late to retreat. "And what is that?"

"Freedom from what you view as a restrictive society. You admire your aunt because of her lifestyle. She has her own money, answers to no one, and is free to come and go by her leave."

He'd discovered her ruse. He knew she was using him. Blinking back the tears, M.J. turned to run but she wasn't quick enough as Samuel caught her upper arm.

"Let me go."

Samuel tightened his grip and turned her around to face him. His free arm curved around her waist. "I can't let you go, M.J. Not now. Not ever."

Burying her face against his chest, she wept without making a sound. "I'm sorry," she sniffled, swiping at the moisture on her cheeks.

"There's nothing to be sorry for." Cradling her chin in his hand, he forced her to look up at him. His thumb caressed her lower lip. "I don't ever want you to apologize to me for something you felt you had to do." He smiled. "Understand?"

"*Sí*," she whispered.

"Good." Lowering his head, he touched his mouth to hers, increasing the pressure when she moaned softly. The kiss ended as quickly as it had begun. "Now, go back inside before there's talk about you traipsing in the garden with your *americano.*"

"What does traipsing mean?"

"Frolicking without a care."

She wound her arms around his waist. "I don't have a care."

Samuel kissed her hair. "Please go, M.J."

"I don't want to, Sammy." She'd sobbed out his name.

The press of her firm breasts awakened the flaccid flesh between his thighs, and Samuel knew if M.J. didn't leave he would take her where they stood. "Either you go inside or I will."

M.J. rested her cheek over his heart. "Kiss me again, and I'll go."

Samuel tightened his hold on her slender body and kissed her with all of the passion he could summon for a woman. His mouth moved to her jaw, eyes, and throat before returning to her moist, parted lips.

He ended the kiss, breathing heavily. "Go! Now!"

M.J. needed no further urging. She'd felt the passion and the fire for the first time in her life. Samuel's mouth had set hers afire and his hardness made the area between her legs moist and pulsing with a desire that frightened her.

She raced back to the house, up the staircase, and into her room, closing and locking the door behind her. She peered into a wall mirror; the image staring back at her was a stranger. Her nipples were distended, her pupils dilated, and her lips swollen.

Walking on trembling legs, she made it to her bed and lay facedown on the embroidered sheets. She buried her face in the pillow, smothering the soft moans as her flesh betrayed her again.

She lay motionless, long after her moans subsided and the pulsing eased. The last thought she remembered before sleep claimed her was, how long would she have to wait before she would be acknowledged as Senora Marguerite-Josefina Isabel Cole?

7

How do I love thee? Let me count the ways.

—Elizabeth Barrett Browning

M.J. walked into the small space off the *sala* and came to an abrupt halt. Sitting on the chair she always occupied when reading or doing needlework was the man whom she'd only glimpsed at the dinner table. Samuel Cole, her houseguest, had spent the past week with her father.

The two men spent hours secreted behind the door to Jose Luis's library, many more hours away from the house, and the night before they'd driven into Havana for a night on the town.

It had become apparent to her that she hadn't needed a chaperone because her father had monopolized all of Samuel's time on the island.

Her gaze lingered on him as he came slowly to his feet. He wore his favored *guayabera* with a pair of off-white cotton slacks and sturdy boots. His face was thinner, the cheekbones more pronounced, which made him look even more like the African masks Antonio collected and included in his paintings.

"*Buenos dias,* senor."

A hint of a smile crinkled the skin around his eyes. "Why so formal, Senorita Diaz?"

She bit back a smile, dimples winking attractively. "You think I should not be formal with you? After all, we hardly get to see each other."

He lifted an eyebrow. "You see me now."

"That I do."

Samuel wanted to tell M.J. that he had deliberately kept his distance
from her because he didn't want a repeat of what had happened in the
garden. Although she regarded herself as a modern freethinker,
Marguerite-Josefina was still a woman bound to her culture and class by
virtue of birth. She was an upper-class Cuban woman who'd willingly
risked her reputation and an opportunity to marry well to consort with
an American.

M.J. lifted her chin and appeared to look down her delicate nose at
him. "What do you want? Why are you here?"

Taking four long strides, Samuel closed the distance between them. "I
was waiting for you."

Her eyes widened. "Why?"

"I'd hoped we would spend the day together."

"So you do remember the reason you returned to Cuba." There was
no way he could mistake her cutting sarcasm.

"I never forgot."

A rush of color darkened her cheeks. "You come and go by your leave,
then when you decide to make time for me you expect me to follow you
like an obedient pet."

Her sudden burst of anger elicited a smile from Samuel. "No, darling,
I don't." The endearment had slipped out unbidden.

If Samuel hadn't realized what he'd called her, M.J. did. A tremor
swept over her as her pulse quickened. "I'm not your darling, Samuel."

"Why not?"

"Because you haven't earned the right to call me that."

Slipping his hands into the pockets of his slacks, he rocked back on his
heels. "What would I have to do to earn *that* right, darling?"

Her flush deepened. "Stop it, Samuel," she chided between clenched
teeth. "I am not a child, so don't play games with me."

"I know you're not a child," he said softly, sobering, "and I'm too old
to play games."

"You're not old," she countered.

"I'm twenty-six."

"That's not old. Thirty-six is old."

"Too old to do what?"

M.J. shrugged a shoulder under the white cotton blouse she'd paired
with tan jodhpurs and brown riding boots. "It's too old for a man who
wishes to call on me."

"I agree. You're barely a child yourself."

"I'll be twenty in four weeks."

Samuel smiled lazily. "I guess that makes you a woman."

M.J. tilted her chin, giving him a saucy grin. "You guess right."

"Are you going riding?"

"No. I just came back."

"Where do you go?"

"One of our neighbors has a stable. Papa got rid of our horses after my mother died in a riding accident." She ran a hand over her damp hair. "If you'll excuse me, I need to change before Papa sees me. He gets upset whenever he sees me dressed like this. It reminds him too much of Mama."

"There's no need to rush to change."

"Why not?"

"Your father really tied one on last night, and I'm willing to bet he won't get out of bed until sometime this afternoon."

A slight frown marred M.J.'s delicate beauty. "What does it mean, 'tie one on'?"

"He had too much to drink. I left him in Havana."

"Where in Havana?" Fear, stark and vivid, glittered in her eyes. How could Samuel return to Pinar del Rio without her father?

"He's staying with your aunt. She said she would drive him back tonight."

M.J. closed her eyes and let out an audible sigh. Although she challenged her father's authority she loved him beyond description. She opened her eyes and saw Samuel staring at her. There was something in his penetrating gaze that made her uncomfortable. Was it because, other than the servants, she was alone in the house with him? Was it because she didn't trust herself or the riot of emotions that assailed her whenever she and Samuel shared the same space?

She stared at his generous mouth. Closer examination revealed that his masculine features were a little off-balance, yet did not detract from his overall handsomeness.

"How did you get back?"

"I drove."

"You drove my father's car from Havana?"

"Yes, ma'am."

"You didn't get lost?"

Samuel shook his head. "No. I stayed on the Autopista Havana Pinar del Rio."

"You're here for one week and already you know how to travel around Cuba. In three months no one will be able to tell that you're not a *Cubano.* All you have to do now is learn to speak Spanish."

There were things Samuel needed to do, and learning a foreign language wasn't a priority. He had to conclude his business in Cuba and return to Florida before the end of January.

"Is there something you wanted to do, Samuel?"

M.J.'s soft voice shattered his reverie. "Yes. I'd like for you to show me your tobacco fields."

"Now?"

He nodded. "Yes, now. But only if it's not an imposition."

She smiled sweetly up at him. "Not at all."

Turning on her heel, she walked out of the room, Samuel following and staring at her narrow waist, hips, long legs, thinking that she looked as good from behind as she did from the front.

He is a farmer, M.J. mused, as she watched Samuel pick up a handful of soil and inhale its scent for several seconds before letting it fall back to the ground. He ran his hand over his cotton slacks, brushing off the minute particles.

Samuel pulled a handkerchief from his pocket and dabbed his moist forehead. It wasn't ten o'clock and the early morning temperature was already eighty-seven degrees. He smiled at the slender woman at his side.

She'd retrieved her set of keys to her father's car and driven to the *vegas* where hundreds of acres of newly transplanted *corojo* and *criollo* tobacco seedlings would mature in another three months. The finest *corojo* tobacco, intended for the outer covering of cigars, was grown under cheesecloth coverings to protect the leaves from the sun's rays. The *criollo*, grown in full sunlight, would be harvested and used as filler.

"What do you think?" she asked.

"The soil is good, moist, and rich. What other crop does your father rotate to maintain the soil's fertility?" He knew of no other crop that depleted the soil of its nutrients faster than tobacco.

"Corn."

He nodded, smiling. "Good choice." Corn was good, but soybeans were even better. He'd discussed the advantages of planting soybeans with Jose Luis, telling him it was the crop of the future for the Western world.

Reaching for her hand, Samuel held it in the bend of his arm as he led her away from the fields and back to the *secaderos* where the harvested leaves were hung to dry over wooden poles to catch maximum sunlight. They entered one and he seated M.J. on a low stool before he sat on a matching one.

"How long does it take before the leaves are ready to be made into cigars?"

M.J. didn't want to talk. She just wanted to sit and enjoy the closeness of the man with whom she was certain she was falling in love. It had been a week since her brazen exhibition; the following day she avoided Samuel until the last possible moment. After dinner he hadn't spoken of the incident and neither did she.

Clasping her hands, she sandwiched them between her knees, and stared at the toes of her boots. "The leaves hang here in the sun for almost two months until they turn from yellow to reddish gold. The cured leaves are then bound together and stacked in piles for a first fermentation that will last about a month. This process reduces the resin in the leaves and makes for a more uniform color."

Samuel reached over and removed her straw hat, anchoring it on a pole; he tugged gently at the braid falling the length of her straight spine. "How many fermentation processes do they go through?"

Turning her head, she smiled at him. "Two. They are moistened and the thickest parts of the stems are stripped out. Then they're stacked again, this time in higher bales, and left for two months for a second fermentation.

"After this, they're unpacked and dried on racks, packed again in special bales called *tercios*, which are covered with yagua bark from the royal palm tree. After several periods of aging, the bales are shipped to the cigar factory."

Samuel leaned closer to M.J. "What happens there?"

M.J. shivered despite the heat as Samuel's moist breath feathered over her ear. "At the factory, the tobacco is shaken out, moistened, and dried again in a special room. . . ." Her words died on her tongue.

"Where's the factory?" he whispered, placing tiny kisses along the column of her long, scented neck.

M.J. closed her eyes as her breath came in short, quick gasps. "Sammy?"

He smiled, but did not stop his assault on her dewy skin. "What is it, baby?"

It was her turn to smile. "I can't think with you kissing me."

His mouth lingered on her nape. "What is there to think about? You've been around tobacco all of your life."

"Then . . . then the leaves are flattened and their central veins removed, dividing them in two. After—"

Samuel's mouth found hers, caressing rather than kissing her. One moment she was sitting on the stool; then without warning she was straddling him, her arms around his neck. His lips seared a path down her throat and over her collarbone. Her skin was opalescent in the brilliant sunlight coming into the *secadero*.

"You are so incredibly beautiful." There was no mistaking the reverence and awe in his voice. "I came to Cuba to see you, then spent the past week running away from you."

M.J. compressed her lips, dimples deepening. "I don't understand."

Samuel stared at the woman on his lap, seeing her for the first time. Her innocence was so palpable it made his heart flip-flop. Under her facade of bravado, outspokenness, her plea for women's rights for egalitarianism, emancipation, and equality was a convent-educated girl masquerading in a woman's body.

He pressed his forehead against hers. "I want you."

She smiled. "You have me, Samuel."

He shook his head. "I'm not talking about holding you. I want you in my life."

She sobered quickly, dots of confusion forming between her eyes. "Why are you are talking in riddles?"

A chilled black silence surrounded them, offsetting the heat of the tropical sun. M.J. breathed in shallow, quick gasps as screams of frustration gathered in the back of her throat. If Samuel wanted her in his life, then why was he running away from her?

Anchoring a hand against his chest, she tried escaping his embrace. "Let me go."

He tightened his hold around her waist. "I can't do that."

There was something in Samuel's voice that frightened M.J. Why did it sound so ominous, threatening? She was alone with a man whom she didn't know anything about other than what he'd disclosed to her. He was her houseguest, yet had spent more time with her father than her. The only time they saw each other for an extended period of time was over dinner.

She'd found herself drawn to Samuel Cole because of his face, soft drawling voice, and exquisitely formed hands.

She'd found herself infatuated with Samuel Cole because he was worldly and ambitious.

And she'd fallen in love with Samuel Cole because he'd offered her a glimpse of the passion and fire she'd read about in the books lining the shelves in her aunt's Havana residence.

"*Porque no?* Why not?" she repeated in English.

"Because I don't want to."

"That is not your decision to make."

"Yes, it is, Marguerite-Josefina."

She pounded his chest with a fist. "I told you before not to call me that."

Samuel's expression did not change. "What should I call you? Mrs. Samuel Claridge Cole?"

M.J. felt as if a hand had closed around her throat, cutting off her breath. She couldn't speak, swallow, and a loud buzzing sound in her head escalated. Samuel's mouth was moving but she couldn't hear any of what he was saying.

Dios mio!

She was going to faint. The man she'd fallen in love with had just proposed marriage, and she was swooning like a silly goose.

The buzzing subsided, her pulse slowed, and by some miracle she regained her composure. "Are you asking for my hand in marriage, Samuel?"

He nodded, smiling. His deep-set eyes were mysterious. "Yes, I am, Marguerite-Josefina."

He was calling her by the dreaded name, but this time she didn't care.

He wanted to marry her, but did he love her? And as much as she wanted to become his wife, it would not happen without love. She refused to become a participant in a loveless union.

"What about love, Samuel?"

"What about it, Marguerite-Josefina?"

"Do you love me?" There was a moment of hesitation, and she panicked, her nerves tensing. It was apparent he didn't love her. But why propose marriage? Was it because he knew she wouldn't share his bed unless she was his wife?

Samuel's expression changed, dark eyebrows slanting in a frown. She didn't know. M.J. did not know how much he loved her, had fallen in love with her the first time he saw her. Everything about her lingered with him across bodies of water: her dimpled smile, her slender, curvy body, her musical, lightly accented voice, the silken feel of her skin, and her distinctive feminine scent that was the perfect complement for her perfume.

"You think I don't love you?"

"Answer my question, Samuel." Her jaw was set in a stubborn line.

"I love you. I love you. I love you," he repeated in a hoarse whisper. "I love you now, and I'll love you sixty years from now."

Her eyes filled with tears. "Only sixty, Sammy? You'll have to promise more time than that if you want me to be your wife."

Lowering his head, he kissed her eyelids, tasting salty tears. "Okay, baby. How about seventy-five?"

M.J.'s arms came up and circled his neck as tears streamed down her face and over her trembling lips. "Yes, Sammy," she whispered. "Yes, I will marry you."

Samuel pulled her closer, his protective instincts surfacing quickly. Delicate and vulnerable, she trembled like a frightened bird, and the last thing he wanted was to frighten her.

After they'd shared their first kiss he hadn't trusted himself to be alone with M.J. Even with her father in attendance he still wanted to touch her, tell her that his feelings for her were intensifying with each sunrise.

He'd almost convinced himself that what he felt for Marguerite-Josefina was lust because he hadn't been with a woman in months, but that was a lie. He may have needed a woman, but just not any woman. He wanted the one cradled to his heart.

M.J. closed her eyes, biting down on her lower lip to stop its trembling. Her brain was in tumult, her emotions spinning out of control.

Madre de Dios! her inner voice screamed.

What had she done? She'd just consented to marry a stranger.

* * *

Samuel stood in Gloria Diaz's *gran sala*, holding a glass of champagne as M.J. moved gracefully around the room, accepting good wishes from friends and her cousins.

They'd left the tobacco fields and returned to the house where M.J. placed a call to Havana to tell her father that she had consented to become Samuel Cole's wife. She'd ended the call, then informed him that her father wanted them to pack a bag with casual and evening attire because Gloria was planning an impromptu gathering to celebrate their *compromiso*.

During the drive to Gloria's house, Samuel surprised M.J. when he stopped at a renowned Havana *joyeria* to purchase an engagement ring. The owner, a tall, rotund man wearing a black skullcap, conducted business in English, Spanish, and Yiddish with his customers and employees.

M.J. had reacted like a marionette being manipulated by invisible strings when she sat and stared at her hand whenever the jeweler slipped a ring on her tiny hand. He retreated to a back room and returned with a black velvet pouch and took out one with an Old Mine Cut center diamond, flanked by two large marquis diamonds and latticework of forty-two additional diamonds. The instant the ring slid over her knuckle, there was a chorus of sighs of approval from everyone watching the momentous event.

While M.J. admired her ring Samuel and the owner retreated to a private room in the rear where the man quoted an exorbitant price. They negotiated and manipulated figures until they agreed on an amicable amount for the exquisite piece. Samuel and M.J. left with the ring, and the jeweler secreted the much-sought-after American gold notes in his safe.

Jose Luis, having recovered from his night of frivolity, refused a glass of champagne from a passing waiter. He walked over to his daughter and kissed her cheek.

He reached for M.J.'s left hand and stared at the shimmering diamonds in a platinum setting. "*Exquisito, Chica*," he said softly. "I wish your mother could've been here tonight."

Shaking her head, M.J. bit down on her lower lip. "Don't, Papa. Not tonight. Not when this is one of the happiest days of my life."

"I'm sorry, *Chica*. Even after all so many years I still miss my Carlotta."

She hugged him. "I know you do. I miss what little I remember of her. Samuel and I have set a date," she said in a soft tone, deftly changing the subject.

"When?"

"New Year's Eve."

"Why not your birthday, *Chica?* That way your husband will never forget his wedding anniversary."

Her dark eyes sparkled with excitement. "You're right, Papa. That means I'll become a married woman four days sooner."

Jose Luis smiled when a dreamy expression softened her delicate features. "You love him, don't you?"

"So much that it frightens me." There was a tremor in her voice.

His smile faded. Her cheeks were flushed. "How many glasses of champagne have you had?"

M.J. hoisted her glass. "I lost count after three."

He eased her fingers from around the stem, placing the wineglass on a nearby table. "Drinking is not going to help you face whatever is bothering you."

She pulled her lower lip between her teeth. "Papa. I need to talk to you," she whispered. "Please come with me."

Jose Luis followed her as she walked stiffly out of the *sala* to a small room where Gloria's visitors waited for an audience with her. Table lamps with colorfully painted globes cast a soft glow in the opulently decorated space. M.J. turned and looked at him with an expression he'd never seen before.

"What's the matter?"

She took a deep breath. "I'm scared, Papa. I know in my heart that I love Samuel, but I'm so frightened."

Jose Luis felt a fist of fear squeeze his own heart as he stared at the young woman who'd suddenly appeared so childlike that he yearned to take her in his arms and cradle her as he'd done in the months following her mother's death.

She'd chosen to wear a fashionable black and white midcalf silk evening gown that skimmed over her slender body. Its sophistication matched the wealth of coal-black hair done up in a twist on the nape of her long, graceful neck. The onyx and diamond earrings in her pierced lobes were a gift he'd given her for her eighteenth birthday.

"What frightens you, *Chica?*"

"I don't know if I can be a good wife to Samuel."

"All you have to do is love him, be supportive, and have a lot of patience."

"You make it sound so simple."

"That's because it is, my child."

"Papa, what I'm going to face is so different from me playing with my dolls and pretending to get them ready because their father had promised he was going to take them out for sweets."

"No one is born knowing how to be a wife, husband, mother, or father. We learn every day in the same manner students learn from their professors every day.

"You were given an excellent education. You were taught the academics as well as how to cook, supervise a household staff. I'm certain you'll make Samuel a wonderful wife."

A tentative smile inched the corners of her mouth upward. "Do you think he'll be a good husband, Papa?"

Wondering how much he should tell his daughter about her future husband, Jose Luis said, "What I believe is that he will bring you great joy."

Her eyes narrowed. "What aren't you telling me, Papa?"

"Your *novio* is young and very ambitious. Which means you must be patient and support him in all his endeavors."

"What endeavors?"

"That you must ask him, *Chica.*"

"What if he won't tell me? Samuel doesn't talk much. The only conversation we've had is about tobacco."

Jose Luis patted her cheek. "That's because I've monopolized your young man. Now that you are engaged, that will change. Beginning tonight, he belongs to you."

"*Garcias*, Papa."

"*De nada, mi amor.*"

Jose Luis escorted her back to the *sala* and placed her hand in Samuel's. They exchanged a look that spoke volumes.

Even before Marguerite-Josefina had taken her vows, her father had relinquished his responsibility to protect her to Samuel Cole.

8

If ever two were one, then surely we.

—Anne Bradstreet

M.J. glanced up from her needlework and froze. Samuel stood under the arched doorway, staring at her. How long, she mused, had he been there? How was it she hadn't heard his approach? His shirt and trousers were dotted with moisture, and it was apparent he'd been caught in the sudden downpour that had slackened to a soft, soothing, and hypnotic tapping against the windows.

"*Hola*," she said shyly.

He nodded, smiling. "Hello."

It had been three days since the announcement of their betrothal appeared in the major newspapers. The news was followed by invitations from Cuba's officious social elite who sought a glimpse of Jose Luis's daughter with her purported well-to-do *americano de color*. Gloria had appointed herself M.J.'s surrogate mother, accepting those she felt advantageous to her niece and future husband.

Samuel extended the hand he'd concealed behind his back. "I brought you a little something."

M.J. laid aside the shuttle, placing it along with the square of linen on the table next to her chair. She'd been working feverishly to tat lace around the edges of a set of six embroidered napkins that matched the tablecloth she'd completed that spring.

Her favorite cousin, whom she'd selected as her only bridal attendant, had helped her go through Carlotta Diaz's heirloom linens, china, stemware, and silver, selecting what she wanted packed and shipped to Samuel's West Palm Beach, Florida, home.

Rising gracefully, M.J. shook her head. "You've given me enough, Samuel."

"That's your opinion," he countered in the soft, drawling tone that never failed to send shivers over her body.

"What do you have?" She watched his approach; his right foot toed in a little and made for a slight swagger in his gait.

He handed her a package wrapped in paper imprinted with colorful butterflies. "Open it and see."

M.J. sank down to her chair and peeled back the paper. A gasp of surprise escaped her. Samuel had given her a bottle of Maja perfume and an exquisite black lace fan. Who'd told him the fragrance was her favorite?

Smiling up at him, she asked, "How did you know?"

"I didn't know until I asked the shopkeeper if I could smell it." He went to his knees in front of her. "It smells delicious on you." The balanced blend of citrus, lavender, spice, and woods was perfect for her body's natural scent.

Reaching out, M.J. ran her fingertips over his damp hair. She loved the feel of the thick, tightly curling strands, finding them soft and springy to the touch. She much preferred when he didn't apply the pomade that made his hair stiff and sticky.

"I like your hair without that stuff you put in it," she crooned, staring deeply into his eyes.

"If I don't put that stuff, as you call it, on my hair I can't get it to lie flat."

"Promise me once we're married that unless you're going out you won't put anything on your hair." Leaning closer she pressed a kiss over one eye, then the other.

Samuel caught her braided hair, wrapping its length around and around his fist. "I promise, but only if you promise not to cut your hair."

M.J. giggled like a little girl. "That's an easy promise to keep."

He released her hair. His expression changed, his face becoming a mask of stone. "Will you promise to love me until death parts us?"

Her eyes widened as she pulled back. "Why would you want me to promise that?"

His stoic expression did not change. "I need to know how much you love me."

"But . . . but I do love you, Samuel."

He lifted a questioning eyebrow. "Why is it you haven't told me?"

"But I have."

Samuel shook his head slowly. "No, you haven't. You asked me if I loved you, and I told you I did. You've agreed to become my wife, but you have yet to tell me that you love me. Until now."

M.J. picked up the fan and placed it near her heart. She snapped it open and covered her eyes. Lowering it, she closed it slowly, then put the handle to her lips.

"I've just told you in fan speak that you have won my love, I love you, I promise to marry you, and that I want you to kiss me."

Samuel pushed off the floor, walked over to the door, and closed it. Retracing his steps, he extended his hand and eased M.J. up from the chair. Slowly, deliberately he brushed his thumb over her mouth until her lips parted, then lowered his head and slanted his mouth over hers; he caught her full lower lip between his teeth, pulling and sucking gently on the tender flesh until she writhed and moaned under the sensual assault.

M.J. curled into the curve of Samuel's body, trying to get closer, close enough where they would become one. She moaned again when his hands moved down her back to cradle her hips. There was no mistaking his hardened flesh throbbing against her middle. Desire rushed headlong down the length of her body, setting her flesh afire.

Instinctively, she arched toward him; a rush of moisture followed by pulsing in the secret place between her thighs began, growing stronger and stronger with each passing second. Her fingernails bit into his shoulders, her breasts grew heavy, and her nipples swelled to pebbly hardness as the foreign sensations made her feel as if she'd lost herself and floated away into nothingness.

Samuel gathered the hem of her dress, baring her legs and thighs. He longed to tell M.J. how much he wanted her; that every morning he woke up in a full state of arousal, something that hadn't happened to him since boarding a warship for Europe.

As a teenage boy he'd been as randy as a goat. He had become not only a regular customer at Miss Lola's sportin' house but also a favorite of her best girl, who always tried to talk him into not wearing a rubber sheath because she said it didn't feel natural. Her pleas had fallen on deaf ears because he'd seen firsthand what the ravages of syphilis had done to men who'd frequented prostitutes.

After the war he never visited Miss Lola again. War had changed him, inside and out, for the better.

He closed his eyes, listening to M.J.'s halting breathing and soft moans. His fingers caressed her inner thigh, searching and finding her moist core. Cupping her femininity, he bit back his own groan when her heated flesh convulsed against his palm. She stiffened, gasping, then shuddered, collapsing against his chest as a warm liquid bathed his fingers.

Eyes wide with shame, M.J. stared up at Samuel. She turned her head so he couldn't see the tears welling up in her eyes. "I'm sorry, Sammy."

He released her, settling her dress around her legs, and smiled.

"There's no need to apologize, darling. You were wonderful. We are so good together."

If M.J. hadn't looked so distressed Samuel would've laughed in her face. His outspoken, flirtatious *novia* was so innocent. He was going to enjoy teaching her about her body.

"But we haven't had sex, Samuel."

He smiled, nodding. "We have, darling. Sex is not just . . ."

"Copulating," M.J. said when Samuel's explanation faltered.

His eyebrows lifted. "You know about copulation, but what about orgasms or ejaculation?"

M.J. thrust her chin at him. "I know about orgasms and ejaculation."

"How?"

"I've read about them."

"Reading about them is not the same as experiencing them."

"And you have?"

Samuel gave her a long, penetrating stare. He wasn't about to tell M.J. that he'd slept with a number of women, and had enjoyed each and every one of them; his past would remain his past.

"Things are different for men and women."

"That is something you don't have to remind me of. A married man can take a mistress and still be looked upon as respectable, while a woman is scorned and denigrated for taking lovers. It's not fair, Samuel."

"Don't look so worried, baby. I promise to always be faithful to you."

She placed her hand alongside his cheek. "Don't make promises, *mi amor*, just do it."

Resting his chin on the top of her head, Samuel stared at the door. "I have to return to Florida for a few days."

M.J.'s body stiffened in shock. "I thought you weren't going back to Florida until after we marry."

"I have to straighten out a few things that can't wait."

"What things?"

"Business, M.J."

"Can't you take care of it with the telephone?"

"No." He dropped his arms. "I'll be leaving in the morning."

M.J. felt his loss immediately. He hadn't left Cuba, and already she felt as if he'd abandoned her.

She nodded. "I'll be here when you get back."

Samuel smiled sweetly, as if he were dealing with a temperamental child. He lowered his head and brushed a kiss over her cheek. "I'll see you at breakfast."

A look of implacable withdrawal came over M.J.'s face as she watched him cross the room, open the door, and then close it quietly behind his departing figure.

He had invaded her sanctuary, eliciting a passion that left her reeling from its intensity, only to walk away leaving her wanting more. Had her response to his lovemaking frightened him so much that he feared losing control and would take her without the benefit of marriage?

She pressed a fist to her mouth. Perhaps it was best that Samuel leave for Florida, because she did not trust herself not to seduce him. He'd awakened something within her that screamed to be assuaged.

December 27 could not come soon enough. On that day she would celebrate her twentieth birthday, become Mrs. Samuel Cole, and experience what it meant to be a woman in the biblical sense.

Three weeks.

It seemed like a long time because only now had she begun to recognize her own needs. However, she did not have time to pine over her *novio's* absence.

Not when she had to finish planning her wedding.

"Stop in front of the third house on your right," Samuel said, as the taxi driver slowed his decrepit vehicle, its engine wheezing and rattling, before coming to a complete stop. "Don't bother to get out."

He reached for his bag, pushed open the rear door, and stepped out onto the sand-littered path leading to his mother's house. A familiar late-model car was parked alongside the one-story structure. Samuel recognized the vehicle belonging to his eldest brother, Mark.

The weather in Tallahassee was at least thirty degrees cooler than Cuba's sultry temperatures; a slight wind blowing in off the Gulf of Mexico was a refreshing change from the intense tropical heat. He walked to the front door and knocked. He heard voices and movements inside the house before the door opened.

Mark Cole stared at his brother as if he were an apparition. Of the three Cole brothers, Samuel and Mark looked enough alike to be taken as twins. The only difference was that Mark favored a mustache, and at thirty-one was graying prematurely.

Grinning, his teeth showing whitely under a trimmed black mustache, Mark pounded Samuel's back. "Get in here, little brother. Let me warn you that Mama's fit to be tied because you missed Thanksgiving Day."

Samuel dropped his bag by the door. "I couldn't make it."

"Why?"

"I was in Cuba."

Mark looped an arm over Samuel's shoulders. "What's in Cuba?"

"It's not a what, but who."

"Who then?"

"My fiancée."

Mark's grin faded quickly. "You're getting married?"

Samuel nodded. "Yes."

"When?"

"Two days after Christmas."

"Aw, shit, brother. That's three weeks away."

"What's in three weeks? And you know I don't abide no cussin' on the Sabbath, Mark Japheth Cole."

Samuel turned, smiling at the tall, rawboned woman with a coronet of silver braids atop her head that made her look as if she were wearing a crown.

Even at fifty-four Belinda Cole was still a very handsome woman. Men had come courting a year after Charles died, but Belinda wouldn't have anything to do with any of them, no matter how good-looking or smooth-talking they were.

She rested her hands on her hips. "So, you do know where your mama lives."

Samuel started toward his mother. "Hello, Mama." He hugged and kissed her. "I'm sorry I missed Thanksgiving."

Belinda curved her arms under her youngest son's shoulders. She'd never told anyone, but he was her favorite. Charles had favored Mark and Thomas, while Samuel was hers.

She smiled up at him. "I'll forgive you, that is, if you don't miss Christmas."

Samuel examined his mother's taupe-brown face, finding it clear and still wrinkle-free. Without the gray hair she could've easily be taken for a woman in her early forties. "I came to tell you that I won't be in Florida for Christmas."

"So, the prodigal son returns," mocked a deep voice behind Samuel. "I guess now we can all sit down and eat."

Belinda peered around Samuel's shoulder, frowning. "Thomas, mind your mouth, son."

Thirty-year-old Thomas had inherited his late father's good looks and irascible personality. He glared at Samuel. "Mama, you know that Genie has to eat every four hours or she'll be sick."

"You should've fed her before she left home," Belinda mumbled under her breath.

Thomas's glare shifted to Belinda. "What did you say, Mama?"

She glared back. "Don't take that tone with me, Thomas Isaac Cole. Not today, and not in my house."

"It wouldn't be your house if I hadn't helped pay for it," Thomas said, his voice lowering until it resembled a growl.

"That's enough, Thomas!" Samuel shouted. He fisted his hands, struggling to control his temper. It was as if Charles had come back from the dead as Thomas.

Samuel had grown up listening to his father's tantrums, blaming everyone but himself for his failures. If his crop failed, it was because his wife and children hadn't helped out enough. If Belinda put too much seasoning in his food, he'd throw his plate against the wall, blaming it on his sensitive stomach. And whenever he stood up to Charles in defense of his mother he'd end up in the woodshed, holding his ankles while Charles whipped his bare behind with a switch Samuel had to cut for the event. After a while, he gathered a supply, leaving them in the shed, and wanting to get the ordeal over with as soon as possible.

The whippings ended before Charles's constant ridicule did. At sixteen Samuel was well over six feet and had begun to put on muscle from backbreaking work in the cotton fields. He'd followed Charles into the shed, but when the older man raised his arm to strike him he caught his wrist. The impasse lasted a full minute before Charles dropped the switch and walked away. Two years later Charles was stricken with influenza; he recovered but only to contract tuberculosis, which lay siege to his weakened body. After a violent coughing episode, he took to his bed and never left it again. He was buried two weeks after Samuel was sworn into the army as a private.

"I don't ever want to hear you say that to Mama again," Samuel warned in a soft, lethal tone.

A deep red flush suffused Thomas's face as his hazel eyes glittered wildly. "I'll say it whenever I feel like saying it. And what the hell do you think you're going to do about it?"

The air hummed with danger that made the hair stand up on the backs of the four participants. Belinda loathed seeing her sons fight, while Mark silently urged Samuel to beat the crap out of Thomas. He had gotten so many whippings from his father that he learned early on to stay out of his way and not talk back. Thomas had become his father's favorite son, exempt from any and all physical and verbal abuse.

Samuel relaxed his hands. A slight smile touched his mouth. "You don't want to know." The retort was soft, threatening.

Belinda saw something in her youngest son's eyes that made her shiver. The last time Thomas had disrespected her, Samuel went looking for him with a gun. Thomas spent a month in Pensacola, waiting for Samuel to be shipped overseas, before he came back to Tallahassee.

Belinda touched Samuel's arm. "Please wash up so we all can sit down to eat before Her Highness faints."

"That's uncalled for, Mama," Thomas countered. "Carrying a baby hasn't been easy for Genie," he said in defense of his wife. "Most times she can't get out of bed."

"Please go, Samuel," Belinda urged quietly.

Samuel made his way to the bathroom while his brothers and mother retreated to the kitchen. He should've known better than to come back to Tallahassee on a Sunday. Although Mark and Thomas were married, they always went to their mother's house for Sunday dinner.

He left the bathroom and walked into a large, sun-filled kitchen.

Belinda had moved into her new home the year before. Samuel had offered to pay for the house with his profits from the sale of the soybean crop, but Mark and Thomas, not wanting to be outdone, each contributed a third.

Smiling, he kissed his sisters-in-law, lingering long enough to congratulate Eugenia on her impending motherhood. She was pretty and diminutive, reminding Samuel of a delicate doll. She'd taught school until she married Thomas, then settled into a life of complete domesticity.

Samuel much preferred Mark's wife, Annie-Mae. Eight years Mark's senior, she had lost her first husband and two young children when a kerosene heater in their home exploded, killing them instantly. She'd escaped death by mere minutes because she'd gone to the chicken coop to gather eggs for breakfast. The tragedy of losing her entire family left her with emotional scars that still hadn't faded.

He sat down at the head of the table facing his mother. Platters and serving bowls were filled with crispy fried chicken, collard greens, corn bread, fried okra, and potato salad. Belinda said grace, and then plates were passed around and filled with the sumptuous fare she'd gotten up earlier that morning to prepare.

Samuel waited until everyone had eaten before he made his announcement. "I'm getting married in Cuba on December twenty-seventh."

Eyes bulged, jaws dropped, and an audible gasp escaped Belinda's gaping mouth. Only Mark smiled.

"You can't!" Eugenia screamed.

Samuel frowned at her agonized expression. "And why not?"

"Because I told my best friend that I wanted her to meet you."

He wanted to tell Eugenia that even if he were desperate for a woman he'd never become involved with anyone associated with her.

"I'm sorry, but I'm no longer available to meet any woman."

"Why Cuba?" Thomas asked. It was apparent he'd gotten over his earlier confrontation with Samuel.

"Because she lives there."

"Is she Cuban?" Annie-Mae asked. Samuel nodded. "Does she speak English?"

Smiling, he nodded again. "She speaks English very well." He hesitated. "You're my family, and I'd like all of you to come to witness my very special day."

Annie-Mae stared at her brother-in-law. "I can't, Samuel. I'm afraid of water."

Reaching over, he patted her hand. "It's okay, Annie-Mae."

Thomas curved an arm around Eugenia's thickening waist. "Genie and I won't be able to make it either. Her doctor has cautioned her about traveling."

"Don't worry, Samuel. I'll be there for you," Belinda said with cool authority. "I wouldn't miss your wedding for all of the money in the world."

Samuel bowed his head in acknowledgment. "Thank you, Mama."

He hadn't expected his brothers to attend his wedding. Mark couldn't leave Annie-Mae, and Thomas had always resented his closeness with their mother.

The only thing that mattered now was that in another three weeks he would exchange vows with a woman he loved, and his mother would be there to witness it.

Belinda opened her eyes as she rocked back and forth in a slow measured rhythm and smiled at Samuel lounging in a matching rocker.

Dinner was over, the kitchen cleaned, and everyone had returned home—everyone but Samuel. He'd informed her that he would remain in Tallahassee for two days before traveling on to West Palm Beach.

"When are you going back to Cuba?"

"Next weekend."

"Tell me about your young lady."

Belinda heard an emotion in her son's voice when he spoke of Marguerite-Josefina Diaz that she'd never heard before. It was soft, almost reverent.

"Do you love her, Samuel?"

He gave her a direct stare. "More than I thought I could ever love a woman."

"Does she love you?"

"Yes, Mama. She's admitted she loves me, too."

"Then you should have a wonderful life together."

Belinda closed her eyes again, and a small smile of serenity touched her lips. Samuel was worth spending her entire pregnancy in bed, and the long, painful delivery she'd gone through to bring him into the world.

9

Maidenhood, maidenhood, whither has thou fled from me?

—Sappho

M.J. felt the muscles tense in the arm under the fabric of an off-white linen jacket. She glanced up at Samuel and held her breath. His countenance was immobile, his gaze fixed on a group of people coming from the area where they'd waited to be cleared to enter Cuba.

She turned and stared at the figure of a tall, thin woman striding regally in their direction. As she came closer, M.J. noticed the exquisite tailoring of a raw silk blue-gray dress with long sleeves and a dropped waistline. A straw cloche in the same blue-gray shade dipped slightly over her left eye. Her nut-brown face was flawless, wrinkle-free.

M.J. smiled when Samuel covered her hand resting on his arm. "That's my mother," he said softly.

Leaning against his side, M.J. glanced up at him. His expression hadn't changed, and at that moment she couldn't tell what he was thinking or feeling.

Samuel had returned to Cuba after a ten-day absence, informing her that only his mother would be able to attend their wedding because one of his sisters-in-law was in the early stages of a difficult pregnancy and the other's fear of water prohibited her getting on a boat.

Of the 112 invited to witness the exchange of vows between Marguerite-Josefina Isabel and Samuel Claridge Cole, only one would share blood with the groom. She'd argued nonstop with Samuel, asking why Mark couldn't attend without his wife, until Samuel finally told her that Annie-Mae had had a mental breakdown and could not be left alone for an extended period of time. This disclosure left her wondering if she would ever be able to form a bond with the women who'd married Samuel's brothers. And she did not expect to see them too often with more than three hundred miles between Tallahassee and West Palm Beach.

She returned her attention to the woman whom she would relate to as Mother. "She's a very handsome woman."

Samuel agreed with M.J. that Belinda looked extremely fashionable. He'd given her money to purchase a new wardrobe for her trip and the wedding. He'd also requested that she come to Cuba days before the ceremony to take in some of the sights on the beautiful Caribbean island. He waited until she'd shown her stamped paper to a uniform guard at a gate before approaching her.

Belinda didn't see her son and the slender woman clinging to his arm until they were several feet away. She'd hardly recognized him in an off-white linen suit and Panama hat. He'd turned the brim down, shading his upper face from the intense winter sun.

She extended her hands, smiling. "Thank you for meeting me."

Samuel hugged his mother with his free arm. "Welcome to Cuba." He kissed her moist cheek and took her single piece of luggage from her loose grip. "I'd like to introduce you to Marguerite-Josefina. M.J., my mother, Belinda Cole."

M.J. eased her hand from Samuel's arm and hugged Belinda. In heels they were the same height. "*Bienvenido a Cuba,*" she said shyly in Spanish, translating Samuel's greeting. Her dimples winked at Belinda. "I said welcome to Cuba."

Belinda smiled at the young woman with Samuel. Marguerite-Josefina was tall and claimed an ethereal beauty rarely seen in a woman. Her hair, under a sunny-yellow straw cloche, was a gleaming blue black, her features delicate and perfectly symmetrical. The double strand of pearls around her long neck, and a matching pair dangling from her pierced lobes, were magnificent. When Samuel told his mother that his future wife came from an upper-class Cuban family it was evident by the poise of the woman who spoke English and Spanish with equal facility.

"Thank you, Marguerite-Josefina."

"Please call me M.J. Marguerite-Josefina takes too long to say."

"You may call me Belinda."

A slight blush swept over M.J.'s lightly tanned face. "May I have your permission to call you Mother? My mother died when I was four, and I'd be honored if you would think of me as your daughter."

Belinda moved closer, hugging and kissing M.J.'s cool, scented cheek.

"Of course, my child." Pulling back, she looked into a pair of large, dark eyes filled with uncertainty. "From this very moment you can consider me your mother and you'll be my daughter."

Samuel offered his arms to the two most important women in his life. "Come, let's get out of the sun."

He led them to where he'd parked Gloria's car. After assisting them into the vehicle, he stored Belinda's bag in the space behind the rear seats. Since returning to Cuba he'd moved in with Gloria Diaz. Her home was situated in the Vedado section of Havana, a quiet old neighborhood where wrought-iron gates and night watchmen guarded classic mansions. Every night at Gloria's was a fiesta with a steady stream of people who ate, drank, debated, sang, and danced to the live music of several bands until the early morning hours. One morning he had to step over a man who'd passed out in the inner courtyard, his fingers still gripping a glass of *fuego liquido*. His single encounter with liquid fire was enough for him to swear off the potent drink forever.

He and M.J. would marry in a nuptial Mass in a Havana cathedral, followed by a formal dinner, then dancing in Gloria's grand ballroom and garden. Belinda had taken him and his brothers to church every Sunday, but it was only when he had to talk to a priest about his Baptist faith that he realized he had become a backslider. He could not remember the last time he had been inside a church. He admitted that he hadn't lost his faith in God; it was just that he did not attend services. The newly ordained priest made him promise to baptize his children as Catholics, and then prayed he would find his way back to the house of God.

Samuel maneuvered away from the waterfront, driving slowly over cobblestone streets. He drove along El Prado, reminiscent of a European boulevard, enormously wide and beautifully designed with an allée of trees, old streetlamps, benches, and grand turn-of-the-century buildings and monuments standing in the brilliant sunlight. The air was bright, clear, and smelled of the sea. Cuba was beautiful, a magical paradise where he'd found the woman whom he'd risk everything to love and hold on to forever.

Havana was bustling with activity. There was a cacophony of sounds from automobile horns, trolley-car bells, the music of street bands, and the voices of people sipping coffee at sidewalk cafés.

"What do you think of Cuba, Mama?" he asked Belinda over his shoulder.

She stared out the car window. "Everything looks so old, but it's very pretty."

Samuel nodded. "That's because they don't tear down their old buildings to put up new ones. It's the same in Europe. The old coexists with the new."

Belinda stared at the colorful awnings shading balconies and door-ways, flowering trees, palms set in massive stone planters, and facades painted shrimp pink, sky blue, or lemon yellow.

Her gaze lingered on buildings with shuttered windows and grillwork balconies. A street band made up of musicians with guitars, drums, and horns played a catchy tune as people in cars, motorcycles with sidecars, and pedestrians slowed to listen. Most men wore Panama hats, while women wore fashionable cloches made of the finest straw.

Havana was a city of color—from the many shades of its inhabitants, to the lushness of its tropical foliage, clear blue sky, and waters. Belinda could see why her son had fallen in love with M.J. Diaz. She, like the country of her birth, was charming and breathtakingly beautiful.

The last haunting note of "Ave Maria" sung by a soprano with an opera company at the Sociedad pro Arte faded away, and a hush fell over the cathedral as M.J., leaning against her father to keep her balance, placed one foot in front of the other and stared through a veil of Belgian lace as he led her down the flower-strewn carpet to the altar where Samuel stood with Cesar Ferrer. Her cousin had offered to stand in as Samuel's best man, while his sister Ivonne had become her sole atten-dant. A nervous smile parted her lips as she glanced at Ivonne, who had teased her, saying she was going to make funny faces, hoping to make her smile.

As the time neared for the wedding she'd had an attack of nerves that left her cloistered in her bedroom. The reality that she would marry Samuel, and a week later leave all she'd known all of her life for a foreign country and a culture so unlike her own, made her short-tempered. Her anxiety only subsided when Samuel came to Pinar del Rio for *Noche Buena.*

Family members who had come from every part of the island for the wedding assisted the household staff decorating trees with colorful lights, tending the pigs roasting on barbecue spits, and setting long tables with festive linen, china, and silver. After filling up on roast pork-*lechon asado,* black beans and rice, yucca with a garlic sauce, salad, and Samuel's favorite, *mojo criollo,* a Creole garlic sauce, she managed to steal away in the garden to meet him for all of three minutes.

They'd held each other, without exchanging a word, then returned to the courtyard to join the others enjoying the Christmas Eve festivities that were repeated throughout the island.

"Are you all right, *Chica?*" Jose Luis whispered close to her ear.

"*Sí,* Papa," she whispered back.

And she was all right. The man she loved was less than ten feet away, waiting to make her his wife. Her smile widened when she saw him staring at her, his dark eyes filled with awe. He looked dashing in a cutaway coat, black-striped trousers, white silk tie, and pearl-gray vest. The lily of the valley pinned to his lapel matched those in her bouquet.

Samuel lowered his chin and glanced away from the vision in white. At that moment he didn't trust himself not to lose his composure. He'd tried imagining how M.J. would look as a bride and failed miserably. She wore a vintage couture dress bought in Paris by her maternal grand-mother's great-aunt in 1870 and a modern, dramatic, flowing, floor-length veil.

He felt her presence, heat, inhaled the heady scent of her bouquet, and turned and stared at his bride. Her features were obscured under the lace. Pinned into her unbound hair, fashioned into tiny curls, was tiny, bell-like lily of the valley.

The priest said something in Spanish and Jose Luis responded, placed M.J.'s glove-covered right hand in Samuel's left one, then stepped back to sit down in the pew assigned him.

Samuel couldn't understand a word of Latin as he found himself standing and kneeling at various times during the ceremony. Everything appeared mystical as the priest offered those who were Catholics a tiny white wafer disc that represented the body of the risen Christ. He switched from Latin to Spanish when it came time for them to exchange vows.

Samuel repeated his vows in Spanish, getting all of the words right, but his pronunciation had a few people close enough to hear him corrupt the language snickering behind their hands or fans.

His hand shook slightly as he slipped a delicate platinum band on M.J.'s finger. She repeated the gesture, and the wide gold band on his finger was a sign that he'd pledged his life and future to her for an eter-nity.

Slowly, deliberately he raised her veil, and smiled. The delicate oval face with the large dark eyes was that of an angel. He touched her lower lip with his thumb, then lowered his head and brushed his mouth over hers.

"I'll love you forever, Senora Cole," he whispered against her moist, parted, reddened lips.

M.J. inhaled the moistness of his breath. "*Te amo, mi amor, mi corazon.*"

Smiling and holding hands, they turned to face the congregants as Mr. and Mrs. Samuel Cole. He raised her left hand to his lips, kissing her fin-gers. The gesture was imprinted in the minds of all who witnessed the in-timate moment.

M.J.'s smile dazzled everyone who watched her traverse the carpet with her new husband. Rumors were circulating that Marguerite-Josefina had married Samuel Cole because he was a distant cousin of an African prince who owned diamond mines, that he'd inherited millions from his ancestors who'd made their money buying and selling slaves, and that Josc Luis had paid him an enormous dowry to marry his daughter to save her from the licentious advances of Antonio Santamaria.

Whatever the reason for Marguerite-Josefina marrying her American they were looking forward to the wedding reception at Gloria Diaz's Vedado mansion. Word had come from someone at the capitol that President Machado was expected to come and pay his respects to the newlyweds.

M.J. stood under the sweeping branches of an acacia tree, Samuel standing behind her, right hand resting on her waist, as they stared directly at the camera lens. Lifting her chin slightly, she smiled as a bright flash, followed by a puff of smoke, captured the excitement shimmering in her dark eyes.

The photographer nodded and she turned to Samuel, her smile still in place. "Thankfully that's over."

They'd spent more than an hour posing for wedding pictures. The photographer had taken frames of them outside the cathedral as they were showered with rice and orange blossoms, with their respective parents, then several with Jose Luis and Belinda, Samuel with Cesar, M.J. with Ivonne, and the wedding party.

Anchoring a forefinger under her chin, Samuel kissed her mouth. "Let's go inside." He was hot, thirsty, and hungry.

Gloria had her cook prepare a monstrous breakfast, but he hadn't been able to eat anything when doubt attacked him without warning. Five hours before he was to be married he struggled with the uncertainty of whether he could be a good husband and father. And it wasn't as if he'd had the best teacher: Charles Cole.

He'd sworn an oath that he would never berate his wife or whip his children, but the what-ifs lingered along the fringes of his mind. What if his United Fruit Company venture failed? What if his quest to become a millionaire never materialized? What if he couldn't give M.J. the comfortable lifestyle she was accustomed to? As much as he tried dismissing the apprehension as premarital jitters, it persisted.

Samuel escorted M.J. into the grand ballroom and they were met with a rousing, deafening applause. Hundreds of lights from two massive chandeliers twinkled like stars as a string quartet played softly in a corner. They were led to a long table while waiters escorted wedding guests to round tables with seating for ten.

M.J. smiled at her father, who was sitting beside Belinda at the bridal table. Samuel seated her, then sat down. Ivonne and Cesar were on his left.

Gloria had hired two well-known Havana chefs to prepare everything from appetizers to main courses, and a plethora of desserts. White-jacketed waiters were busy filling glasses with chilled wines and champagne as waitresses with crisp white aprons set out platters of *empanadas, mariquitas de plantanos,* yucca, crab, and black-eyed pea fritters with the ubiquitous sauces: *mojo vinegreta* and *mojo criollo.*

M.J. removed her veil, handing it to Ivonne. Smiling at her younger cousin, she said, "Save it for your wedding." She would wrap the vintage wedding gown in tissue paper and save it for the daughter she hoped to have. She placed her hand over Samuel's, catching his attention.

"Yes, darling?"

Angling her head closer to his, she said, "There's something we *have* to talk about."

He lifted his eyebrows. "Here?"

M.J. hesitated. "Well . . . yes."

Samuel reversed their hands, giving her fingers a gentle squeeze. "What is it?"

A blush found its way up the high neckline of white lace to her midnight-black hair. "Babies," she whispered.

A hint of a smile played at the corners of Samuel's wide mouth. "What about them?"

Her embarrassment escalated, and she chided herself for broaching the subject. "Do you want them?"

Samuel stared at his wife, wondering why she would ask him such a preposterous question. Wasn't that why people married? So they could start a family?

"Of course I want children. Why would you ask me that?"

"Because," M.J. said in a hushed tone, "we've never talked about it."

"We don't have to talk about everything, baby," he said softly, shaking his head.

"I don't want you to think of me as presumptuous."

"That will never happen. And to let you know how much I want you to be the mother of our children, would you mind if we start tonight?"

"No," she whispered, "I don't mind at all."

She glanced away as the heat in her face moved downward, settling between her legs. Gloria had spoken to her at length about what to expect on her wedding night, showing her drawings of men and women in various sexual positions. Her aunt told her that she would probably endure some pain the first time, but if she learned to relax she would experience pleasure so intense that it would leave her breathless.

When M.J. asked her aunt why she hadn't married or become a mother, the older woman said she did not have the proclivity to be a faithful wife, so therefore she chose to remain single.

Samuel saw a becoming blush stain M.J.'s cheeks. December 27, 1924, was to become a day of milestones for Marguerite-Josefina Isabel Diaz Cole: her twentieth birthday, wedding day, and the day she would offer her virginity to her husband.

The strains of a waltz grew louder and he pushed back his chair and eased M.J. to her feet. He bowed from the waist. "May I have this dance, Mrs. Cole?"

She tilted her head back and a wealth of curls grazed her hips. "Yes, you may, Mr. Cole."

A swollen hush fell over the assembled guests as they watched Samuel lead his wife to the middle of the marble floor. He twirled her around and around, the tails of his cutaway coat lifting with the motion. Tiny petals from the flowers pinned in her curls floated to the floor as Samuel and M.J. moved smoothly together as if gliding on ice.

Jose Luis rose to his feet, offering his hand to Belinda. Tall and silver-haired, they made their way onto the dance floor and joined their children. Belinda was stunning in pale gray—a tabard of antique beaded lace over a satin slip dress. She'd had her hair straightened and styled into an elaborate chignon on the nape of her long, smooth neck.

"Our parents look nice together," M.J. said, smiling up at Samuel.

"True, but my mother will never marry again."

"Neither will my father, but perhaps they will become friends."

Samuel pulled her closer to his body. "Matchmaking, darling?"

"No. It's just that we're so happy, so why can't everyone else be?"

"Because it's just not that way." His voice had taken on the tone one used when speaking to a child. "People have to find their own happiness. I can't give you what you need to make you happy, or vice versa."

Her smooth brow furrowed in confusion. "But you do make me happy, Samuel."

"I make you happy because I happen to be what you were looking for in a husband. And you make me happy because you have everything I want in a wife. And because you are who you are I thank God for making me a man."

M.J. rested her forehead on his shoulder as he spun her around and around until others joined the two couples on the dance floor.

The silent, efficient waiters served course after course, while premium champagne flowed like water. The sumptuous banquet ended with cake and delicate confectionaries and cups of strong Cuban coffee. The reveling continued well into the night as the guests left the ballroom and gathered in the courtyard and gardens for dancing under the stars. The soft strains of the waltz gave way to a band playing the African-inspired samba.

Samuel stood near the acacia tree, watching his wife as she lifted the hem of her gown and danced in wild abandon with a step-close-step, then dipped and sprang upward with each beat of the drums. Only a few flower petals and curls were left in her hair as she lost herself in the hypnotic rhythm. The music had reached inside her, connecting her with her African ancestors.

"Your wife is very spirited."

Samuel glanced down at Gloria. He hadn't heard her approach. "I see that."

"Whatever you do, Samuel, promise me you won't break her spirit."

He felt the pounding of the drums in his ears and in his chest, feeling what M.J. felt. The sensations were powerful, frightening in their power to transport him across an ocean to a continent where his ancestors lived for centuries before outsiders began carving up their homeland.

He met Gloria's challenging stare, eyes gleaming like glassy volcanic rock. "I promise."

"Good." She rested a hand on his sleeve. "I came to tell you that your driver is waiting in the courtyard to take you and your wife to the pier where a yacht will take you to Cayo Largo del Sur."

The yacht belonged to a Boston financier who'd begun wintering in the Caribbean after the war. A widowed grandfather, he and Gloria had conducted a liaison spanning a decade.

"How can M.J. and I thank you for your generosity?"

Gloria patted his arm. Her dark eyes misted. "You can thank me by making my niece happy. Now go and change. I'll get Marguerite-Josefina."

Samuel searched the garden for his mother. He wanted to tell her he was leaving for his honeymoon. He found her in the ballroom, sitting at one of the round tables talking quietly with Jose Luis.

Bending over, he kissed her forehead. "We're leaving now. I'll see you after we're settled."

Touching his cheek, Belinda smiled. "God bless you, son."

Jose Luis stood up, extending his hand. "I'll see that your mother gets home safely." He shook Samuel's hand. "*Bendicion, mi hijo.*"

Samuel nodded. "Thank you." He walked out of the ballroom, feeling two pair of eyes boring into his back. His mother was scheduled to sail back to the States New Year's Eve because she wanted to celebrate the new year on American soil. Jose Luis and Gloria had promised him they would look after Belinda until the time of her departure.

He and M.J. would honeymoon on Cayo Largo del Sur for a week before returning to Pinar del Rio. Two days later they would leave Cuba for Florida to begin to live out their lives as husband and wife in the United States.

*   *   *

The ship's captain greeted Samuel and M.J. with a snappy salute, his sky-blue gaze lingering on Mrs. Cole. Her rose-pink traveling suit enhanced the olive undertones in her tanned face. Several strands of black hair lifted and touched her cheek in the sea breezes sweeping over the deck of the yacht.

"Welcome aboard, Mr. and Mrs. Cole. I'm Captain McLaughlin. We'll be sailing with a small crew, who are here to see to your every need." His Irish brogue sounded like music.

Samuel inclined his head, smiling. "Thank you, Captain. When do you expect to drop anchor at Cayo Largo del Sur?"

"Sometime after sunrise. Will you and your missus be wanting breakfast in your cabin?"

Samuel met M.J.'s questioning gaze. He hadn't expected them to spend their wedding night onboard a ship. "Yes."

Captain McLaughlin snapped his fingers at a skinny, barefoot boy. "Take these bags below." He turned back to Samuel. "If you and your missus follow Bobby he'll show you to your cabin."

Samuel gathered M.J. in his arms, carried her down the narrow stairway, and into a cabin reeking of extravagance so opulent he felt slightly nauseated. A bed covered in gold silk and large enough for four took up more than half the space. Soft yellow light from wall sconces illuminated African mahogany walls, Persian rugs, and a Cluny tapestry wall hanging. A sterling tea set, a crystal bowl filled with ice, and a bottle of champagne sat on an antique rosewood table with two pull-up chairs. Delicate bone china, crystal stemware, and decanters of liquors filled a massive china cabinet. The cabin had all of the amenities of a room at any luxury hotel.

Waiting until the cabin boy placed their luggage on a padded bench and walked out, closing the door behind him, M.J. wrinkled her delicate nose. "What do you think?" she asked, seeing a glint of amusement in her husband's eyes.

"It's a little showy for my tastes," Samuel admitted.

Tightening her grip around his neck, she brushed her mouth over his. "I think ostentatious is a better word, don't you think?"

Samuel went completely still. Nothing moved, not even his chest as he held his breath. He'd found it hard to believe that the woman in his arms was his; she belonged to him to love and cherish forever. And there wasn't anything he wouldn't do to make her as happy as she appeared now.

"I think you're perfect."

M.J.'s lashes fluttered wildly as she anticipated what she would come to share with the man holding her to his heart: her life, selfless love, and virginal body.

She closed her eyes against his intense stare. "I love you."

Making his way to the bed, Samuel placed M.J. gently on the silk coverlet, his body following hers down. Cradling her face between his hands, he caressed her mouth until her lips parted. Slowly, tentatively he eased his tongue into her mouth; she opened wider to permit him full possession. His splayed fingers tunneled through strands of ebony silk spread out over gold silk.

M.J. reveled in the tongue exploring the roof of her mouth, the ridge of her teeth, and the inside of her cheek before it curled around hers. It evoked sensations that were new and exciting. She'd thought kissing was the touching of lips, but this was different, electrifying.

She caught the tip of Samuel's tongue between her teeth, suckling it gently until he moaned as if in pain. She released his tongue, replacing it with his lower lip, pulling it into her mouth. His hardness surged against her middle, and she arched.

Go easy with her, because it's her first time. The litany played over and over in Samuel's head; he forced himself to slow down as his fingers tightened in her unbound hair. He didn't know how long he could continue to kiss her and not explode.

Rolling off her body, he left the bed. "I'm going up on deck," he said, slipping out of his jacket and tie. "As soon as we're under way I'll be back." Samuel leaned over and ran the pad of his thumb over her lower lip. "Don't run away."

M.J. smiled. "That's something you don't ever have to worry about. I will never leave you."

Samuel gave his wife a long, penetrating look. "Nor I you, Marguerite-Josefina." Turning on his heel, he left the cabin, closing the door.

Minutes later he found himself on deck, watching the crew as they prepared to sail away from Cuba's mainland for the tiny piece of land dotted with palm trees, lush vegetation, caves, and lagoons.

He sat on a deck chair, staring up at the darkened sky. The smell of the sea and Cuba wafted in his nostrils. He never would've imagined when he'd come to the Caribbean island two months before that he would fall in love with a woman and the country of her birth. He'd told Arturo Moreno that he had no intention of living in Cuba. But what he hadn't known at the time was that he *would* come back again and again because of his wife.

He would give M.J. time to get into bed before joining her.

M.J. tossed back a small amount of brandy, grimacing as heat settled in her chest. Placing the snifter on a table, she climbed into bed and pulled a sheet over her. The rustle of her silk nightgown against the satin sheets reminded her of the sound lizards made whenever they scurried into the bushes for safety. She was exhausted from eating, drinking, dancing, and celebrating her birthday and wedding.

It was a day she would never forget.

Samuel walked into the cabin, encountering darkness. M.J. had extinguished all of the lights. Feeling his way, he managed to make it to the tiny bathroom without falling or knocking something over.

The smell of M.J. permeated the space. A shelf held bottles and vials of lotion, creams, and perfume. He smiled. She'd unpacked his toiletry bag and placed his grooming supplies on a lower shelf.

He brushed his teeth, stepped into the cramped shower stall, and turned on the hot water faucet. "Shit!" The curse slipped out as a stream of ice-cold water pelted his body. M.J. had used up all the hot water. The next time, either he would shower first or they would shower together.

"What's the matter?"

Samuel peered over a low wooden door. M.J. stood in the bathroom, eyes wide with fright.

The light from a lamp on the vanity showed the outline of her body under a diaphanous white, lace-trimmed nightgown. His stunned gaze lingered on the soft curves of her hips, slim thighs, and long legs.

"Nothing. Go back to bed."

"Why were you cursing?"

Samuel swallowed another expletive. His penis had hardened so quickly that he feared spilling his passions in the shower. He held his engorged flesh tightly, struggling to stop the flow of semen straining for release.

"It's nothing, M.J. Please go back to bed." He was pleading with her, and didn't care if she knew it.

There was a moment of silence. "Okay, Samuel."

She left the bathroom, yet her sensual image lingered. He washed his hair and body in record time. Pushing open the louvered door, he reached for a towel. He hadn't realized his hands were shaking until he peered into the mirror to blot the moisture from his hair.

He'd slept with women whose faces or names he couldn't remember, yet a slip of a woman-girl he'd claimed as his wife had him close to losing control.

Even when Charles Cole whipped him Samuel never cried. He would've forfeited his life before he'd permit his father to control him. He loved M.J., but she was never to know that she'd come close to controlling him.

Walking on bare feet, he left the bathroom and made out the bed. M.J. had opened the curtain covering a porthole. He slipped into bed and pulled her close to his body. She was trembling.

Samuel kissed her forehead. "Baby, we don't have to do anything tonight. I'll give you all of the time you need to get used to sleeping with me."

M.J. shifted, burying her face against his chest. She wrinkled her nose, smiling. The hair on his chest tickled her nose. "I'm okay, Sammy."

He kissed the top of her head. "Are you sure, baby?"

"Yes, I'm sure."

"Then kiss me."

She obeyed; pressing her lips to his, she inhaled his breath, his scent. Samuel smiled. "Good."

Waiting until her trembling subsided, he swept back the sheet and removed her nightgown. Supporting his weight on his arms, he began at her hairline, trailing kisses over her forehead, the end of her nose, mouth, jawline, throat, breasts, belly, thighs, legs, and feet before reversing a path over the expanse of her velvety, fragrant skin.

M.J. could not stop the moans escaping her parted lips, the rush of moisture bathing the folds at the apex of her thighs, could not keep her hips from writhing or her legs from shaking. Samuel's mouth was driving her crazy.

"Now I want you to touch me, darling."

"Why?"

Samuel's soft chuckle filled the space. "Because I've touched you. Reaching for her hand, he pressed it to his groin and tightened his grip when she attempted to pull away. "No, baby," he crooned against her ear. "Feel how much I want you. That's it," he continued as her fingers closed on his erect penis. "Move your hand like this." He guided her hand in an up-and-down motion.

M.J. felt the heat, the flow of blood, and the throbbing against her palm. "You want me and I want you, Sammy."

He suckled her lower lip. "I don't want to hurt you."

Curving an arm under one shoulder, she kissed his throat. "I've been told that it will only hurt the first time."

"I'll try to be gentle."

Sighing, M.J. closed her eyes. "Don't talk, Sammy." She opened her legs. "Just do it! Please." She'd sobbed her entreaty.

Spreading her legs wider with his knee, Samuel guided her hand and eased his penis into her vagina. Her gasps, one overlapping the other, escalated as her tight flesh stretched to accommodate his sex.

"Do you want me to stop?" He'd asked the question when it was the last thing he wanted to do. M.J.'s feminine heat, her smell, tightness made him feel as if he were losing his mind. He'd thought perhaps it was because he hadn't been with a woman for some time, but knew differently. It was the woman to whom he'd given his name and pledged his protection.

M.J. shook her head. She wanted it done so the pain could stop. Samuel was big, much larger than the men in the drawings she'd glimpsed in her aunt's books. Closing her eyes, she prayed for the burning to stop, and miraculously it did.

Samuel froze. He was only in halfway. Gritting his teeth, he thrust his hips forward, tearing the maidenhead his wife had offered as the ultimate gift.

He buried his face between her neck and shoulder. "Thank you, darling. Thank you for saving yourself for me."

Tears flooded M.J.'s eyes and flowed down her cheeks as she recalled the words of the Greek poet Sappho: *Maidenhood, maidenhood, whither has thou fled from me?*

She nodded, unable to form the words locked in her throat. She had become wife and woman in the twentieth year of her life.

Samuel moved slowly, tentatively, as if testing how much he could thrust into her newly opened flesh. His hands traced a sensual path down her ribs and hips. He took his time, arousing her until she squirmed and writhed in an age-old rhythm that needed no tutoring. Passion and lust pounded the blood through his head, heart, and loins.

M.J. gloried in the scent of her husband's freshly showered skin, the feel of his skin against hers, his touch that sent tingles up and down her body, and the hardness sliding in and out of her body, setting her afire.

He quickened his thrusts, M.J. following his pace. Heat shot through her like an electric current; throwing back her head, she screamed, not a high-pitched sound but a low growl that subsided to long, surrendering moans. A deep feeling of peace entered her being as Samuel collapsed heavily on her body. The sound of their breathing competed with the rush of water lapping against the yacht as it sailed toward their honeymoon destination.

M.J. closed her eyes. A man who'd offered her his love, his heat, and his passion had awakened the dormant sexuality of her body, a man who'd become her husband; a man, she prayed, who would become the father of her children.

PART 2

1925

Everett Kirkland

Success is never so interesting as struggle.

—Willa Cather

10

In the United States there is more space where nobody is than where anybody is.

—Gertrude Stein

"*Por Dios*! What did you do to yourself?"

M.J. halted in the task of placing earrings, necklaces, rings, and bracelets into velvet pouches, and glanced up. Ivonne Ferrer stood in the doorway, a hand covering her mouth and an expression of shock distorting her pretty face.

M.J. rolled her eyes at her cousin. "Say it, Ivonne."

Diminutive, with unruly bright red curls and dark blue eyes, Ivonne lowered her hand. "You've ruined your skin."

Ivonne's reaction was similar to those who saw her since she'd returned from her honeymoon. She and Samuel had spent the week swimming, eating, and sometimes sleeping on the beach where the sun had darkened her face and body. The first day she'd burned so badly that she couldn't bear for Samuel to touch her. But instead of peeling, her tan deepened until she was as brown as some who worked long hours in the tobacco fields.

M.J. lifted her expressive eyebrows. "Why? Because I now look like *mi bisabuela*?"

Ivonne lowered her hand. "She really wasn't your great-grandmother. She was your *bisabuelo's* mistress."

"She was my father's grandmother, and therefore *mi familia*."

Ivonne blushed. "And I'm not?"

"Yes, Ivonne, we are family because our mothers were sisters."

Walking into the bedroom, Ivonne held out her arms, tears shimmering in her eyes. "I didn't come here to fight with you, *m'ija*, but to say good-bye."

M.J. hugged her. "It's not good-bye. You promised you would come visit me."

"And I will. But first I'm going to let you get used to your new husband."

"I'm already used to him."

"How is he?" Ivonne whispered.

"He's wonderful."

Ivonne held M.J.'s hands. "How was it?"

"What?"

Ivonne blushed again. "You know what I'm talking about."

Pulling her fingers from her cousin's loose grip, M.J. went back to packing her jewelry. She'd decided not to put the heirloom pieces with the other items that were to be shipped to her new West Palm Beach home.

"Are you talking about sex?"

"Don't say it so loud." M.J. gave her a sidelong glance. "So . . . was it . . . good?"

A small smile of enchantment touched M.J.'s lips. "No, it's not good." She ignored her cousin's gasp. "It's wonderful." Her hands stilled as she tried ignoring the rush of heat making its way down her body. "I can't get enough of him, Ivonne," she whispered coconspiratorially. "We finish, rest a few minutes, then do it again. I'm like someone . . . someone possessed, or addicted to . . . to opium."

"*M'ija*, I'm so happy for you." The tears in Ivonne's eyes sparkled. She sat down, watching M.J. as she closed a large carved jewelry chest. "I hope when I marry I will find a man like your Samuel."

"Don't worry, Ivonne, you will. You're only eighteen, and you have time before people will start calling you a *solterona.*"

"I have no intention of becoming a spinster. Now, tell about your honeymoon."

The two women sat on a chaise, M.J. holding Ivonne's rapt attention as she described in vivid detail the beauty of Cayo Largo del Sur and the house where she and Samuel stayed that belonged to a wealthy American. Her voice softened considerably when she revealed how she and Samuel lingered in bed until midday, took their meals under a copse of pine trees, several hundred feet from the pristine blue-green waters of the Caribbean, and ended the day sitting on the beach watching the sun set.

She didn't tell Ivonne that she and her husband had swum naked in a secluded lagoon, then fallen asleep in the tropical sun. That would remain their secret.

Ivonne's face had taken on a dreamy expression. "Did you cook for Samuel?"

"No. A cook, maid, and gardener were there to take care of all our needs."

"It's probably going to be very different for you once you move to the United States."

Vertical lines appeared between M.J.'s eyes. "Why would you say that?"

"Will you have what you have here in Cuba? Who's going to cook for you, clean your house, or take care of the flowers you love so much? Will you have as much land as you have here?"

M.J.'s face clouded with uneasiness. "I don't know."

"Have you not asked your husband these questions?"

Biting her lip, M.J. glanced away from her cousin, uncomfortable with the fact that she'd spoken the truth. The apprehension she had experienced after accepting Samuel's offer of marriage was back—this time stronger than before.

She wanted to believe that Ivonne was jealous because she had what she had—a man who loved her enough to claim her as his wife. And all Ivonne ever talked about was becoming the wife of a rich man. She wanted to live in a grand house and host grand parties that would become the talk of all of Cuba.

Tilting her chin, M.J. stared down her nose at her younger cousin. "I'm certain Samuel can give me whatever it is I want."

"What is it you want, darling?"

Both women turned and stared at the tall figure standing in the doorway. Neither had heard his approach.

M.J. moved off the chaise, closing the distance between her and her husband; at the same time Ivonne jumped up, her face flushed with embarrassment.

Samuel glared at Ivonne Ferrer as she brushed past him. He hadn't meant to eavesdrop, but had managed to hear the spiteful woman's taunt. He and M.J. were only married a week and he did not want someone filling her head with doubt, doubt as to whether he could provide for her, and whether he would make her a good husband.

Rising on tiptoe, M.J. brushed her mouth over his. "I want only you, darling."

Curving an arm around her waist, he stared down at the face the shade of a newly minted penny. He found M.J. exotically stunning with her sun-browned skin, glossy black hair, and luminous large, dark brown eyes, and it was not the first time he'd been awed by the beauty of the woman who'd become his and his alone.

"I came to tell you that we have to leave now." He'd made arrangements with the captain of an American fishing boat to take them directly to West Palm Beach. Once there he would pick up the car he'd left in a warehouse on the pier.

Smiling, M.J. pulled out of his loose embrace. "I just have to get my jewelry." Returning to the bed, she picked up a leather drawstring pouch.

Samuel's eyes widened. The handbag was the size of a small feedbag. "What on earth do you have in *that*?"

Looping the ties around her wrist, M.J. said, "My mother and grandmother's jewelry. I'm saving them for my daughters."

She'd said it so confidently that he wondered whether his wife knew something he didn't. He'd waited two days for her tender flesh to heal, then made love to her like a man possessed, and there was the possibility that he could've gotten her pregnant on their honeymoon.

M.J. had mentioned daughters when it was sons he wanted. Sons he would relate to and rear differently than his father had him and his brothers. He'd taken a solemn oath never to whip his children or berate them. He would praise their successes and provide support during their failures.

Dismissing the memories of his tortured childhood, he smiled. "What if we only have boys?"

"Then I'll give them to my granddaughters."

Samuel extended his hand, grinning broadly. "Let's go, little mama."

Tilting her chin, M.J. stared down the narrow bridge of her nose, the gesture the epitome of haughtiness. "My children will not call me Mama. It will be Mother."

Samuel's eyebrows lifted. It was the second time she'd referred to their children as *my children*. "Your children?"

"Okay, Sammy. Our children."

He grasped her free hand, tucking it into the bend of his elbow. "That's better."

As he led M.J. down the staircase Samuel recalled the arguments between his parents. Belinda always claimed her children were "my sons," while Charles referred to his sons as "your bastards."

It was something he could never understand. Why had Charles called his sons bastards when he'd married their mother and fathered them? Samuel did not want to dwell on the past, not when he looked forward to a future filled with things he'd dreamt about all of his life.

West Palm Beach, Florida—January 12, 1925

M.J. successfully concealed her disappointment when she walked into the living room in the house that was her new home. It was half the size of the house where she'd grown up, the land on which it was erected was smaller than her garden in Pinar del Rio, and the only thing that evoked memories of Cuba was a copse of palm trees shading the front of the one-story, stucco property.

Wooden crates that were shipped from Cuba lined a wall in the sparsely furnished space. Samuel's revelation that he hadn't furnished or decorated his house was an understatement.

"How long have you lived here?"

"Not long."

"How long is not long?"

"Four . . . maybe five months. Why?"

She met his questioning gaze. "Because it doesn't look lived-in. It's a house, not a home, Sammy."

He lifted wisps of hair sticking to her moist cheek. "I'll leave it up to you to make it look like a home. You can purchase whatever you need. I have a woman who comes in twice a week to clean and dust."

"Does she cook?"

"No."

"Who cooks for you?"

"I cook for myself."

"Are you good?"

Samuel angled his head, forcing back a smile. "I've never gotten sick."

M.J. moved closer, tilted her chin, and flashed a seductive moue. "I'll do the cooking, and your *woman* can continue to clean."

"She's not my woman."

"Did you not say, 'I have a woman who—"

His mouth stopped hers in an explosive kiss that stole the breath from her lungs. Samuel Cole was a thief. Without warning he'd come into her life and stolen her heart, and she knew she would love him forever.

He cradled her face and kissed the end of her nose. "Would you like to see the rest of your house?"

M.J. traced the outline of his lower lip with the tip of her tongue. "No."

"Why not?"

"I have tomorrow, the next day, and all the days after to see and decorate the house."

Samuel moaned softly. "Baby."

"I love your mouth, Sammy," she crooned. "The way it feels, the way it makes me feel."

He stopped her words a second time, deepening the kiss and wanting to absorb her into him. His blood heated with unbidden memories of making love to her.

"What do you want, darling?"

M.J. writhed against him like a cat in heat. "I want you. I will always want you."

Samuel gazed deeply into his wife's eyes. She'd declared what he was feeling and would always feel with her. There would never be a time when he would not want her.

Sweeping her up in his embrace, he carried her across the living room, past the dining room, a large kitchen, and down a wide hallway leading to the bedrooms.

The house was one of twelve newly built homes in an area populated by professional Negroes, all who were college graduates. His lack of a higher education was offset by his status as a businessman. His former marital status had served him well when several of the older couples considered him a suitable catch for their young daughters. However, that would change because he'd returned to West Palm Beach with a wife.

He carried M.J. into the master bedroom, a knowing smile parting his lips when he heard her soft gasp of surprise. The bedroom and an alcove in the adjoining dressing room were the only furnished areas in the house. When at home he spent most of his time there. The exception was when he took his meals in the kitchen.

"It's beautiful, Sammy."

"You like it?"

"I love it."

And she did. M.J. stared at the four-poster mahogany bed draped in delicate white lace and a mahogany pedestal table with two matching chairs covered in white petite point. Nightstands with table lamps flanked the large bed. The white-on-white embroidered coverlet and matching pillows would've appeared feminine if not for the heavy dark furniture. The walls were covered with paper dotted with sprigs of soft blue forget-me-nots, and the floor with a pale sisal rug.

"Who decorated this room?" M.J.'s eyes shimmered with excitement.

Samuel set her on her feet and rested his chin on the top of her head. "My mother. I wanted it to look like a bedroom I once saw in a French chateaux."

"You were in France?" There was no mistaking the surprise in her voice.

"Yes. It was during the war."

Her expression sobered quickly. "You were a soldier?" He nodded. "Did you kill any Germans?" Turning her in his embrace, Samuel gave her a cold stare that pebbled her flesh although the air inside the house was warm.

"I'm only going to say that I did whatever it was I had to do to come back alive. This will be the last time we speak of my past."

M.J. opened her mouth to tell him that she knew very little of his past, except that he was the youngest of three sons born to Belinda Cole, and he made his money importing and exporting produce, but then closed it quickly. This was not the time to challenge him. After all, they were married and living together. As his wife she doubted whether he would be able to conceal too much from her.

"What's in there?"

"A dressing room and my study."

M.J. left the bedroom, walking into a spacious dressing room with two facing ornately carved armoires, a highboy, and a dressing table and bench. Tucked away in an alcove was an antique secretary with compartments for letters, drawers for stationery, and a blotter-covered surface for writing. A telephone sat to the right of a supply of fountain pens. Framed photographs and bottles of ink lined the top shelf of the mahogany piece. The shelves behind the glass doors of a built-in Chinese chest were filled with novels and titles on crops and animal husbandry.

Her earlier assessment that the house was too small vanished quickly. If she chose her furnishings with meticulous care, there was no doubt her home would be an exquisite showplace.

She turned back to Samuel and wrapped her arms around his waist. "I love the house. I know I'm going to enjoy decorating it."

Smiling at her childlike enthusiasm, Samuel pressed a kiss to her forehead. "I'll put some money into an account for you to run the house."

"I don't need your money."

"Why not?"

"My father's solicitor transferred money from a bank in Havana to one in West Palm Beach for me."

He stiffened, his expression a mask of stone. "When were you going to tell me this?"

M.J.'s quick temper flared. "I didn't have to tell you at all, Samuel."

He struggled to rein in his temper. "Are we going to begin our life together keeping secrets?"

"No," she spat out. "My aunt convinced Papa to set up an account in my name so that I can retain a modicum of independence to come and go by my leave."

"Married women don't come and go by their leave, M.J.! No more than I will come and go by my leave now that I'm married."

"I'm not going to go off and not let you know. I plan to use the money to buy whatever it is I want for the house."

"I can afford to take care of you!" Samuel shouted, his voice rising with his increasing frustration.

M.J. stared at her husband as if he had taken leave of his senses. "Don't take that tone with me, Samuel. I'm not accusing you of not being able to take care of me." Her hand came up and she trailed a fingertip over his cheekbone and down to his strong chin. "We've been married for ten days, and already we're fighting about something so inconsequential as money."

His fingers curled around her wrist like manacles. "Money may be inconsequential to you because you never had to concern yourself with it. It was very different for me. My grandfather was a sharecropper who literally worked himself to death to save enough money to buy his own land. I worked in the fields before going to school, missed classes during cotton-picking season, and then I had to bust my ass to catch up with my schoolwork so I could be promoted to the next grade with the other kids. I've done things I didn't want to do so that I'd be able to take care of my wife *and* my children."

M.J. heard the passion in his voice, passion and fear. Her heart turned over in compassion. "Sammy, *mi amor, mi corazon,*" she crooned. "Whatever I have is yours. Don't ever forget that."

Samuel gathered her to his chest, a smile slicing through the lines of tension ringing his mouth. "And whatever I have is yours, baby. Do you think you can remember that?"

Lifting her chin, M.J. gave him a dazzling dimpled smile. "I don't know. I think I'll need some extra instruction."

"How?"

Going on tiptoe, she brushed a light kiss across his mouth. "Like this."

His hands moved down her body and cupped her hips. "Like this?"

M.J. couldn't stop the moan escaping her parted lips. "Yes."

"And this?" Samuel nuzzled the side of her neck as he pushed his groin against her hips.

"Yes, Sammy," she whispered, opening her mouth to his probing tongue. Anchoring her arms under his shoulders, M.J. writhed as the familiar sensations rippling through her belly settled between her legs. "Yes, yes, yes," she repeated over and over as he swung her up in his arms and returned to the bedroom.

It didn't matter that it was the middle of the afternoon, that she hadn't unpacked any of her clothes, that she had yet to examine the other rooms in the house, or that she hadn't eaten anything in twelve hours. The only thing that mattered was that the man in whose arms she lay was going to remind her why she'd been born female.

Samuel pulled back the coverlet before placing M.J. on the bed. His gaze held hers as he undressed, leaving his clothes on the floor, then undressed her. His eyes moved with an agonizing slowness over her tanned face and body. He still was unable to believe she was his.

He lay down and eased her over his body. He'd found that she liked being on top, and he preferred her on top because it prolonged his pleasure until the last possible moment.

M.J. buried her face between her husband's neck and shoulder, smiling. "*Que tu quieres?*"

Samuel closed his eyes and smiled. That he understood. Whenever she straddled him she always asked what he wanted. "Anything, baby."

She kissed him, her lips trailing from his mouth to his chin, his breastbone, and down his flat belly. The tip of her tongue tasted the moisture clinging to the tight curls in the inverted triangle of coarse hair between his thighs.

Samuel felt her hot breath near his penis, and he sat up and caught her hair. "No!" His protest bounced off the walls; his erection went down as if he'd been doused with ice-cold water.

Her head jerked up, M.J. staring at him as if she'd seen a ghost. "What's the matter?"

"Don't do that."

She sat back on her heels, totally bewildered by Samuel's behavior. "Why?"

He didn't drop his glare. Didn't she know? She was his wife, not a whore. He only permitted whores to take him into their mouths. "I don't like it," he lied smoothly.

"But you do it to me." Samuel had brought her to orgasm the first time he made love to her with his mouth. A flicker of apprehension coursed through M.J. as she tried understanding the complex man she'd married.

Samuel's thunderous expression softened as he reached for his wife. "I do it because bringing you pleasure makes me happy." He kissed her passionately as he reversed positions. His erection had returned. "Let me love you, baby."

Nodding, M.J. closed her eyes, opened her arms and her legs, moaning softly when Samuel's hardness filled her. Her hands caressed the length of his back, the firm flesh over his buttocks, her body arching to meet his powerful thrusts, her breasts tingling against the hair on his chest.

It was flesh against flesh, man against woman, husband and wife. Ecstasy swept over them like the waves crashing over the Malecon, and they shared a pleasure so pure and explosive that for several seconds they had actually become one.

11

Our life is composed of love, and not to love is to cease to live.

—George Sand

The shrill ring of the telephone shattered Samuel's concentration. Capping a fountain pen, he picked up the receiver. The operator's nasal voice came through the earpiece.

"I have a call from a Mr. Kirkland for Samuel Cole."

"Put the call through."

"Go ahead, Mr. Kirkland," the operator instructed the caller on the other end of the line.

"Samuel?"

"Yes, Everett."

"I've been calling you once a week over the past month, but no one answered."

Samuel leaned back on his chair. "I've been out of the country," he said quietly, explaining his absence, because he'd instructed his housekeeper never to answer his telephone. "I take it you're settled in," he continued.

"Yes," Everett confirmed.

"Where are you?"

"I'm in Winter Park."

"Do you think you can spare some time and come down to West Palm Beach?"

"All I have is time," Everett admitted. "When do you want to meet?"

"What are you doing next weekend?" He was anxious to reunite with the accountant.

He would've had Everett come sooner, but he and M.J. were invited to their first soiree as a married couple by one of their neighbors. One or two of the women had caught a glimpse of M.J., and there was no doubt she'd aroused a great deal of curiosity.

"Nothing."

"Good. I'd like you to come down Friday and stay over until Monday."

"Where do you live?"

Samuel gave Everett his address before he ended the call. Minutes after he'd hung up he thought about M.J. It would be the first time they'd have a houseguest.

It had taken four weeks for her to turn the house into a home. He had spent all of his free time driving her to furniture warehouses where she selected pieces for the kitchen, living, dining rooms. Furnishings for one of the guest bedrooms were scheduled for delivery later that afternoon. Walking out of his study, Samuel found M.J. in the kitchen.

"Where's Bessie?"

M.J. glanced up from her task of peeling green bananas. She'd been overjoyed once she found a store that carried tropical produce. "I sent her home."

Samuel forced himself not to scowl. "Why?"

"She wasn't feeling well."

"What's wrong with her *now?*"

M.J. heard the sarcasm in her husband's voice. They'd been married a month and a half, and with each passing day she'd found herself more and more in love with him.

But she'd also discovered he was solitary, spending long hours in his study writing letters, reading reports, or making and receiving telephone calls; but on the other hand whenever she sought him out he'd put aside whatever it was he was doing to drive her to the market or the antique shops she favored.

"Why would you ask me that, Sammy?"

This time he did frown. "Because Bessie gets sick an average of once every two weeks. And always on a Friday."

"She told me she was having a problem with her monthly."

Samuel sat down across from M.J., shaking his head. "I thought women have their monthlies once, not twice a month."

Heat flared in M.J.'s face. Although married, she felt uncomfortable discussing the function of a woman's body with Samuel. It had taken her hours before she garnered the nerve to tell him that with her show of menstrual blood she wasn't pregnant.

"You can't expect me to challenge her, Sammy."

His frown deepened. "What I expect is for you to make certain she does what I pay her to do. This is your house, M.J., and you're responsible for everything that goes on here. If she isn't doing her job, then I want you to either chastise or fire her. The decision is yours."

"I'll talk to her."

"When?"

"When she comes again on Tuesday."

"May I make a suggestion?"

"Yes, you may, Sammy."

"Start looking for her replacement. When you talk to some of the other women tomorrow night you can inquire about who they use to clean their homes."

She lifted a shoulder. "I'll think about it."

There was no way M.J. was going to let those women know that she wasn't able to run an efficient household. She'd noticed several peering through their curtains or whispering to one another whenever she ventured outdoors to check on the progress of the garden that was under construction at the back of the house.

The gardener had planted orange, lime, and lemon trees, and put in flowering shrubs of frangipani. A retractable awning shaded an area with a table with seating for four. She'd wanted to erect a gazebo, but changed her mind; it would've made the garden area appear too crowded.

Leaning over, Samuel kissed the side of her neck. "Don't think too much, darling."

She smiled up at him. "I won't, darling."

"What's for dinner?"

"*Camarones al ajillo.* Garlic shrimp," she translated before he could ask.

"It sounds good." He kissed her again.

"It is," M.J. said confidently, watching Samuel as he walked out of the kitchen.

Pleasing her husband in the kitchen and bedroom was something she was able to do with little or no effort. But whenever they didn't share a bed or a meal she found Samuel standoffish. On more than one occasion she came into the house to find him sitting in his study in the dark, and even when she turned on a lamp he did not move or acknowledge her presence. If she hadn't loved him as much as she did she would've fled the house, Samuel, and Florida, because there was something about her husband that frightened her.

She felt a presence and looked around. The object of her musings had silently returned to the kitchen. Placing a hand over her chest, M.J. let out an audible sigh. Her heart was pounding an erratic rhythm.

"Don't do that!"

Samuel stared mutely at his wife. "What?" he asked after an uncomfortable silence.

"Spy on me."

"What makes you think I'm spying on you? What do you have to hide?"

"Nothing. I look up and you're there."

He smiled and nodded. "Okay. Next time I'll make some noise before coming up on you. I forgot to tell you that we're having a houseguest next weekend."

Her mouth dropped open. "Sammy, no!"

"I forgot to tell you, baby."

M.J. glared at him. "We can't have guests now. The house isn't ready."

Samuel walked over to the table, eased the knife from M.J.'s hand, and pulled her gently to her feet. "Don't worry about the house. It looks beautiful, darling. Besides, our guest is not coming to judge our home."

"Why is he coming?" A slight frown wrinkled her smooth forehead. "Is the guest a *he*?"

"Yes. Everett Kirkland and I have business to discuss."

"Does he have a wife?"

Samuel shook his head. He doubted whether Everett would've married since their last encounter. "I don't believe he does."

Placing her hands on her husband's chest, M.J. rolled her eyes at him. "I suppose I should thank you for giving me a week's notice."

He smiled. "Don't worry too much. I'll help you out. Now all you have to do is get that triflin' Bessie to do her job."

"What is this triflin'?"

Throwing back his head, Samuel laughed until tears rolled down his cheeks. He'd forgotten that English, and in particular southern vernacular, wasn't M.J.'s first language.

"It's the same as lazy or good-for-nothing."

"Why didn't you just say that?" Her vexation was evident.

"Because it's easier to say triflin'."

"You shouldn't tease me."

He pressed the pad of his thumb to her mouth, parting her lips. "I don't mind if you tease me."

"What if I tell you that I ordered a piano?"

"You're teasing, aren't you?"

Dimples deepened with her beguiling smile. "No, my husband. I'm not teasing. It will be delivered today along with the other furniture."

Samuel threw up his hands, scowling. "I don't believe you."

"What can't you believe? I told you I wanted the piano."

"And I told *you* this house isn't large enough for a piano."

M.J. poked him in the middle of his chest with her forefinger. "Then get me a larger house."

"No! This house isn't a year old."

"It's too small for the things I want to buy."

A slow, rising rage knotted Samuel's stomach muscles. She'd deceived him. M.J. had spent the past month humming and singing as she had him arrange and rearrange pieces of furniture until he was fearful of entering any of the rooms without turning on a light.

"I asked you if you liked this place, and you said you loved it." He was hard-pressed not to yell at her. "You didn't have to lie to me."

M.J. stared at the protruding veins in her husband's neck. "I didn't lie to you," she retorted angrily. "I do love this house, but it's much smaller than what I'm used to."

"I'm sorry, madam, if I didn't grow up in a mansion."

"Don't be condescending, Samuel."

"I'm not being condescending. I'm only saying what is the truth. If you opened the front door you could see clear through to the back door. It was what we call a shotgun house. I've worked my ass off to get where I am today because I want better for my family and for my children." He leaned closer, close enough for his moist breath to whisper over his wife's face, his frown deepening. "We are going to live *here*, in *this* house, until we outgrow it."

Samuel's words were as bitter and acrid as gall. Tears filled M.J.'s eyes but didn't fall. They shimmered like polished jet as she continued to stare up at the man she loved beyond reason, a man to whom she'd committed her future, and a man whom she'd trusted to protect her in a country where she felt like and was an alien.

She wanted to curse him—in English and in Spanish—and say all of the coarse, ribald words she'd learned from the girls at the convent. But she decided not to challenge Samuel, not today, and not when she couldn't seduce him. M.J. had learned quickly that if she used her body she could get most of what she wanted from him.

"Okay, Samuel," she said in a tone swollen with resignation. "I will send the piano back."

Regret assailed Samuel when he saw his wife's tears and heard her declaration of defeat. He'd become Charles Cole, bullying and berating those he'd sworn to love and protect. He extended his arms, but she moved beyond his reach. Her rejection twisted like a knife in his heart.

"Baby. Please . . . don't."

She shook her head. "Don't touch me, Samuel. Not now."

Eyes wide, Samuel angled his head. Didn't she know? Did she not know how much he loved her, how much he wanted to please her? Taking two long strides, he caught her around the waist and pulled her to his chest.

"It's all right, my darling. You can have your piano."

Eyelids fluttering, M.J. stared up at him. "Really?"

He kissed the end of her nose. At that moment M.J. appeared more like a little girl than a woman. "Yes, baby. Really."

Throwing her arms around his neck, she pulled his head down and kissed him. "Thank you. *Mil gracias, mi amor, mi corazon.* I will never defy you again," she murmured, placing featherlike kisses over his parted lips. "If you say no, then it will be no."

Cupping her hips, fingers splaying over the firm mounds under a lightweight, flower-sprigged dress, Samuel pulled her even closer. He stared down at the dark brown pools that reminded him of the tiny cups of Cuban coffee he'd grown so fond of.

"Why is it that I don't believe you?"

M.J.'s expressive eyebrows lifted. "Why should you not believe me?" She'd answered his question with one of her own.

"Because, wife, something tells me that you will defy me again and again in spite of my protests."

"That is not true."

"Yes . . ." Samuel's retort trailed off as the doorbell chimed. "I'll get it," he volunteered.

M.J. nodded, biting back a smile as Samuel walked out of the kitchen. She'd gambled and won.

M.J. felt the chill the instant she and Samuel were greeted by their hostess, while the gazes of men and women crowding the living room were trained on her as she clung to her husband's arm. It was their first social outing as a couple, and she had taken particular care with her appearance.

Earlier that morning she'd washed her hair, sectioned and twisted it around strips of fabric, then sat in the sun waiting for it to dry. The result was a cascade of curls that touched her waist.

She wore a tabard of black lace and shimmering bugle beads over a satin slip dress. Sheer black silk stockings, two-inch silk-covered pumps, and a small evening purse with bugle beads rounded out her winning look. Her only jewelry, aside from her rings, was a pair of dangling onyx and diamond earrings in her pierced lobes. Samuel looked incredibly handsome in a midnight-blue suit, stark-white shirt, and dark-blue-and-white-striped tie. Tall and slender, they made a striking couple.

"Good evening, Samuel. I'm so glad you could make it."

Samuel felt M.J.'s fingertips bite into his arm over the sleeve of his suit jacket. Winifred Mansfield had deliberately ignored his wife.

His mouth was smiling, but his eyes were cold. "Marguerite and I are pleased you've invited *us* to your lovely home."

Winifred, a petite woman with velvety dark skin, rested a hand over her ample bosom, sighing heavily. "I'm so sorry, Samuel. I did not mean to slight your lovely wife." She stepped aside. "Please come in and meet everyone."

Gaudy.

It was the only adjective M.J. could think of to describe the Mansfield home. It was the same layout as her house, but a gigantic crystal chandelier covered more than half the living room ceiling area. An oversize brocade sofa and matching chaise and chairs took up nearly all of the floor space.

Couples were either seated or stood around holding drinks, talking softly to one another while the sounds of a saxophone, drum, and muted trumpet came through the speaker of a Victrola.

M.J. leaned closer to Samuel. "Isn't alcohol illegal in America?"

Lowering his head, he pressed his mouth to her ear. "Yes. But a lot of folks manage to get around the law."

She glanced up at him. "How?"

"Rumrunners and bootleggers bring it in from Canada and the Caribbean by boat," he whispered. Her mouth formed a perfect O that elicited a soft chuckle from Samuel. His attention was diverted when he spied Basil Mansfield striding toward them.

Basil, a large man with a perpetual flush suffusing his redbone complexion, was the complete opposite of his snobbish wife. "Samuel, my boy, how nice of you to come."

His gray-green eyes shifted to the slender, raven-haired woman clinging possessively to his neighbor's arm. Winnie had nagged him constantly to host a dinner party so she could meet Samuel Cole's young wife. Now that he'd given in to her whining he was glad he had.

"Samuel, your wife is lovely."

Covering the hand on his arm, Samuel inclined his head. "Thank you, Basil. I'd like to introduce you to my wife, Marguerite-Josefina. M.J., this is Basil Mansfield, our host and closest neighbor."

M.J. removed her hand from her husband's arm, offering it to Basil. "Nice meeting you, Mr. Mansfield."

Basil switched the glass filled with a golden liquid to the opposite hand, tilting it at a precarious angle. Grasping M.J.'s fingers, he squeezed them tightly. "My, my, my, Marguerite-Josefina. You are as beautiful as your name." His admiring gaze swept over her face. "Are you Spanish?"

M.J. forced a polite smile. "No, sir. I'm Cuban."

"Is there a difference, little lady?"

"Yes, there is. Spanish is a language."

Samuel felt the stiffness in M.J.'s body and knew it was time to circulate. He reached into the breast pocket of his suit jacket and withdrew three cigars. "Basil, these are for you. Compliments of M.J.'s father." He smiled at her. "Darling, may I get you something to drink?"

"Yes, please."

Samuel nodded to Basil. "We'll talk again later."

"Thank you, darling," M.J. whispered, as Samuel led her to where a bartender stood behind a portable bar mixing drinks.

"You're very welcome, my love."

Samuel and M.J. shared a passionate look that made those close enough to witness the exchange smile.

M.J. glanced up over her shoulder, smiling at Samuel as he seated her. She watched as he rounded the long, rectangular table and sat opposite her. Her gaze shifted to the place card next to her wineglass: *S. Cole. Guest.*

A slight frown furrowed her smooth forehead. The word had gotten out in the private residential enclave that Samuel Cole had returned to West Palm Beach with a wife, yet Winifred Mansfield had referred to her as Samuel's guest. Why not Mrs. S. Cole? She'd spent less than an hour under the Mansfield roof and knew unequivocally that she and Mrs. Mansfield would never become friends.

"Winnie can be so gauche at times," said a soft feminine voice on M.J.'s right.

Turning, she stared at a woman with a liberal sprinkling of freckles dotting her light brown face, finding her very pretty. Her hair was styled in a fashionable bob. Large round dark eyes, a pert nose, and a heart-shaped mouth made her appear doll-like.

"I don't understand."

The woman leaned closer. "I'm Margaret Carson, but everyone calls me Peggy."

M.J. flashed her dimpled smile for the first time since entering the Mansfield residence. "I'm Marguerite-Josefina Diaz Cole, but all of my friends call me M.J."

The skin around Peggy's eyes crinkled as she smiled. "May I call you M.J.?"

"Of course. But only if I can address you as Peggy."

"Sure."

M.J. angled her head. "What were you saying about Winnie?" she whispered.

"She hates it when anyone calls her that, but I do it just to mess with her."

M.J.'s eyebrows lifted. "Mess?"

"It's means to annoy. Where are you from?"

"Cuba."

Peggy nodded. "I thought I heard an accent. Your English is very good."

"My Spanish is much better," M.J. admitted. "Samuel says words I don't understand, and I have to ask him to translate them for me."

"That's because here in the South we use different words for something that will mean the same thing elsewhere. An example is that we'll say 'tote' instead of carry."

"It's the same in my country."

"Did you and Samuel meet in Cuba?"

"Yes."

"You should know that once the word got out that he was married a lot of women had hissy fits. That means a tantrum."

M.J. waited until a waiter filled the water goblet at her place setting before asking, "Why?"

Peggy stared at M.J. as if she'd lost her senses. "Do you have any idea of what a catch your husband is? He's young, handsome, ambitious, and a successful businessman. Everyone sitting at this table, with the exception of Daniel Williams, who has his own law practice, works for someone else. Most are teachers, one is a pharmacist, another a dentist, and the rest work for banks and insurance companies. Samuel Cole is the only entrepreneur. In other words, he's his own boss, makes his own hours, and doesn't have to share his profits."

M.J. digested what the chatty woman had just told her. It was apparent Peggy knew more about Samuel's business than she did, and she attributed that to her upbringing. Upper-class Cuban women were afforded the security necessary to focus all their attention on their home, not on their husband's business dealings.

"Were there a lot of women flirting with my husband?"

Peggy rolled her eyes. "Child, they were downright shameless. Winnie's fast-ass daughter, who's not here because she's in college, took the rag off the bush. She was so loose that folks were beginning to refer to her as a hussy."

M.J. decided she liked Peggy even if she couldn't understand half of what she'd said. "Sammy never spoke to me of his other women."

Peggy sucked her teeth. "That's because there were no other women that I know of. He usually keeps to himself. But if someone invited him to a soiree he'd come, but always alone."

An expression of satisfaction shimmered in M.J.'s eyes as her confidence spiraled appreciably. There was no doubt Samuel would remain a faithful husband, because she did not want to spend her time agonizing that he was having affairs with other women whenever he embarked on a business trip.

One night he'd disclosed that he planned to go to Costa Rica to confer with a representative of the United Fruit Company. When she asked when he was leaving he'd admitted he was awaiting a telegram before he could confirm a departure date.

Most conversations halted as platters of baked ham, fried chicken, potato salad, collard, mustard, and turnip greens, candied sweet potatoes, rice, and giblet gravy were passed around the table. It was M.J.'s first introduction to a southern-cooked meal.

"Everything tastes so good," she said to Peggy.

"You've never eaten southern food?"

M.J. shook her head. "No."

"What do you cook?"

"Cuban dishes."

Peggy placed a hand over M.J.'s. "If you want, I can teach you to cook our dishes."

A ripple of excitement swept through M.J. "I'd love that. But don't say anything to Samuel. I want to surprise him once I make cold-lard greens."

Peggy laughed when M.J. said "cold-lard" for collards. "Don't worry. It will be our secret. Why don't you join the rest of us on Wednesday afternoons for our bid whist parties?"

"I don't know how to play card games." Although her aunt held weekly card parties at her Havana residence, M.J. never participated. She'd found the gatherings too smoky and boisterous.

"That's okay. I'll teach you."

"Thank you, Peggy."

Peggy smiled. "You're welcome, M.J."

"You smell so good that you should be on the table, beautiful lady."

M.J. ignored the comment from the man on her left; he'd tried unsuccessfully from the moment he'd sat down next to her to engage her in conversation. He'd had too much to drink and most of his comments were not only inappropriate, but also disrespectful. It did not matter that his daughter overheard him or that M.J.'s husband sat less than three feet away.

Samuel's expression was one of strained tolerance. He'd sat for more than an hour watching his wife recoil each time the intoxicated dentist leaned close enough for their shoulders to touch. He didn't want to make a scene, and there was a possibility M.J. would become socially involved with the other women, but enough was enough.

Once dinner concluded, he pushed back his chair, circled the table, and came up behind Dr. Cyrus Rhodes. He tapped him on his shoulder, then leaned down until his mouth was inches from the older man's ear.

"May I have a word with you?"

Cyrus glanced up, training bloodshot eyes on Samuel. Although he'd whispered to him, his voice sounded abnormally loud in his ear. "Can't it wait?"

"No, it can't," Samuel countered, his voice rising slightly. He smiled at M.J. "I'll just be a few minutes. I need to speak to Cyrus about something."

Cursing under his breath, Cyrus rose to his feet and walked out of the dining room, Samuel following. He stopped in the living room and turned to face Samuel, who'd caught his upper arm in a punishing grip.

"We'll talk outside."

"Now, just wait a damn minute, Cole, I—"

"Outside, Rhodes," Samuel warned quietly. "I don't think you'd want your daughter to witness me kicking your ass in someone else's house. It's your choice."

It took the forty-two-year-old dentist a full minute before he was able to process Samuel's threat. His life had been on a downward spiral since losing his only son in an automobile accident three years before. His occasional drinking escalated until he started and ended his day with a drink; he'd lost his private practice, and Mrs. Rhodes had taken to her bed, never to venture outdoors again.

Cyrus opened the door, stepping out into the cool early February night. "What do you want?"

Samuel glared at the man whose good looks were ravaged by alcoholism. "I want you to leave my wife alone," Samuel said with a lethal softness that sent shivers up Cyrus's spine.

"I don't know what you're talking about."

"Don't touch her, and don't say anything to her."

Cyrus weaved back and forth, spittle forming at the corners of his slack mouth. "You're full of shit, Cole," he slurred.

Forcing himself not to grab the drunken man by the throat, Samuel pushed his hands into the pockets of his trousers. "If you touch my wife again, or even breathe on her, I will beat the shit out of you."

That said, he turned and walked back into the Mansfield house to tell M.J. it was time they returned to their home. If he remained, then there was the possibility that he would physically assault a man unable to defend himself.

He found M.J. in the living room where coffee, tea, liquors, and trays of cake, pie, and sweet pastries awaited the dinner guests.

"Let's go home."

M.J. caught his meaning immediately. She'd had enough of the Mansfields and their supercilious guests. The only one she could relate to was Peggy Carson; they'd set a date when they would get together again.

She pressed the back of her hand to her forehead. "I am feeling rather tired."

Samuel dropped a kiss on the top of her head. "Go wait for me outside while I make our apologies to Basil and Winifred."

"Don't make me wait too long, Sammy."

Running a finger down the length of her nose, he winked at her. "I won't."

M.J. made her way through the crowd to the front door. She didn't have to wait long when Samuel joined her. "That was quick."

They walked hand in hand in silence, both lost in their private musings. M.J. knew she would never become a part of her husband's social milieu. The women did not like her, the men liked her too much, and for the first time since she'd left Cuba she felt like crying because she missed her homeland.

She'd sought out Samuel, fallen in love, and married him because she wanted to live as a liberated woman, but was forced to face the harsh realties of life. The price she had to pay to determine her own destiny was now too painful to bear.

Swallowing to relieve the tightness in her throat, she stopped and stared up at Samuel. She couldn't see his expression in the shadows of the streetlamps. "I need you to promise me something."

Releasing her hand, Samuel cradled her face. "What's that?"

"Please don't stop loving me."

His expression stilled and grew serious. "Where is all of this coming from, darling?"

"I don't know why, but right now I feel so alone."

"You're not alone, baby. You have me. You will always have me."

Curving her arms around Samuel's waist, M.J. rested her cheek on his chest. "You're right, Sammy. I have you."

But for how long? a silent voice whispered inside her head.

12

When you depart from me, sorrow abides, and happiness takes his leave.

—William Shakespeare

The doorbell chimed and M.J.'s head came up as she stared at Samuel. "He's here." Her voice was a whisper. Everett Kirkland had arrived.

Samuel, resting a hand on the small of her back, leaned over and kissed the side of her neck. "Everything looks beautiful. You are beautiful. And try to relax, baby," he crooned, walking out of the kitchen to answer the door.

She wasn't concerned with how the house looked. Instead of asking Peggy for a recommendation for a cleaning woman, she confronted Bessie about her frequent absences, who admitted she'd begun taking Lydia Pinkham, a special tonic for female ailments, and that she was feeling much better.

Bessie had cleaned the house thoroughly and a hundred hours of instruction at the convent school should have prepared M.J. for this moment, but the sound of the doorbell had momentarily shattered her confidence. Playing hostess for her father had not counted because she was merely a substitute for Carlotta, dress rehearsals for when she would become mistress of her own household.

Within minutes Samuel returned to the kitchen—alone. "It wasn't Everett."

Unconsciously M.J.'s brow furrowed. "Who was it?"

"Someone from Western Union."

She met her husband's steady gaze, her heart pounding a runaway rhythm. "Is it the telegram you were expecting?"

"Yes."

"When are you leaving?"

Samuel glanced away. "I'm not sure."

"That's not an answer, Samuel."

"It's the only answer I have right now. I have to wait and see if I can book passage on a ship sailing to Costa Rica."

Feeling his loss even before his actual departure, M.J. nodded. "How long will you be away?"

"At least a week, maybe more. I'm going to ask Bessie to stay here with you until I come back."

"No, Sammy," M.J. said, shaking her head. "I'm not a child who needs to be looked after. I'll be all right staying here alone. Besides, Bessie should be home with her children at night."

He lifted questioning eyebrows. "Are you sure?"

"Very sure," she lied smoothly.

She did mind, but didn't want him to think of her as immature. It was to become the first time she would stay alone for an extended time. She'd lived with her parents, but a year following her mother's accident she was sent to the convent school. Then she lived with her aunt while attending classes at the *universidad.*

"I have my books, piano, working in the garden, and the radio to entertain me. And if I get really bored, then I'll go shopping and spend your money. Remember, I still have another bedroom to decorate."

A hint of a smile played at the corners of Samuel's mouth. "I thought you wanted to wait and turn it into a nursery."

A shadow of color appeared on her cheeks. "I'm just going to look for wallpaper patterns."

"Just don't pick out anything that's too frilly for my son."

"What makes you think I'm going to have a boy first?"

He ran a finger down the length of her delicate nose. "Because there hasn't been a girl baby in my family for thirty years."

"Maybe . . ." The words died on M.J.'s lips when the doorbell chimed for the second time that afternoon.

Samuel's gaze fused with his wife's. "That must be Everett."

Everett Kirkland stared at the door, waiting for an answer to his ring. He'd spent hours in the back of a bus during the ride from Winter Haven to West Palm Beach, one time having given up his seat to a white passenger, only to arrive at an enclave where Negroes lived as grand as those who'd once enslaved their ancestors.

Samuel Cole's home was a one-story, Spanish-style Colonial with a red-tiled roof. A wry smile twisted Everett's mouth. It was apparent the cotton-turned-soybean farmer was a visionary.

Unfamiliar with soybeans, he'd researched everything he could find about them, and there was no doubt the legume would become a crop for the twentieth century.

He hadn't believed Samuel when he'd asked him if he wanted to become wealthy, because there was something about the younger man that reeked of arrogance and self-importance. It had only taken Everett seconds to recognize that Samuel Cole was totally lacking in humility. The door opened, and the object of his musings stood in front of him. Samuel looked the same as he had in Costa Rica. He wore a guayabera, sharply creased tan slacks, and a pair of leather sandals.

Samuel smiled, extending his right hand. "Come in, Everett."

Everett shook his hand and stepped into the spacious entryway. "Thank you. Good seeing you again, Samuel."

Samuel's sharp penetrating gaze swept over the man he had come to think of as his accountant. Everett had put on weight. He appeared well groomed and had added a clipped mustache to his clean-shaven face.

"You're looking well."

"I'm feeling much better."

Samuel's smile widened as he patted his back. "Once you've eaten my wife's cooking you're going to feel wonderful."

Everett froze, his expression mirroring his shock. "I . . . I thought, I . . . I didn't know you were married."

He was angry with himself for stuttering. It had taken years of choosing his words carefully before taking deep breaths to control the stutters that had made him an object of constant ridicule as a child and young adult.

"I wasn't married when we met in Costa Rica."

"Look, Samuel, I can always come back another time. I don't want to intrude on you and your new wife."

"That's nonsense," Samuel countered, reaching for Everett's single piece of luggage. "You're here because I need you. Come let me show you to your room where you can unwind before we sit down to dinner."

Everett nodded as if in a trance, following Samuel through a living room, a formal dining room, and down a carpeted hallway to the rear of the spacious house. Each table, lamp, and rug had been selected to harmonize with the structure's Spanish architecture.

Samuel stopped at the first bedroom on the right. "This room is yours. The bathroom is across the hall." He handed Everett his bag. "Take your time settling in."

Everett didn't know why, but he felt a profound well of emotion sweep over him. It was the second time Samuel Cole had offered him a chance to redeem himself. Firstly, he had given him enough money to escape an existence wherein he was dying slowly—a minute at a time. Now he had invited him into his home because he claimed he needed him.

Samuel didn't need him. Everett Joshua Kirkland needed Samuel Claridge Cole.

Shaved, showered, and dressed in a white shirt and black slacks and shoes, Everett walked out of his bedroom, looking for his host and hostess. The mahogany sleigh bed in his bedroom had beckoned him to come and lie down; although exhausted he had resisted. He hadn't gotten much sleep during the ride down, sandwiched between two oversize passengers, both whose snores reverberated throughout the rear of the bus.

He found the kitchen. Samuel stood at the stove with a woman, his arm around her waist as she sprinkled something into a large pot. There was a tightening in the nether region of his body as he stared mutely at the long black hair caught on the nape of a long slender neck with a white ribbon. She turned and smiled up at Samuel, her lips touching his in a brief kiss.

Everett felt like a voyeur watching the couple; shame assailed him as if he were a thief; his body had betrayed him; he was lusting after another man's wife, a woman under whose roof he would reside, a woman whose food he would eat, a woman whose husband had promised him an opportunity to fulfill his dreams.

The changes going on in his body reminded him that he hadn't slept with a woman since he'd contracted tuberculosis. He saw a young prostitute a few times while he waited for Eladia to return to Puerto Limon, but after he exhibited all of the signs of the disease even she refused to share a bed with him.

He had recently celebrated his twenty-ninth birthday and gained ten of the thirty pounds he'd lost; the hardness in his groin signaled a return of his virility; he was alive and ready to embrace life.

He backed out of the kitchen, waiting for his penis to return to a flaccid state. He waited and swore a solemn oath. There wasn't anything he would not do for Samuel Cole. Humming softly to make his presence known, he reentered the kitchen.

"Something smells wonderful."

Samuel and his wife turned, both smiling. Everett felt as if he'd been poleaxed when he saw the face of the woman with the black waist-length hair. She was young *and* breathtakingly beautiful.

M.J. wiped her hands on a cloth, extending the right one. "Hello, Everett. I'm Marguerite-Josefina, but I'd prefer that you call me M.J." She hadn't waited for Samuel to make the introductions.

Everett closed the distance between them and grasped her fingers. "I'm honored to make your acquaintance."

M.J. smiled up at the man who appeared as if a strong wind would blow him down. His face was made up of sharp angles that made it look as if it had been haphazardly put together. His light brown eyes, flecked with gold, were warm and friendly.

She lifted an eyebrow. "Are you always so formal?"

He looked awkward. "Yes, ma'am. My parents were both in their forties when I came along, and after they passed I lived with an elderly aunt."

Samuel saw M.J. grimace. Everett had referred to her as *ma'am*. "Do you think you can put aside your upbringing and relax this weekend?"

"I'll try," Everett said, smiling broadly.

"Good. I hope you brought your appetite, because M.J. has really outdone herself preparing tonight's dinner."

"Sammy, darling, could you please take the roast into the dining room?"

Samuel patted Everett's back, winking. "If you want to eat you'll have to work." He handed him a soup tureen. "Follow me."

The two men made short work of carrying dishes from the kitchen into the dining room. M.J. had set the table with one of two patterns of china she had shipped from Cuba that had belonged to her mother and grandmother. She and Bessie had spent hours polishing silver, washing and drying china and crystal glassware.

Samuel seated M.J. on his right, then sat down at the head of the table, leaving Everett to sit on his left. There was a moment of silence as the three bowed their heads to say grace.

Picking up a pitcher of chilled lemonade, Samuel filled M.J.'s goblet. He stared at his guest. "If you want something stronger I could always ask one of my neighbors if they have a bottle they're willing to part with."

"Please no," Everett insisted. "I haven't had anything to drink since I've come back." America's ban on alcohol had helped him recover his health more quickly than he would have if he'd continued to drink. Whenever he drank he usually lost his appetite.

"Where were you?" M.J. asked.

"Costa Rica." Everett took another spoonful of creamy pumpkin soup.

Her gaze lingered on Everett. "Are you going to accompany my husband when he leaves for Costa Rica?"

"M.J." Samuel's voice, though soft, held a thread of warning. "You know we do not discuss business at the table."

"It's not business, Samuel," she retorted, her dark eyes flashing fire. "I was merely asking Everett a question."

"It is a question I can't answer, Mrs. Cole, because your husband and I have not discussed it," Everett said, hoping to diffuse an uncomfortable situation.

M.J. offered Everett a supercilious smile. "Thank you, Everett, for being so direct."

A shadow of anger swept over Samuel's face as he kept his gaze glued to his plate. Not only had his wife defied him, but she had done so in front of a stranger. He'd established the rules the first day of their honeymoon: they would never talk about his business when dining. He wanted to sit down and enjoy his food and his wife's company.

Everett broke the uncomfortable silence that ensued when he asked M.J., "Where in Cuba are you from?"

She flashed a dimpled smile. "How did you know I was from Cuba?"

"The black beans and rice."

"I see you recognize our *moros y cristianos*. Do you speak Spanish, Everett?"

He nodded. "A little."

"I've been tutoring my husband."

"How are the lessons coming, Samuel?" Everett asked.

"Very slowly," he admitted, unable to meet M.J.'s gaze.

What he couldn't tell Everett was that their lessons were always at night whenever they were in bed together. The assignment wasn't learning a new word or phrase, but a passion in which the result would be the beginning of a new life. Samuel wanted children, but more for M.J. than himself. Caring for a baby would fill up the hours when he had to travel or attend business meetings. He'd spent the past week mulling over options for Cole International, Ltd., and had reached a decision to move his business out of his home and into an office building.

M.J. listened intently as Samuel and Everett discussed sports and the absence of Negroes in professional baseball before the topic segued to national and world politics. Dinner ended and even after she'd cleared the table they still hadn't moved.

Usually Samuel helped her clean the kitchen, but tonight was the exception. He had a friend, someone whose interests were similar to his, someone with whom he could discuss *business* at the table.

She washed dishes, pots, silver, glassware, then put everything away. She left the kitchen and made her way down the hallway to her bedroom.

A sense of strength came to M.J. as she prepared for bed. She'd defied her father to marry Samuel, live in a foreign country, and become an independent woman.

And that meant she couldn't throw a tantrum whenever Samuel informed her he had to leave her. Peggy had extended an invitation for her to join the other wives in their enclave for their regularly scheduled Wednesday bid whist luncheon, but she had declined. Everett Kirkland's presence had changed everything; she would accept their invitation to join them for their next get-together.

Climbing into bed, she lay on Samuel's pillow, the lingering smell of his aftershave wafting in her nostrils. She would join the ladies, but would invite them to meet at her house. It was time they were introduced to some Afro-Cuban cuisine and hospitality.

Everett sat on the patio, enjoying the fading warmth of the sun on his face. He'd slept soundly, not waking until late afternoon. Samuel and M.J. were the perfect hosts. His room was spacious and sun-filled while M.J.'s cooking skills were without equal. He'd shamelessly requested two and three helpings of everything she prepared.

Samuel stepped out onto the patio with tiny cups of strong black coffee, placing one in front of Everett. "How long can you stay?" he asked, sitting opposite him.

"As long as you want. I have nothing waiting for me back in Winter Park."

Once he returned to the States he hadn't known where he wanted to settle, but decided on Winter Park because he'd spent a week there with a college buddy. He got a room in a boardinghouse usually frequented by migrant workers. The room was clean, the rent reasonable, and the food hardy and filling. There were several occasions when he considered looking for a job, but wanted to wait until he heard what Samuel was offering.

Samuel sat down and took a sip of the thick brew. "I want you to come back to Costa Rica with me."

Everett sat up straighter. "Why didn't you say something last night?"

The softness in Samuel's face changed, as his expression became a mask of stone. "I'd hoped you understood me when I said I don't discuss business at my table."

"But we'd eaten," Everett said in a quiet voice.

"It's not about food, Everett."

And it wasn't about sitting down to eat. It was about Charles Cole, who used the dinner table as his soapbox to rant about his cotton crop. Night after night he had complained incessantly about the cycle of hiring workers who quit because they were too lazy to work hard, the brutal heat waves, weevil infestation, erratic weather conditions, and that he wouldn't have to spend money hiring more workers during harvest time if his sons weren't so *fuckin' lazy.*

Everett stroked his mustache with a forefinger. "What is it about then?"

Leaning back on his chair, Samuel gave his guest a long, penetrating look. "It's about you respecting my wishes as my employee."

Everett stared at Samuel, his pulse racing and heart pounding. "I didn't know I was an employee."

"Why are you here?"

"Because you asked me to come."

Samuel's open hand came down on the table, rattling the cups and a vase filled with fresh flowers. "Cut the bullshit, Kirkland! You called me because you want something."

Pushing back his chair, Everett stood up and leaned over the table. "And you asked me to call you because you need me."

A half smile tilted the corners of Samuel's mouth. "Sit down, Kirkland, stop the theatrics, and let me know whether you're going to Costa Rica with me. Sit down," he ordered again between clenched teeth when the accountant hesitated.

Everett sat down, gold eyes narrowing. There was a pregnant silence filled with a tension so thick it was palpable. "Yes, Samuel. I will accompany you to Costa Rica."

"As the accountant for Cole International, Limited?"

He nodded. "Yes. As the accountant for Cole International, Limited," he repeated.

Samuel picked up his demitasse cup, touching it to Everett's. "I'll drink to that."

The tense moment over, Everett picked up his cup, repeating the gesture. "When do I start?"

"Today."

"How much?"

"Sixty dollars a week, with a year-end bonus based on a percentage of profits. Your responsibility is to maximize profits, save taxes without evading them, and provide me with everything I'll need for possible expansion."

"What about investments?"

"What about them, Kirkland?"

"Do you intend to invest in the stock market?"

Samuel shook his head. "No. I'm not a gambler, and to me playing the market is nothing more than gambling."

A smile parted Everett's firm lips. "I agree. How about banks, boss?"

"What about them?"

"Do you like them?"

Angling his head, Samuel pulled his lower lip between his teeth. "No, but they serve a purpose for keeping one's money safe."

"What do you know about the Panic of 1893?"

"Not much," he admitted honestly.

"There was economic disaster. Businesses failed, and a lot of folks lost everything."

Samuel remembered his grandfather boasting that he was glad he hadn't put his money in a bank like most of the other farmers. They were wiped out completely, whereas he was left with his small but hard-earned savings.

"What are you suggesting?"

Everett leaned forward, as if he were telling a secret. "Put your money where it's safe. But leave enough to cover expenses for a year."

"Is this advice or a warning?"

"It's more of a hunch," Everett admitted. "We're currently in a postwar boom that's like a balloon getting bigger and bigger, but the day is coming when it's going to pop and we're going to experience an economic crash that will make the eighty-seven and ninety-three panics look like a three-year-old's birthday party."

Samuel studied the face of the man who'd just predicted economic disaster for the United States. He wanted to tell Everett that he was being pessimistic, but decided to reserve comment on the subject.

"Haven't we always had little recessions?"

"Yes."

"Then we'll just have to wait and see if your hunch is right, won't we?"

Everett, sure of himself and his rightful place in the universe now that he'd secured a position earning three times the salary of most working-class Americans, inclined his head and pressed his hands together in a prayerful gesture.

"We will not speak of this again until the time is right for you to withdraw your money."

Samuel drained his cup, then dabbed at the grounds on the tip of his tongue with a napkin. He recognized a quiet assurance in Everett Kirkland that hadn't been there before. Did his number man know more than he was disclosing? Was he a con man whose intent was to get him to take his money out of the bank so he could rob him?

Although he'd hired the accountant to oversee his books and Everett had given him the information he needed to negotiate with the representative of Puerto Limon's United Fruit Company, he still had to prove that he could be trusted. He would follow Everett's advice and withdraw some of his funds, albeit slowly for an extended period of time, and leave them with the only person he entrusted with his life: Belinda Cole.

"I hope that time never comes," he said in a quiet tone.

"So do I," Everett concurred.

13

Let us have wine and women, mirth and laughter, sermons and soda-water the day after.

—George Gordon, Lord Byron

Samuel Cole and Everett Kirkland left West Palm Beach at dawn Tuesday, February 17, 1925; the following morning they boarded a merchant steamship in Miami for Costa Rica while M.J. prepared for her first Wednesday bid whist luncheon. She'd informed Peggy Carson that although she didn't play she was willing to host the gathering.

Samuel had gotten up early, M.J. offering to cook breakfast for him and Everett, whom she'd come to like and respect. Intelligent, polite, and still a little too formal with her, Everett had become a welcome guest. Both men declined, saying they would eat onboard the ship.

Glancing at a clock on a kitchen shelf, she noted the time. It was 7:10. In less than five hours the four women who had committed to attend would walk through her door. Hoping to take advantage of the warm weather, she'd elected to hold the get-together on the patio overlooking the garden. She'd given Bessie Tuesday off in lieu of coming on Wednesday.

"Watcha fixin', Miz Cole?"

Turning around, M.J. smiled at Bessie Wright. The thirty-five-year-old mother of ten affected a grin that showed her teeth, four of the upper ringed in gold. Short and full-figured, she'd just completed the eighth grade when she married a neighbor's son who'd begun courting her at thirteen. She gave birth to her first baby at fifteen, then one every other

year for the next ten. Bessie cleaned houses and her handyman husband
held down several jobs to earn enough to care for their family.

"I'm making *frituras de cangrejo.*"

"Say what?" Bessie drawled.

"Crab fritters," M.J. translated, smiling.

Bessie bobbed her heard. "Sounds good. I loves me some crabs." She
placed her handbag on a high stool. "What do you want me to do?"

"Make the beds, clean the bathroom, and dust everything. By the time
you're finished I'll need your help setting up outside."

Bessie rolled her eyes and sucked her teeth. "I hope you ain't makin' a
mistake invitin' dem high-fluentin' heifers to yo place," she mumbled
under her breath as she made her way over to a closet where she kept her
cleaning supplies.

She liked working for Mrs. Cole. Maybe because she was a foreigner
she was different from the other women whose houses Bessie cleaned.
They tended to talk down to her, not at her, and they thought she didn't
know that they checked their silver and jewelry regularly to make certain
she hadn't taken anything. What they didn't understand was that she
needed to work to put food on the table for her family, not get arrested
for stealing stuff she wouldn't use or need.

"If you want help cookin' somethin' jest holler," Bessie said, opening a
closet to retrieve a mop and pail.

The two women shared a knowing smile. Bessie always offered to help
with the cooking even though Mrs. Cole fixed foods with funny names
and even stranger ingredients.

"Thank you for asking, but I'm okay."

M.J. put together a menu she hoped would please her guests. Most
were classic Cuban recipes passed down through the centuries. Four
hours after entering the kitchen she finished with her preparation, then
made her way to the patio where she and Bessie set the table with an heirloom tablecloth and napkins, china, and silver.

M.J. stood back and surveyed the table, finding it to her liking. She returned to the house, finding everything immaculate, and the clean scent
of lemon oil mingled with the tantalizing smells of tropical herbs and
spices. She had less than half an hour to take a bath and dress.

She had just secured the last pin in the chignon pinned on the nape of
her neck when the doorbell rang. The clock on the dressing table beside
her vanity chimed the hour. It was exactly noon.

M.J. had instructed Bessie to greet the women, escort them out to the
patio, and serve liquid refreshments until she joined them. What she
hadn't wanted was for Winifred Mansfield to think she was *that* thrilled

about seeing her again. If Winnie, as Peggy referred to her, hadn't been responsible for forming the group, M.J. wouldn't have invited her, knowing the woman had sought to make a match between Samuel and her daughter.

A short-sleeved pale pink dress in delicate georgette with a dropped waist and handkerchief hem was perfect for the afternoon garden party. Uncapping a tube of lipstick, M.J. applied a deep rose-pink color to her lips. Her tan had faded. Her face was now the color of a newly ripened peach.

Staring at her reflection in the mirror, she took a deep breath, pinched her cheeks to create the illusion that she'd applied rouge, then turned on her heel and left her bedroom. For a brief moment she wished Samuel were there with her. But he was hundreds of miles away on a ship heading for Puerto Limon, a city situated along Costa Rica's Caribbean coastline.

She heard the women before she saw them. One was exclaiming excitedly that she'd never seen a rose that particular color. M.J. knew she was referring to a deep red purple hybrid.

Stepping out onto the patio, she affected a warm smile. "Welcome, ladies. Thank you for coming to my home," she said softly.

Peggy, holding a glass filled with a citrus drink, turned and returned her smile. "Hello, M.J." She waved her free hand. "I believe you've met the others, but let me introduce you to them again. Winifred Mansfield, Shirley Yates, and Edna Burgess."

She nodded to the trio. Peggy told her that Winifred and Shirley were former schoolteachers, and Edna had been a nurse before she married her pharmacist husband. She'd also confided that the women had attended college with the hopes of finding a suitable husband, and once married were content to become housewives and mothers.

Winifred stepped forward. "Before we sit down to eat, could you please give us a tour of your lovely home?"

M.J.'s smile was dazzling. "Of course. We'll begin in the living room."

She led the women through the kitchen and into the living room, exchanging a knowing glance with Bessie. All of the ladies, with the exception of Winifred, complimented M.J. on the meticulous care with which she'd chosen items for her home. The eclectic mix of country French and Spanish provincial furnishings gave each room its own distinct personality.

Shirley pointed to the piano. "Do you play, Marguerite?"

"Yes, I do."

Edna ran her fingertips over the side of the black concert piano. "Please play something for us."

An attractive blush spread over M.J.'s face. "Perhaps another time."

Winifred studied a framed painting on a wall between two tapestry-covered chairs of Jose Luis with his grandparents. "Who's the woman in this picture?" she asked M.J.

"She was my great-grandmother."

Eyes wide, Winifred straightened and stared at M.J. "So, you're an octoroon," she said cheerfully, as if uncovering a secret.

M.J. glared at Winifred. She'd never denied her African blood. In fact, she was proud of it. "Mulatto, quadroon, or octoroon. It doesn't matter what you call me because in Florida I'm still a Negro."

"You talk as if you don't have racism and segregation in Cuba," Winifred spat out, her words dripping with venom.

"We have racism and segregation. But what we don't have is cowards who hide their faces behind bedsheets and hang black Cubans for sport." She forced a smile. "I'm certain you did not come here to debate international politics, so please let us retire to the patio."

Peggy lagged behind as Shirley, Winifred, and Edna made their way to the rear of the house. "We've learned to ignore Winnie because she's going through her changes. She's so prickly that she and Basil are now sleeping in separate bedrooms."

"How do you know this?" M.J. whispered.

"Our housekeepers are cousins. And you know how hard it is for hired help to keep their mouths shut. So, if you have something you don't want Bessie to know, then don't speak of it in front of her."

Digesting this information, M.J. instructed Bessie to begin bringing out the food. The crab fritters, potato and shrimp puffs, and empanadas had been left warming in the oven. Potato and green plantain chips were used to scoop up the potent *mojo criollo*, the Creole garlic sauce, which also accompanied the warm miniature *pan con lechon*, Creole pork sandwiches.

She'd made an exception and prepared one fried dish: *masitas de pollo frito*—fried chicken morsels. M.J. served the crisp, tender chicken with white rice and the garlic sauce.

There was little or no conversation as the four women sampled foods that were as pleasing to the palate as to the eye. Winifred removed a flask from a large sack, passing it around the table. Peggy, Edna, and Shirley added a generous amount of scotch to their lemonade. Within minutes they were as animated as circus monkeys.

M.J. refused the liquor because she'd found its taste unpleasant. She much preferred wines: sherry or champagne. If her guests drank illegal alcohol, then there was no doubt they also smoked cigarettes.

Shirley leaned back in her chair. "I think I ate too much."

"Me too," Edna concurred.

"Where did you learn to cook like this?" Peggy asked M.J.

She dabbed the corners of her mouth with a napkin. "At school."

Winifred shot her a look of disbelief. "What kind of school did you attend?"

M.J. stared at the women ranging in age from midforties to late twenties. Peggy, at twenty-nine, was closest to her in age. She told them about growing up in Cuba, attending the convent school, and the courses she'd taken that were taught by nuns.

"What about college?" Winifred asked.

"I've completed two years."

"What were you studying?"

"Latin American history and philosophy."

"What did you plan to do with that?" Shirley asked.

"I hadn't made up my mind."

Winifred put down her drink. "How old are you, Marguerite-Josefina?"

"Twenty."

"Twenty!" Shirley, Edna, and Winifred chorused in unison.

"I thought you were at least twenty-eight," Shirley admitted.

Winifred placed a hand over her bosom. "Good Lord! Samuel married a child."

Peggy rolled her eyes at Winifred. "M.J. is only a year younger than your Celeste."

"We are not discussing my daughter, Margaret!"

"What's wrong with you, Winnie?" Peggy snapped angrily.

"There's nothing wrong. And don't call me Winnie, you spiteful bitch!"

Peggy recoiled as if she'd been slapped. "How dare you!"

Winifred pushed back her chair and stood up. "You're impossible to be around since you found out that you are barren."

Tears welled in Peggy's eyes. "You didn't have to say that."

"Well, I did," Winifred retorted, sneering.

M.J. stood up so quickly her chair tipped over. "*Bastante*! Enough!" she repeated in English. "Mrs. Mansfield, I want you to leave my home." Her eyes shimmered like bits of volcanic rock. "I'd like for all of you to leave. Now."

Winifred snatched her large purse off a stone bench. "Who do you think you are? You're nothing but a foreigner trying to put on airs. Samuel Cole only married you because you're the closest he'll ever get to a white woman without getting lynched. Why couldn't you stay in Cuba or marry one of your own men?"

Shirley patted Winifred's back as if to comfort her. "Come, honey. You need to lie down and rest."

Peggy blinked back tears. "I'm sorry, M.J."

Turning her back, M.J. stared at a blooming rosebush. She wanted them all gone—even her new friend. Something had told her the night of the Mansfield soiree that the women didn't like her. They'd viewed her as a foreigner, an interloper who had taken one of their most eligible bachelors. She righted her chair, sat, and stared into space until Bessie came and cleared the table.

"Don't pay them no mind, Miz Cole. They ain't nothin' but heifers who ain't happy and ain't never gonna be happy. They mens buys them fine houses but fool around wit other women. They only marry them because they talk all fancy like. You be the youngest, but you the lady they alls want to be."

M.J. forced a smile that made her face ache with the effort. "Thank you for all of your help today."

She sat at the table long after the sun had moved behind a copse that left the patio and the garden in the shade. She hadn't moved when Bessie came to tell her that she was leaving.

When she did finally get up and go into the house Marguerite-Josefina Isabel Diaz Cole was not the same as when she'd gotten up that morning. It was as if she had to grow up within a matter of hours.

There was no more girl left in her.

She'd become a woman in every sense of the word.

Samuel and Everett checked into the Casa del Caribe three days after leaving West Palm Beach. It was only mid-February, and the heat was brutal. Both craved a shower, clean clothes, and a cold drink.

The proprietor remembered Samuel, offering him his best room. This time he would have a private bath. Ironically, Everett was given the same room Samuel had occupied during his previous visit.

Samuel checked his watch. "I'll meet you down here in an hour."

Nodding, Everett picked up his bag. He couldn't tell Samuel that he didn't have a watch, that he'd sold it to buy rum, but it would be the first thing he'd buy once Samuel paid him.

"Aren't you going to check the time, Everett?"

He gave his boss a direct stare. "I would if I had a watch." A perceptible nod and a slight lifting of an eyebrow were Samuel's only reaction to his revelation. "I won't be late."

Turning, he headed for the staircase, feeling the heat from Samuel's gaze on his back. It wasn't until he unlocked the door to his room that Everett was able to relax. He'd spent a week with Samuel, yet knew nothing more about the man than what he'd gleaned in their first meeting.

It was as if there were two Samuels—one the businessman who listened intently and remembered everything, the businessman who offered to pay him three times what Henry Ford gave his assembly line workers. (Ford had increased the prevailing $1.75-a-day wage to five dollars to counter resignations and firings.) The other man was husband and host who was relaxed, friendly, and adored his wife. His demeanor and voice changed whenever he was in M.J.'s presence. And it was obvious his adoration was reciprocated.

Opening his luggage, Everett removed a change of clothes. A wry smile softened his mouth. He'd left Puerto Limon as the "American," and with his return he would be known only as Everett Joshua Kirkland.

He and Samuel had discussed the meeting with Nigel Cunningham, head of finance for the United Fruit Company. Cunningham's telegram indicated he wanted to discuss increasing the rates for shipping goods to the States.

Everett had asked Samuel if he could chair the meeting on behalf of Cole International, Ltd., because he was familiar with the man who at one time had been his boss. He hated the supercilious, condescending, bigoted son of a bitch who'd fired him months before he was diagnosed with the debilitating disease that had almost cost him his life.

A knowing smile curved Everett's mouth under his mustache. It was now payback time.

Samuel and Everett sat at the end of a long table facing Nigel Cunningham and Trevor Richards. Lacing his fingers together, Samuel leaned forward, his gaze fixed on the stoic expressions of the two men seated at the opposite end.

"I did not spend three days on the water to come here and shout to be heard. Either we sit closer together or this meeting is over." Pushing back his chair, he rose to his feet, Everett rising at the same time, as if they'd rehearsed and orchestrated the motion beforehand.

Nigel stood up quickly. "Mr. Cole . . . please don't leave. We have much to discuss."

Everett, sensing the advantage, spoke up. "If that's the case, *Nigel*," he spat out, using the effeminate man's given name for the first time, "then perhaps you and Trevor can sit closer to Mr. Cole and myself." He beckoned as a feral smile parted his mouth. "Come, come, gentlemen. I can assure you that Mr. Cole and I won't devour you, in spite of the stories coming out of darkest Africa about our people being cannibals."

Trevor's face reddened as Nigel's paled. "Look, Everett," Nigel said, protesting.

Everett shook his head slowly. "I don't work for you, Nigel, and I'd appreciate it if you'd address me as Mr. Kirkland."

Trevor Richards, hoping to diffuse what would've become a volatile situation, rose to his feet and approached Samuel and Everett. He was Nigel's superior, and in no way would he allow the man's insecurity to get in the way of United Fruit Company's success. He sat down on Everett's right, leaving Nigel to sit at Samuel's left. The Americans shared a surreptitious look. There was only the sound of measured breathing as the four men regarded one another.

Everett, with a perceptible nod from Samuel, stared at Nigel. "You mentioned in your cable something about an increase in shipping rates."

Nigel nodded. "That is true. The workers are threatening a work slow-down if they're not offered better housing and medical care. We're also facing a massive sanitation program to combat the tropical diseases that undermine the workers' efficiency and threaten the well-being of company managers."

Samuel smiled as Everett pushed far enough back from the table to loop one leg over the opposite knee. The cuffs of his suit jacket were slightly worn, as was the collar of his white shirt, but the shabbiness in no way detracted from the overall appearance he presented as a formidable negotiator.

"Correct me if I'm wrong," Everett said softly. "You plan to address the issues of health and social inequities by raising shipping costs to offset United Fruit's efforts to establish a network of hospitals and housing for your workers."

"You are correct," Nigel stated emphatically.

Everett's golden eyes glittered dangerously. "Why don't you use a portion of your profits? And don't tell me you've been losing money, since I was summarily discharged because you couldn't stand to work with a black man who knew more than you."

Nigel cast his gaze downward.

Trevor drummed his fingers nervously on the surface of the table. "We have stockholders to answer to."

"How unfortunate for you," Samuel replied sarcastically. "Fortunately for Cole International, Limited, we answer only to ourselves. And I'd like to inform you that United Fruit isn't the only company interested in soy-beans nowadays." He'd lied, but said it with such conviction that he almost believed his own lie.

Everett picked up on Samuel's untruth. "I'm certain you two gentle-men remember Mr. Marcus Garvey's visit to Limon back in twenty-one."

Trevor Richards shook his head. "Mr. Cunningham was assigned to meet with Mr. Garvey."

"What was your impression of Mr. Garvey, Mr. Cunningham?"

Nigel fixed his gaze on a pencil beside his right hand. "I heard he was quite satisfied with the results of his visit here. Mr. Garvey told the work-ers that the work given them by the United Fruit Company meant their bread and butter. They would receive the same respect as United Fruit once they had farms, railways, and steamships of their own and showed that they could operate them."

Everett inclined his head. "Did he not say that in order to operate such an enterprise they must have money and that in order to get money they had to work?" Trevor and Nigel nodded.

"There is another group of men," he continued smoothly, "who are of the same belief as Mr. Garvey."

"Who are these men?" Nigel asked.

"I cannot reveal their identity," Everett said, his expression closed, and it took all of his self-control not to laugh in the faces of the two greedy North Americans. "However, Mr. Cole is a member *and* an officer of this organization that has become the cornerstone of a vision for black economic independence. The corporation was created with the goal of supporting businesses that would employ African-Americans and produce goods to be sold to black consumers. They have black-owned factories, retailers, services, and other businesses. The result will be a network strong enough to empower and sustain an all-black economy with world-wide significance.

"If you intend to raise the shipping costs for goods handled by Cole International, Limited, then we'll be forced to pull out completely and turn everything over to this organization."

"But . . . but you can't!" Nigel sputtered.

"But *we* can," Samuel said quietly. "Have you forgotten the clause in our contract that our prevailing shipping costs are fixed for the next five years? However, if you want out, then you'll have to pay me. . . ." His words trailed off as he met Everett's amused stare. "Mr. Kirkland, have you come up with a figure that would satisfy us for this breach of contract?"

"At least one million."

"You're crazy if you believe United Fruit will give two niggers a million dollars!" Nigel shouted.

Schooling his expression not to react to the slur, Samuel glanced around the large room. "Who are these niggers you speak of, Nigel?"

Everett wasn't as successful in reining in his temper. "If you ever utter that word in my presence again you'll find yourself picking up your teeth with a rake."

Trevor's open palm came down hard on the table. "Gentlemen, *please.*" He glared at Nigel. "Leave us, Cunningham."

Nigel blanched. "Trevor, you can't take their side."

"I'm not here to take sides," he countered. "I'm here as a vice president of the United Fruit Company. In case you've forgotten, our role is to protect the company. I'll take it from here."

Samuel lowered his head rather than let the others see the smirk stealing its way across his face. Nigel and Trevor were both from the American South, but that was the only similarity. Nigel had worked as an accountant for the owner of several West Virginia coal mines before he signed on a merchant steamship heading for Central America, whereas Trevor left Alabama to escape his tyrannical banker-father.

Waiting until the door closed behind Nigel, Trevor turned his attention on the two men who'd managed to shake the accountant's composure. The skin around his soulful-looking brown eyes crinkled when he smiled.

"I'm sorry about Nigel. There are times when he forgets himself during the heat of negotiations."

"There's no need for you to apologize," Everett said harshly.

Samuel placed a hand on Everett's sleeve. "Everett, let's hear what Mr. Richards has to say."

Trevor inclined his head. "Thank you, Samuel. May I call you Samuel?"

Samuel nodded. "Yes."

Trevor smiled at Everett. "Everett?"

"Yes, Trevor."

Clasping his hands together, Trevor stared at the shiny surface on the oak table. "Gentlemen, I need to take something back to my superiors that is palatable. Are you willing to help me out?"

"Do you smoke, Trevor?" Samuel asked.

His light brown eyebrows lifted. "Cigarettes?"

"No. Cigars."

The middle-aged man smiled, the gesture making him appear years younger. "I like a good cigar."

Reaching into the breast pocket of his jacket, Samuel withdrew a cigar and handed it to Trevor. "Try this one, and let me know what you think."

Three minutes later Trevor, leaning back in his chair, blew a series of blue-gray smoke rings, his eyes widening in surprise. Removing the cylinder of tightly rolled tobacco leaves from his mouth, he shook his head.

"Nice."

"You like it?" Samuel asked.

Trevor nodded. "It's the best cigar I've ever smoked. Where did you get it?"

"Cuba."

"A lot of cigars come from Cuba."

"That's true," Samuel conceded. "What if I arrange for the exportation of Cuban cigars to this region in exchange for a small percentage of the profits you'll derive from their sale? We can begin with a small quantity, and if the demand increases so will the supply."

Everett picked up quickly on Samuel's new scheme. "Your company's stockholders never have to know about the cigars. The profits can be used to offset the costs for your hospital and housing projects."

Trevor's features became more animated. "Let me talk to my boss. Do you happen to have another one for him to sample?"

Reaching into his pocket, Samuel took out the last two remaining cigars and handed them to Trevor. "When will you get back to me?"

Trevor sucked in another mouthful of sweet tobacco. "Can you wait?"

"How long do you want us to wait?" Samuel asked.

"Hopefully, I can get back to you before the end of today."

Samuel checked his watch. The end of the day wouldn't come for another two hours. "Contact me at my hotel."

"Where are you staying?"

"The Casa del Caribe."

The meeting ended with the three men shaking hands, and when Samuel and Everett stepped out into the brilliant sun, their smiles were triumphant.

Samuel rested a hand on Everett's shoulder. "What made you come up with that secret organization hoax?"

"Those two hillbillies have been away from home too long to concern themselves with black men seeking to change the status quo. Are you serious about the cigars?"

Samuel nodded. "Quite serious. M.J.'s father is a cigar manufacturer. We can export the cigars without a broker."

Everett's eyebrows lifted a fraction. "Do you think they're going to accept it?"

"They're too greedy not to."

Everett hoped Samuel was right, because it was a scheme wherein United Fruit's owners stood to make a lot of money without having to share the profits from the sale. They were known for exporting bananas, not importing cigars.

Samuel dropped his hand. "A word of caution, Everett. Never show your opponent your weakness."

"What are you talking about?"

"You got personal and lost your temper when Nigel called us niggers. If Richards hadn't stepped in when he did, then we'd be going home with nothing."

Smarting from his boss's reprimand, Everett clenched his jaw. "It will not happen again."

Samuel patted his cheek. "Now let's go get something to eat."

"I thought we were going back to the hotel," Everett said when Samuel started out in the opposite direction.

"Patience, Everett," he said in a soft voice.

Patience, he repeated to himself as he followed Samuel to a restaurant frequented by tourists.

Samuel and Everett sat on the sand and toasted each other with Jamaican rum. They'd returned to their hotel to find a typed letter signed by Trevor Richards. The executives of Puerto Limon's United Fruit Company were willing to negotiate with Cole International, Ltd., for the importation of Cuban cigars.

"You're a genius," Everett said reverently.

"No, I'm not," Samuel countered. "It's called appealing to one's greed."

"*Hola, Americano.*"

Everett glanced over his shoulder to find the woman he'd slept with while he waited for his photographer-lover's return, smiling at him. Petite, dark-skinned, and very pretty, Paullina Michael was an expert when it came to pleasing a man. Her tightly curling hair floated to her shoulders like a dark cloud.

Both men rose unsteadily to their feet.

Everett nodded. "Hello, Paullina."

Her gaze strayed to Samuel before it returned to Everett. "Would you like company?"

Everett stared at Samuel, who nodded his approval. He wanted to stay and celebrate with his boss *and* he wanted to go with Paullina, because it'd been too long since he'd lain with a woman.

"Samuel, this is Paullina Michael, Paullina, Mr. Samuel Cole." The two shook hands, exchanging the perfunctory greetings. "Would you like something to drink?" Everett asked the garishly dressed Paullina.

She sat down, gesturing to the bottle of rum. "I'll have what you're having."

Samuel signaled for a waiter under a makeshift bar to bring another glass. He was ready to retire for bed. He'd been headed there when Everett suggested they go out and celebrate their unexpected windfall. They found a little shack less than a hundred feet from the ocean, ordered a bottle of potent Jamaican rum, and sat silently drinking and watching the sun sink lower and lower.

His mind, before the onset of drunkenness enveloped him, was filled with plans on how he would approach Jose Luis to have him sell a portion of his cigar production to his son-in-law to export to Costa Rica; and he still had to weigh the advantages of having the cigars shipped directly from the Pinar del Rio factory.

Samuel hadn't realized that he'd closed his eyes until Everett shook him roughly. "What is it?"

"Paullina wants to know if you want a friend."

He squinted at the beautiful face awash in the red-gold glow of the setting sun. "Friend?"

Paullina smiled, displaying small, white, even teeth. "Yes. I have a friend who would like you very much."

Weaving slightly, Samuel affected a wide grin. The rum had dulled his senses. "How much?"

"For you—only a few American dollars."

All he had in his pocket were a few American dollars. He'd left most of his money and his gold watch in a safe at the hotel. Dressed in his favored *guayabera*, slacks, and sandals he could be taken as a local—until he opened his mouth.

Demon rum, the tropical heat, the sound of a trio playing steel pans, and because he'd bested the United Fruit Company in their scheme to breach their contract made him euphoric, cocky, and reckless.

"Ish . . . is she clean?" His words were slurring.

Paullina's eyes widened. "Of course she's clean. She would never lie with a man without a rubber sheath."

It took two attempts before he was able to come to his feet and stand unaided. He did not remember leaving the beach, or in which direction Paullina had led him and Everett.

He did not remember the face of the woman whose talented mouth left him moaning in the most exquisite pleasure he'd ever experienced.

He did not remember how he'd gotten back to the hotel or who'd put him to bed.

What he did remember fourteen hours later when he sat on the side of his bed was that the woman who had suckled his penis while he ejaculated was not his wife.

14

Drunkenness is simply voluntary insanity.

—Seneca the Younger

Samuel paid the taxi driver and walked up the path to his home. He unlocked the door, moved into the entryway, and left his luggage on the floor beside a small bench. He'd been away nine days, although it felt longer.

The house was quiet even though it was the middle of the day. M.J. couldn't have gone far because his car was still in the driveway. Streams of bright sunlight glinted off the tables. The house was spotless.

Samuel found his wife in her garden. Crossing his arms over his chest, he smiled at the figure she presented in a pair of slacks, one of his shirts, and a battered straw hat. Kneeling, she used a trowel to loosen dirt around a flowering rosebush.

"*Hola, mi amor.*"

"Sammy!" M.J. dropped the trowel and launched herself at him, her arms going around his neck. Picking her up, he fastened his mouth to hers and spun her around.

"Why didn't you let me know you were coming home early?"

He'd sent her a telegram indicating he wouldn't be home for another week.

"I needed to see you. I needed to feel you. I needed to smell you." His voice and gaze lowered as he stared deeply into the dark eyes filling up with tears.

M.J.'s lower lip trembled with an emotion that made drawing a normal breath difficult. Her gloved hands cradled his stubbly cheeks. "I love you, I love you, I love you," she whispered against his mouth.

She'd confessed to Samuel that she loved him, but this absence had forced her to face her true feelings. She had married Samuel Cole for all the wrong reasons; he'd offered a freedom the men in Cuba couldn't, and for that she was grateful. But what she felt for her husband wasn't gratitude. It was love, a love that made her look forward to the next sunrise, a love that left her with a sense of fulfillment and peace that made her able to face any obstacle.

After her aborted Wednesday bid whist luncheon she'd kept her distance from the other women. She instructed Bessie to inform Peggy that she wasn't accepting visitors when she'd come to see her. She didn't blame Peggy for Winifred's behavior, but she had expected her new friend to at least chastise the pompous Mrs. Mansfield for her insults. And like a coward she'd waited two days to come to offer her apologies.

Marguerite-Josefina Isabel Diaz-Cole did not need Winifred, Peggy, Edna, Shirley, or any of the other heifers, as Bessie tended to call them, in their so-called exclusive residential enclave. All she needed was her husband, Samuel Claridge Cole.

She smiled, her dimples deepening. "I've missed you so much."

"Really?"

"Yes, really," she said, wrinkling her delicate nose.

"Do you want to show me how much?"

Her smile faded. "I've told you. How can I show you?"

His expression mirrored confusion. Samuel didn't know why, but there were times when he forgot how young and inexperienced his wife actually was. Tightening his grip under her knees, he left the garden and reentered the house.

"It looks as if I'll have to show you how much I've missed you."

M.J. let out a small shriek when he carried her into the bathroom. It took less than a minute to relieve her of her clothes and remove his own. Standing under the spray of a warm shower, they reunited and reconciled in the most intimate way possible.

Samuel luxuriated in the water spilling over his body washing away the residue of salt clinging to his hair and skin, and his hardness moving in and out of his wife's body eradicated the memory of another woman who'd taken him into her mouth when he refused to penetrate her. Passions spent, they lay motionless, waiting for their heartbeats to resume a normal rate.

"Is this what I can look forward to whenever you return from your business trips?"

"Not for a long, long time."

Her smooth brow wrinkled. "What are you talking about?"

"I'm taking you with me when I go to Tallahassee, then to Cuba."

"When are we leaving?"

"Tomorrow."

M.J. screamed in childish delight, then placed tiny kisses over his stubbly cheeks.

Samuel had booked passage on a tanker sailing from West Palm Beach to Mobile, Alabama. It'd rained nonstop and he and M.J. were forced to spend the trip in a cramped cabin no larger than their bathroom.

By the time the ship sailed into the warmer water of the Gulf of Mexico the rain had tapered off to a light drizzle. They disembarked at Apalachee Bay where he hired a driver to take them north to Tallahassee.

He'd followed through on Everett Kirkland's hunch and withdrawn half of his savings from the bank. The manager of the West Palm Beach branch of the Sun Trust wanted to know if anything was wrong with their services, if any of the employees had displeased or insulted him in any way, but Samuel reassured him that everything was well, and that he planned to loan the money to a relative to start up a new business. He'd secured the money in a waterproof case, then in a canvas bag.

Belinda opened the door to Samuel's knock. Reaching up, she hugged her son. "You made good time, especially with the weather."

Samuel kissed his mother's cheek. "We're just glad we made it safely."

Smiling at her daughter-in-law, Belinda offered her hands. "Please come in and rest yourself. You must be exhausted after spending so many hours on the water."

M.J. grasped Belinda's hands and kissed her on both cheeks. "Thank you, Mother. It's good seeing you again."

Belinda stared at the tall, slender woman with a wealth of black hair tucked into a tight twist on the nape of her long neck sporting a stylish navy cloche that was the exact match of a lightweight traveling suit. She and Samuel were the perfect couple, tall, slender, and stylishly attractive.

"I'm so glad Samuel decided to bring you." She tightened her grip on the delicate fingers. "Come, let me show you to your room. Would you like something to eat?"

M.J. shook her head. "No, thank you. All I want is a warm bath and a comfortable bed."

Samuel watched as his mother led M.J. to the room they would share for their stay. He left to pay the driver and assist him with the luggage, instructing him to leave the bags by the door. He lingered long enough to remove the case containing thousands of dollars. Tucking it under his arm, he made his way into the kitchen, putting it on a pantry shelf. He would let Belinda know what the case contained, and together they would determine where to hide it in the event of a bank failure.

Samuel had hired Everett based on a sixth sense, the same sixth sense that made him get into black marketeering toward the end of the war, and the same sixth sense that made him forgo growing cotton in lieu of soybeans.

He knew he was paying the accountant more than what most men with families earned each week, but felt it crucial he ensure Everett's trust and loyalty. Before leaving Puerto Limon to return to the States he'd given Everett a three-month advance in salary with an edict that he relocate to West Palm Beach, and purchase a wardrobe befitting his position as finance officer for Cole International, Ltd. He also allowed Everett a month to finalize his move and to make preparations to begin working in an office.

He planned to spend two weeks in Tallahassee with his mother, brothers, and in-laws, and another two in Cuba so that M.J. could see her relatives. Once he returned to West Palm Beach, Florida, he would begin to fulfill his own role as president of his company.

Samuel sat at the kitchen table with Belinda, talking softly. M.J., who'd readied herself for bed, promised not to fall asleep until he joined her.

"I want you to put the money where it will remain dry and animals can't get after it."

Vertical lines appeared between his mother's eyes. "Are you sure you know what you're doing taking your money out of the bank?"

"Very sure," Samuel said confidently, even though he still had to convince himself what he'd done would protect his future business endeavors.

"I have a place," Belinda said in a quiet voice. "I'll hide it down in the root cellar behind my preserves. There's a loose board in the wall. It will be safe there."

"Does anyone know about it?" Belinda shook her head. Pushing to his feet, Samuel leaned across the table and kissed his mother. "Thanks, Mama. I'm going to bed now."

Belinda caught his wrist. "How's married life?"

Samuel smiled. "It's wonderful. M.J. is the perfect wife."

"When can I expect grandchildren from the two of you?"

He lowered his gaze. "We're working on it."

Her smile was dazzling. "That's good, son."

He kissed her again, staring into a pair of dark eyes so much like his own. "Good night, Mama."

Belinda held his gaze. "Good night, Samuel."

Samuel slipped quietly into bed next to M.J. Her soft snores indicated she'd fallen asleep. He smiled. She'd promised to wait up for him.

M.J. is the perfect wife. He'd told his mother the truth while he was living a lie. He hadn't been the perfect husband; he'd been unfaithful when his wife had given him no reason to seek out another woman.

He lay motionless, staring up at the shadows on the ceiling, while listening to the steady beating of his heart. But had he really been unfaithful to his wife?

Could he be deemed an adulterer because he paid a woman for sex?

Sighing, he closed his eyes, turned over on his side, and went to sleep, feeling as if he'd done nothing wrong.

"When do I stop stirring, Mother?"

Belinda peered into the pot of hominy grits on the stove. "Give it another minute, then lower the flame and cover the pot." M.J. had asked whether she could teach her to cook the southern dishes Samuel had grown up eating.

M.J. covered the pot, making certain the flame was low enough to finish cooking the ground corn kernels. "I'll fry the fish." Belinda had coated filleted whiting with flour and coarse cornmeal seasoned with salt, black pepper, and cayenne pepper.

Belinda smiled at the eager young woman. She found M.J. different from her two other daughters-in-law. Eugenia and Annie-Mae Cole had never offered to help her, so when she visited their homes she did not reciprocate. She watched as M.J. scooped up a serving spoon portion of lard from a tin and dropped it into a large cast-iron skillet.

"Make certain it's hot, but not so hot that it will burn."

M.J.'s dimples deepened in a knowing smile. "We do use lard when we fry in Cuba." There was a hint of laughter in her voice.

Nodding, Belinda removed a container of chicken liver from the refrigerator. She was the only woman in her neighborhood to have a refrigerator rather than an icebox. And with the onset of the sweltering summer heat a block of ice usually didn't last more than a couple of days, but the electric refrigerator had changed that dramatically, preserving meat and dairy products for longer periods of time.

"Maybe before you and Samuel leave you can teach me to cook some of your foods," Belinda suggested.

M.J. hugged her mother-in-law. "I find many of our foods are similar. It's the seasonings that give them a different taste."

She fried the fish to a crispy, golden brown, placing them on a plate covered with brown paper to drain while the tantalizing aroma of sautéed flour-dredged chicken liver with onion, green bell pepper, and chopped garlic filled the kitchen.

"Now, isn't this a sight to behold? The two women I love most cooking together," drawled a deep voice some distance away.

Belinda and M.J. turned to find Samuel standing under the entrance to the kitchen, smiling.

He walked into the kitchen. "I thought you'd be in church by now, Mama." He kissed Belinda's cheek, then M.J.'s mouth.

Belinda's gaze swept over his face, seeing things she hadn't noticed the night before. There were streaks of gray in his hair. Samuel would turn twenty-seven in August, yet there was something about her youngest that made him appear years older, even older than Mark. She couldn't shake a nagging feeling that his insatiable craving for money, fame, and power had replaced the humility that she'd always admired in him.

She forced a smile. "Church will always be here when you and M.J. leave. By the way, how long do you plan to be here?"

Samuel stared at M.J. and smiled. "Two weeks. We're going on to Cuba from here."

Belinda glanced at her daughter-in-law. "Will it be your first visit since marrying Samuel?"

M.J. nodded, smiling. "Yes. I'm looking forward to seeing Papa and my aunt Gloria."

"Do you miss Cuba, M.J.?" Belinda asked the young woman.

There was a moment of silence. M.J. nodded again. "Yes, I do."

She wanted to tell Belinda that she was homesick, that there were nights when Samuel was in Costa Rica that she'd cried herself to sleep, and the days when Bessie did not come to clean the house she only got out of bed when nature forced her. In a moment of weakness she'd regretted marrying Samuel Cole and leaving her home, believing it would've been better to marry one of the men her father had selected for her if only to offset the isolation and loneliness.

Samuel wound an arm around M.J.'s waist, pulling her to his side. "After I open the office and get everything running smoothly M.J. and I will take frequent trips to Cuba."

Surprise siphoned the blood from M.J.'s face. *Office.* Samuel hadn't mentioned that he was going to open an office. She thought he was more than content conducting business out of their home. Resentment swelled in her until she felt light-headed.

She'd married a man who continued to confound her. He wouldn't discuss business at their table, and didn't discuss his business with her away from the table. Did he believe she was so unintelligent or disinterested in what he did that he felt it necessary to keep secrets from her?

She remembered what her father had told her: *Your novio is young and very ambitious. Which means you must be patient and support him in all his endeavors.*

She did support her husband and she was patient—very, very patient. But she was almost out of patience. Some of the stiffness left her; she had

enough patience to wait until they were on their way to Cuba. That way
her husband wouldn't be able to evade her questions.

M.J. stood next to Samuel in the parlor, smiling when she was introduced to her brothers-in-law and their wives. Her smile faltered slightly
when she saw Thomas's wife's rounded belly, wishing it were she carrying
Samuel's child.

Annie-Mae, Mark's wife, leaned forward and kissed M.J.'s cheek. "You
have no idea how shocked we were when Samuel told us he was getting
married."

M.J. liked Annie-Mae. "I was just as shocked when Samuel proposed."

Thomas Cole rubbed Eugenia's belly, his hazel gaze roving over M.J.
as if she were a delectable sweet. If nothing, his youngest brother had
chosen well. Not only was Marguerite-Josefina beautiful, but there was no
doubt she'd come from a good family. He knew men who'd married foreign women to rescue them from a life of poverty or servitude.

"How long did you know my brother before he asked you to—"
Thomas's query stopped abruptly when Eugenia elbowed him in the
ribs.

Samuel and M.J. shared a smile. "Not long," they chorused.

Eugenia placed a hand over Thomas's as the child in her womb moved
vigorously. "Why did you marry so quickly? You don't look as if you're
with child."

An attractive blush covered M.J.'s face. "I only wish I were. I married
Samuel because I fell in love with him the first time I saw him."

"That's really romantic," Annie-Mae crooned.

Eugenia sighed. "I agree." She had been prepared not to like Samuel's
wife because she'd sung his praises to her best friend, but could find no
fault in the woman who'd become her sister-in-law. M.J., as she'd asked to
be called, was pretty, articulate, although she spoke English with a hint of
an accent, and fashionably dressed. And seeing her and Samuel together
was evidence enough that he was in love with her.

Belinda entered the parlor, drying her hands on a towel. She touched
Mark's arm. "Why are you here so early?"

He kissed his mother's forehead. "Thomas suggested we leave church
early. We thought something had happened to you when you didn't show
up." Belinda Cole never missed Sunday morning services—rain or shine,
hot or cold, well or unwell.

Belinda looped her arm through Mark's. "Thanks for worrying about
your mama. M.J. asked me to teach her cook some down-home dishes, so
I guess I lost track of time."

"What did you cook, M.J.?" Annie-Mae asked.

"I learned how to make grits and biscuits. I also found out that Sammy loves grits with chicken liver for breakfast." Everyone exchanged knowing glances when she referred to Samuel as Sammy.

"Speaking of food, I'm ready to eat," Eugenia said loudly.

Thomas massaged her belly over a pale blue linen tunic. "When aren't you hungry, Genie?" he teased.

She rolled her eyes at him. "Keep running off at the mouth, Thomas Isaac Cole, and you'll find yourself sleeping at Miss Sally's Boardinghouse."

"Damn," Samuel whispered under his breath, "I know you're not going to let your woman put you out of your own home."

"Samuel," Belinda admonished, glaring at her youngest, "you know I don't abide swearing on the Sabbath."

"Sorry, Mama," he mumbled as he averted his head so she wouldn't see his smile.

"You're forgiven," she said softly. "Annie-Mae, you and Genie can help me and M.J. put the finishing touches on dinner."

Eugenia and Annie-Mae exchanged puzzling glances, then followed Belinda and M.J. into the kitchen.

Waiting until the women left the parlor, Samuel went over to a side table and selected two cigars from a wooden box, clipped the ends, and handed them to his brothers. "I want you to try these and tell me what you think."

Mark put the cigar to his nose, inhaling deeply. His teeth shone whitely under his mustache. "Damn, Sam. It's sweet," he said, low enough not to be overheard by the women in the kitchen. "Where did you get this?"

"From Jose Luis Diaz."

"Who the hell is that?" Thomas asked.

"My wife's father," Samuel said proudly.

Mark's eyes widened. "Her father is a tobacco farmer?"

Samuel nodded. "He also has a cigar factory."

"Shit," Thomas drawled, drawing out the expletive into four syllables. "It looks as if you hit the mother lode, little brother. I can see why you married your little senorita."

Suddenly Samuel's expression went grim. "Her father's money has nothing to do with why I married her."

Thomas's handsome face twisted into a scowl. "Do I look that stupid to you, Samuel? Now I know why you wanted out of our business, because you had your own little enterprises going on behind our backs."

Samuel's temper flared. "I wanted out because of your bullshit! I got tired of arguing with you. What I should've done was leave you picking cotton for the rest of your life. You call yourself a businessman when you're still nothing more than a cotton-shopping sharecropper wearing a fancy suit."

Thomas swung at Samuel, but he wasn't quick enough when he found his throat caught in a savage grip. "This is the last time you'll raise your hand to me, brother," Samuel snarled close to his face. "If Genie wasn't carrying my niece or nephew I'd kill you where you stand. So, think twice about coming at me again, or I'll forget and make your wife a widow." Shaking him as if he were an annoying puppy, he released Thomas's throat.

Mark stared at Samuel as if he were a stranger. There was something in his brother's eyes that frightened him. And at that moment he believed Samuel could kill Thomas with his bare hands.

Dropping an arm over Samuel's shoulders, he pulled him close. "Let's go for a walk. I need to sample my cigar."

Samuel glared at Thomas rubbing his throat, then turned and picked up his cigar and followed Mark to the door. Once outside he closed his eyes, aware of how close he had come to murdering his brother.

And he hadn't lied about why he'd severed his business relationship with his brothers. Thomas's vacillating moods kept him off balance, and there were times if he had been carrying a gun he would've shot him. Thomas was too much like Charles in appearance and in temperament.

At first Samuel felt guilty about abandoning Mark, but knew his personality was better suited to dealing with Thomas than his. It wasn't until he lit the cigar and drew in a mouthful of flavorful tobacco that some of the rage left him.

He'd given Mark and Thomas the cigars because he'd contemplated making them partners in the United Fruit-Diaz cigar proposal; however, that all changed with Thomas's outburst.

Ten percent of the profits would go to Everett Kirkland, and the remaining 90 percent would be targeted for future investments.

15

Marriage is primarily an economic arrangement, an insurance pact.

—Emma Goldman

M.J. closed her eyes, shutting out the flickering candles throwing long and short shadows on the cabin walls and ceiling. A violent thunderstorm had swept over the Gulf, downing wires carrying electricity into Panama City and as far north as Tallahassee. The sound of the rain beating against the porthole, and the motion of the ship, made her sleepy. The warm body in the bed beside her moved closer.

"Did you enjoy visiting with my family, baby?"

She shifted on her side and pressed a kiss to Samuel's bare shoulder. "*Sí, mi amor.*"

She'd been truthful with him. Belinda had become the mother she'd lost, and Eugenia and Annie-Mae the sisters she never had. She'd spent the two weeks cooking with her mother-in-law and shopping with her sisters-in-law.

Samuel pulled her closer and eased her leg over his. "My mother is very fond of you."

"I feel the same about her," M.J. said, rubbing her nose against the crisp, curling hair on his chest. "Samuel?"

"Yes, baby?"

"Why didn't you tell me that you planned to open an office?"

There was a long pause before he said, "I didn't think you'd be interested."

Pulling out of his loose embrace, she sat up. "Interested? I'm your wife, Samuel. Everything you do, every decision you make is of interest to me. I would hope that you would confide in me."

"There's nothing to confide, darling. I decided it was best not to continue to work out of our home. If I have to hold meetings I don't want strangers knowing where I live. I want my private life kept separate from my business affairs." He tugged on the single braid resting between her breasts. "Does that answer your question?"

She smiled. "Yes, it does."

"What else do you want to know?"

"Do you still love me?"

His muscles tensed, then relaxed. "Why are you asking me that?"

"I just need to know, Sammy." She needed to know because during their stay in Tallahassee he hadn't touched her.

His fingers caressed a firm breast under her silk nightgown. "Yes, darling. I love you."

M.J.'s hand trailed down his chest to his groin. "Show me, then."

His penis hardened quickly as she lifted the hem of her nightgown and spread her legs. They sighed in unison as flesh met flesh; there was only the sound of their labored breathing joining the howl of the wind, the lashing rain, and the rush of water against the hull of the ship as it rode out the storm.

M.J. forgot her former annoyance with her husband for keeping secrets as she lost herself in the rising passion threatening to tear her asunder.

Samuel quickened his thrusts as he forgot the night in Puerto Limon wherein drunkenness had rendered him voluntarily insane. Without warning, pleasure, pure and explosive, hurtled him to a place that left him hot *and* cold as he surrendered to the exquisite ecstasy that bound him to the woman in whose scented embrace he wanted to lie until he breathed his last breath.

All of Havana's social elite turned out for the return of Jose Luis Diaz's daughter and her American husband to the country of her birth. Those who had known Carlotta Diaz remarked how much Marguerite-Josefina looked like her at the same age.

Samuel sat under the shade of an acacia tree, watching his wife greet friends and relatives who'd attended their wedding. Her dimpled smile, her tinkling laugh, and the way she seemingly floated about Gloria's garden were some things he hadn't seen since before they were married. She'd missed Cuba.

"She looks happy, Samuel."

Glancing around, he nodded to his father-in-law. "She *is* happy, Jose Luis."

The older man sat on a nearby chair, crossing one leg over the other. "And for that I must thank you, my son."

Samuel's gaze narrowed. "There is nothing I wouldn't do for her."

Jose Luis brought his hands together in a prayerful gesture. "You sound so serious."

"That is because I am when it comes to *my wife*."

He hadn't lied to Jose Luis. He did not realize how much he'd come to love M.J. until they were reunited after his last Costa Rican trip. He hadn't planned to take her with him to Tallahassee or stay the two weeks, but he was glad he did. She'd charmed his mother in a way Eugenia and Annie-Mae were unable to.

His lids lowered as he stared at her laughing at something Ivonne whispered close to her ear. Samuel smiled as if he, too, were privy to their conversation.

What was there about M.J. that made him want to risk all he had to keep her? And it wasn't the first time the question had nagged at him, and the answer was always the same: *everything*.

"Are you not feeling well, Samuel?"

Jose Luis's query broke into his thoughts. "I'm quite well, thank you. Why do you ask?"

"You haven't eaten anything."

Samuel smiled. "I'll eat something later."

"You said you wanted to talk to me about a business arrangement."

"I do."

"Talk, Samuel."

He raised a questioning eyebrow. "Here?" Samuel expected his father-in-law to conduct business indoors, not in a garden.

Jose Luis waved a hand. "Why not? There is no one close enough to overhear us."

Leaning over the small table separating them, Samuel told him about his trip to Costa Rica and his meeting with the representatives of the United Fruit Company. Jose Luis's eyes widened when he told of their interest in his cigars.

"What is it you want, Samuel?"

"I want to purchase cigars from you and export them under a company I intend to set up as ColeDiz International, Limited."

Jose Luis ran a hand over his mane of white hair. "I am committed to selling all of my cigars to one company."

"Is it possible to hold out a small amount for your daughter's husband?" Samuel asked in a quiet tone. "These can be sold under another brand name. I'll leave it up to you to come up with a name that exemplifies its reputation as the finest quality Cuban tobacco leaf."

A knowing smile parted Jose Luis's lips as he shook his head. "You have really thought this out, have you not?"

Samuel nodded. "I think better on an empty stomach. Let me know if we have an agreement before I faint from hunger." The expectation of starting up another enterprise had him feeling so anxious that his stomach roiled whenever he attempted to put something into his mouth.

Jose Luis angled his head, seemingly deep in thought. "I could harvest some under the name of *Presidente.* Those who smoke the cigars will have to wonder which Cuban president I'm referring to." He glared at Samuel under lowered eyebrows. "I'll be ruined if anyone finds out that the cigars come from the same harvest as El Supremo."

"Is there someone you can trust with this information?"

"My factory foreman."

"Double his pay to keep his mouth shut."

Eyes wide, Jose Luis shook his head. "I cannot afford to do that. The workers are constantly demanding higher salaries even though my profits are lower."

"I'll do it," Samuel said softly.

"You will pay him?"

Samuel nodded. "I've learned that everyone has a price. I'll pay your foreman, buy your Presidente cigars, and in turn sell them to certain individuals in Costa Rica. There's a lot of money to be made in things that make people believe they're happier if they have them. Bootleg alcohol, cigars, cigarettes, automobiles, moving pictures, and sporting events. They're the extra little things we tell ourselves we need whereas in reality if they vanished like a puff of smoke we as human beings would continue to exist.

"We only need food, clothes, and shelter, Jose Luis," Samuel continued softly. "So there is going to come a time when all of the so-called items of happiness will mean naught. And just like the price of sugar in 1920 that fell from twenty-two dollars and fifty-one cents a pound in May to five dollars and fifty-one cents in December of the same year, your cigars, which are touted as the finest in all of Cuba, will suffer the same fate, as will those who profit from illegal alcohol sales when the U.S. government repeals the Volstead Act. We have to make our money now because things are changing all over the world as we speak."

Jose Luis's expression was grim. "You are right, Samuel. Unions have workers going out on strikes everywhere, the Communists are now in China, the Fascists and Socialists are fighting each other in Italy, there are trains that run under tunnels in big cities, and people now take airplanes to travel from one place to another. You turn a knob on a box called a radio and music comes out. The world is moving much too fast for me to keep up with the changes."

Closing his eyes, he affected a wistful smile. "I'm going and you are coming, Samuel. The way I used to do business is over." He opened his eyes, his penetrating gaze fusing with his son-in-law's. "I will sell you my cigars."

Samuel was hard-pressed not to jump up and hug his father-in-law. He inclined his head instead. "*Mil gracias,* Jose Luis."

A hint of a smile touched the corners of Jose Luis's mouth. "No, Samuel. It is you I must thank. I can now go to my grave knowing that my daughter will be happy and well provided for."

Samuel was still sitting under the tree long after Jose Luis left and M.J. came to take his place.

"Are you okay, Sammy?"

Reaching out, he ran the back of his hand over her cheek. "Yes, baby."

Her fingers circled his wrist. "You haven't eaten anything all day. Do you want me to bring you a plate?"

He stood up, pulling her up with him. Lowering his head, he cradled her face between his hands and brushed his mouth over hers. "No, baby. I don't want you to wait on me."

She moved closer to him. "But here in Cuba it is a wife's duty to wait on her husband."

His gaze lingered on her lush mouth before he smiled. "Okay. But only in Cuba."

Rising on tiptoes, M.J. kissed him. "Only in Cuba," she repeated breathlessly.

The protective cocoon of love and being loved lingered with M.J. long after she returned to West Palm Beach with her husband. Whereas she'd been overwhelmed with the ongoing activity of interacting with her Tallahassee relatives, it'd been the complete opposite in Cuba.

Aside from the soiree her aunt had hosted to welcome their return, she and Sammy slept late, took their meals in the garden of her family's estate, walked together once the intense tropical sun began its descent, and talked about what they wanted for their futures.

Samuel told her of his dream of building a family empire rivaling those of Rockefeller, Carnegie, and J.P. Morgan. This disclosure had rendered her mute, and it wasn't until two days later that she was able to broach the subject with him, quoting the Bible verse: what profit a man to gain the world only to lose his soul? Much to her surprise Samuel laughed and countered with: wealth you get by dishonesty will do you no good, but honesty can save your life. His pronouncement was enough to put her mind at ease as to whether he would seek his fortune through fraudulent dealings.

M.J. halted brushing her hair, meeting the gaze of Samuel in the dressing table mirror. As he leaned against the open door, arms crossed over his chest, a slight smile softened his firm mouth. He wore a suit, which meant he'd planned to go into the office he'd rented in a new two-story building in West Palm Beach's Colored business area.

She continued brushing the coal-black strands until they shimmered like satin. "Is there something you want?"

Samuel didn't move from his leaning position. "Yes, I do."

Shifting on the vanity stool, M.J. stared at him. "What is it, Samuel?"

"Have you made plans to do anything today?"

"Not really. Why?" She had planned to work in her garden and try a new recipe Bessie had given her.

His smile widened. "I'd like for you to come to the office with me."

With her eyes wide, her mouth formed a perfect O. "Why, Sammy?" she asked once she recovered her voice.

Pushing off the door, Samuel closed the distance between them. Cradling her elbow, he eased her to her feet. "Why? I need your help."

"You want me to work for you?"

Throwing back his head, he laughed loudly. "No, baby. I already have a secretary. What I need is your decorating talent."

He'd hired a middle-aged woman with exceptional business skills. She was not only articulate, but also proficient in dictation and typing. It had taken two months of interviewing more than twenty applicants until he and Everett agreed that Nora Harris would meet the administrative needs of Cole International, Ltd.

A slight frown creased her smooth forehead. "You want me to make your office pretty for you?"

It was Samuel's turn to frown. "Not pretty, M.J. I want it elegant and tasteful like our home, but with a businesslike ambiance."

"Ambiance?"

"Feeling, atmosphere—impression," he explained.

"Why couldn't you say that, Sammy?"

He forgot there were occasions when what he said couldn't be literally translated, and that frustrated his wife, who he knew still thought in her native language.

Combing his fingers through her hair, he cupped the back of her head and massaged her scalp. "I'm sorry, sweetheart. Do you want to come with me?"

Her smile was dazzling. "Of course." Easing out of his comforting grasp, she slipped off her dressing gown and walked over to the armoire filled with her clothes.

Samuel felt as if he'd been punched in the gut. He held his breath until he felt his lungs exploding before he was forced to exhale. He stared at his wife's naked body as she slipped into a pair of silk underpants. Her breasts were fuller, her normally pale nipples a darker rose pink.

Did she know and hadn't told him? Or was it possible that she didn't know? In another two weeks they would celebrate their six-month wedding anniversary and he suspected M.J. was pregnant.

She'd been going to bed early and rising later than usual. This past week he'd been the one to prepare breakfast while she lingered in bed.

"How are you feeling?" he asked as she pulled a slip over her underwear.

Tossing her hair back over her shoulders, M.J. smiled. "Good. Why?"

"When was the last time you had your period?"

The flush that began in her face spread to her chest. "Sammy!"

"Don't Sammy me, M.J. Just answer my question."

Biting down on her lower lip, M.J. narrowed her eyes as she tried recalling her last show of blood. She'd had one in Cuba, but that was in mid-March. It was now June . . .

"*Dios mio!*" she whispered softly. Her flush deepened. Her husband knew before she did. Her heart pounded a runaway rhythm and she couldn't stop her hands from shaking.

"Hurry and get dressed," Samuel ordered in a quiet voice. "I'm taking you to the doctor."

"I . . . I thought you wanted to go to your office."

"Damn it, Marguerite-Josefina! Get dressed!"

Before she could tell him not to swear at her or call her by the insufferable name, Samuel had walked out of the dressing room, leaving her staring at the space where he'd been.

What Samuel had suspected was verified three days later. His wife *was* pregnant, and he could look forward to becoming a father early the following year.

M.J. crawled onto his lap and hugged him. Her lips feathered over his jaw. "Why are you being so stubborn, Samuel?"

"I'm not being stubborn, baby. You know what the doctor said about taking it easy the first couple of months."

She tightened her hold around his neck. "You promised me I could decorate your office."

"That was before I discovered you were having *my* baby."

"What does my having *your* baby have to do with looking at furniture? Nothing," she said, answering her own question. "The doctor said I could do everything I still do, but in moderation." She buried her face against his neck. "Please, Sammy. If I'm not feeling well, then I promise to take to my bed."

Turning his head, he stared at her delicate features, wondering which of them their child would favor. There was no doubt he or she would be tall, and have dark eyes and hair.

He glared at her under lowered lids. "You promise you'll let me know if you're not feeling well."

She smothered a yawn behind her hand. "Yes, Sammy. I promise." Curving his arms under her knees, he lifted her effortlessly. "Where are you taking me?"

He carried her into their bedroom. "I'm putting you in bed for a nap." Parting the sheer fabric falling around the four-poster, he placed her on the mattress.

"I'm not sleepy," she mumbled around another yawn.

Smiling, Samuel bent down and brushed his mouth over hers. "Try to get some rest. I have to leave now because I have a meeting at the office. I'll try to get home early. Then we can celebrate in grand style."

M.J. closed her eyes. "Can we celebrate at home?"

"What do you have mind?"

She shrugged a shoulder. "I don't know. I'll think of something before you get back."

Samuel kissed her again, increasing the pressure on her mouth until her lips parted. "Thank you, my darling. Thank you for making me the happiest man in the whole damn state."

Her eyes opened. "Only Florida?"

"No, baby. The whole world."

M.J. smiled. "That sounds better." Sighing audibly, her chest rising and falling heavily, she closed her eyes again as a secret smile curved her mouth.

Her prayers had been answered with the life growing inside her.

She was going to have a baby—a son or daughter she would love with every fiber of her being, a baby that would make her perfect life complete.

16

Now I am alone—oh, how alone!

—Mary Shelley

Samuel parked his late-model Duesenberg in an unpaved lot behind the building housing his office, then took a back staircase to the second floor. He inserted a key into the lock of a door with PRIVATE painted on the glass in gold letters. He'd made it a practice never to use the front door or entrance.

Removing his hat and jacket, he hung them on a coatrack affixed to a wall. He opened the door separating his office from a spacious waiting area. Several feet beyond the alcove sat Nora Harris, guarding his privacy like a sentry with his general. Everett's office was fifty feet away, the windows facing the front of the building. At any time of day or night the accountant could be found there adding up columns of numbers on an adding machine as a continuous stream of paper floated to the floor like ribbon.

Samuel picked up the telephone messages Nora had left on his desk. One was from a man he was to have met to discuss his acquiring a one-hundred-acre lot on which he wanted to build a new home for himself.

He swore under his breath. Merrill Wright had canceled their meeting for the second time. Reaching over, Samuel pressed a button on the box next to his telephone. "Mrs. Harris, please call Mr. Wright and let him know I'm no longer interested in the property. And if he calls back, do not put him through."

"Okay, Mr. Cole."

He released the intercom. He had no intention of wasting any more time rescheduling meetings with the fickle real estate broker. Picking up the signed and executed contract outlining the terms between the United Fruit Company and ColeDiz International, Ltd., Samuel leaned back in his chair.

"I thought you had a meeting with Merrill."

Samuel's head came up. Everett stood in the doorway, cradling a folder under his arm. "We did, but he called to cancel again." He motioned to him. "Come in and close the door."

Everett walked in and sat down on the chair beside the large oak desk. The sunlight pouring into the room through the wooden Venetian blinds shimmered off his stark-white shirt. It had taken him less than six months to acquire the persona of a businessman.

He'd relocated to West Palm Beach, rented a small cottage on the property of a well-to-do funeral director, purchased a new wardrobe, and now drove a 1923 Stutz Bearcat.

Shaking his head, Everett placed a file folder on the edge of the desk. "He's playing with you, Samuel."

"No, he's not. I just told Mrs. Harris that I'm no longer accepting his telephone calls."

"Good." Everett stroked his neatly barbered mustache with a forefinger. "How's M.J.?" Samuel had informed him the night before that he had to take his wife to the doctor.

"Good. Real good." The warmth of his smile echoed in his voice. "She's pregnant."

Everett patted Samuel's shoulder. "Congratulations to you and M.J."

Samuel smiled. "Thank you."

"When is the big day?"

"Early next year." He laced his fingers together. "We're going to have to change our travel schedule."

Everett stared at his boss, complete surprise on his face. They'd spent weeks, sending a dozen telegrams to finalize a schedule wherein they would meet with the representatives of United Fruit. Now Samuel had suggested they change it—yet again.

Shaking his head, Everett ran a hand over his face, blowing out his breath. "What do you want?"

"It's not what I want as much as what I can't do."

Schooling his expression not to reveal his frustration, Everett said, "What?"

"I can't leave M.J."

"I thought you said she's okay."

"She is," Samuel confirmed.

"Then what's the problem, Samuel?"

"The problem is I don't want to leave M.J. for extended periods of time. I want you to see if we can't accelerate the meetings."

"Tell me what you want," Everett repeated. He was annoyed and didn't care if Samuel knew it.

"I want you to sit in for me."

"Nigel Cunningham will never agree to meet with me. And if you insist, then we'll be courting trouble." Everett was certain the man still harbored a grudge because two Negroes had bested him, one a former employee whom he'd fired. "I think you should reconsider your decision."

Samuel shook his head. "I can't."

"You don't have to leave M.J. You can take her with us."

"No, Everett. I will not expose her to the possibility that she could come down with a tropical disease for all of the money in the world."

Everett had worked with Samuel Cole long enough to know when to argue a point and when to retreat, and Marguerite-Josefina Cole was one subject that was never up for debate.

Turning on the leather chair, Samuel stared at the glass on the door bearing his name and title. "I'll do July and October. But I'm not going to commit to December."

"That's when all of the big shots from Boston go to Puerto Limon with their families to escape the cold weather," Everett argued in a quiet voice.

Samuel turned again to face Everett. "It's too close to the time when she's to have the baby."

Everett felt as if he'd won a partial victory. He'd gotten Samuel to agree to accompany him on two of the three trips to Costa Rica. He had plans for Cole International, Ltd., that would make it comparable in scope to Standard Oil and American Telephone and Telegraph.

He and Samuel spent one day each week poring over the business section of every major U.S. newspaper to keep up with acquisitions and mergers. He also perused the stock listings although he eschewed playing the market. Investors were hoping for a repeat of the November 1924 record-setting 2,226,220 shares in a total of 526 issues that topped five consecutive business days of bullish trading. The average price of fifty representative shares had topped the previous record set in 1919.

Crossing one leg over the opposite knee, he gave his boss a direct stare. "I've been giving your notion of opening a string of hotels some thought."

Samuel smiled at Everett. "Talk to me, Kirkland."

Everett ignored the quip. He'd also learned to gauge Samuel's mercurial moods, and today he was in a good one. "The word is that Flagler plans to rebuild the burned-out Breakers Hotel, this time with concrete instead of wood."

This news did not surprise Samuel. Henry Flagler, who in partnership with John D. Rockefeller when they formed Standard Oil, had erected hotels and built railways that turned Florida's swampland into a vacationer's paradise.

"It never should've been constructed of wood in the first place. But Flagler let his ego get in the way when it was touted as the world's largest wooden structure."

"You're right," Everett concurred. He opened the folder and removed a sheet of paper covered with penciled numbers. "I've come up with some construction costs if you decide to build in Cuba."

Samuel shook his head. "Not Cuba."

"Why not, Samuel? It would be perfect. You have a connection with the island because of M.J."

"I said not Cuba." His voice was soft and lethal. "Building in Cuba would be akin to a dog going back to wallow in its own vomit." Arturo Moreno's refusal to sell him his sugarcane fields still smarted.

Though puzzled by the cryptic statement, Everett decided it was better not to know why Samuel refused to invest in his wife's homeland. "Where do you want to build?"

"Costa Rica. Mexico or even Puerto Rico."

"What about the States?"

Samuel's eyes filled with contempt. "Never here. Not as long as we're viewed as second-class citizens. Not in a country that we built with the blood of our ancestors so that others who didn't have a boot to piss in or a window to throw it out of could come here and spit on us."

The gold-flecked eyes met a pair so dark and burning with resentment that it sent a shiver up his spine. He agreed with Samuel about racial prejudice in America, but didn't take the same view about his refusal to invest in the country of his birth.

Everett supported Marcus Garvey's and W.E.B. DuBois's belief that an aggressive strategy toward black integration into the political and economic systems was key to the Negro achieving equality in the United States.

He dropped his gaze, his mouth thinning in frustration. If he knew with a certainty that he could get another position earning close to what Samuel paid him he would've gotten up and walked out. However, he swallowed his resentment and forced a smile he didn't feel. He couldn't leave—not until he'd become a rich man.

"I'll work on the figures for the construction and labor costs in these countries." Not waiting for a reply from Samuel, Everett rose to his feet and walked out of the office, closing the door softly behind him.

Samuel stared at the door. He knew he'd angered the number man because of his reluctance to invest in a U.S.-based enterprise. He'd had Merrill Wright investigated, and knew the man was meeting with a group

of white businessmen who also wanted the property. They'd either offered him more than the land's actual worth, or intimidated him enough
to sell it to them rather than a Negro. The investigator's report indicated
that two of the six men in the group were Klansmen.

Shaking his head, Samuel grunted under his breath. It was a different
country, but the events were the same. A group of bigoted men had gotten to Merrill Wright as those had with Arturo Moreno.

He had refused to invest in Cuba, and now it was the United States.
And he had no intention of changing his mind until the social injustices
facing his people were eradicated.

He pressed a button on the intercom. "Mrs. Harris, please ring my
mother's exchange."

"Certainly, Mr. Cole," came the firm efficient voice.

He sat, waiting for his secretary to place the call, certain that Belinda
Cole would welcome the news that she was going to have another grandchild.

Three minutes later Nora's voice came through the intercom's speaker.
"I'm sorry, but there is no answer. Do you want me to try later?"

Samuel pressed the button again. "No, thank you. I'm going to be out
of the office for the rest of the afternoon. If you need me for anything,
then call me at home."

"Good afternoon, Mr. Cole."

"Good afternoon, Mrs. Harris."

He placed the contract in a folder where the secretary would file it
away, then stood up and retrieved his jacket and hat from the coatrack.

He left the office the way he'd come, taking the back staircase.

Twenty minutes later Samuel maneuvered into a parking space off
Worth Avenue to make a purchase for the woman who'd become his
whole world.

M.J. turned over and gasped. Her heart pounded painfully in her
chest. "What are you doing here?"

Samuel draped an arm over her waist, pulling her closer. "I live here."

Her lids fluttered wildly as she stared at her husband smiling at her. "I
know you live here, but—" Her words were stopped from the pressure of
his mouth capturing her breath.

He sat up, bracing his back against a mound of pillows, and shifted her
to straddle his bare thighs. "I thought I'd surprise you and come home
early."

M.J. smiled, looping her arms around Samuel's neck. "I like the surprise."

"Do you really like it?" he whispered, nuzzling her neck.

Throwing back her head, she bared her throat. "Yes. Do you want me
to show you how much I like it?"

He kissed the column of her neck. "Yes."

Reaching down, M.J. caught the hem of her nightgown and pulled it over her head; the pale pink silk garment fell off the bed and pooled on the floor. A wave of heat washed over her as she caught her husband staring at her breasts. They were fuller, the nipples so sensitive that she couldn't bear to touch them. When he cupped them in his hands, she closed her eyes and gritted her teeth.

Samuel saw the slight flaring of her delicate nostrils as he gently squeezed the mounds of flesh filling his hands. "Do they hurt, baby?" She nodded. "A lot?"

M.J. pulled her lower lip between her teeth. "They are very sensitive."

"Where?"

She smiled. "The nipples."

The word was barely out of her mouth when Samuel's mouth replaced his hands. Throwing her arms around his head, M.J. held on to her husband as his tongue and teeth worshipped her breasts. The pain was followed by a pleasure so intense that it elicited a spontaneous throbbing between her thighs.

She forgot that it was the middle of the afternoon, that she sat on her husband's lap writhing against his hardness sliding in and out of her body, that it was the most exquisite passion she'd ever experienced, and that each breath she took she thought was going to be her last.

Samuel dug his fingers into the soft flesh covering M.J.'s buttocks, holding back the whimpers that had reduced him to a hapless mass wherein he had surrendered everything he was and hoped to be to the woman in his arms.

Burying his face in the fragrant hair flowing down her back, he let out a low growl of erotic pleasure, giving in to the ecstasy, leaving him with an amazing sense of completeness as M.J. breathed out the last of her passion against the side of his neck.

M.J. rested her head on his shoulder, savoring the intimacy of the act that made them one. A soft sigh escaped her parted lips as a deep feeling of peace entered her being. "I think I could get used to you surprising me in the middle of the day."

Samuel chuckled. "It doesn't take much to spoil you, does it?"

"No. All I need is love."

"That you have. And this." Reaching under his pillow, Samuel grasped a flat box and handed it to M.J.

Her fingers shook slightly as she raised the top. The sparkle of flawless diamonds and bright green emeralds winked at her. Testing the weight of the bracelet, she knew the stones were set in platinum.

"Why, Samuel?"

He took the bracelet, fastening it around her left wrist. "I don't ever want to forget the day I found out that I was going to be a father."

Looping her arms under his shoulders, M.J. rested her cheek on his chest and listened to the strong, steady beating of his heart. They sat silently, holding each other, offering love, and being loved.

M.J. alternated sitting on a hard wooden bench and pacing the concrete floor of the stiflingly hot structure. She'd lost count of the number of times she'd checked the watch pinned to her bodice. Her cousin's Miami–West Palm Beach bus connection was more than an hour late, and she loathed having to use the less than adequate bathroom facilities again in the depot's Colored waiting room.

Snapping open her fan, she wielded it savagely. She'd alternated pacing and sitting with fanning and dabbing her moist face with what once had been a crisp linen handkerchief; it was now wrinkled and damp.

Once her pregnancy was confirmed she'd called her father and aunt to give them the news, then written to Ivonne Ferrer to let her know she was to become a mother early the following year, and extended an invitation for her to come to West Palm Beach.

Her pacing and fanning came to an abrupt halt when the sounds of an approaching bus brought those in the waiting room to their feet. Opening a parasol, she headed outside into the suffocating heat and humidity.

Ivonne was the third passenger off the bus. Her dark blue eyes searched the crowd until she saw her cousin. Smiling, she grasped the handles of a large tapestry-covered bag and made her way toward her.

As she neared Marguerite-Josefina her smile widened. Her older cousin, who'd been a pretty girl, was now a beautiful, elegant woman. The fabric of a delicate oyster-white dress banded in satin matched the parasol she held over her head to shield herself from the blistering summer sun.

Dropping her bag, she gently hugged M.J., mindful of her condition. "You look wonderful, *mamacita*."

M.J. closed the parasol and kissed Ivonne's cheek. "Thank you, Ivonne. And thank you for coming."

Ivonne pulled back and stared up at her cousin; there were tears in M.J.'s eyes. Unconsciously, her brow furrowed. "What's the matter, *m'ija*?"

M.J. sniffled. "I'm hot and very tired. I just need to lie down." She was ten weeks into her confinement and had experienced a fatigue so intense that she spent most of her days in bed.

"Where's Samuel?"

"He's not here."

"What do you mean he's not here?"

"I will tell you in the car."

"You're driving now?" Ivonne asked as she bent down and picked up her luggage.

M.J. smiled. "Yes. When Samuel bought a new car I got his old one. How long can you stay?" she asked as they neared her car.

"As long as you want me to stay."

Slowing her pace, M.J. stared at Ivonne. "You are making a joke?"

The younger woman's dark blue eyes sparkled like sapphires. "No, *m'ija. No es la broma.*"

M.J. wagged a finger at her. "If you're going to stay with me, then you should practice speaking English."

"There's no need for me to learn English, because I don't plan to marry an American."

Reaching out, M.J. touched Ivonne's arm. "Do you think I did wrong marrying an American?"

"No, *m'ija.* You married a man you love who just happens to be an American."

The two women were silent as they climbed into the car. M.J. had parked under the sweeping fronds of a palm tree. The tree, abundant all over Cuba, was being planted throughout Florida in record numbers. She started up the car, shifted into gear, and drove away from the depot.

"He's made you very happy."

M.J. took her gaze off the road for several seconds. "Why would you say that?"

"It shows."

Concentrating on her driving as she shifted gears, M.J. nodded. Samuel Cole had made her very, very happy, but the happiness was marred with his frequent absences.

"You're right, *prima.* Samuel has made me happy, but . . ."

"But what?" Ivonne asked when she didn't finish her statement.

"I'm left alone so much that I've begun talking to myself just to hear another voice."

Ivonne touched M.J.'s shoulder. "What do you mean he leaves you alone?"

"I suppose some of it is my fault."

"Has he taken a mistress?"

M.J. shook her head. "Samuel would never take a mistress. And it should be that simple. We share a house and a bed, but we hardly see each other. When Samuel comes home I'm asleep, and when I wake up he's gone. The last time we spent more than two hours together was when we picked out furniture for his office.

"It's his business, Ivonne. It's like he's obsessed with making money. When I spoke to him about it he said he has to make it now because the economy is going to change. I told him that economies have gone up and down since the beginning of time."

A swollen silence filled the vehicle. "What did he say to that?" Ivonne asked.

"He said as his wife I should not concern myself with things I'm not involved in."

There was another moment of silence before Ivonne spoke again. "He's right, M.J. If you'd married a *Cubano* he would've said the same thing."

An angry flush darkened M.J.'s face. "He's not Cuban, and this is not Cuba."

"Did you think because you married a *norteamericano* and moved here that things would be different for you? No, *m'ija,*" she said, answering her own question. "Men are the same all over."

"What do you know about men, Ivonne?"

"Enough to know they live their lives by their leave and then tell us how we should live ours."

"Samuel doesn't tell me what to do!"

Ignoring her sharp tone, Ivonne said, "He doesn't have to, *m'ija.* When he told you not to concern yourself with his business he meant that your responsibility is to take care of his home and his children. It is that way with my mother, it was that way with your mother, and will be the same with you. If you'd wanted to be like *Titi* Gloria, then you never should've taken a husband."

"But I want children."

"Then you should be content with your life. You've married a man you love, and you're going to have his child."

You should be content with your life. Ivonne's words stayed with her until she maneuvered into the driveway leading to her home. They came back later that night when she lay in bed—alone, crying herself to sleep.

17

Why is it married folks always become so serious?

—Mary Todd Lincoln

Samuel lay in bed, resting his head on folded arms, and stared up at the slow-moving blades of the ceiling fan working futilely to dispel the buildup of heat. He and Everett had spent ten days in Limon, yet had not met with Nigel Cunningham or Trevor Richards.

Both men were sequestered with other *Mama Yunay* officials. United Fruit Company, referred to as "Mommy United" by the locals because of their monopolistic grip on the export of tropical fruits and their covert involvement in Central American politics, had been hit with a general strike in Panama.

He'd thought about returning to the States until the labor unrest was resolved but changed his mind, because he'd committed to leaving M.J. one more time before she delivered her baby. A light tapping on the door caught his attention. Swinging his legs over the side of the bed, he went to answer the knock.

"Yes?"

"Kirkland."

Samuel opened the door and made his way back to the bed as Everett walked in, flopped down on a cushioned rattan chair, stretching long legs in front of him. A pair of walking shorts, sandals, and a *guayabera* had become his daily attire.

"How are you holding up?" he asked Samuel.

Shaking his head, Samuel blew out his breath. "Not good. I feel as if I'm losing my mind." The inactivity played havoc with his concentration, and he alternated sleeping with pacing the floor of his hotel room like a caged cat.

"I've already lost mine," Everett admitted. "And I've never known it to be this hot."

Midafternoon temperatures topped out at the one-hundred-degree mark. The intense heat only abated with the unexpected thunderstorms, and returned when the rains stopped. Steam rose above the trees from the nearby rain forest teeming with exotic plants, flowers, and jungle wildlife.

Shifting his position on the bed, Samuel smiled at Everett. "I thought you were passing the time with Paullina."

"I told her that I'll see her later at her brother's place for a friend's birthday celebration. Unless you have something more exciting than hanging out here, I suggest you come with me. Daisy will be there."

Samuel closed his eyes, recalling the woman with the talented mouth. He'd tried not thinking about her, but failed miserably. The moment he'd set foot on Costa Rican soil, memories of their time together came rushing back.

He and M.J. hadn't made love since the day her pregnancy was confirmed. Her passion wilted as her body bloomed with the life growing inside her. It'd become torture for him to see her fuller breasts and hips and not feast or gorge on them. She retired to bed before he arrived home, and did not wake up until after he left to go into the office.

The doctor had explained what M.J. could possibly encounter during her confinement: fatigue, nausea, an increase in weight and appetite were the most obvious changes, and occasionally some women experienced a decrease in sexual desire. His wife experienced all with the exception of nausea.

"Sure. I'll go with you."

Everett pushed off the chair. "I'll meet you downstairs at ten." He walked to the door, then stopped and peered over his shoulder. "I don't know how true it is, but there are rumors that Nicaraguan rebels out to topple Diaz's regime have attacked several U.S. missions."

Samuel shook his head. There was no doubt President Coolidge would send U.S. troops to the region to protect American lives and property. It'd happened in Panama, Cuba, and now Nicaragua. A cynical smile twisted his mouth. Which Latin American country would be next?

Samuel held two glasses above his head as he wound his way through the throng in Stephen Michael's small house. The odors were distinct, the closely packed bodies, the flowery fragrances, and the mouthwatering smells of oxtail stew, curried goat, codfish, *ceviche, patti*, a spicy meat patty, and callaloo.

The sounds of drums, guitars, and steel pans playing a rhythmic Caribbean beat had most moving their feet while they stood around eating or talking to one another in small groups.

He handed Daisy one of the glasses. "Rum for the very pretty lady."

She touched her glass to his. "What are you drinking, Samuel?"

"Rum." It *was* rum, but liberally diluted with water. He took a deep swallow, looking around for Everett. His accountant had braced a hand on a wall over Paullina's head. He leaned forward and said something close to her ear.

Daisy swayed back and forth in time with the music as she sipped her drink. She tugged on Samuel's free arm. "Are you ready to leave?"

He lifted an eyebrow. "Are you?"

Her dark eyes in an equally dark face crinkled in a smile. "I am always ready for you."

Samuel caught her double meaning immediately. He placed his glass on a table and followed Daisy. Hand in hand they walked in silence along the stretch of beach before climbing a slight rise that led to the house she now shared with Paullina.

Letting go of Samuel's hand, Daisy unlocked the door. He stood motionlessly as she moved around in the darkened space. A bright glow followed the scrape of a match. Within seconds a flickering flame from a kerosene lantern provided enough illumination for them to make their way into one of the two bedrooms. She struck another match, lighting a short, fat candle.

Daisy turned, walked over to Samuel, and pressed her breasts to his chest. "Do you like me?"

Samuel tried making out her expression in the flickering light. "Yes, Daisy, I like you." He liked her pretty face, compact body, and lilting Caribbean accent.

She rose on tiptoe, her mouth mere inches from his. "If you like me, then why do you not want me to make love to you?"

He held her shoulders, stopping her from kissing him. "You do make love to me, Daisy."

"Not the real way."

His fingers tightened on her soft flesh under a sheer blouse. "Because that was the way I wanted it."

"It is because you are married?" The gold band on his left hand was a constant reminder that he belonged to another woman.

"No. It's not because I'm married." The first time he slept with any woman he always had her perform fellatio.

She smiled, flashing small, straight, white teeth. "Come to the bed. I remembered and changed the sheets just for you."

He had refused to get into the bed the first time he came to her house because she hadn't had any clean sheets. He'd sat on a chair, lowered his trousers while she knelt and suckled him until he released his passion in a tremendous shudder that left him gasping.

Samuel dropped his hands, smiling as Daisy unbuttoned his shirt. Within minutes she'd undressed him, then herself. Like someone in a trance, he permitted her to lead him to the bed. There wasn't enough rum in his body to render him voluntarily insane; he knew where he was, who he was with, and what he wanted to do. He paused to slip on the condom, then lay on his back, extended his arms, and welcomed Daisy into his embrace as he reversed their positions and entered her body.

Everything about the woman writhing under him was different: her smell, the feel of her skin, the Jamaican pidgin she whispered as she urged him do it harder, faster; he overlooked the differences between her and his wife as he surrendered yet again to one of the deadly sins: lust.

Putting aside the tiny white linen dress tatted with lace around the collar and sleeves she'd made for Mark and Eugenia's infant daughter, M.J. stared at Ivonne as she read the letter that had been delivered moments before.

"What's the matter, Ivonne?"

Ivonne folded her mother's letter and returned it to the envelope. She combed her fingers through her hair, pushing the unruly red curls off her forehead. "Mama wants me to come home."

M.J. felt her pulse quicken, and she placed her hand over her belly in a protective gesture. "Why?"

Ivonne saw fear in M.J.'s large dark eyes. "Everyone's okay."

"Then why does she want you to go back to Cuba?"

An attractive blush washed over the redhead's freckled face. "She says Alfonso Rivera has asked permission to call on me."

M.J. leaned closer, smiling. "Tell me about him."

"He's a lawyer. He works with his father and uncle."

"How old is he?"

"Twenty-six or seven."

"Handsome?"

Ivonne affected a mysterious smile. "*Muy guapo.*"

M.J. clapped her hands. "I'm so happy for you. So, when are you going back?"

Her cousin had been in the United States for two weeks, and she'd become the perfect companion during Samuel's absence. They cooked to-

gether, went shopping, and spent hours talking and laughing about any-
and everything.

The younger woman's smile faded. "I don't know."

"What is there not to know?"

"I don't know if I like him."

"You will never know if you don't permit him to call on you."

Ivonne waved a hand. "I'm not ready to—"

"Miz Cole, you have a telegram." Bessie's appearance stopped Ivonne's
words. "The messenger said he was to wait for your reply." She handed
M.J. an envelope.

M.J. opened it, unaware that her hands were shaking; she expelled a
sigh of relief once she saw who'd sent her the cable. She thought it had
come from Cuba. Since leaving the island she'd begun the practice of
writing to her father and aunt every week.

TO: MARGUERITE-JOSEFINA COLE
FROM: SAMUEL COLE
DELAYED IN LIMON BECAUSE OF LABOR UNREST. WOULD LIKE
TO STAY. DO YOU NEED ME?

She nodded to Ivonne. "I'll be right back."

M.J. left the patio and walked into the house to the study. Sitting at the
desk, she reached for a pen and blank sheet of paper. The point of the
pen was poised over the engraved stationery before she wrote:

TO: SAMUEL COLE
FROM: MARGUERITE-JOSEFINA COLE
STAY AND FINISH YOUR BUSINESS. I DO NOT NEED YOU NOW.

She reread what she'd written, then blotted the ink, folded the mis-
sive, and slipped it into an envelope. Rising from the chair, she gathered
several coins from a crystal dish. Samuel had a habit of emptying his
pockets of loose coins at the end of each day. Retracing her steps, she
handed the envelope and money to a young boy who sat waiting on a bi-
cycle outside the front door.

Samuel's extended stay in Costa Rica had solved M.J.'s dilemma of attending a social gathering unescorted. Edna Burgess's housekeeper had
delivered an invitation to the Coles requesting their presence for a celebration of their son's acceptance into the United States Military Academy
at West Point. George Burgess was one of two young men who would become the prestigious military college's only Colored cadets this upcoming school year.

She reentered the study and penned a declination to the Burgesses.

She and Samuel would not attend, but she planned to purchase something suitable for the young man to take with him before he left Florida for New York.

M.J. found Bessie in the dining room running a cloth over the top of the buffet server. "I'd like for you to take this over to Mrs. Burgess." She handed her the envelope.

Bessie took the envelope, put down the cloth, and stared at her employer's wife under lowered lids. "Do you want me to do it now, or can I take it when I'm done here?"

"Now, please."

Rolling her eyes and sucking her teeth, Bessie stomped out of the dining room as if her shoes were weighted with cement. M.J. had noticed a change in the housekeeper's attitude within days of Ivonne's arrival. It was apparent the two did not get along—Ivonne admitting she did not understand anything Bessie said, and vice versa. She'd begun the practice of speaking only English to her cousin, who in turn replied in Spanish. It was apparent Ivonne was hesitant to speak English.

M.J. felt as if her life were tilting precariously like a boat in a storm. Her husband was away and she didn't know when he would return, and her body was changing rapidly. She'd lost her waistline, her breasts were so tender she couldn't bear to touch them, and her cousin and employee were wary *and* resentful of each other.

It was apparent the bid whist ladies had forgiven her; otherwise she wouldn't have received an invitation from Edna. They'd extended the olive branch, unaware she'd sworn a vow never to step foot into any of their homes again.

A steady tapping against the windows caught her attention. It had begun raining. The rains came every day, seemingly at the same time, quenching the thirsty earth and allowing only a temporary respite from the heat. Once the rain stopped and the sun reappeared, so did the heat.

M.J. would wait for the rain to stop, and then she would take Ivonne with her into Palm Beach to select an appropriate gift for Army Cadet George Burgess Jr.

Samuel sat in the rear of a truck with Everett, watching the changing topography. They'd left the Caribbean side of the country for a region south of San Jose, the country's capital, and the intense jungle heat. It was early August and the rainy or "green" season.

Slouched in his seat, a straw hat covering his face, Everett moaned audibly each time the truck hit a rut in the unpaved road. "When are you going to tell me where we're going?" he asked under the hat.

Samuel smiled when he spied two large colorful parrots perched on the branch of a tree copulating. "When you stop pouting because I interrupted you and Paullina this morning."

"I'm not pouting," Everett retorted quickly, as he sat up and removed the hat.

Samuel lifted a questioning eyebrow. "Would sulking be a better word for your bad mood?"

Everett's gold eyes glittered dangerously. "You'd be in a bad mood if I pounded on your door while you were fucking Daisy."

"That's where you're wrong."

"And why not?"

"Because she is a whore, Everett."

"You say that because you're married."

"Even if I wasn't married, it still would not change the fact that she is a whore," Samuel said softly, with no expression on his face. "I pay her a lot more than she's worth to do whatever it is I want her to do, which means I can take her *and* I can leave her with no guilt."

He hadn't lied to Everett. After the second time he'd slept with Daisy he hadn't permitted himself to wallow in the guilt from their first encounter. She was someone to pass the time with, fill up the empty hours while he waited for a face-to-face meeting with the representatives of *Mama Yunay.*

As the head of Cole International and ColeDiz International, Ltd., he was at an impasse. He wanted to leave and return to Florida, but he also did not want to miss an opportunity to increase his cigar exports.

"Paullina is not a whore, Samuel."

"I didn't call her one."

"But you implied—"

"I implied nothing of the sort," Samuel said sharply, interrupting Everett. He leaned forward and stared intently at the accountant. "Don't ever tell me what I'm thinking or implying, or you'll find yourself looking for another job."

He hadn't raised his voice, but the effect was the same as Everett's eyes narrowed. The two men glared at each other for a full minute, hostility as thick as the haze that hung over the jungle after a thunderstorm.

The interchange signaled a change in Samuel and his association with Everett Kirkland. He'd broken the most important of Charles Cole's rules: never mix business with pleasure; in other words do not fraternize with an employee.

One harvest Samuel had befriended a young boy whose family brought him along to pick cotton, and Charles had punished him severely.

He'd socialized with Everett and slept with Daisy. He hadn't given it much thought as to why, because it still would not change the fact that he, as a married man, had shared a bed with a woman who was not his wife. There were the pat excuses for being an unfaithful husband—loneliness, frustration, or revenge. He'd experienced none, so his sins were his own to claim.

Everett was the first to look away. His boss's stare was chilling and intimidating. It was the first time he and Samuel had disagreed, and what bothered him was that it was because of a woman—a woman whose body and company he really enjoyed. Unlike Samuel, he did not have a wife to go home to each night—a wife he could discuss his day's events with, a wife whose body he could have whenever he wanted it, and a wife whom he did not have to pay for her sexual favors.

He'd defended Paullina, arguing that she wasn't a whore when she was. Although he shared her bed, so did many others. Paullina's rule of "first come, first served" had him waiting patiently for her summons. She had finally made time for him when Samuel pounded on his hotel room door ordering him to be ready within the hour because they were going south. Turning, he stared out the mud-spattered window. And if he argued with Samuel Cole again it would *not* be because of a woman.

The truck driver maneuvered down a rutted road to a valley where thousands of small plants dotted the lush hillside. Realization dawned as Everett sat up straighter and stared at the sight unfolding before his startled gaze.

"What do you think?" Samuel asked. His voice was as soft as sterile cotton.

Everett didn't trust himself to blink, because he thought what he'd seen would disappear. "Well, I'll be damned. Coffee."

Placing a hand on Everett's shoulder, Samuel nodded. "Yes. Coffee."

Smiling for the first time since their confrontation, Everett looked at Samuel, seeing an expression of supreme confidence radiating from his near-black eyes.

"Is it for sale?"

"We'll find out when we meet the owner," Samuel said cryptically. "When I went to send the telegram to M.J. I overheard two men talking about a coffee plantation near San Isidro. Judging from their accents they sounded German, and because folks haven't forgotten the war entirely, I thought while the Germans are arguing about whether they want to become coffee growers, we'd come down and a take a look."

"Coffee is different from soybeans, Samuel."

He nodded. "And soybeans are different from cotton."

Everett laughed softly. "Why is it I always forget that you're a farmer?"

"I don't know," Samuel countered, as the driver slowed the truck, stopping in front of a sprawling hacienda, "because I never forget that you're a number man."

Both men reached for the jackets folded across their laps, alighted from the truck, and walked toward the house where they were met by a tall, slender, blond man with piercing blue eyes. He shook Samuel's, then Everett's hand. The two men were complete opposites of the Germans who were interested in his coffee fields.

"Welcome. I'm Anthony Jones-Smythe." His accent was distinctly British.

Samuel inclined his head, taking the initiative. "I'm Samuel Cole, and this is Everett Kirkland, partner and accountant for ColeDiz International, Limited."

"Before I welcome you into my home, I need to know if you are serious about going into the coffee business."

Samuel gave Everett a sidelong glance. The accountant nodded. "More serious than two German gentlemen I happened to overhear talking about your property in a telegraph office."

The blue eyes hardened like chips of ice. "I wouldn't sell a lump of coal to those two Krauts if they were freezing to death. The bastards killed my brother during the war." His mood changed like quicksilver when he smiled and stepped aside. "Please come in, gentlemen."

He wanted to sell his coffee-growing enterprise and return to England with his family. Malaria, dengue fever, and a venomous snakebite had claimed the lives of three of his four children, and now that his wife was pregnant again he did not want to risk burying another loved one in the jungle.

It took less than four hours for Samuel Claridge Cole and Anthony Jones-Smythe to tour the plantation and agree on a selling price.

As Everett manipulated numbers, Samuel drafted the paperwork to transfer ownership of an eight-hundred-acre Costa Rican coffee plantation located in a fertile valley five thousand feet above sea level from an English farmer to an American farmer.

"I will retain your foreman," Samuel told Anthony. "He can move his family into the main house, and I'll use the guesthouse whenever I come for a visit."

Everett stopped making notations in a small notebook. "I'm going to need financial statements, payroll records, schedules of duties imposed by Costa Rica and foreign countries for the past three years."

Anthony nodded. "I will have my accountant and solicitor send you whatever you want."

A diminutive Indian woman walked into the room and nodded to Anthony. He removed a watch from his vest pocket. "The time seems to have gotten away from us. I'd be honored if you would spend the night.

My driver will take you back to Limon tomorrow." He stood up, and Everett and Samuel rose with him. "Whatever you'll need in grooming aids will be in the guesthouse. We have talked enough. Now it is time to eat."

Samuel and Everett shared a knowing glance. There was no need to wait out United Fruit Company's labor unrest. They could do that back in the States.

18

The chances of a strong-minded woman becoming a good wife to a man able and anxious to dominate her are few.

—Elsa Schiaparelli

Everett hesitated, his hand resting on the door handle, as he looked over his shoulder at Samuel. "I'll see you Monday."

Samuel nodded, his expression impassive. "Monday."

Pushing open the passenger-side door, Everett picked up the bag sitting between his feet and alighted from the car. Cradling his luggage in one hand and a Panama hat in the other, he walked to the small cottage that had become his home. He hadn't unlocked the door when he heard the sound of a car's fading engine.

Spending the past three days in close quarters hadn't eased the bad feelings toward each other. They'd argued about a woman, a woman he liked although she openly slept with other men, a woman Samuel labeled a whore.

But none of their hostility was apparent when they'd negotiated with Anthony Jones-Smythe to acquire his coffee plantation. It was as if they'd read each other's mind, knowing which questions to ask, what terms to demand that would result in greater profits for the company.

As businessmen they were incomparable. As social companions they were incompatible.

This trip would signal the last one wherein Everett would mix business and pleasure.

Samuel parked his car in front of the storefront with a red-and-white-striped pole and walked into Goode's Barbershop. He'd varied his routine. Usually he drove directly home after disembarking, but this time he wanted to stop for a haircut and professional shave before reuniting with his wife. He also wanted to take her out to eat to celebrate his impending coffee plantation acquisition.

Thinking of M.J. quickened his pulse. He missed her, couldn't wait to see the changes in her body. A smile parted his lips. A baby. His wife was going to have a baby—his baby. The prospect of becoming a father was exciting and frightening. And it wasn't for the first time that he wondered how much of Charles's personality he had inherited when it would come to raising his children. There was one thing he was certain of and that was he would not beat his children as Charles had done him and his brothers. Charles had taken "spare the rod and spoil the child" literally.

Samuel decided to allow M.J. to discipline their children; he would only become involved with her permission, or if the situation exceeded her control. A knowing smile softened the angles in his lean, bearded face. He doubted whether his stubborn, independent, willful wife would *not* be in control of any situation.

Tobias Goode nodded to Samuel as he walked in and sat down on a chair. Barely five-two, Tobias stood on a small stool as he wielded his scissors and clippers with an unusual skill that had most Negro men in Palm Beach County standing in line for him to cut their hair. There were arguments when he'd hired several assistants, so he let them go and continued to cut hair without help.

"Afternoon, Samuel. I'll be with you directly."

Samuel smiled at the elderly barber. "Good afternoon, Mr. Goode."

He was glad he wouldn't have to wait long. There was only the customer in Tobias's chair ahead of him. The first Saturday he'd come to Goode's Barbershop he'd waited almost two hours for a haircut. Not wishing a repeat of his introduction to having the skillful barber cut his hair, he now usually came in any day other than Saturday.

The bell over the door tinkled musically as it opened. Tobias Goode nodded to his latest customer. "Afternoon, George. I'll be with you directly."

Samuel smiled at George Burgess as he sat down beside him. He offered his hand. "How are you?"

George shook Samuel's hand, his gray-green eyes warm and friendly. "Well enough, Cole. I hope you and your wife are coming to my boy's farewell soiree tomorrow night."

Samuel's expression showed confusion. "What's happening?"

"Didn't your wife tell you?"

"Tell me what?"

"Edna sent your wife an invitation to come help us celebrate George Junior making it into West Point. She declined, saying you were away on business."

"I was."

"If she knew you were coming back, then why did she decline?"

A shiver of annoyance snaked its way up Samuel's back. "Are you questioning my wife's actions?"

The eyes that were warm and inviting became suddenly cold, the gray replacing the green until they appeared frosty. A rush of color had also darkened George's high-yellow face at the same time the nostrils of his thin nose flared.

"No, Samuel," the pharmacist said between clenched teeth. "It's just that my wife and the other women have tried to make your wife a part of their group, but she has declined all of their overtures. I've made it a practice of not getting in womenfolk business, but you need to know that they regard her as a snob."

Samuel flashed a feral smile. "I, too, try not to get involved with the goings-on of womenfolk, but I will make it my business to get involved if their menfolk are. First of all, M.J. didn't know when I'd be back in the country, and secondly, perhaps her being in the family way precludes her from socializing with the other women at this time."

The flush darkening George's face deepened even more. Samuel Cole had chastised him in a way a father would his son. Embarrassment replaced annoyance. He'd listened to Edna go on about Marguerite-Josefina Cole, unceremoniously dismissing her and the other women as if they were beggars looking for a handout. She'd also complained that Samuel Cole's wife refused every invitation they'd extended for their Wednesday bid whist luncheons.

"I'm sorry, Samuel. I didn't know she was breeding. "When's the big day?"

Samuel accepted the backhanded apology with a barely perceptible nod. "Early February."

George offered his right hand. "Congratulations."

It was several seconds, but Samuel shook the proffered hand. "Thank you. And congratulations to your son for getting into West Point."

"Thanks. It wouldn't have happened if it hadn't been for Congressman Phelps. He's my mother's first cousin on her white daddy's side of the family."

"I suppose you have to use any advantage that you can in order to get what you want," Samuel said sagely.

"You're right, Cole. My mother said it was the only time being a white man's bastard worked to her advantage."

All conversation ended when Tobias summoned Samuel to sit in his chair.

Samuel walked quietly into his home with a close-cropped haircut and a smooth jaw from a professional shave. He left his bag near the door in the entryway. Raising his head, he sniffed the air and smiled. Something smelled good. Whatever it was would have to be put aside for the next day. Tonight he and M.J. were dining out.

He made his way through the living room, past the dining room, and into the kitchen. M.J. stood at the sink, her back to him. A single braid hung down her back. His gaze lingered on a loose-fitting colorful peasant dress ending at her ankles. Her tiny feet were bare.

Moving closer, he looped an arm around her waist and swung her up in an embrace. She let out a shriek seconds before she looped her arms around his neck, her eyes widening in shock.

"Why didn't you tell me you were coming home?"

Samuel lifted his eyebrows. "Whatever happened to nice to see you? Or I'm glad you're home?"

Tightening her grip around his strong neck, M.J. touched her nose to his, then brushed a kiss over his firm mouth. "I should geld you for being away so long," she whispered softly.

He chuckled. "What, and make that baby in your belly an only child?"

She kissed him again. "Never."

M.J.'s gaze moved slowly over her husband's face. It was leaner; it was also darker than when they'd spent their honeymoon on Cayo Largo del Sur, and she noticed more flecks of gray in his close-cropped hair. A forefinger traced the length of his nose, the outline of his wide mouth, and the stubborn set of his strong chin.

"I love you, Samuel Claridge Cole."

Smiling down at M.J. from under lowered lids, Samuel said, "Not as much as I love you, Marguerite-Josefina Isabel Diaz Cole." He shifted her body. She'd put on weight. "Turn off the stove and put away whatever it is you're making. I'm taking you out to a restaurant for dinner."

M.J. pushed against his chest. "I can't"

Ignoring her request, he tightened his hold under her knees. "Why not?"

"We have a houseguest."

Samuel went completely still as he stared at M.J. as if she'd taken leave of her senses. "A houseguest?"

She nodded. "Yes. My cousin Ivonne is staying with us."

Struggling to contain his temper, Samuel drew in a deep breath. "For how long?"

M.J. lifted her shoulders. "For as long as she'd like to stay."

Samuel lowered her bare feet to the linoleum. "You invited her?"

"Yes."

"Without asking me?"

A spot of red appeared on M.J.'s fuller cheeks. "I didn't think I'd have to ask your permission to invite family to come and stay with us. You didn't ask my permission when you invited Everett Kirkland to come and stay with us."

"Everett was only here for a few days. How long has Ivonne been here?"

"She came two days after you left. And I told her she could stay as long as she wanted."

Samuel's temper exploded. "You wait for me to leave, and then you invite your family to come live with us."

"I didn't wait for you to leave, so don't make it sound as if I plotted behind your back. My cousin has been here when you weren't. Anything could've happened to me while you're out seeking your fortune."

"I sent you a cable asking if you needed me."

M.J. rose on tiptoe, thrusting her face close to his. "And if I did need you I would've been dead before you got back. I feel like a widow with a husband who's still alive. When you go away you have Everett Kirkland to keep you company. Who do I have, Samuel?"

Samuel held her shoulders, pulling her closer. "What about the women who live here? They've made overtures to befriend you, but you push them away with your snobbery and high-handedness."

Her eyes filling with tears, M.J. struggled to free herself from Samuel's loose grip. "How dare you come to me with something you know nothing about! Those so-called women whom you think so highly of are nothing but a pack of jackals. I invite them into my home and they repay me by insulting me to my face. They were rude, Samuel, and I don't want to have anything to do with them."

"Why didn't you tell me they insulted you?"

"Why!" she screamed at him. "What would you do, Samuel? Confront them directly? Tell their husbands?" She shook her head when he did not reply. "I thought not. They hate me, and I hate them. Ivonne will stay as long as she pleases. And if you send her back to Cuba, then I'm going with her. I'll stay there until my child is born. After that I'll decide whether I want to come back."

Samuel's hands curled into tight fists, his eyes narrowing to slits. "You will not leave me."

M.J. was too incensed to register the low, ominous quality in Samuel's threat. "You cannot make me stay. What are you going to do? Chain me to the bed like a slave? What's going to happen when you leave again on another one of your business trips? Will you pass the entire time wondering if I'll be here when you get back? Do not threaten me, Samuel Cole, because this is one deal you cannot win. And as surely I stand here and profess my love for you I will leave you."

"You will *not* leave me," he repeated so softly she had to strain her ears to hear. Turning on his heel, he stalked from the kitchen.

Covering her mouth with her hand, M.J. stumbled over to a chair and sat down heavily, willing the tears filling her eyes not to fall. Instead of welcoming her husband home with open arms and passionate kisses she had talked of leaving him.

He did not understand. While he went off seeking his fortune she was left at home to entertain herself. It was different whenever he went into his office, because she knew he'd come home at night. But his trips abroad were different. She didn't know whether he'd arrive safely unless he cabled her. And he was never certain how long he would be away. It could be a week or even a month, and when he returned he expected her to be the same as when he'd left her.

Sniffling, she shook her head. No! She wasn't the same woman who'd exchanged vows with Samuel Cole in Havana almost eight months before. She was not a puppet to be manipulated by a man who sought to bend her to his will. She was a soon-to-be mother and wife to a man she loved enough to defy her father to marry, and a man whom she loved enough to sacrifice her life to keep safe from all harm.

She sat until the smell of burning food propelled her to her feet. Snatching the pot off the stove, she threw it into the sink, chipping the porcelain.

She cried silently, her shoulders shaking. The words she'd thrown at Samuel came rushing back as she gripped the edge of the sink to keep her balance.

Turning on trembling knees, she saw Samuel standing under the entrance to the kitchen watching her. He'd showered and changed his clothes. She took a step and before she could take another one she found herself in his arms, his mouth covering hers and cutting off her breath.

"Where's Ivonne?" he asked softly.

"She's taking siesta."

He smiled down at her. "It's time you took siesta."

Burying her face against his warm throat, M.J. sank into the comforting strength that communicated she was safe and would always be protected by the man cradling her gently to his chest. He carried her out of the kitchen, and into their bedroom at the rear of the house. The door to the guest room was closed. Samuel placed her on the bed, then moved over her, M.J. watching his expression change from indifference to desire. She held her breath as his hands went to the many buttons on the front of her dress.

"What are you hiding from me under this?" he whispered, deftly undoing the buttons. The garment parted and he sat back on his heels marveling at the changes in the body. Everything about her was ripe with the life growing inside her.

He placed his palm over her rounded middle, then lowered his head, his mouth replacing his hand. Samuel trailed kisses over her belly, along the curve of her fuller breasts, mindful of their sensitivity. He undressed her before worshipping every inch of her body with his tongue, not stopping until M.J. breathed out the last of her passion into his mouth.

Pulling M.J. to his chest, Samuel held her until she fell asleep in his arms. He hadn't expected to return home to find M.J.'s cousin living with them. He wanted to enjoy his wife and the privacy of his home without having to censor himself. What he hadn't expected nor would he accept was M.J. threatening to leave him—leave him and take his unborn child with her.

Her leaving him was not an option, and if he had to make her his prisoner, he would. He had scheduled one more trip to Costa Rica before the end of the year. Ivonne could stay until his return, and then he wanted her gone.

19

A woman is born to bear children, and I went through hell to do it.

—Sophia Loren

Ivonne boarded a ship to return to Cuba two weeks before Thanksgiving Day, but only after her father issued a mandate that he was going to disown her if she did not come home.

Samuel slipped into bed next to M.J. and placed a hand over her distended belly. "I can't believe we have the house all to ourselves."

She returned his smile. "You're a selfish man, Samuel."

His eyebrows lifted. "Selfish? I can't walk around my own house assnaked, and I can't make love to my wife whenever and wherever I want. And you call me selfish?"

M.J. covered the hand on her stomach where her baby kicked vigorously. She was in her eighth month of confinement and each day she found it more difficult to do something as simple as bending down to tie up or buckle her shoes.

"You shouldn't want to make love to me."

"Why not?"

"Because I look hideous."

Samuel pressed his mouth to her ear. "You look beautiful, baby."

M.J. made a moue. "I'm fat, Samuel."

"You're pregnant, M.J."

I'm still fat, she mused. She'd gained twenty-two pounds, but it could've been twenty-two hundred. Her daily routine had changed when she went for early morning walks to relieve the cramps in her back and legs. At night she slept with her legs resting on a pile of pillows.

"I spoke to your mother this morning."

Samuel nuzzled her scented neck. "What did she say?"

"She wanted to know how I was feeling, and I told her that I was getting bigger, the baby moves a lot, and that I couldn't wait to become a mother. She wanted to know if we were coming to Tallahassee for Christmas."

Rising on an elbow, Samuel stared down at his wife staring back at him. "What did you tell her?"

"I told her I couldn't ride in the car that long."

"Would you like to see her?"

A hint of a smile softened her mouth. "Of course. I always enjoy spending time with your mother."

"What if we invite her to come here for Thanksgiving? We could also invite Mark and Thomas."

Pushing into a sitting position, M.J. ran her fingers through the hair on Samuel's chest. "Didn't you just say something about having your house to yourself?"

He nodded. "I did, but because we're not going to see them for Christmas, I think it would nice to have them here for Thanksgiving."

Looping her arms around her husband's neck, M.J. kissed him tenderly on the mouth. "That is very generous of you."

"I'm not really that generous."

"Yes, you are," she whispered softly.

The last time he'd come back from Costa Rica he'd brought a set of ivory pins and combs for her hair. Easing back, she searched his face, wondering what he was thinking at that moment. They were nearing their first wedding anniversary, and she still did not know any more about her husband than she had before they left Cuba.

During a rare moment when they lay in bed together he disclosed the extent of his business holdings in Central America. He'd purchased a coffee plantation, imported his brothers' soybean crop, a portion of her father's cigars, and in turn exported bananas to the West Coast region of the United States. He was forthcoming when she asked his net worth, the amount far exceeding her imagination.

"Where is Everett celebrating the holiday?"

"I don't know. Why?"

His gaze had lowered as did his voice. He and Everett had managed to maintain a strictly business association during their last trip to Limon. He didn't know whether the accountant saw Paullina, and did not care one way or the other if he did.

However, Daisy had come to his hotel room asking to see him, but he sent her away without opening the door. Sleeping with her and having her do things to him he wouldn't permit M.J. to do had lost its appeal.

"If he's not going anywhere, then I'd like you to invite him to share the holiday with us."

"Why don't you invite him? It would look better coming from you than me."

She broke into a wide, open smile. "I will write a formal invitation to-morrow." Her smile faded as quickly, lines of consternation wrinkling her brow. "Do you think he will decline?"

Samuel pressed the pad of his thumb over her lower lip, parting her lips. "Don't worry so much, darling." He kissed her softly before increasing the pressure. Her tongue darted out to meet his, igniting a passion only she could assuage.

He entered her slowly, carefully, always mindful of the baby, and made love to her that was so measured and unhurried that when he finally released the desire that had been building for what seemed like months he felt as if his heart and the top of his head had exploded.

Lying facedown on the bed, one arm thrown over M.J.'s thighs, Samuel waited for his respiration to return to a normal rate. He'd been a fool to sleep with Daisy. Nothing she could do to and with him would ever come close to what he felt for the woman who carried his name and his child.

Samuel closed his eyes when he heard the screams. M.J. had been in labor more than sixteen hours and each time she let out a bloodcurdling scream he weakened.

He was on his feet with the next scream, racing for the bedroom door only to find Everett blocking his way. "Get out of my way!"

Everett shook his head. The midwife had told him that under no circumstances was he to let Samuel enter the room. "I'm sorry, Samuel."

Samuel swung at him, but Everett was faster and sidestepped him, his hand crashing into the wall. "Shit!" Shaking out his hand, he glared at his accountant, unaware of the tears streaking his face or that he hadn't slept in hours. "I've got to go to her."

Curving an arm around his boss's neck, Everett led him back into the kitchen. "There's nothing you can do to help her. Women go through this every day."

Samuel's eyes glittered wildly. "This is my woman, Everett. Mine! Do you understand what I'm saying?"

Patting his back, Everett forced a smile. "I understand. Sit down and relax. It will be over soon."

Sitting down like an obedient child, Samuel covered his face in his hands, rocking back and forth as if in a stupor.

When Samuel hadn't called or come into the office, Everett had become concerned that something had happened to him. He'd called the Cole residence, and when he hadn't gotten an answer he decided to drive over.

He found Samuel sitting on the side of the bed holding M.J.'s hand. She was in the early stages of labor, and they had to wait until the pains were closer together before summoning the midwife. He called Mrs. Harris and instructed her to cancel everything on the day's calendar.

The night before, he'd completed the year-end balance sheet and profit and lost statements for Cole International, Ltd., and ColeDiz International, Ltd.; the bottom line figures were staggering. He would give Samuel the good news—after the birth of his son or daughter.

The rosary beads left deep impressions on M.J.'s palm. She gripped them tightly, unable to pray as the pains came so hard and fast that she felt as if someone had stabbed her.

Her eyelids fluttered wildly. "I need a priest." She didn't recognize her own voice. Her throat was raw, her voice hoarse.

The dark, smiling face of the midwife hovered over her. "Why would you want a priest?"

M.J. closed her eyes, her head rolling back and forth on the pillow. "I'm dying."

Willa Lee placed a hand over her swollen belly, timing the contractions. "You're just fine, honey. You're young and in good health, and you're going to give your husband a lot more babies."

"I don't want another baby!"

The midwife knew better. Once Samuel Cole's wife delivered her baby she would forget all she'd gone through to give birth to it. M.J. let out a scream that made Willa's hair stand up. Moving quickly to the foot of the bed, she smiled. Water washed over the rubber bedsheet. Minutes later she saw a head with lots of black hair. The baby was coming!

Looping leather straps around her patient's ankles, she secured them to the bedposts. "When you feel the next contraction I want you to push hard like you're going to the bathroom."

"I can't."

"Yes, you can. I see your baby's head. Now I'm going to need your help getting it out."

A contraction ripped through M.J. and she clenched her teeth and pushed and pushed. It seemed as if she was slipping away into darkness until she heard the faint cry. It was followed by two slaps, and then a full-throated cry filled the room.

"It's a boy!"

Those were the last words she remembered before succumbing to exhaustion.

* * *

Samuel and Everett stared at each other when they heard the baby's cry. They shared a smile similar to one they exchanged whenever successfully negotiating a new deal.

Everett reached over and patted Samuel's shoulder. "Congratulations."

Closing his eyes and whispering a silent prayer of gratitude, Samuel nodded. "Thank you."

Pushing back his chair, Everett stood up. "I have something hidden under the seat of my car that would do nicely right about now."

Samuel opened his eyes, grinning broadly. "Bring it in, Kirkland." He forced himself not to get up and go to the bedroom. He wanted to make certain his wife was okay, and he also wanted to meet his son or daughter for the first time.

Everett returned with a bottle of scotch smuggled in from Canada. Both men toasted each other with the illegal spirits, tossing it back in one swallow.

"Don't drink too much of that stuff, Mr. Cole. I can't have you dropping your son."

Samuel turned to find the midwife cradling a tiny infant in the crook of her arm. "My son," he said reverently. "Is he okay?"

Willa Lee handed him the baby. He stared at the tiny face, his heart softening and turning over when his son's mouth made sucking sounds, indicating he wanted to be fed.

"He's perfect, Mr. Cole. Mrs. Cole is a little tired, but she's going to be just fine in a couple of days."

Samuel peered closer at the red-face baby. "He looks like his mother."

Willa nodded. "He's her spitting image. I'm going to clean up your wife, and then you can see her." She held out her arms for the baby. "It's going to be a few days before all of her milk comes in, but she'll be able to give him enough to keep him from being too hungry."

Samuel relinquished his son to the midwife. Shaking his head, he fell back down to the chair he'd vacated. He extended his glass to Everett. "Give me one more."

"No, Samuel. You need to be sober when you see your wife."

Running a hand over his face, he nodded. "You're right."

"Have you and M.J. come up with a name for your son?"

"Martin Diaz Cole."

"Who selected the name?"

"M.J. She wanted him named for Martin de Porres, a sixteenth-century Peruvian priest who ministered to the sick and poor. She predicts the Church will canonize him as a saint one of these days."

Leaning back on his chair, Everett shook his head. "Wonders never cease. A southern Negro boy named for a Spanish priest."

"It's not a joke, Everett. When I married M.J. I had to agree to raise our children as Catholics."

"Do you have a problem with that?"

"Not at all. I would've agreed to anything to marry her. I love her just that much."

Everett straightened, staring at his boss as if he'd never seen him before. Suddenly it hit him. He'd found Samuel Cole's weakness, his Achilles' heel. It was his wife—Marguerite-Josefina Diaz Cole.

He hadn't known Eladia was his weakness until after she left him. Even after so many years he still missed her. He still loved her.

The two men sat silently, each lost in his private thoughts, until Willa Lee returned to the kitchen to let Samuel know that he could see his wife.

Samuel walked into the bedroom. The sight that greeted him would be imprinted on his brain forever.

M.J. sat up in bed, her hair flowing around her face and shoulders, cradling Martin to her bared breast. Dark smudges under her eyes did not detract from her overall beauty. She was the quintessential Madonna with child.

"How do you feel?" He didn't know what else to say.

"Tired, Sammy. Very, very tired." M. J. closed her eyes. "Thank you, *mi amor.*"

He moved closer to the bed, sat down, and combed his fingers through her mussed hair. "What for, darling?"

She opened her eyes, meeting his dark fathomless gaze. "For making me so very happy."

Samuel pressed a kiss to her forehead. "I live to make you happy."

"We're going to have to do this again."

His fingers stilled. "You want another baby after what you just went through?"

A mysterious smile curved her mouth. "Yes. We need a daughter. Who else am I going to give my jewelry to?"

Samuel laughed under his breath. "You can always give it to your daughter-in-law."

Shifting slightly, M.J. rested her head on her husband's shoulder. "That's true. But I don't want Martin to become an only child. Not like me."

"And he won't," Samuel promised. "We'll wait two years, then try again."

What he didn't tell M.J. was that he had put together a five-year plan. Within five years he hoped to build a house that would become a West Palm Beach showplace, and in less than five his income would give him millionaire status.

He lay beside M.J. watching her sleep while their son fed. After a while he, too, fell asleep. Reaching over, Samuel removed the sleeping infant from M.J.'s breast; he held him close to his chest, feeling his warmth, and inhaling the smell exclusive to babies.

He didn't want to put his son down, yet knew holding the baby would make life difficult for M.J. Walking to a corner of the bedroom, he placed Martin in a cradle. He stood, arms crossed over his chest, losing track of time, as he made plans for his firstborn.

Then he remembered he'd left Everett in the kitchen. Retracing his steps, he found the kitchen empty. His gaze lingered on a wall calendar. Someone had circled the date. It had to be Everett.

January 31—a day he would never forget, the day he'd become a father. Going to one knee, he rested his forehead on a chair and prayed. He said a prayer of thanksgiving, and he prayed for strength. He would need the strength to become a better husband *and* a good father.

PART 3

1929

Teresa Maldonado

Single women have a dreadful propensity for being poor, which is one very strong argument in favor of matrimony.

—Jane Austen

20

It is not by spectacular achievements that man can be transformed, but by will.

—Henrik Ibsen

Havana, Cuba—veintiuno de diciembre 1928

Marguerite-Josefina sat on a cushioned love seat next to Jose Luis, enjoying the smell of blooming flowers in the garden of the mansion in the Vedado neighborhood.

"Everything is so beautiful, so peaceful here."

Jose Luis heard the wistfulness in his daughter's voice. "Is it not beautiful and peaceful in Florida, *Chica?*"

She let out a soft sigh. "It is, Papa, but it is different."

A light breeze off the ocean stirred wisps of hair that had escaped the single braid. There were a few occasions when she talked about cutting her hair like millions of other women worldwide, but Samuel had pleaded with her not to. She'd acquiesced, because there weren't that many things he asked of or from her.

"Different how?" Jose Luis asked. "Did you not tell me that the house Samuel built for you is one of the finest houses in all of West Palm Beach?"

A knowing smile parted her lips. "It *is* the finest. When we return I plan to host the grandest gathering just to give those *putas* who hate me so much something to talk about."

"*Chica!*"

M.J. rolled her eyes while sucking her teeth, a habit she'd picked up from her housekeeper. "They are bitches, Papa. I threatened Samuel that I would divorce him if he told any of their husbands that we were building a house."

Jose Luis chuckled. "What did they say when you moved away?"

"There wasn't much they could say. While the house was under construction I ordered the furniture I wanted. The pieces were delivered one week, and we moved in the next week. One morning I put Martin and Nancy in the car and drove away. Samuel and Bessie stayed behind to monitor the movers when they loaded everything from our old house onto a truck. Our housekeeper has a cousin who works for one of these *vacas* and she said they were so upset that some of them took to their beds once they realized Samuel and I owned the property."

Jose Luis shook his head as he smothered a laugh. "Which one are they, *Chica*? Putas or cows?"

M.J.'s grin matched her father's. "Both." She sobered quickly. "When are you coming to visit with me and your grandchildren?"

She had written and called her father so often that she'd lost count, inviting him to come and spend time with her son and daughter in the U.S. Three months after Martin's birth, she and Samuel sailed to Cuba to introduce Jose Luis to his first grandchild. Thereafter she and Samuel visited Cuba every six months.

The exception had been the year Martin celebrated his second birthday when she found herself pregnant again. This pregnancy was different from her first because she'd been plagued with nausea. Her labor was long and difficult, but once she saw her daughter M.J. knew she would willingly do it again.

In less than a week she would celebrate her twenty-fourth birthday and fourth wedding anniversary. Her life had changed from the time she'd sat in the Moreno garden flirting with Samuel Cole. He'd changed her when he made her his wife and a mother. And it was being a mother that she revered most. She loved her husband, but her children more.

"I don't know," Jose Luis said after a pregnant pause.

M.J. peered closely at her father. He was thinner. "Are you okay, Papa?"

"*Sí*," he replied much too quickly.

Her forehead furrowed. "I don't believe you." Her tone was sharp, waspish.

"You forget yourself, daughter!" Jose Luis snapped angrily. "I am still your father."

She refused to back down. "And I am your daughter, and I have a right to know if you're not well."

Jose Luis was saved from responding to M.J.'s accusation when Samuel walked into the garden with his dark-haired, dark-eyed daughter sitting on his shoulders. Martin, who would turn three in a month, raced ahead of his father and sister.

"*Abuelo*," he shouted excitedly, "Titi gave me *papas fritas!*"

Luis reached out, picked up his grandson, and settled him on his lap. "You like fried potatoes?" he asked him in English. The child nodded and smiled. Matching dimples creased his cheeks like thumbprints.

"Please speak Spanish to him, Papa," M.J. chided in a quiet voice. She'd promised herself that her children would be raised as Catholics and would be equally comfortable speaking Spanish and English.

Jose Luis ruffled the boy's coal-black curly hair. "Don't worry so much, Marguerite-Josefina. The boy will learn Spanish."

"That's what I told her," Samuel said, swinging Nancy from his shoulders and putting her down. She opened her mouth and let out an ear-piercing shriek. "No, Dada. *Arriba!*"

"Don't, Samuel," M.J. ordered when Samuel reached out for Nancy, who'd pressed her tiny fists to her eyes and wailed loudly. "You've spoiled her so much that she's become impossible."

Samuel ignored his wife's grumbling. "Who's Daddy's big girl?"

Laughing hysterically, her open mouth displaying a dozen tiny teeth, Nancy clapped her hands over her head. "Nay-Nay."

"Yeah!" Samuel and Nancy crowed in unison.

M.J. leaned over and kissed her father and son. "Good night. I'm going inside." She stood up, glaring at Samuel. "You can put the children to bed."

Jose Luis watched his son-in-law as he stared at M.J. until she disappeared. "Are you still away from home a lot?"

Samuel froze. It was the first time Jose Luis had broached the subject with him, and it was apparent M.J. had complained to her father about his business trips.

"No," he answered honestly. "I only took two business trips this year, and so far I only have one scheduled for next year."

The nostrils of Jose Luis's aquiline nose flared. "I should not have to remind you that you are not only a husband, but also a father. Children need to see their father, especially sons, Samuel."

Swallowing a rush of rage, Samuel counted slowly to three. "Don't ever chastise me in front of my children again."

Jose Luis offered a hint of a smile. "Put them to bed. Then we will talk."

Samuel nodded. "Come, Martin."

Martin wound his arms around his grandfather's neck. "I want to stay with *Abuelo*."

Jose Luis shook his head. "You must obey your father. Now go with him. You and *Abuelo* will go for a walk along the Malecon tomorrow. We'll see if we can't outrun the waves coming over the seawall."

Martin's smile was as bright as the rising sun. "I'm not going to get wet, Grandpa," he said in English.

"That remains to be seen, *nieto*," Jose Luis teased. Hugging his grandson, he kissed him on both cheeks. "Good dreams."

Martin repeated the gesture, kissing his grandfather's cheeks. "Good dreams," he repeated in Spanish before scrambling off the elderly man's lap and running to catch up with his father and sister.

Samuel found Jose Luis sitting where he'd left him. The sky still bore streaks of red, orange, and blue as nightfall descended on Havana. He'd managed to cool his anger when he bathed Martin and Nancy, then dressed them for bed. As he passed the *sala* Gloria asked if he wanted to join her and M.J. for coffee, but he'd declined because he wanted to clear the air between himself and his father-in-law.

"Sit down, Samuel," Jose Luis ordered unceremoniously. "Do you have a mistress?"

Samuel froze as if he'd been shot or impaled with a sharp instrument. "What!"

"Answer me!"

"Hell—no! And why would you ask me that?"

Jose Luis's left hand shook slightly, and he gripped his knee to conceal the tremor. "Because that is the only reason I could come up with why you leave my daughter alone so often."

"That was before . . ." His words trailed off.

The older man's impassive expression did not change. "Before what, Samuel?"

"When I was setting up my businesses."

"Are you saying it's different now?"

Crossing his arms over his chest, Samuel focused on a profusion of frangipani. He nodded. "Very different. I have coffee holdings in Costa Rica, Mexico, and Jamaica, and I'm currently in negotiations to acquire a failing banana plantation in Puerto Limon."

He hadn't lied to his father-in-law about other women. He hadn't been unfaithful to M.J. since becoming a father. And his love for her deepened each time he returned to find her and their children waiting to welcome him home.

"What about your United Fruit-Cole Brothers soybean contract?"

"It expires the end of March."

It was due to expire and he and Everett had agreed not to renew it. Mark and Thomas had received offers from several European food-processing companies who'd expressed an interest in their soybean crop. He'd suggested they consider a more global market, but Thomas was apprehensive about expanding beyond the Northern Hemisphere. The meeting ended with Mark's and Thomas's deciding to renegotiate with their former Mexican food processor.

"Has it been five years already?" Jose Luis asked.

Samuel lifted his eyebrows, nodding. The years had passed so quickly that whenever he returned from a business trip he found his children changed. It was the reason he'd curtailed his traveling.

"Are you a millionaire?"

Attractive lines fanned out around Samuel's eyes. His aim had been to become a millionaire by age thirty, but he had exceeded his own goal by a year. Everett had worked well into the night, completing the profit and loss, balance sheet, and the upcoming year's quarterly projections for Mrs. Harris to type when she came in the next day.

Samuel knew something was afoot when Everett presented him with the financial statements, instead of his secretary. There was only the sound of their breathing when he read and reread the figures. It had taken only three years for his newly renamed ColeDiz International, Ltd. Inc. to net more than a million.

"I was before I built and furnished the new house," he admitted.

Jose Luis released his knee and ran his hand over his hair. "I'm sorry if I implied that you were keeping another woman, but I had to know before I tell you something."

Lowering his arms, Samuel stared directly at Jose Luis. "What?"

"I'm dying, Samuel."

There came a long, thick silence that grew more uncomfortable with each passing second. Samuel looped one leg over the opposite knee, struggling not to break down. Jose Luis had become the father Charles couldn't or did not know how to be.

"We're all dying, Papa."

Jose Luis stared at the younger man as if he were a stranger. It was the first time he related to him like family and not a business partner. Samuel had changed. He wasn't the arrogant and brash man who'd come to Cuba five years ago. But after marrying his daughter the brashness was tempered by confidence—confidence and a boldness that seemed to make him invincible.

However, it was fatherhood that had made the greatest impact on Samuel; he'd openly lavished affection on his children and they worshipped him as if he were a god. Jose Luis knew Samuel loved Marguerite-Josefina as she did him, and that he would always provide for his daughter and grandchildren.

"That is true, but I am dying," he repeated, his voice quivering with fear and dread. "It's my heart. There are times when it stops beating for a few seconds, causing me a great deal of pain. The doctors say there is nothing they can do for me. They tell me not to do anything strenuous, and that I should take a lot of rest. That is why I cannot travel."

Samuel closed his eyes and swallowed painfully. "Have you told M.J.?"

Jose Luis placed a hand on Samuel's shoulder. He opened his eyes with the slight pressure. "No. And I don't want you to tell her." A muscle twitched in Samuel's jaw. "Swear to me on your children that you won't tell her."

"Don't bring my children into this."

The hand on Samuel's shoulder tightened. "Swear it!"

It was a full minute before either man spoke again. Samuel was the one to break the impasse. "I swear."

M.J. woke up the morning of her twenty-fourth birthday and fourth wedding anniversary to find her husband staring at her. Her lips parted in a smile that always softened his heart wherein he could not refuse her anything.

"Happy birthday, baby."

"Thank you, *mi amor,* for five years of the most exquisite happiness any woman could ever hope for."

Tiny lines fanned out around Samuel's eyes when he threw back his head and laughed. "Five down and seventy to go."

M.J. stared at the man she'd married. She still found his features interesting. His lean face had filled out, softening the sharp angles of his prominent cheekbones and along his jawline. His salt-and-pepper hair gave him an air of sophistication not attributed to thirty-one-year-old men.

What hadn't changed were his eyes. Dark, deep-set, and penetrating, they seemed to see everything in one sweeping glance. His deep voice was the same, and she discovered he didn't have to raise it to prove a point.

Although she hadn't liked his traveling so much, she'd reconciled that as an international businessman this was what Samuel had to do. He had his companies and employees, whereas she had her home and children.

Looping an arm around her waist, Samuel pulled M.J. atop him, her legs sandwiched between his. "What do you want for the next five years, darling?"

She rested her chin on his breastbone and stared up at him staring down at her. "I don't know, Sammy. I can't think of a single thing. I have the house I've always wanted, I get to have you home practically every night now, and I have my children. What more could I want?"

"Do you want more children?"

Her expressive arching eyebrows lifted. "Why are you asking me this? After Nancy was born I remember you saying that with a son and a daughter our family was complete."

Samuel closed his eyes. "You're right. It's just that every time you go into labor I keep thinking that I'm going to lose you." He opened his eyes, meeting her startled gaze.

"You are not going to lose me, Sammy."

"But the pain and—"

"Stop it," she whispered, halting his plea. "If it will make you feel better I'll have the next one in a hospital."

"You want another baby?"

M.J. nodded. "Of course. I want more of *your* children."

He frowned. "Children?"

"Yes. I want to teach all of them to speak, read, and write Spanish. I want them to learn to play the piano, go to college, fall in love, get married, and give us lots of beautiful grandchildren."

Samuel cupped her hips, massaging the firm flesh under her silk nightgown. "You've really planned our future, haven't you?"

"Don't you make projections for your business projects?"

"Yes—I do."

She offered her husband a confident smile. "That means we're very much alike, my darling. You take care of your businesses, and I take care of my family."

The fingers of Samuel's right hand gathered fabric as he bared M.J.'s thighs. "When do you project we start increasing our family?"

M.J. moaned softly as the flaccid flesh between Samuel's thighs stirred. "I want to wait until Nancy turns three."

Without warning, Samuel reversed their position, supporting his greater weight on his elbows. "I don't want to wait that long."

Lowering his head, he trailed kisses along the column of M.J.'s scented neck. "Let's start now."

Her eyes widened. "Really?"

"Really," he repeated, easing her nightgown to her waist. He took his time arousing M.J. until she pleaded with him to take her. Samuel complied, sheathing his penis in her warm, moist, throbbing flesh.

He forgot everything and everyone as pleasure, pure and explosive, sucked him into an abyss from which he did not want to escape. Making love to M.J. wasn't merely filling a moment of physical desire and release, but a communion of love and life that would continue long after they'd ceased to exist.

Waves of ecstasy washed over him, drowning him in a fiery explosion wherein he surrendered all he had and all he wanted to be to the woman he'd sworn to love forever.

21

Wife and servant are the same, but only differ in the name.
—Mary Lee, Lady Chudleigh

West Palm Beach, Florida—May 1, 1929

Samuel held his breath as he watched the Pan American Airways plane touch down in a bumpy landing on a runway in Key West, Florida. He'd been waiting hours for the plane to arrive. An early morning thunderstorm had delayed the flight originating in Havana.

A smile softened the lines of tension ringing his mouth as his wife, son, and daughter deplaned. His family had come home following a four-month mourning period.

Jose Luis Diaz de Santiago had died in his sleep on New Year's Day at the age of sixty-nine, and his passing had taken its toll on M.J. She refused to believe her father was gone and wasn't coming back. The funeral Mass was interrupted twice when she fainted, and it was the first time in Samuel's life that he felt completely and utterly helpless.

Out of respect for his wife's relatives, he stayed a month longer than he'd planned to remain on the Caribbean island. Most days it was he who'd gotten up with Martin and Nancy, feeding, washing, and dressing them. M.J. would not get out of bed, refused food, and wouldn't see anyone. It was when she lost her temper, screaming at the top of her lungs at Martin because he'd knocked on her bedroom door, that Samuel was forced to take action.

He unlocked the door, picked her up, and forcibly held her under the stinging spray of a cold shower until her teeth chattered and her lips turned blue. Tears that she'd held back, when informed of her father's death, fell. He'd comforted her as he would a child until she crawled atop him and went to sleep in his protective embrace. She woke up hours later asking for food and water. It was a fragile beginning; he'd broken through the wall of grief to reconnect with his wife.

Martin saw him first. He ran toward him, arms outstretched. "Daddy!"

He caught his son in midair, swinging him around and around. At four, he was taller, heavier, and the hot sun had darkened his skin to a gleaming copper brown.

Martin's arms tightened around his neck as M.J., clutching Nancy's hand, came closer. A shaft of sunlight slanted across M.J.'s face, and Samuel felt his composure slip. Dressed entirely in black, she appeared thinner, a specter of her former self, but her face radiated a maturity that had come from a healing he hadn't been able to offer her. Closing the distance between them, he went to his knees and hugged his wife and daughter, struggling not to weep with joy.

He'd given in to M.J.'s wishes and hadn't returned to Cuba after his extended stay. She claimed she needed to be alone, to commune with her ancestors, and to reconcile with her country of birth.

"My baby. My sweet, sweet baby," he whispered over and over. He pressed his mouth to Nancy's fragrant silky hair.

"No!"

Samuel felt a small fist hit his chest. His eyes widened when he stared numbly at his daughter. Her large dark eyes were filled with tears. Standing, he looked at M.J. "What's wrong with her?"

M.J. patted his shoulder as she rose on tiptoe and brushed her mouth over his. "Please be patient with her, Sammy. She cried when I told her she had to leave Cuba."

Samuel's eyes grew hard. "What about you, M.J.?"

She flashed her dimpled smile. "I'm here, aren't I?"

"You didn't answer my question."

Her smile faded. "And I'm not going to. You asked us to come back, and here we are. I'm tired and the children are tired. We were up early to catch the plane, but had to wait three hours before we could take off. Please take us home."

Samuel set Martin on his feet, one hand going to the small of M.J.'s back. He glanced at her delicate profile under a stylish black cloche. "I've chartered a boat to take us up to West Palm."

The driver Samuel Cole hired to drive him to the airport got out of his taxi with their approach. In less than five minutes he stored luggage in the trunk and drove away from the airfield for the short ride to the pier where a boat awaited their arrival.

*   *   *

Samuel, M.J., Nancy, and Martin lay together on a large bed in a spacious cabin of a sleek cruiser. The rocking motion had put the children to sleep as soon as their heads touched the pillows.

"Martin needs a haircut," Samuel said softly as he ran a hand over his son's curly hair. "I'll take him with me when I go next week."

M.J., having removed her hat, dress, and shoes, stretched like a cat. "There's something you need to know about the children," she said cryptically.

"What is it?"

"They haven't spoken English in months. In fact, I can't get them to speak it."

Samuel recoiled as if he'd been slapped. "What do you mean you can't get them to speak English?"

M.J.'s serene expression did not change. "If I say something to them in English they reply in Spanish."

"What the fuck have you done! How the hell am I supposed to communicate with them?"

M.J. came to a sitting position as if jerked upright by an invisible wire. "Don't ever use that gutter language in the presence of my children as long as you live!"

Samuel waved a hand. "They're asleep, M.J."

She pushed her face so close to his he could feel her breath on his throat. "I don't care if they are unconscious, Samuel Cole. Don't do it again!"

"How do you expect me to react? You've kept them away from me for so long that Nancy doesn't want me to touch her. She doesn't see me as her father, but a stranger. And whenever I spoke to you to tell you that I was coming back to Cuba your response was, 'Please, Sammy. I need more time.' I can understand you wanting to mourn the loss of your father, but not at the risk of alienating me from my children. This will be the last time you will keep me from my children."

"My children," she mimicked nastily. "It's always your children, Samuel. They are not trophies or priceless baubles you can put on display whenever you want to solidify your standing as West Palm Beach's Negro Man of the Year."

The resentment within Samuel that had been building for months surfaced, boiling and spilling over when he said, "If I can't have my wife, then I'll settle for my children."

Her eyes widened until he could see their chocolate-brown centers. "What are you implying?"

"I can't say it in Spanish, so you'll have to settle for the English equivalent."

Without giving M.J. a chance to come back at him, Samuel slipped off the bed, walked out of the cabin, closing the door behind him. He'd waited months to be with his wife and children, but what should've been a warm reunion was marred with accusations and blame.

He couldn't remember the last time he'd denied M.J. anything, but this time he wasn't going to compromise. She would never take their children away from him again.

Samuel and M.J. were like two strangers as they sat in the backseat of the chauffeur-driven Model J Duesenberg, flanking Martin and Nancy, who chattered incessantly to each other in Spanish.

The chauffeur was one of six on the payroll of ColeDiz International, Ltd. Aside from his private secretary, Nora Harris, he had hired a book-keeper to assist Everett, a typist/file clerk fluent in English and Spanish, the chauffeur-mechanic, and a maintenance man.

Everett had suggested they move the office to one of the high-rise of-fice buildings going up in the middle of downtown West Palm Beach, but Samuel was hesitant to relocate. He and his accountant had continued their routine of reading the business sections of major newspapers, while closely monitoring the trading on the New York Stock Exchange. Another record was broken on November of the prior year when the governing committee of the exchange ordered a suspension after the trading vol-ume reached 6,954,020 shares. Those wishing a seat on the Stock Exchange now had to pay $550,000 for the privilege.

Two weeks later the market went into a sharp decline with Radio Corporation of America, International Harvester, and Montgomery Ward as heavy losers.

Samuel closed his eyes and rested the back of his head on the leather seat. He'd preferred risking the future of his empire on the turn of a card or a roll of the dice to gambling with Wall Street. Since going into business for himself he'd learned to keep his business expenses separate from his personal, paid his taxes, and kept a large amount of cash in a vault built beneath the floor of a room in his home.

"Samuel. Wake up, Samuel. We're home."

The sound of M.J.'s voice woke him. He hadn't realized he had fallen asleep. He looked out the side window. The bright orange rays of the set-ting sun reflecting off the lake threw a strange fiery glow on coral columns and every light-colored surface of the large house designed in Spanish and Italian revival styles. Barrel-tiled red roofs, a stucco facade, balconies shrouded in lush bougainvillea, and sweeping French doors that opened onto broad expanses of terraces made for an imposing showplace. The magnificent structure was surrounded by tropical fo-liage, exotic gardens, and the reflection of light off sparkling lake waters.

The day M.J. had informed him that she was pregnant again he con-tacted an architect to draw up plans for a house to be erected on a twenty-acre lot he'd purchased after Martin's birth. It took six months to

finish building the three-story, twenty-four room, four-bedroom suite
house. Nancy had celebrated her first birthday when M.J. completed decorating the interior. Putting in the gardens—tropical, exotic Japanese,
and boxwood—had become an ongoing project. M.J. would've expanded
her gardens if he hadn't sold off eight acres to a man who built a golf
course for Negro golfers.

He'd given his wife the children she wanted, a house with enough
room for family and other guests to come and stay for an extended period of time, and a staff to ensure a well-run household.

All Samuel wanted from M.J. was her love and understanding. He'd
curtailed his traveling and hadn't slept with another woman since the
birth of his son.

She professed that she wanted more children, but that was not possible if they lived apart. He wanted more children—as many as M.J. would
be able to give him—but before that became a reality they would have to
resolve a few issues.

Eddie Grady had opened the passenger-side door for him. Samuel
stepped out and scooped Martin off the seat. He stared at the curious
dark eyes staring up at him. "You're home, son."

Martin gave him a tentative smile, the dimples he'd inherited from his
mother deepening with the gesture. Both children looked like M.J. His
only contribution to their gene pool was his coloring and hair.

A chill raced over him when Martin took his hand. Even if his daughter hadn't remembered him, his son did. Mothers had their daughters,
while fathers had their sons. At that moment life couldn't have been better for Samuel Claridge Cole.

Samuel used a guest room to shower and ready himself for bed. Tying
the belt to his robe around his waist, he made his way down a wide hallway to the suite he shared with M.J.

The sight that greeted him stopped him in his tracks. "What's going
on here?" M.J. lay in bed with Martin and Nancy asleep beside her.

"Hush, Sammy, or you'll wake them up."

He failed to be aroused by the soft swell of breasts rising and falling
under the revealing décolletage of an ivory-white nightgown, or the
loosely braided raven-black hair falling over her shoulder.

"Why aren't they sleeping in their own bedrooms?"

"They're used to sleeping with me. It's going to take time before they
go back to sleeping by themselves."

Samuel glared at her as if she had taken leave of her senses. "Let me
know when you want *me* in your bed again." Turning on his heel, he left
the bedroom and made his way to one at the opposite end of the hallway.

M.J. stared at the space where her husband had been. Hot tears
pricked the backs of her eyelids. He didn't understand. He couldn't understand how bereft she was. The death of her father, and her aunt

Gloria's decision to leave Cuba and marry her longtime lawyer-lover, twenty-two years her junior, and live with him in Spain, signaled a complete break with her island homeland.

She still had relatives on the island, but it was different without Papa and Tia Gloria. Ivonne had married, become a mother of two young boys, and was expecting her third before the end of the year. Everyone had made plans for their futures whereas she gathered her children close to her bosom, holding on to them as if she feared they would disappear.

She smothered them with hugs and kisses until they screamed in protest. The love she should've shared with her husband she lavished on Martin and Nancy. She thought it would've ended once Samuel issued an ultimatum that if she did not return to Florida he would come to Cuba and get her.

She loved Samuel with all of her heart, but somehow along the way she had come to love her children so much more.

A single tear trickled down her cheek and into the valley between her breasts. M.J. knew she had to do something quickly, or she would lose her husband. Making certain her son and daughter were still asleep, she slipped out of bed and padded on bare feet down the carpeted hallway, looking into each bedroom.

She found Samuel in bed with a mound of pillows supporting his head and shoulders. An open book lay on his lap. His head hung at an awkward angle, indicating he'd fallen asleep.

A smile found its way around her expression of uncertainty as she walked to the bed. Lifting the sheet, she slipped in beside him. He moaned softly, shifted, but did not wake up. M.J. reached over and turned off the lamp on the bedside table, then settled down to sleep with her husband.

Samuel came awake before dawn, all of his senses on full alert. At first he thought he'd imagined her—her smell, the velvety smoothness of the slender leg thrown over his. His fingers touched the silky curtain of hair spread out on his pillow.

She'd come to him.

Lowering his head, he trailed a series of kisses over a bared shoulder, down the length of her arm. Turning her hand over, he licked her palm. Her fingers quivered. He licked it again, eliciting a gasp from her.

Samuel glanced up to find M.J. smiling at him. "Don't stop there," she whispered.

His smile matched hers as he moved over her. "What are you doing here?"

Her beautifully arching eyebrows lifted. "I live here."

"Why is it I don't recognize you?"

Trailing her fingertips down his chest, M.J. closed her eyes. "Perhaps I can do something to help you remember who I am."

This was the M.J. Samuel loved, soft and teasing. "What?"

"Let me up and I'll show you."

He could not imagine what his wife had in mind until she divested herself of her nightgown and lay flush over his body. Heart to heart, flesh to flesh, breaths mingling, they'd become one.

M.J. kissed him, tentatively at first, until her kisses grew bolder. Moving down the length of his body, she alternated kissing and licking his furred chest, flat belly; she breathed her hot breath on the triangle of tightly curling hair at the apex of his thighs, eliciting a deep moan and shudder from him.

Samuel couldn't move, breathe. He wanted to stop M.J. but it'd been months—too long since they'd slept together. He bellowed as if someone had branded him with a heated iron when her mouth closed around his rigid sex.

No!

She can't!

She's my wife.

She's not a whore!

His silent entreaty went unspoken as he gave himself up to the exquisite sensations wrought by her moist, hot mouth and rapacious tongue. Somewhere between sanity and insanity he found the strength to stop her before he ejaculated.

Reaching down, Samuel fastened his hands in her hair and tugged gently until she released him. His sensitized penis bobbing between his thighs, he pushed her onto her back and entered her in one sure thrust of his hips. He rode her like a man possessed, her feet anchored on his shoulders.

It was M.J.'s turn to moan and sob. Samuel's hands, mouth, and hardness reminded her of what he was to her, what she'd missed. *Love me, Sammy. Please love me*, she chanted to herself as flutters of desire pulsed through her core, growing stronger and longer with each pounding thrust of Samuel's hardness that made her aware of why she'd been born female. She gasped, her body arching as ecstasy, strong and turbulent, ripped her asunder.

M.J. did not remember crying or babbling how much she loved Samuel when she woke up in a bedroom she did not recognize as her own. When she finally found the strength to get out of bed she discovered walking was difficult. It had been a long time since the muscles along her inner thighs ached with every step she took.

Some time later, after she'd showered and completed her toilette, she went down to the kitchen to find Samuel, Martin, and Nancy sitting at the table in a breakfast nook, eating the pancakes Bessie flipped deftly at the stove.

Bessie smiled at M.J. "Good morning, Miz Cole. It's nice to have you back. Your babies are growing like weeds."

Closing the distance between them, M.J. hugged her housekeeper. "It's good to be back." She glanced around the large kitchen. "Why are you cooking?" She'd hired a cook while Bessie had stayed on to supervise the other women who were responsible for keeping the house clean and running smoothly.

"She cut her hand yesterday, and she called to say she had to go to the doctor this morning."

Walking over to Samuel, M.J. kissed his mouth. "Good morning, *mi amor.*"

"His name is Daddy, not My Love," Martin chimed up, waving a fork with a piece of pancake hanging from the tines.

Reaching over, Samuel ruffled his son's hair. "So, you do know how to speak English."

Martin's black eyes were brimming with laughter. "Of course I know how to speak English, Daddy."

He sounded so mature that Samuel had to laugh. M.J.'s laughter joined his, and soon Nancy and Martin were laughing.

Bessie turned back to the stove. She flipped another pancake. It had been a long time since she'd heard the sound of laughter in the enormous house.

Now that Miz Cole had returned with her children, the house could once again become a home.

22

You can do anything in this world if you are prepared to take the consequences.

—W. Somerset Maugham

Samuel sat at a small round table in the corner of his office with Everett going over the report of the Costa Rican coffee harvest.

He massaged his forehead with his fingertips. "Something is not right. We plant four hundred acres of arabica seeds and the harvest yields two."

Bracing his elbow on the table, Everett rested his chin on his fist. He did not have an answer for Samuel. He only dealt with real numbers, whereas his boss knew unequivocally the amount of any crop an acre would yield.

"Maybe they had an infestation problem."

Samuel shook his head. "No, Everett, they didn't. I told them to try a technique that has been used in Kenya where they intersperse trees with the coffee bushes. The poro tree is perfect because its roots grow deep, preventing soil erosion, and it attracts insects from and provides shade for the coffee bushes."

"Did he plant them?"

"He said he did."

Everett gave Samuel a sidelong look. In less than ten years Samuel Claridge Cole had become a hands-on gentleman farmer. He hadn't earned a college degree, yet he was one of the smartest men Everett had come to know.

Fastidious to the point where it could be interpreted as obsessive, Samuel had all of his clothes made-to-order. He now had a barber and manicurist come to his home each week, and paid a chemist for specially blended cologne.

Samuel was always open to Everett's suggestions, a patient listener, and a voracious reader. When he purchased his first coffee plantation he hadn't known anything about the crop. But within three months he knew enough to question those who'd been cultivating the crop their whole life. A modern-day visionary, he knew instinctually what people needed to make their lives more pleasurable. Their latest project was to erect vacation villas for the wealthy throughout the Caribbean.

However, there was another side of Samuel he rarely exhibited, except if crossed. Trust and loyalty forgotten, he'd become a dangerous and deadly foe.

"Do you think he's skimming?" Everett asked.

A frown marred Samuel's smooth forehead. "I know he is. Not only is Aquilar greedy, but he's also a stupid son of a bitch. I offered him ten percent of the harvest and he goes behind my back and takes fifty. Did he actually think I wouldn't know?"

"He counted on your not knowing."

Leaning back in his chair and crossing his arms over the front of a crisp white shirt, Samuel stared at a gelatin silver print of an Emancipation Day parade photographed in St. Augustine by Richard Aloysius Twine.

Straightening, he shifted his gaze to his accountant. "I can't leave M.J. and the kids now." It'd been only two weeks since they'd returned from Cuba, and he looked forward to going home each night and sharing the evening meal with his family.

"I'll go," Everett volunteered in a quiet voice.

Lacing his fingers together, Samuel nodded, smiling. "You know what to do." The question had come out as a statement.

A hint of a smile curled the accountant's upper lip. "I'll stay until I can secure a replacement for Aquilar. After that I'll take a look at that property you're interested in at Dominical."

Sighing, Samuel inclined his head. When he saw Dominical for the first time he felt as if he'd ventured into an idyllic paradise. White sand, clear blue water, and tropical foliage provided the perfect setting for a string of pastel-colored villas.

"Thank you, Everett."

A strange light lit up Everett's gold eyes. "Remember, we're in this together."

He was as close as one could get to becoming a partner in ColeDiz

International, Ltd. Samuel had kept his promise to give him 10 percent of the company's year-end profit, but had shocked him when he handed him the deed, free and clear, to the house he'd lived in with M.J. before they moved into the mansion overlooking a lake.

Everett saved the handwritten note attached to the deed. *I couldn't have done it without you—SCC.*

Samuel had offered him his gratitude, whereas it should've been Everett J. Kirkland thanking Samuel C. Cole.

Individually they were unique, and together they'd become invincible.

A buzzing sound from the desk caught the attention of both men. "Mr. Cole, there is a Mr. Salazar from Havana on the line. The gentleman speaks only Spanish, so I think Miss Maldonado should help you with this call."

Rising to his feet, Samuel walked to the desk and pressed a button on the intercom. "Please send her in, then put him through." He glanced over his shoulder. "This is a personal call," he said to Everett, who'd stood up and gathered the pages of the harvest report.

"I'll have Mrs. Harris make reservations for my trip."

Samuel nodded and sat down behind his desk. Vertical lines formed between his eyes as he pondered why his late father-in-law's attorney wanted to talk to him. Why hadn't Ibrahim called M.J.? The man had informed M.J. that Jose Luis hadn't wanted the contents of his will disclosed until six months following his death. He glanced at the wall calendar: Monday, July 1, 1929. It had been six months.

"Mrs. Harris said you wanted me to translate for you."

Samuel looked at the young woman who stood in the doorway cradling a pad to her chest. Nora Harris had hired Teresa Maldonado to assist her with typing and transcribing dictation, filing, and answering the switchboard. The part-time clerk-typist was hired not only for her office skills, but also for her fluency in spoken and written English and Spanish.

He stared at the petite young woman with shimmering silver-blond hair and mesmerizing pale green eyes. Her café au lait complexion made her eyes appear much lighter in color. There was something about Teresa that always reminded him of a cat.

"Please sit down, Teresa. I have a call coming through from Havana, and I'm going to need you to take down everything my wife's attorney says, then translate it for me."

Charcoal-gray lashes lowering, Teresa sat down on a soft leather chair beside the ornate oak and rosewood desk. The only time she'd ever entered Samuel Cole's office was to leave a telephone message on his desk. Each time she lingered longer than necessary to examine the photographs on one wall, those of his family on a credenza, and the many books lining a floor-to-ceiling mahogany bookcase. She'd never met her boss's wife, but had spoken to her once when she called to speak to her husband. She'd discerned a slight accent in the soft, husky voice that identified her as of Cuban ancestry, the same as her own.

She gave Samuel a shy smile, pencil poised over her pad. "I'm ready, Mr. Cole."

Pressing a button on the intercom, Samuel said, "Please connect him, Mrs. Harris."

"Senor Cole. I am Ibrahim Salazar, and I represent the estate of Jose Luis Diaz de Santiago," came a deep masculine voice in Spanish through the speaker box.

Samuel nodded to Teresa. "Ask him why he didn't contact my wife."

Teresa translated for Samuel, while at the same time jotting down the lawyer's and her boss's dialogue. "He said he was instructed by Jose Luis to deal directly with you."

"Why?" Samuel asked.

When Teresa translated Samuel's query, Ibrahim said, "Because that is the way he wanted it. Several months before he passed away, Jose Luis arranged for the sale and transfer of ownership of his tobacco fields, house, and surrounding property, effective six months following his death, to Ricardo Puente."

Listening to his employee's translation, Samuel sat stunned when she told him that Jose Luis had set up trust funds for his two grandchildren while leaving the remainder of his estate to his only child and sole heir.

His shock was compounded when Ibrahim informed him a codicil had been added to the will, stating that Samuel would have complete control of the money bequeathed to Marguerite-Josefina Diaz Cole.

"The transfer of funds will be initiated tomorrow morning."

Teresa's hand shook noticeably when she wrote down the amount quoted by the attorney. If her boss hadn't been a millionaire, he definitely was now. The conversation ended three minutes after it had begun, and she sat without moving, staring at the impassive expression on Samuel's face. For a man who'd suddenly inherited more than two million dollars he hadn't given any indication that he was pleased with the news.

She, the daughter of Cuban immigrants, who wanted a better life for herself, had no intention of spending her life working long hours in a factory, or as a housekeeper, nursemaid, or cook for a rich *norteamericana.*

She'd studied very hard in school, and it paid off when she was granted admission into a local college's nursing program; working for

ColeDiz International, Ltd., was an answer to her novenas because she earned enough from her part-time position to pay for her studies and help out at home.

Samuel studied Teresa with his enigmatic gaze for an extra moment. "Please type up your notes and leave it on my desk."

She smiled. "Yes, Mr. Cole."

"Thank you, Teresa."

Pushing off the chair, she walked out of the office, past the area where Mrs. Harris sat, and into the reception area. Inserting a sheet of paper into a typewriter, she placed her fingers on the keys and closed her eyes.

Although Samuel sat more than two hundred feet from her, she still could smell his intoxicating cologne, see the crispness of his starched shirt, his exquisitely shaped hands with long, delicate fingers, and hear his melodious, deep voice. He was her boss, a married man with children, *and* she was besotted with him.

Teresa enjoyed what she did at ColeDiz because the work was interesting, and at times challenging. Whenever she came in on Mondays, Wednesdays, and Fridays she found her wooden basket filled with memorandums for typing. She did not mind typing, but hated filing because of paper cuts and an occasional broken fingernail.

She seldom saw Joseph Hill, the part-time bookkeeper. Also a college student, he worked on Tuesdays and Thursdays, the days she attended classes. Her interaction with Everett Kirkland was limited to typing his financial reports. He was the only employee with unconditional access to Samuel Cole. This angered Mrs. Harris, who was forced to bite her tongue whenever he walked past her and into her boss's office without being announced.

Teresa had mixed feelings about Nora Harris. A short, stout woman with flawless sable-brown skin, the forty-three-year-old widow with three adult children reminded Teresa of a vicious dog guarding her master's property.

She did not get to see as much of Samuel as she would've liked because he always used the back staircase, but all of that would change in three days. Samuel and his wife had invited the ColeDiz employees and their families to join them at their home for a Fourth of July celebration. They would be paid for the holiday and given Friday off with pay. Teresa had invited her parents to come with her, but they declined with the excuse that their limited English would make them feel uncomfortable. Her parents had been in the United States twenty years, yet had not learned more than a few rudimentary words of the language. And because she did not want to go alone, she'd asked her best friend, Liliana, to accompany her.

* * *

Eddie Grady maneuvered along the circular driveway, stopping in front of Samuel Cole's residence. He cut the engine, stepped out, and came around and opened the rear door for Samuel.

"What time should I call for you?" he asked, his solemn expression in place. It was what he considered his professional persona.

He'd driven for a white bank president for years, until his untimely death. Eddie asked his cousin Nora Harris if Samuel Cole needed a driver, and was surprised when Nora told him Samuel could use his services on a short-term basis because her boss spent a lot of time out of the country. Short-term had become permanent once Mrs. Cole and her children returned to the States.

Samuel placed one foot on the slate path, then the other. He got out of the car and stared up at the place he now called home, a place he expected to live out his life. Shifting his gaze, he smiled at the thin, dark-skinned man with salt-and-pepper hair. Eddie Grady was an excellent driver, and had become an invaluable employee.

"I'll call you," Samuel said, noncommittally because he'd planned to take the rest of the week off. He'd told Everett that he was in charge of the office, and if there was something he could not handle, then he was to call him at home.

Samuel felt as if he were in a runaway freight train without brakes. Since he'd come back from Cuba he hadn't stopped long enough to enjoy what he'd worked so hard to acquire.

He got up early to go into the office, and did not return home until nightfall. He had Mrs. Harris make travel arrangements for trips to Costa Rica, Mexico, and Jamaica, where he'd purchased tracts of land between Mandeville and Ocho Rios to cultivate a green coffee bean known as Jamaican Blue Mountain.

His coffee plantations were yielding higher than expected profits, but it would be a while before the Puerto Limon banana venture would prove to be either a success or a failure.

"Make certain you bring your missus and children by on Thursday," he said to the chauffeur.

Eddie flashed a rare smile. "Will do, Mr. Cole."

Samuel unlocked the door, stepping into the entryway with an African slate floor. An ebony and gilt table dating to the eighteenth century cradled a crystal vase with a profusion of snow-white roses. M.J. had decorated their home with the skill of a professional decorator.

Cradling a leather case under his arm, Samuel took one of the twin staircases leading to the second floor. His footsteps were muffled in an oriental runner lining the hallway leading to his suite of rooms. He stopped to peer into the bedroom where Nancy slept. It had taken several weeks for her to adjust to her own bed. She cried herself to sleep for several nights, and when her mother did not come for her she stuck her thumb in her mouth and went off to sleep. Leaning over her crib, he touched a fat, black curl falling over an ear. Playing outdoors had darkened her skin until she was as brown as a berry.

"What are you doing in here?" asked a familiar voice in a hushed whisper.

Turning, he smiled at M.J. She was dressed for bed. "I just came to look in on the kids."

M.J. folded her arms under her breasts. She wanted to scream at Samuel that if he didn't spend all day and half the night at his office, then he'd be able to see his children before they were bedded down for the night. But she held her tongue because arguing with Samuel would not change who he was or what he'd become.

He didn't interfere with her decision as to how to run their household and rear their children, so she'd decided to compromise: she would not question the drive it took for him to maintain his status as a successful businessman.

"I put them to bed early because they didn't take a nap today."

Samuel walked toward M.J., caught her chin, and brushed a kiss over her parted lips. "Are they giving you a hard time?"

Shaking her head, she smiled. "No. They're good children."

He led her out of the nursery, past Martin's bedroom, and into their suite of rooms. "They're good because you give in to their every whim. You're spoiling them, darling."

"And you don't?" M.J. countered.

He lifted his eyebrows. "No."

M.J. sucked her teeth. "That's horse stuff, Sammy."

"Don't you mean horseshit?"

"No. I don't want our children growing up using bad language."

"Either they hear it at home or they'll pick it up once they go out into the world. Take your pick."

"I'd rather they not use it at all." Rising on tiptoe, M.J. kissed him. "Come to bed."

Samuel looped an arm around her waist, smiling and pulling her closer. "As soon as I shower, I'll join you."

M.J. nuzzled his throat, her breath warm and sweet. "I'll be waiting, *mi armor.*"

His smile became a full grin. It had been more than a week since they'd made love to each other. That always foretold of a coming together that was certain to be passionate, unrestrained, wherein they bared their souls and held nothing back.

"Sammy, get up or you're going to be late for work."

Samuel burrowed deeper into the pillow. "I'm not going."

M.J. placed a cool hand on his bare shoulder. "Are you not feeling well?"

Groaning, he wanted her to go away and let him sleep. "I'm okay. I'm taking a few days off."

"Why?" she asked close to his ear.

Rolling over on his back, Samuel glared up at his wife. "Damn it, woman! I didn't know I had to get your permission to stay home."

Shrieking, M.J. jumped on him, her arms going around his neck. "Why didn't you tell me last night?"

A smile replaced Samuel's frown. "I tried, but you told me not to talk."

M.J. had been insatiable, her desire matching and surpassing his when they made love using every inch of the large bed. She screamed, cried, moaned, and begged him not to stop. And he didn't, not until both were sated. They fell asleep, limbs entwined, until they woke before dawn and made love again.

"I have something to show you."

Leaning over to the table on his side of the bed, he opened the leather case and took out the pages Teresa had translated and typed. She'd surprised him when she transcribed his conversation with Ibrahim Salazar in English and in Spanish. He handed the Spanish copy to M.J.

Samuel watched for a reaction from his wife, but there was none as she read the typed pages. She finished, then smiled. "I didn't know Papa had so much money."

"I had no idea he wanted me to handle your money."

M.J. shifted, sitting on Samuel's lap as his arms circled her waist. "It's not *my* money, darling. It's ours. Yours, mine, and our children's." Samuel closed his eyes, enjoying the pressure of the soft body curving into his. He'd made it, had accomplished all the objectives on his wish list, but it was of little consequence because Charles Cole wasn't alive to witness his youngest son's success.

"*Ay, Dios mio,*" Teresa whispered under her breath. "I didn't know he lived in a mansion."

Liliana Martinez leaned forward on the rear seat of the taxi, handing the taxi driver his fare. Her warm brown eyes sparkled with excitement. "Let's go, *muchacha,* I want to see up close how the rich live."

When Teresa asked Liliana to come to an Independence Day celebration at her boss's house, she'd jumped at the opportunity to spend time away from her own home. Since her grandmother and three cousins had come from Cuba to live with her family she felt smothered. Twelve people living together in a small three-bedroom house made her resent the lack of privacy.

The two women stepped out of the taxi and walked to the entrance. A solid brass door knocker, shaped in the head of a lion, rested against a gleaming black door. Teresa knocked twice. The door opened and a Negro woman wearing a pale pink uniform smiled at them.

"Please, come in."

Teresa gave Liliana a sidelong glance as they followed the woman through an entryway with a ceiling rising thirty feet to a clerestory window through which pinpoints of light shimmered off a black slate floor like diamonds. She hadn't realized she'd been holding her breath until she felt the constriction in her chest. She could not have imagined living in a house like the one Samuel Cole occupied with his wife and children. The small house where she lived with her parents and two brothers could fit into the Cole mansion four times. The house wasn't a home—it was a showplace.

Teresa and Liliana walked through a door at the rear of the house and were met with a plethora of sounds and smells. Dozens of people sat at long tables under three large white tents. Teresa searched the crowd for Samuel and found him holding a small child as he shared a laugh with Everett Kirkland.

She affixed a smile she'd practiced over and over, and made her way over to him. It wasn't until she was less than five feet away that Samuel noticed her. His laughter faded as his eyes widened. Teresa was hard-pressed not to laugh aloud. She'd achieved the reaction she sought from her boss. The white slip-dress in delicate georgette banded in satin with a handkerchief hem skimmed her petite curvy body. She hadn't pinned up her hair and it floated around her shoulders like a pale mane.

Samuel shifted Nancy from one arm to the other, extending his right hand to Teresa. "Welcome. I'm glad you could come."

She shook his hand and leaned forward. The gesture elicited the response she sought when Samuel's gaze lingered briefly on the soft swell of her breasts rising above the revealing décolletage. The shopkeeper who sold her the garment said it was perfect for an afternoon garden party. What the woman didn't know was that it was the perfect dress for seduction.

"Thank you, Mr. Cole, for inviting me."

Samuel released her hand. "None of that Mr. Cole today. We're not at the office." He glanced over her head. "Did you bring someone with you?"

Throwing back her head, silver-blond hair sweeping over her bared shoulders, Teresa smiled up at her boss through a fringe of long lashes. "I brought my best friend." She beckoned to Liliana. "Liliana, this is my boss, Samuel Cole. Samuel, Liliana Martinez."

Liliana smiled at the man whom Teresa could not stop talking about. Dressed in a white *guayabera*, linen walking shorts, sandals, and a Panama hat, he looked nothing like the wealthy man Teresa bragged about who wore custom-made suits, shirts, and imported footwear. His dark eyes were friendly, his smile warm and genuine. She found that he wasn't as good-looking as he was attractive. What she did not understand was how her friend could fantasize about a man, one who wore a wedding ring.

Samuel nodded to the young woman who'd come with his clerk. Her round, brown face was framed with a profusion of short black curls that gave her a doll-like look. "Welcome, Liliana."

Teresa rested an arm over Liliana's shoulder. "This is Everett Kirkland. We also work together. Everett, my friend, Liliana."

Liliana offered Everett her hand, smiling up at him. This man was someone she could like. His gold eyes with their dark brown centers were mesmerizing, and, unlike Samuel Cole, he did not wear a wedding band.

"My pleasure, Everett."

He did not release her hand, tucking it into the bend of his elbow. "Are you hungry, Liliana?"

Angling her head, she flashed an attractive moue. "Starved."

Teresa watched Everett lead her friend to a table and seat her. She shifted her gaze back to Samuel. "Is this your daughter?"

Samuel patted the back of the little girl who'd fallen asleep on his shoulder. "Yes. This is Mistress Nancy, who happens to be the indisputable boss in the family."

Green eyes narrowed as they moved slowly over the young child in Samuel's arms. Black curls clung to her moist forehead, and although asleep she continued to suck the thumb she'd pushed into her mouth.

"She's beautiful, Samuel."

"Thank you, Teresa."

His gaze lingered on Teresa Maldonado as if seeing her for the first time. And it was the first time he'd seen her hair loose, and so much of her body exposed. When she was at the office her hair was always fashioned into a bun. Her business attire was white sailor-type blouses, dark skirts, and functional leather shoes.

He forced himself not to stare at her when he spied M.J. talking to Belinda. His mother, brothers, sisters-in-law, and two young nieces had come from Tallahassee to spend the holiday weekend in West Palm Beach.

M.J. had softened considerably when she extended invitations to those who'd ostracized her when they lived in Palm Grove Oval. He got to see another side of his wife's personality when she led them in and out of rooms in the opulently decorated house like a tour guide in a museum. Marguerite-Josefina Cole had exhibited a charm that would've made her father proud. It was unfortunate that Jose Luis hadn't lived long enough to see his daughter display the grace and deportment befitting a woman of her station.

"Come, Teresa. I want to introduce you to my wife."

Turning around, Teresa looked for the woman who claimed the man she wanted as her own. Her heart sank when she saw her. The child Samuel held to his heart had the same delicate features as the woman coming in their direction. Dressed in a pale yellow shirtwaist dress and matching straw hat that protected her face from the sun, she was tall, slender, with a hypnotic dimpled smile and black hair tied with a yellow satin ribbon that touched her waist. Teresa found Samuel's wife stunning!

M.J. wound an arm through Samuel's. "Why don't you give me Nancy so that I can put her to bed?"

Lowering his head, Samuel kissed M.J.'s cheek. "I'll put her to bed, but first I'd like you to meet the person who translated Ibrahim's telephone call. Teresa, this is my wife, Marguerite-Josefina. M.J., Teresa Maldonado."

M.J. smiled at Teresa. "*Hola*," she said in Spanish. "My husband has been singing your praises," she continued in the language. "He says you're an invaluable employee."

Teresa felt her pulse accelerate. Samuel had told his wife about her! She hadn't been able to tell what Marguerite-Josefina was when she'd first looked at her photograph, thinking perhaps she could have been a member of one of the Indian tribes from Florida, but when she heard her speak she knew she was Cuban. Again, she found it hard not to laugh. It was apparent Samuel Cole was attracted to Cuban women.

"You and your husband are very kind," she said shyly, "to invite me to your home. And working for ColeDiz is like a dream come true."

"I hope Samuel isn't working you too hard."

A wave of heat swept up Teresa's neck to her hairline. "Oh no, Mrs. Cole. Your husband is a wonderful boss."

Samuel winked at M.J. "Please make certain Teresa gets something to eat. I'll introduce her to everyone after I put Nancy to bed."

A warm glow flowed through Teresa, and it had nothing to do with the heat of the day. Samuel wanted to make the introductions, which meant she was special, special enough for him to have spoken of her to his wife.

And she knew there was something special about Samuel the instant she saw him. He embodied everything she wanted in a man, and there was nothing or no one that could stop her from having him.

23

Woe be to them that for a loved one must wait in longing.

—Anonymous

Teresa sat with her feet on the seat of the wooden rocker, her arms wrapped around her knees, staring at lightning bugs through the mesh of the screened-in porch. "What do you think of him, Liliana?"

Liliana lay on a discarded sofa that had once graced her family's living room. It had become her bed because she didn't want to share her bedroom with three younger girl cousins.

"Everett Kirkland?"

"No, silly. Samuel Cole."

"What's there to think about? He's rich *and* he's married."

"Don't you think he's cute?"

Liliana rolled her eyes. "He's too old to be cute."

"He's only thirty-one."

"And, he's too old for you, Teresa. You're only nineteen, and may I add, a virgin? And why would you want a married man? Your Samuel Cole is not going to leave his wife for you. All you have to do is look at her and see that."

Teresa lowered her bare feet to the wooden floorboards. "Are you saying she's prettier than I am?"

"No, I'm not." Liliana sat up, glaring at her best friend and neighbor. "What's wrong with you? You're pretty and smart, and you hope to be a nurse one day. Don't ruin your life wishing for something that is not going to happen, *muchacha*. Why would Samuel Cole want you when he has a wife, a wife he's in love with?"

"How do you know that?"

"Did you see how they looked at each other?"

Teresa pushed out her lower lip. "No."

"That's because you don't want to see what is so obvious between them. They are in love." Moving off the sofa, she sat on the floor in front of the rocker. "I'm going to tell you something I've never told anyone. Not even the priest I go to for confession."

Teresa sat down beside Liliana, wondering what it was her friend was hiding. "What is it?"

Her shoulder touching Teresa's, Liliana closed her eyes. "Please don't make the same mistake I made, Teresa. I fell for the sweet talk from a man who was betrothed to another. I believed him when he said he didn't love her, but he had to marry her because their fathers were in business together.

"One night I snuck out of the house to meet him. He gave me something to drink. Then we started kissing, and the next thing I knew he was inside me. I let him make love to me knowing that I could never claim him as my husband. We met a few times after that. It ended when he married his *novia*."

Eyes wide, Teresa stared at Liliana. "Did you get to see him after he married?"

Liliana shook her head. "No. He refused to see me. What he did was send me a letter saying he was trying to be a faithful husband. He threatened me, saying I must never attempt to contact him again or he would tell everyone that I tried to seduce him."

"But . . . but it was he who seduced you."

"Who do you think people are going to believe?" She stared at the floor. "I trusted him and he deceived me. I don't ever want to get married."

Wrapping her arms around Liliana's waist, Teresa shook her head. "Don't say that."

"What? That I am not soiled? Men want to marry women who come to them untouched."

"You can't tell me that all couples wait until their wedding night to sleep together. It's not the way it used to be, Liliana," she argued softly so as not to be overheard by those inside the house. "Have you heard of Margaret Sanger?" Liliana shook her head. "She is a pioneer in birth control for women. She helped organize the first international birth-control conference less than two years ago. This means you can sleep with a man and not get pregnant."

"Why would I want to sleep with a man?"

"Did you not enjoy your friend?"

A dreamy expression softened Liliana's lush mouth. "After the first time it was wonderful."

"And it could be wonderful again if you decide you want to have an affair with a man."

"Why would I want to have an affair?"

"Why not?" Teresa asked, answering Liliana's question with one of her own. "Don't men have them?"

"Yes, but—"

"But nothing," Teresa interrupted. "We are Cuban, but we are also American women. We vote, go to college in greater numbers than years ago, work outside the home, and now we can control our own bodies."

"But we're so different from men," Liliana argued quietly.

"How?"

"I don't know."

"The only thing that is different is physiology. They may be stronger, but that's it. I'm willing to bet you that I can get Samuel Cole to marry me."

Liliana let out a loud gasp. "No, Teresa. What you plan to do is a sin."

"And what you did wasn't?"

"No. We weren't married when we shared a bed. Samuel is married, and it's not like you don't know that he is."

Teresa's expression hardened, becoming a mask of stone while her eyes narrowed to cold green slits. "I don't care. I want him, and I'll do anything to get him."

Liliana crossed her chest and said a silent prayer for Teresa. When she went to church on Sunday she would light a candle for her friend. Teresa Maldonado had everything she could wish for, so why would she embark on an undertaking where the result was certain to end in disaster and heartbreak—for her?

Pushing off the floor, she returned to the sofa. Lying down, she rested her head on folded arms and stared up at the peeling porch ceiling. "Do you have to work tomorrow?"

"No. I have the day off. What about you?"

Liliana worked at a hotel in the housekeeping department. "I have to go in from eight to six."

"Do you want to go out dancing after you come home?"

"Sure."

Even though she knew she would be exhausted from mopping floors, cleaning bathrooms, and making beds, Liliana preferred going out to staying home where she couldn't linger in the bathroom because someone was always knocking on the door.

Teresa stood up and walked down the porch steps. "I'll see you tomorrow night."

"*Adios*," Liliana whispered long after her neighbor returned to her house where she didn't have to share her bed or bedroom.

She'd always thought that Teresa was the more levelheaded of the two of them, but her quest to take a married man away from his wife was crazy. She hoped her best friend would come to her senses before it was too late.

Liliana thought Everett Kirkland was a better choice for Teresa. He was intelligent, single, and he was Samuel Cole's right-hand man. And with his gold eyes and her green ones, there was no doubt their children would have extraordinary looks. She'd wait before she'd try to convince Teresa to shift her attention from Samuel Cole to the controller of ColeDiz International, Ltd.

Samuel glanced at the clock on his desk. It was minutes before six. Pressing a button on the intercom, he waited for his secretary's voice. Mrs. Harris never left the office before her scheduled six o'clock departure.

"Yes, Mr. Cole?"

"Is Teresa still here?"

"Yes, she is."

"Please send her in."

Teresa appeared in the doorway, pencil and pad in hand. "Yes, Mr. Cole?"

She still favored her white blouses and dark skirts, but the bun was missing, in its place a mane of pale hair tied back with a black ribbon. Today she looked like a schoolgirl.

He beckoned to her. "Please come in. I need you to take down a letter in Spanish."

Her gaze was steady as she walked into the office and sat down on the chair she'd occupied the week before. Everything that was Samuel Cole swept over her, and she pressed her knees together to still the unexpected pulsing at the apex of her thighs. Liliana had tried unsuccessfully to convince her to let go of her pursuit of Samuel, but she would not relent.

"Do you want me to type it tonight?"

He gave her a direct look. "Yes. I'll pay you extra, and make certain you get home."

She wrote down the date, using her shorthand symbols. "I'm ready."

Leaning back in his chair, Samuel rested his hands on the arms and stared at Teresa's bowed head. Her hair was more silver than blond, which made the contrast between it and her golden-brown complexion more startling. However, it was her eyes that held him spellbound. The color changed with her moods from a pale near-transparent green to a darker, almost moody, emerald hue.

"This letter goes to Senor Juan Redondo at the Mexican National Association of Coffee Exchange. I am in receipt of your report on the recent harvest of the *maragogype* bean. I have also received reports from the broker, and from a variety of tasters.

"The beans were compared to those from Brazil, Cameroon, Colombia, Costa Rica, and Kenya. The result is a flavor that is smooth and fragrant with good, mellow depth, good to excellent acidity and balance, and excellent as a high roast.

"Currently the average yield is about 560 pounds per acre, and at this time I cannot honor your request to increase planting. Therefore, I am authorizing you to decrease production and the workforce for the next planting season by fifty percent. My conservative stance is predicated on the instability of daily trading on Wall Street. I know you will use the utmost discretion with regard to layoffs. This action should be initiated in stages over the next three months.

"I have scheduled a trip to visit your beautiful country in the coming months. I will contact you prior to my arrival."

He paused, as did Teresa's pencil. "Use my usual closing." Her head came up. "Type a copy for my file, the general file, and one for Everett."

Nodding, Teresa stood up and walked to the door, feeling the heat of Samuel's gaze boring into her back. She turned suddenly and caught him staring at her. A hint of a smile parted her lips, and to her surprise he returned it.

Swiveling on the chair and turning his back to the doorway, Samuel stared out the window. Everett was in Costa Rica, and had reported that he'd fired the foreman and evicted him and his family from the main house. The man had offered to give back the money he'd stolen to keep his position, but Everett refused, saying he did not negotiate with thieves. Samuel's number man wasn't certain how long it would take him to find a replacement, but hoped it would be soon because of a recent malaria outbreak.

Samuel's thoughts shifted to the week he hadn't come into the office. He stayed in bed beyond sunrise, played nonstop with Martin and Nancy, and for the first time in his marriage he helped M.J. in the kitchen. He rolled out crusts for pies and cobblers while she prepared the fillings. Their working together ended when she snapped a towel at him after he pilfered peach slices from a bowl; he picked her up and took her upstairs to their bedroom, stripping her naked in under a minute. Peach and apple pies and cobblers were forgotten when they came together in a passion that had eluded them since they'd celebrated their anniversary.

His family arrived July 3 and stayed the weekend. Belinda was overjoyed having all of her grandchildren together at the same time. She babysat her grandson and three granddaughters Saturday night when their parents went out for dinner and to a movie.

Teresa walked into Samuel's office; she watched him staring out the window. Who or what was he thinking about? She was more than aware that they were the only ones in the office. Everett was out of the country and Mrs. Harris had left for the day.

"Samuel?"

He turned at the sound of his name. If he was surprised that she'd called him by his given name, his expression did not indicate it. "Yes?"

"I'm finished."

Samuel pushed back the chair, stood up, and closed the distance between them. He held out his hand. "Please sit down." She handed him the letters and envelope, then sat down beside his desk.

Teresa watched Samuel pace as he read what she'd typed. Her gaze caressed the width of his broad shoulders under his shirt, moving down slowly to his trim waist and hips, ending with a pair of highly polished wing tips. She noticed a swagger in his gait as his right foot toed in slightly.

"Did it bother you that I called you Samuel?"

Samuel stopped pacing and stared at the woman sitting next to his desk. "Excuse me?"

Teresa was certain he could hear her pounding heart. She'd opened Pandora's box, and now she had to deal with what had escaped: brazenness.

Her gaze caught and held his questioning one. "I called you Samuel instead of Mr. Cole. Are you bothered by that?"

Samuel shook his head. "No, Teresa."

"Will it bother you if I call you Samuel in front of the others in the office?"

Vertical lines appeared between his eyes. "No. Why?"

"It's just that Mr. Cole sounds so formal for a company this size."

"Who told you to call me Mr. Cole?"

"Mrs. Harris."

"If Mrs. Harris says anything to you about calling me Samuel, then tell her I said it's okay."

Her smile was one of triumph. She'd broken through the formality. "Thank you."

Samuel nodded, then went back to reading the letter. It was perfect. There wasn't one typographical error. "How can I be certain the Spanish version reads the same as the English?" he said teasingly.

Teresa rose to her feet, smiling. "You'll just have to take my word that it is the same, won't you?"

He returned her smile. "You're right about that."

She angled her head, baring her throat, bringing his gaze to linger there. "You're married to a woman who speaks Spanish, yet you don't know the language."

"I know a few words, but not enough to carry on an in-depth conversation."

"I suppose that's why I was hired," Teresa said softly. "I'm more than willing to help out whenever you need me."

An explicable look of withdrawal came across Samuel's face, and she chided herself for making it seem as if she would be *that* available when it was exactly what she wanted to be. She wanted to be what Marguerite-Josefina was to her husband—and much more.

She wanted to be mistress and wife, mother and confidante. She would willingly travel with him, acting as interpreter, transcribing and typing his reports while providing him with companionship.

Teresa did not know why she'd fallen in love with Samuel, but her heart refused to listen to what her head was telling her. She planned to seduce a man, a married man with children, become pregnant with his child, then issue an ultimatum: leave his wife and marry her. Whether it was vanity or recklessness, she refused to believe he would be able to resist her.

She'd learned as a young girl how to charm, flirt with, and seduce the opposite sex. She charmed the men and boys in her family, and flirted shamelessly with those who weren't, stopping only when it came to relinquishing her virginity. That she would save for the man whom she planned to marry.

"I'll make certain to keep that in mind," Samuel said after a noticeable pause. He walked over, picked up the telephone, and dialed a number, hoping to contact his chauffeur, who hung out at a nearby social club where the members came and went, playing cards and checkers. A voice he didn't recognize answered the phone. Samuel identified himself, then asked for Eddie Grady, who answered the call within seconds.

"Eddie, I need you to bring the car around and take Miss Maldonado home. Once you return I'll be ready to leave."

He ended the call, then reached into a pocket in his trousers and withdrew a money clip. Peeling off a twenty-dollar gold note, he handed it to Teresa. "Thank you."

She stared at the bill as if it were a venomous reptile. Samuel was offering her more than she earned in a week. "It's too much."

Reaching for her hand, Samuel placed the money on her palm, forcibly closing her fingers over it. "You're worth a lot more. Now take it and go. Mr. Grady is waiting downstairs to drive you home."

Teresa successfully curbed the urge to throw her arms around Samuel's neck, pull his head down, and kiss him. She lowered her lashes in a demure gesture. "Thank you, Samuel."

"You're quite welcome, Teresa."

She watched as he sat down while she stood paralyzed, transfixed by the man who'd occupied her every waking moment.

His head came up and he stared at her, brow furrowing. "Is there something else you want?"

The sound of his soft, drawling voice shattered the spell. She wanted to scream, *Yes, Samuel, there is something else. I want you.* Teresa shook her head. "No. Good night, Samuel."

"Good night."

When he lowered his head again, Teresa went to retrieve her pocketbook. She planned to give the twenty dollars to her mother so she could buy something pretty to wear. Silvia Maldonado made all of her family's clothes, and it was on a rare occasion that she purchased a store-bought garment.

Her footsteps were muffed in the reception area as she closed the self-locking front door behind her and skipped down the staircase to the street level. Parked several doors away was Samuel's gleaming black Duesenberg. His chauffer leaned against the rear bumper, waiting for her. She believed Eddie Grady had the easiest job of anyone at ColeDiz. All he had to do was drive his boss whenever and wherever he instructed him. Eddie straightened and opened the rear door for her.

She settled onto the soft leather seat, the lingering scent of Samuel's cologne enveloping her in a cocoon of longing. Sinking lower, she closed her eyes. The image of her and Samuel sitting together in the backseat made her smile.

"Where to, Miss Maldonado?"

Her eyes opened quickly. She gave him her address. "Do you know where that is?"

He nodded. "Yes, ma'am."

A hint of a smile curved her mouth. Eddie had called her "ma'am" as if she *were* Mrs. Cole. Her smile faded quickly, replaced with an expression that paled her eyes. Marguerite Cole. Oh, how she hated the woman who'd clung to Samuel's arm while smiling at him with the adoring look on her too perfect face. Everything about Marguerite was perfect: flawless complexion, shiny black hair, manicured hands, and a tiny waist that belied her claim of birthing two children.

Teresa's eyelids fluttered wildly before they closed. The pictures in her head came back, more vivid than before. She would be every inch the grand lady in a suit designed by Coco Chanel. Strands of luxurious pearls graced her neck, and brilliant jewels bedecked her wrists and fingers. Her magnificent diamond engagement ring would surpass the one on Marguerite's hand by several carats.

Her eyes opened and she stared at the back of Eddie's head. She couldn't wait for the day when Samuel had to tell the *puta* that he no longer wanted her, that he didn't love her, and all the money in the world wouldn't make him stay.

Teresa felt as if she were falling, deeper and deeper, into a world wherein all of her wishes were granted just by asking. She wanted to marry Samuel, have his babies, and like the princesses in fairy tales—live happily ever after.

"Miss Maldonado. Wake up, Miss Maldonado. You're home."

Teresa came awake. She'd dozed off. She must have been more tired than she realized. Eddie held the door open for her. Extending a hand, he helped her out. A triumphant grin crinkled her luminous eyes when she saw the number of people coming out of their homes to stare at her getting out of the luxury motorcar.

"Thank you, Mr. Grady."

He touched the shiny brim of his black cap. "Have a good evening, ma'am."

Amusement lit up her face. "You too, Mr. Grady."

Turning on her heel, she walked slowly toward her house where her mother, father, and two younger brothers stood together on the porch, eyes wide and mouths gaping. They parted as if she were a queen and in single file followed her into the house.

"Where have you been?"

"What were you doing in that car?"

Her father and mother were questioning her as if she had done something wrong. "Mr. Cole asked me to work late, so he had his driver bring me home." She opened her pocketbook and thrust the gold note at her father. "He also gave me this."

Ramon did not move. He just stared at the money. Choking sounds came from Silvia Maldonado before she managed to say, "He gave you *that?*"

Teresa smiled. "*Sí, Mami.*"

"But it is so much money."

"That's because Mr. Cole has a lot of money."

"Take it, *Mami,*" Teresa urged, "and buy something pretty for yourself. When was the last time you had a new dress?"

Silvia looked at her husband, who nodded his approval. "*Mil gracias,* Teresa."

She kissed her mother, then her father. "I'm going to my room."

"Don't you want to eat?" Silvia asked. "I made your favorite—*ropa vieja.*"

Teresa shook her head. "I'm not hungry, *Mami.*"

"I will put it in the icebox. You can eat it tomorrow."

"Okay," she said over her shoulder as she made her way toward her bedroom. She wanted to be alone and relive the time she'd spent with Samuel, replay their conversation, rehearse what she would say to him the next time they were alone together.

Latching her bedroom door to keep her twelve- and fourteen-year-old brothers from barging in, Teresa lowered the shades to keep out prying eyes. She hadn't turned on a lamp, preferring to undress in the dark.

Undressing had become a nightly ritual, beginning with her hair. Instead of the usual pins, tonight it was only a ribbon keeping the flaxen waves in place. She untied the ribbon and shook out her hair. With her glittering green eyes and pale hair she looked like a lioness.

Her shoes were next, followed by her blouse. Her fingers never faltered as each button slipped smoothly from its fastening. There were more buttons—two on her skirt's waistband and eight along the left side of the hem. Off came a pair of garters, silk stockings, slip, chemise, and underpants.

Stepping away from the pile of discarded clothes, Teresa walked over to her bed and lay atop the cool sheets. She cupped her breasts and closed her eyes.

Her breathing deepened, her chest rising and falling in a measured rhythm. It was only in the privacy of her bedroom, behind a locked door, that she ceased to be Teresa Maldonado. She became whoever she wanted to be, and for the past two months she was Mrs. Samuel Cole.

It was she, not Marguerite, who woke up beside Samuel, sat across the dinner table from him, attended civic and social dinner parties on his arm, and nursed their babies.

Her hands inched down her body to the area between her thighs. Parting her knees, Teresa massaged the swollen nub until her hips lifted off the mattress. Applying pressure with her fingertips, around and around, faster and faster, she pleasured herself until she convulsed. Then she lay motionless—spent.

A smile spread over her moist face as she closed her eyes. "I love you, Samuel." It was only in the dark, behind a locked door, that she felt completely free—free enough to live out her fantasies.

24

Sex and love are like tea and milk. They can be mixed or they can be taken straight.

—Joyce Brothers

"Teresa, open the door!"

"Go away, Jesus!"

"No! There is a man here for you."

Teresa sat up, splashing water over the sides of the bathtub. "What man?" she asked her younger brother.

"I don't remember his name. He is driving the same car that came yesterday."

"Let him know I'll be out soon." A flicker of concern wrinkled her brow. Why had Eddie Grady come to her home on her day off?

"Should I tell him to wait, Teresa?"

"*Sí*, Jesus!" she shouted. "*Estupido!*" she whispered under her breath. Her father accused Jesus of having *caca*, or shit, for brains, and this was one time she was forced to agree. The twelve-year-old could not remember anything. His teachers always sent home notes saying that Jesus was smart, but that he daydreamed in class.

Teresa stepped out of the tub, reaching for a towel. Even though Ramon and Silvia did not say it often, she knew they were proud of their children. Though they were Cuban immigrants who spoke no English, their U.S.-born children were going to have a piece of the American dream. She had graduated from high school and was now studying for a nursing degree, fourteen-year-old Pedro excelled in his studies and in school sports, while Jesus, lost in his own world of fantasy, was a top math and science student.

After drying her body, she dusted it with a scented powder she'd bought from a local store that sold everything from canned foods to meat. She'd been drawn to a small section where a shelf was crowded with tubes of lipstick, face powder, and fragrances. She'd wanted to purchase a bottle of cologne, but felt the body powder would last longer than the liquid.

Not bothering to run a comb through her damp hair or putting on shoes, she pulled a flower-sprigged cotton dress over her underwear. Unlocking the bathroom door, Teresa walked on bare feet to the living room.

Samuel sat on a chair in the Maldonado living room, staring at the pattern on the threadbare rug under his feet. The air inside the small house was stifling.

"My sister said to wait for her.".

He glanced up and smiled at the young boy with hair the color of wet straw. "Thank you."

Samuel wanted to tell Teresa's brother that he would wait on the front porch, but did not want to appear discourteous. Moisture had formed on his upper lip and under his armpits.

His gaze shifted to a photograph. The photographer had captured a gelatin silver print of a couple in their wedding finery. Peering closer, he realized the man and woman were Teresa's parents. She'd inherited her father's eyes and hair.

"Samuel?"

He sprang to his feet, as if struck by a bolt of lightning. Teresa stood less than six feet away, her feet bare, damp hair falling around her face, and glowing green eyes filled with unanswered questions. His gaze moved from her face to her chest. Light coming in through a window behind her showed the outline of her body through her dress. The faded cotton fabric had been washed so many times that it was almost transparent. He forced himself to look away, but it was too late. The flesh between his legs stirred as if rising from a long slumber. Shifting slightly so she wouldn't be able to see his erection, Samuel cleared his throat.

"May I speak to you . . . outside . . . on the porch?"

Teresa nodded as if she were a mute. And at that moment she couldn't speak. When she'd left the bathroom she'd expected to see the ColeDiz chauffeur, not the company's president.

"I . . . I need to put on my shoes." She needed not only her shoes, but also a slip.

Turning, she walked to her bedroom, her heart beating a rhythm that made her feel light-headed. "What is he doing here?" she asked the door after she'd closed it behind her.

After she'd touched herself again earlier that morning, bringing herself to completion, she'd lain in bed fantasizing it was Samuel's hands and his hardness that made her feel things so wonderful that she never wanted to leave his side.

Opening a drawer in a highboy, Teresa took out a slip. There was no doubt she would become the talk of their neighborhood if anyone saw her talking to a strange man wearing a well-worn dress and no undergarments.

She put on the slip, ran a comb through her hair, and slipped into a pair of sandals. Opening the door, she saw Jesus. "Stay here," she ordered, as he attempted to follow her. Teresa ruffled his coarse hair and kissed his cheek. "I'll be right back."

This time when she stepped out onto the porch she was better prepared for Samuel Cole. He'd removed his suit jacket; his shirt was pasted to his chest and back; she knew why he wanted to talk on the porch. His house, with ceilings rising upward to twenty feet, was cool and comfortable, whereas hers retained the heat for days whenever she or her mother used the oven. Now she understood why some Cuban homes were constructed with separate kitchens.

Her face flushed with humiliation, Teresa stared up at him staring down at her. The longer Samuel looked at her, the more uncomfortable she became. The color in her face drained slowly when a silent voice said, *He's going to fire you.*

Would he let her go because she'd been too forward? Had he rethought his decision to allow her to address him by his given name? Had he figured out that she'd flirted with him, and as a married man he would not tolerate her brazen behavior?

"You've come to fire me." Her question was a statement.

Standing on the porch waiting for Teresa helped Samuel regain control of his body. He did not know what it was about her that elicited the unexpected physical reaction.

The sound of her husky voice shattered his reverie. "You believe I've come here to fire you?"

Tears sparkled in Teresa's eyes before she shuttered her gaze from Samuel's startled one. "Yes."

She could not imagine not working at ColeDiz, not waking up on Mondays, Wednesdays, or Fridays and going into the office just to catch a glimpse of him. She would work for no money if it meant being close to Samuel Cole.

Samuel took a step, leaving less than a foot between them. He curbed an urge to reach out and touch Teresa because she appeared so fragile, so very vulnerable. "Now why would I do that when I need you?"

Her eyes opened, moisture spiking her lashes. "What?"

Lowering his head, Samuel said softly, "I came here to ask you if you can put in a few more hours."

She clapped her hands as would a small child, threw back her head, and laughed, the sound bubbling with the joy that had replaced the sadness in her eyes. "You . . . you want me to work with you?"

Shaking his head in amusement, Samuel affected a wide grin. "Yes, Teresa." He sobered quickly when he remembered why he was standing on the Maldonado porch. "I need you to fill in for Mrs. Harris."

"Why?"

"She has a family emergency in Arkansas that required her immediate attention. Eddie went with her."

Nora Harris had woken him with the news that her son had been shot in the head by revenue agents. He lay unconscious in a prison hospital close to death. He'd been arrested along with several cousins, who'd also been shot, but their wounds were superficial in nature.

"You want me to do what Mrs. Harris does?"

"I need you to cover the office, Teresa. I need you to work five days instead of three. Let me know if you're available. Otherwise I'll try to find someone else."

"No," she said a little too quickly. "Please don't look for someone. I'll do it."

He lowered his head and his voice. "Are you sure, Teresa?"

She tingled as he said her name. Samuel was so compelling, his magnetism so potent, that she couldn't tear her gaze from him. An enchanting smile parted her full, lush lips.

"Very sure, Samuel. When do you want me to come in?"

"Now."

"Now?" she repeated.

"Yes."

"Ah . . . oh. I have to change my clothes. I have to let my brothers know I'm leaving. Then I have to leave a note for my parents." She was rambling, but she didn't much care. Her wish had been answered. She was going to see Samuel—every day.

She turned to go back into the house, but Samuel caught her upper arm in a firm grip. "I'll adjust your pay for the extra time, and if you have to work beyond six, then I'll bring you home."

Teresa suffered the warm hand on her bare skin. There was nothing sexual in his touch, but her body refused to listen to the dictates of her brain. She jerked her arm away. "I have to get dressed."

The screen door opened, closed, slamming loudly against its frame. One minute Teresa was there; then she was gone, and for a reason Samuel could not fathom, he missed her. He missed her moonlit hair falling in sensual disarray around her perpetually tanned face, missed the mysterious glow in her incredible eyes, and her sweet musky feminine scent that lingered in his nostrils long after she'd disappeared.

Folding his body down to a rocker, Samuel stretched out his legs and waited for the woman whose affect on him was puzzling. She was the complete opposite of M.J. His wife was tall, slender, dark-haired, dark-eyed, whereas Teresa was petite, fair-haired, light-eyed, and with a lush body that was undeniably feminine.

They were so different, yet their physical impact on him was the same. He knew he had to be careful, very, very careful around Teresa now that they would be spending more time together.

"Am I going too fast for you?"

Teresa gave Samuel a sidelong glance. "No."

He'd been reading and dictating telegrams for nearly five hours. He was trying to avoid making a trip to Puerto Rico. A hurricane had swept the island, causing extensive damage to one of his two coffee plantations. His island representative was urging him to come and survey the damage.

Leaning back in his chair, he focused on the wall plaques. Most of them honored ColeDiz International, Ltd., for its contribution to various civic and social organizations. His company was solvent, he'd achieved the rank of a multimillionaire, and the company still did not list one domestic holding. Whether it was Oklahoma, Kentucky, or Texas, racial inequality continued throughout the U.S. The NAACP had reported that the lynching of nine Negroes in 1928 was the lowest figure in forty years. They were one-third into the twentieth century and his people were still being hanged from trees.

"As at your urging," he continued, "I will see you early next week. I remain, Samuel." He smothered a groan. Everett was still in Costa Rico, which meant he *had* to go to Puerto Rico. "Please make certain to get this to the telegraph office before they close today," he told Teresa.

"Yes, Samuel."

She pushed her pencil into the bun she'd pinned up on the back of her head, and left to transcribe and type the cablegram. Samuel stared at her retreating back. She was back to the severe, old-fashioned hairstyle.

It was their third day working together, and to his surprise he got along better with Teresa than he did with Mrs. Harris, who tended to question him even when he didn't solicit her opinion. Perhaps it was the age difference that made the older woman assume the stance, but it had not been that way with Teresa.

She came in early and stayed beyond her quitting time. Samuel paid for her lunch and drove her home. Their relationship was one of employer and employee, and nothing more.

He picked up the telephone and dialed his home. The connection was broken after the fourth ring. "Cole residence.."

"I'd like to speak to Mrs. Cole," he whispered into the mouthpiece.

"This is Mrs. Cole."

"Mrs. Cole, this is your secret admirer. Perhaps I can interest you in having dinner with me in the garden this evening."

A soft laugh came through the earpiece. "That all depends on who my secret admirer is," M.J. crooned, playing along with him.

"Accept my invitation and you'll find out who he is."

There was a slight pause. "Okay. What time do you want to meet?"

Samuel glanced at the clock on a corner of his desk. "Is seven-thirty too early?"

"Make it eight and you're on."

He smiled. "I'll see you at eight."

M.J. could not get used to eating dinner before eight o'clock. The evening meal in Cuba usually began at that time, or some times as late as ten. He made it a practice to ready himself for bed at ten.

He was still a farmer—early to bed and early to rise.

Samuel maneuvered along the unpaved road to the house where Teresa lived with her family in a racially mixed community of poor whites, Negroes, and several immigrant Cuban families. The many small children, who attended segregated schools, played with one another without regard to race. Their parents, on the other hand, all worked at a local cotton mill.

"It looks as if you've become quite a celebrity," he said in a quiet tone as he stopped in front of her house. People were gathering on their porches just to watch Teresa Maldonado get out of his car.

Teresa angled her head, lowered her eyelids, and affected a pose that reminded Samuel of a Hollywood actress. "Thank you, darlings, for your applause." Lowering her sultry voice to a throaty growl, she'd affected a Spanish accent.

Resting his right arm over the back of her seat, Samuel chuckled. "You are incredible."

Her mood changed like quicksilver. She went completely still, smile fading. "Am I, Samuel?"

"Are you what?"

Their gazes met, and a shock raced through Teresa. She was going to ruin it. Other than her calling Samuel by his name, nothing had changed between them since she'd begun filling in for Mrs. Harris. She and Samuel spent hours together, alone, yet she could not summon up enough nerve to seduce him.

"Nothing," she mumbled. She didn't wait for Samuel to get out and come around to open her door.

Dozens of eyes followed her until she opened the door to her home and disappeared inside. They whispered softly among one another before dispersing. Most were curious as to why this time the tall man hadn't gotten out of his car to assist Ramon and Silvia's daughter.

Samuel waited a full minute before he shifted into reverse and backed slowly away from Teresa's house. It was obvious he'd said something that had disturbed her, and by the time he maneuvered into an expansive garage, parking next to M.J.'s car, he still hadn't come up with an answer as to her abrupt change in attitude.

M.J. moved closer to her husband on the bed, pressing her chest to his back. "We have to do it again, *mi amor*."

They'd shared dinner secreted behind a high hedge in the boxwood garden as the sun began its descent. They lingered after streaks of blue and orange feathered the darkening sky and stars dotted the heavens. It had been their time together to "talk" without words.

"When?"

M.J. placed light kisses along the curve of his spine. "Saturday."

"It can't be Saturday." Samuel's voice was muffled in his pillow.

"Why not?"

"I may have to go to Puerto Rico Saturday."

M.J. sat up and switched on the table lamp on her side of the bed. "When were you going to tell me, Samuel?"

Rolling over on his back, he looked up at her. Her face was flushed with color. "I said I *may*, M.J."

"When will you know?"

"Probably tomorrow."

She folded her arms under her breasts. "How long do we have to be married before you'll trust me?"

"What makes you think I don't trust you?"

"Because you never talk to me about your other life. I can't plan anything because I never know if you're going to be around. Mrs. Harris, Everett, and Mr. Grady see you more than I do. Your secretary knows your every move while I have to guess as to whether I should wait dinner or even stay up for you."

Pushing into a sitting position, Samuel shook his head. "Why are you doing this, M.J.?"

"Doing what, Samuel?"

"Ruining a wonderful evening with your nagging."

With her eyes wide, her jaw dropped. "Oh! You think I'm nagging?"

"Yes."

"You think I shouldn't be upset? Well, I am, Samuel Cole. And as your wife I believe I'm entitled to more than three days' notice that you are planning . . . no, you *may* go away."

"Why are you carrying on like this?"

Her eyes filled with tears. "I want my husband, Sammy."

Reaching out, he pulled her into the circle of his arms. "You have me, baby."

"But for how long?"

"What the hell are you talking about?"

The sharp edge M.J. despised had crept into her husband's voice. Whenever they disagreed about something he was quite adept at making it look as if he were the wronged party.

Bracing the heels of her hands against his chest, she freed herself. "You're here, yet you're not here. When I get up in the morning you're gone. I go to bed, and you're still not home. Yet when I ask you about it you say you're working. Working doing what or with who?"

Samuel decided to ignore her innuendo that he'd lied to her. "Have you forgotten that my businesses aren't in West Palm? It would be easier if they were in Florida. My only means of communication is either by telephone, mail, or telegram. Then there is the matter of different time zones and the custom of siesta. Have you been away from Cuba so long that you've forgotten that no one conducts business during siesta?"

"No, I haven't."

"So, why are you complaining?"

"I don't see you enough. The children don't see you enough. And I'm tried of talking to you about it," she said through clenched teeth.

Samuel threw up a hand while shaking his head. "I will never understand you. You wanted to be married, and I married you. You wanted to live in the United States, and you're here. You complained that the house in Palm Grove Oval was too small, so I built you a new one. Not once did I complain when you said you had to have this icon or that heirloom piece."

Her eyes narrowed. "I used my money, Samuel."

"Let me remind you that the money your father gave you as a wedding gift wasn't enough to decorate this house. You ordered whatever you wanted, and I paid the bills. You wanted children, and I've given you those. What the hell else more do you want from me?"

"I want you, Samuel." The four words were pregnant with emotions running the gamut from frustration to fear.

The clock on the bedside table ticked off the seconds as they glared at each other. The uncomfortable hush swelled with each passing tick.

Samuel broke the silence when he said, "You have all the me I'm able to give you at this time."

M.J. felt her stomach roil, and she thought she was going to be sick. She suspected she was pregnant again, but wanted to wait until she was certain before telling Samuel.

Her menses was a little more than a week late, and if she was pregnant, then this confinement would be similar to when she carried Nancy. She tired easily and her breasts were very sensitive. Within minutes of waking and her feet touching the floor she'd found herself racing to the bathroom to involuntarily purge her stomach. She wanted this baby *and* she wanted her baby's father. It was something she refused to negotiate.

"That is not acceptable, Samuel."

He slid down to the mattress, turning his back to her. "I'm sorry about that, M.J., but that's the way it is, and will be for some time."

It wasn't what Samuel said that caused a shiver to rush over M.J.'s body, but how it was said. It held a tone of finality that would not permit her to come back at him. He was telling her she did not have to like it, but that she had to accept it.

Reaching up, she turned off the lamp, plunging the room into darkness. Moving closer to the edge of the bed, she withdrew from her husband, physically and emotionally.

Samuel picked up the telephone and placed a call to the manager of the Sun Trust branch where he had his business account. "I'd like to make a cash withdrawal," he said quietly.

"How much, Samuel?"

"Everything but twenty thousand."

A choking sound crackled through the earpiece. "That's a lot of money, Samuel. It's going to take about a week to get that much cash."

"I'm aware of that," Samuel countered, as he drew interlocking circles on a pad. "I'm going to be out of my office for a few days, so there's no rush. I'll call you when I get back."

"I can have it delivered to you."

"That's okay. I'll pick it up myself."

"No problem, Samuel. You can be assured I'll use the utmost discretion with your transaction."

Of course you will, you greedy bastard, Samuel mused. Whenever he withdrew large sums of cash he always gave the manager a cash gift for his *discretion* when he counted and bundled the bills in their corresponding denominations.

"I'm sure you will," he concurred. "I'll call you again next week." That said, he ended the call.

Withdrawing money from a bank paled in comparison to what lay ahead of him. Teresa had translated the cable from his Puerto Rican coffee broker that had been delivered to the office an hour ago. He had to go to the island country to inspect his coffee crop, and it was recommended that he bring his own translator. That wasn't possible because Everett was still in San Isidro.

With the exception of Jamaica, every business holding of ColeDiz International, Ltd., was in a Spanish-speaking country; the irony was that the head of the company was unable to speak or understand the language of the laborers who harvested the crops that afforded him great wealth.

A light tapping on his door caught Samuel's attention. Teresa stood in the doorway, clutching a folder. He stood up. "Yes."

"I just thought of something."

"What is it?"

"I can act as your translator when you go to Puerto Rico."

Samuel stared at her as if she had grown an extra head. "No, Teresa."

"Why not?" she asked, stepping into the office.

"It wouldn't be appropriate."

"Is it not appropriate for you to travel with Everett?"

"That's different," Samuel countered.

"Why? It is because he is a man, and I'm not?"

"Yes."

"You want to punish me because of my sex?"

Samuel felt as if he'd been chastised. The coffee plantation in Adjuntas was his first American investment, and he was determined to make it a success.

"No, Teresa, I'm not punishing you."

"Then let me accompany you to Puerto Rico," she said with a quiet firmness. "I will record everything, act as your translator, and if I take a typewriter I can type up the reports while we're there."

A tentative smile found its way across his face. He had to admire Teresa. She had an air of calm and self-confidence, which he liked. He'd rejected her offer because she was a woman, a very attractive woman.

"When did you come up with this plan?"

Cradling the file to her chest, Teresa wrinkled her nose. "When I translated the telegram to you." She closed the distance between them. "You need me and you know it."

Samuel shook his head slowly. "No, Teresa, I don't need you. ColeDiz needs you."

An unwelcome blush crept into her cheeks. "I stand corrected. ColeDiz needs me."

He saw the eagerness and a glint of amusement in her eyes. Teresa was right, ColeDiz did need her. "Okay, Teresa."

Her pale eyebrows lifted. "Okay?"

"You can come with me. I want . . ." His words trailed off as he reached into a pocket of his trousers. He slipped two twenties from his money clip and handed them to her. "I want you to take the afternoon off and buy yourself something to wear." He returned the clip to his pocket. "Let

25

The serpent beguiled me, and I ate.

—Genesis 4:13

The stabbing pain in the back of his right hand began with the loss of altitude as the aircraft made its descent; it banked to the left before leveling off in preparation for a landing at the San Juan, Puerto Rico Airfield. The Pan American Airways aircraft had taken off in West Palm Beach in bright sunlight and was scheduled to touch down in rain-soaked San Juan.

Reaching over, Samuel captured Teresa's left hand. Her sharp nails had left four distinct half-moon impressions on his skin. Her eyes, wide with fear, were fixed on the seat in front of her. It was her first flight, and it had become a harrowing experience when the plane flew into a violent thunderstorm.

He patted her shoulder. "It's over, Teresa."

Shifting in her seat, she stared at Samuel, her eyes brimming with tears. "I'm not flying back to Florida."

Leaning closer to her so the other passengers wouldn't overhear their conversation, he whispered, "We have to."

She blinked once. "You can go back to Florida on an airplane, but I'm not!"

A muscle in Samuel's jaw twitched as he clenched his teeth. "We'll talk about it later."

"There is no later, Samuel."

His fingers snaked around her upper arm, holding her in a firm grip.

your father know I'll be by later on tonight to explain why we'll be traveling together."

Teresa took the money as panic knotted her stomach muscles. She'd forgotten about her father. She had to formulate a plan that would convince Ramon Maldonado that private secretaries usually accompanied their bosses on business trips.

"Do not challenge me, Teresa. And in case you've forgotten why we are traveling, let me remind you that this is a business trip, not a holiday jaunt. This is the first and hopefully the last time that I'm going to remind you that as the head of ColeDiz International, Limited, I give the orders. Do you understand what I'm saying?"

Sudden anger fired Teresa's eyes, the green orbs paling and clawing his arrogant face like talons. How dare he talk to her as if she were an imbecile! Within seconds all of the love she had for him was replaced with a seething rage. At that moment if she'd had a knife she would've plunged it into his heart. She compressed her lips, her mouth thinning into a hard, straight line, and without warning a single tear found its way down her golden cheek.

Teresa closed her eyes, biting back the hot rush of tears welling up behind her lids. "Yes, Samuel. I understand quite well."

Samuel swore under his breath. He'd become his father, threatening and bullying those he sought to control. Pulling a handkerchief from his jacket's breast pocket, he touched it to Teresa's cheek.

"I'm sorry, Teresa."

He was sorry, and she couldn't stop crying. She had permitted the man she loved to see her as weak, helpless. Leaning to her left, she pressed her face to his shoulder.

He smelled and felt so good. Her heart softened as she melted into Samuel's strength. "Hold me. Please," she pleaded. Tears streamed down her face, tears of love and a joy so full that she feared blurting out what lay in her heart.

Samuel held her, his chin resting on the top of Teresa's head. He did not know what it was about the young woman in his arms that tugged at his heart in a way no other woman had done before. He saw her more as a girl than a woman. At nineteen, she was the same age M.J. had been when he'd first met her.

Convent-educated Marguerite-Josefina's involvement with political dissidents, university intellectuals, artists, and her worldly aunt's influence had afforded his wife a sophistication Teresa lacked.

Turning his head, he pressed a kiss to her fragrant hair. "It's all right, baby." The endearment had slipped out unbidden, but it was too late for Samuel to retract it.

Teresa felt a measure of relief that Samuel couldn't see her triumphant expression. Her plan to seduce Samuel had taken an about-face; he had become the seducer.

Samuel eased her back, blotting her face with his handkerchief. "Look at me," he said softly when she attempted to turn away.

Teresa covered her face with her hands. "No, Samuel. I must look horrible."

He pulled her hands down, his fingers tightening around her tiny wrists. "Let me be the judge of that." His mouth curved into an unconscious smile. "You give new meaning to the word *horrible*. You should cry more often because your eyes are breathtakingly beautiful. Right now they look like polished emeralds." Her spiky wet lashes framed a pair of eyes that had darkened to a deep, rich green.

She blushed to the roots of her silver-blond hair. "You need glasses."

"There's nothing wrong with my eyes. You are an incredibly beautiful woman." She averted her gaze, charming Samuel with the demure gesture.

The flirtatious repartee ended when the airplane's wheels touched the ground, bumping several times before the aircraft came to a stop.

Samuel turned away from Teresa to stare out the tiny window; the fat drops sliding down the window reminded him of the tears of the petite woman sitting beside him. Why had her tears disturbed him so much?

Conversations that had ended with the plane's descent started up again, the chatter escalating to excitable shrieks. Samuel unbuckled his belt, waiting for Teresa to do the same.

Forty minutes later they were seated in a taxi, the driver taking a route that led to Viejo San Juan.

Samuel listened intently to the conversation between Teresa and the hotel manager, understanding little of what was said. They'd checked into an establishment that was a fifteenth-century convent-turned-hotel.

He stared at her delicate profile, unable to tear his gaze away from her animated features when she leaned forward, laughing at something the man said to her. It was as if they'd shared a private joke, and for a brief moment Samuel wondered if he was the object of their humor.

I need to learn to speak Spanish. M.J. had offered to teach him, but it was as if he never could find the time to sit with her. He hadn't had the time because he was too engrossed in making money.

He recalled his wife's accusation about not seeing enough of him, but what she failed to understand was his obsession, an uncompromising desire for success, and at any cost.

He'd given his wife everything she'd asked for, and some things she hadn't. He had enough money not only to take care of his wife and their children for the rest of their lives, but also for his grand- and great-grandchildren. He couldn't claim the honor of being the first black millionaire, but he could, if he continued on the same course and at the same pace, become the first black billionaire.

Teresa turned to Samuel. Droplets of water shimmered in his close-cropped hair. She forced herself not to stare at him or he would see the longing in her gaze. "Our rooms are on the top floor, in the back overlooking the courtyard. We'll have to share the bathroom that connects the two rooms. Is that okay with you?"

"Sure."

At that point Samuel would willingly agree to any room. He was exhausted. He'd gone to bed after midnight, and woken three hours later to discover M.J. in the bathroom on her knees, retching.

His first impulse was to postpone the trip, but she convinced him that her upset stomach was the result of eating something that hadn't agreed with her. He'd carried her back to bed and stayed with her until Martin and Nancy came to the bedroom to see why their mother hadn't come down to the kitchen to eat breakfast with them.

"Are you all right, Samuel?" Teresa said when she noted his faraway expression.

"Yes," he answered much too quickly. "I'm just a little tired." He forced a smile. "This is one time I'm totally in favor of taking siesta."

A slender man with distinctive Indian features gathered their bags. Bending slightly, Samuel picked up the case containing Teresa's typewriter.

"Please tell the manager that if any messages come in for me, he's to bring them to my room."

Teresa translated for Samuel, and together they climbed the staircase, following the baggage handler.

Her room was small, clean, and functional. It contained a bed, straight-back chair, and chest of drawers. Walking to the window, she opened the shutters, stepping out onto a balcony with a wrought-iron railing. Resting her arms on the railing, she spied a marble fountain in a corner of the courtyard under the broad leaves of a banana tree. The smell of wet earth and the cloying scent of orchids growing in abandon filled the air.

She returned to the room and discovered Samuel in the doorway, arms folded over his broad chest. There was something about his relaxed stance that made her mouth go dry. He'd removed his jacket and tie, and had unfastened several buttons on his shirt. He gave her a slow smile.

"How do you like it?"

"It's nice."

Samuel lowered his arms. He agreed with Teresa. Their rooms were clean while the rear courtyard was available to hotel guests to take their meals or just relax in.

"I came to tell you that if you want you can use the bathroom first. Just knock on my door when you're finished." Turning, he left as quietly as he'd come.

Teresa crossed the room, closing and locking the door behind him. She opened her single piece of luggage and withdrew a dressing gown she'd purchased with the money Samuel had given her. Liliana had accompanied her on her shopping outing, and together they'd selected several shirtwaist dresses, frilly undergarments, and shoes. Before walking out of the store, she made a final purchase.

She opened the door separating their rooms. It wasn't a bathroom, but a water closet. There was no bathtub, just a toilet and a makeshift shower.

Her heart sank. She loathed showers. When Samuel instructed her to make reservations for two with private baths, she never thought to ask if the bathroom had a tub. How was she to know? After all, this was her first business trip, and the first time she'd traveled out of the United States.

Aware that Samuel was waiting to use the bathroom, Teresa picked up a small cotton drawstring bag containing her soap, toothbrush, and tooth powder. Fifteen minutes later, she knocked on the door to his room.

What she'd noticed when standing under the spray of the cool water was that there were no locks on the doors leading into the bathroom.

Samuel knocked on Teresa's door, listening intently for movement on the other side. He knocked again.

"Are you looking for me?"

Samuel turned around, and then went completely still. He'd recognized the voice, but the woman standing before him did not look like the one who'd come to Puerto Rico with him.

Teresa Maldonado had cut her hair.

He blew out a breath. "Wow!"

The smoldering flame in Samuel's eyes startled Teresa. She hadn't expected this reaction to her new hairstyle. "You like it?"

Attractive lines fanned out around his dark eyes when he smiled. "Yes. You look fabulous."

Her cheeks coloring under the heat of his gaze, Teresa touched the silver waves on the nape of her neck. "It's going to take some getting used to." Her heart thumped uncomfortably when Samuel continued to stare intently at her. "You wanted to see me about something?"

He blinked once, as if coming out of a trance. "Yes . . . yes, I did." Reaching inside his jacket, he handed her the cable from Rodolfo Hernandez, the plantation foreman.

Teresa translated, saying, "*Will send a car and driver Tuesday. Be ready at ten. Bring work clothes and boots.*"

Samuel pondered the cable. It was Saturday, which meant he and Teresa would have two full days in San Juan before they would be driven to the mountain region.

"I didn't bring work boots," Teresa said, handing the cable back to Samuel.

He saw her look of distress. "Don't worry. I'll buy you what you need. We'll go shopping Monday."

Her face brightened. "I like shopping."

Throwing back his head, Samuel laughed loudly. "What woman doesn't?"

Teresa couldn't control the heat stealing across her face and darkening her burnished gold skin. He was laughing at her. Opening her pocketbook, she grasped her key and put it into the lock. She had to get away from Samuel before she broke down.

She doubted whether he laughed at Marguerite when she told him she was going shopping. Not Her Highness, his beautiful Cuban princess. Her hands were shaking so much that the key wouldn't turn.

Moving closer, Samuel brushed Teresa's hand away and turned the key. The lock opened silently. "What's the matter?" he asked close to her ear.

Shivering from his warmth, his smell, and the wall of his chest against her back, Teresa swallowed the moan quivering in her throat. Didn't he know? Did he not know how much she loved him, wanted to lie with him?

"Nothing, Samuel," she lied softly.

"Are you sure?"

"Yes." The word came out in a whisper.

Curbing the urge to touch the pale strands falling in precise waves on the nape of her neck, Samuel closed his eyes for several seconds. He didn't know what it was about Teresa Maldonado that made him reckless, reckless enough to give in to the strong passion she elicited just by sharing the same space.

"Change into something pretty," he crooned close to her ear. "I'm taking you out. I'll meet you downstairs."

Nodding numbly, Teresa removed the key from the lock, pushed open the door, and closed it behind her without turning around. She hadn't realized she'd been holding her breath. Gasping, her breasts rising and falling as if she'd run a grueling race, she stumbled on trembling legs to the bed and fell across it.

Samuel rose to his feet, eyes wide, and stared at the vision in green seemingly floating toward him. If it hadn't been for the pale moonlit hair, he wouldn't have recognized Teresa Maldonado.

A dress the color of the Caribbean skimmed her body like liquid silk. The hue was the perfect complement for her complexion. Narrow straps held up a barely modest décolletage. His gaze moved down her body, caressing every inch of her bared flesh. He stared at the slender legs encased in silk and her feet in a pair of high-heel pumps. The shoes had added at least three inches to her diminutive height.

Teresa shuddered visibly under his slow, agonizing perusal. Men had stared at her, but none had ever undressed her with their eyes. Once she was back in control of her senses, she'd showered again, taking special care to pluck away any visible hair not covered by the dress. Having inherited her father's light hair color had its advantages. A light dusting of face powder, a few strokes of a gray eyebrow pencil, black mascara applied only to the tips of her lashes, and a coat of dark red lipstick completed her makeup application. She and Liliana had experimented over and over applying makeup until they achieved what they thought were perfect results. She knew not to use dark colors on her eyes because they made her look possessed.

Smiling, she curtsied gracefully. "Pretty enough?"

Samuel took her left hand, raised it to his mouth, and kissed the back of it. "You are incredible."

Teresa lost count of the number of times he'd said she was incredible, and she wanted to ask him incredible how. Was he drawn to her because he thought her pretty, smart, or because she was a woman? She prayed it was the latter.

Lowering her lashes, she smiled. "Thank you, Samuel."

Tightening his grip on her hand, Samuel tucked it into the bend of his elbow over the jacket of his custom-tailored white linen suit. "You're welcome, Teresa." He lifted his eyebrows. "Are you ready?"

She met his mysterious, dark eyes. "Where are we going?"

Running a forefinger down the length of her delicate nose, he shook his head. "No guesses. You'll find out when we get there."

Teresa tried extracting her hand from his firm grip. "Wait a minute, Samuel Cole. How did you make arrangements to go somewhere when you admit to not speaking Spanish?"

Samuel smiled and angled his head. "I told you I can't carry on an in-depth conversation, but I do know enough to ask where's a good place to eat." Teresa gave him a look that said she didn't believe him. "We're going to El Café Americano. It's a place not far from here, and a lot of Americans from the States congregate there. It's also a popular hangout for sailors on shore leave. Does that satisfy your curiosity?"

She flashed a sensual moue. "A little."

"What else are you curious about, *Chica?*"

A slight frown furrowed Teresa's smooth forehead. Was he calling her *Chica* because he thought of her as a little girl, or was it an endearment? Her frown faded as quickly as it'd appeared. She did not want to ruin her time with Samuel by questioning and analyzing everything he did or said.

"*Nada, Papi,*" she teased.

It was Samuel's turn to frown. "I'm not old enough to be your father."

Teresa pressed her body to his. Tilting her chin, she gave him a long, penetrating stare. "I know that. I used it as a *como se dice*, a *sweet nothing.*"

"Like *Chica?*"

"*Sí, Papi.*"

"*Que bueno,*" Samuel countered, grinning from ear to ear.

* * *

El Café Americano was crowded with Americans from the mainland, and those who'd made the island their home since Congress passed the Jones Act in 1917, making Puerto Rico a U.S. territory and its inhabitants U.S. citizens.

Samuel wound an arm around Teresa's waist, holding her close to his side in an attempt to protect her from the crush of bodies waiting to be seated inside the popular dining establishment. The sound of a live band playing a Latin rhythm competed with loud voices speaking English and Spanish.

The promulgation of the Volstead Act extended to the island, but alcohol flowed as freely as water. It was obvious the owners of the establishment had paid off federal agents to look the other way.

"Do you want something to drink?" he whispered, his warm, moist breath sweeping over Teresa's ear.

She peered at the glasses of those waiting to be seated, filled with a liquid that looked like milk. The well-dressed men were boisterous, laughing loudly while telling ribald jokes. After a few sips of the beverage, their attractive female companions laughed and flirted shamelessly. There was no doubt they were feeling very good.

"Yes." She'd said yes when she'd never drunk anything alcoholic in her life, and because she did not want Samuel to see her as a gauche ingénue. She'd cut her hair to appear older and sophisticated.

Samuel patted her back. "Don't run away."

Teresa watched Samuel weave his way through the throng. What did he mean, *don't run away*? She could not imagine running away from Samuel—not now, not ever.

Samuel sat at a small, round table with Teresa, mesmerized by her transformation. The sleek hairdo had replaced the matronly bun, and the silk dress that teased more than covered had taken the place of her perpetual white blouse and shapeless shirt. The effects of the *coquito*, a tropical eggnog, was evident by her lowered lids, parted lips, and high color in her cheeks.

He knew if he did not get her up, she was going to fall asleep. Rising, he came around the table and eased her to her feet. "Let's go, *Chica*."

"No, Samuel. We can't go yet."

"Why not?"

Teresa pressed her breasts to his chest, eliciting a soft gasp from him. "The band is wonderful, and we haven't danced together."

Everything and everyone at the restaurant was wonderful: the friendly staff and patrons, the food, the music, and a "moonshine" rum the locals called *canita*, or *mample*. They'd shared a platter of *carne empanadas, lechon asado, tostones de platano*, and a stuffed avocado salad.

Samuel stared down at the woman smiling up at him, lashes feathering over the top of her high cheekbones. His gaze, soft as a caress, followed the outline of her full, lush mouth, the short, straight nose, and the arching sweep of her tawny eyebrows.

"Do you really want to dance—here?"

Teresa sobered immediately. She was under the influence of the delicious rum-laced eggnog but not enough to be intoxicated. Leaning closer, her breasts flattening against his chest, she wound her arms around his waist inside his jacket. Samuel's body heat burned her palms through his shirt. He was on fire!

"Where do you want to dance, *Papi*?" she crooned, her voice lowering to a purr.

Aware that he'd become a willing participant in a web of seduction in which even if there had been a way to escape, he did not want to.

Lowering his head, he brushed his mouth over hers. "Back at the hotel."

Rising on tiptoe, Teresa opened her mouth, kissing Samuel in a way she'd practiced countless times whenever she pressed her lips to the mirror in her bedroom. She'd perfected an open-and-closed-mouth kiss until she could perform the action at will.

Samuel jerked as if he'd been burned with a red-hot poker. His eyes alone betrayed his ardor. Not taking his gaze off Teresa, he reached into his pocket and dropped a bill on the table.

He rested a hand in the small of her back as a vaguely sensuous light passed between them. She wanted him as much as he wanted her.

"Let's go, *Chica*."

26

I have come to believe . . . that there are some people—men and women alike—who should not be married at all.

—Marya Mannes

Samuel led Teresa into the hotel, then swung her into the circle of his arms, taking the stairs two at a time. He shifted her slight weight long enough to unlock the door to his room. Using his shoulder, he pushed it open, stepped inside, then kicked it closed. Light from the courtyard inched through the louvers on the shuttered windows, providing enough illumination for him to discern the bed.

He placed Teresa on the mattress, his body following hers down. Her heat, her sweet musky scent, the velvety feel of her tiny, compact body sucked him into a vortex of desire and longing he was powerless to resist.

Teresa had prayed for this moment and now that it was happening she couldn't believe it. She was in Samuel Cole's bed, in his embrace, his hardness pressing against her middle, and she was paralyzed with wonder and fear.

She'd rehearsed seducing him, learned to bring herself pleasure, practiced kissing techniques all within the privacy of her bedroom, but she wasn't back in the small hot house in a poor West Palm Beach neighborhood. She was in an Old San Juan hotel room with the man with whom she'd fallen in love.

They were so close, breaths mingling, flesh touching. Shyly, tentatively, she kissed Samuel's smooth jaw, smiling. "You smell wonderful."

He chuckled, the sound rumbling from his chest like far-off thunder. "So do you, *Chica.* I love the way you smell, the way you feel, and the way you kiss." Cradling her face between his palms, he moved his mouth over hers, devouring its softness. The kiss deepened, his tongue parting her lips.

Teresa gasped, shocked at the roughness of the tongue filling up her mouth, but her shock was short-lived, as it moved in and out in a slow hypnotic cadence that had her close to fainting away.

Blood coursed through her veins like hot oil.

Her body vibrated like liquid fire.

Her breathing grew shallow when his fingers feathered up her legs and thighs, sending waves of delight washing over her. A fog of desire clouded her as the harsh uneven rhythm of her own breathing resounded loudly inside her head.

"Do you want me, *Chica*?"

Teresa closed her yes. His query had penetrated the erotic haze. "*Sí, Papi*," she whispered. "I want you so much."

Samuel slowly and methodically undressed Teresa: shoes, garters, dress, stockings, slip, and panties, then himself. She lay before him, her smooth khaki-brown skin shimmering in a ribbon of remaining daylight.

Moving over her, he took her face, held it gently, and showered kisses around her lips, along her jaw, down the column of her neck. He released her face, lowered his head, and suckled her breasts, licking and biting gently on the nipples. Her gasps became hiccupping sounds as he journeyed lower; his tongue mapped a path over her flat belly, and still lower.

Positioning his thumbs against the blond down, he spread the folds to her vagina and pushed his face against the moist, pulsing flesh. He alternated licking and rolling the swollen nodule between his teeth.

Teresa moaned, sobbed, and screamed at him not to stop. He couldn't stop even if he'd wanted to. The woman between whose legs he lay had bewitched him. It took only a single glance and he'd found himself sucked into and drowning in a morass of lust that made him crave her when he didn't want to.

Everything he'd professed when sleeping with a woman was forgotten as he guided his blood-engorged penis into her vagina.

Gasps echoed in the stillness of the room—his and Teresa's. She was tight, tighter than any woman he'd slept with. He thrust into her, eliciting another soft gasp from Teresa. Sweat poured off his face and body and onto her trembling breasts.

"I can't!"

Teresa's fingers tightened around his wrists, her sharp fingernails biting into the tender flesh. "*Sí, se puede*. Yes, you can," she translated. "You must, Samuel. You can't leave me like this. Wanting you so much that my heart hurts."

Supporting his weight on his arms, Samuel kissed her tenderly. "I want you, too," he confessed truthfully. "But I don't want to hurt you."

"You won't."

"What if I tear you?"

"It will heal, *Papi.*"

"*Chica*—"

Teresa cut off his words with a kiss that belied her sexual inexperience. Her tongue plunged into Samuel's mouth, mimicking his hardness sliding in and out of her. She knew she'd achieved her intent when he groaned loudly. Growing bolder, she moved her hands down his moist back and cupped his firm hips.

The hardness poised at the entrance to her femininity swelled, stretching her virginal flesh. And with one powerful thrust of his hips, Samuel tore through the barrier that had kept him from full possession of what had become his latest obsession.

A bloodcurdling scream exploded from the back of Teresa's throat, only to be swallowed up by Samuel when he covered her mouth with his at the precise moment he ripped her hymen asunder.

He went completely still, savoring the moment when he and Teresa had become one. "I'm sorry I hurt you," he crooned near her ear. "I just wish it could've been easier, but you are so small, baby."

Tears leaked from under her tightly closed eyes and streamed into her hair. "Maybe I'm not that small. Maybe it is because you are so big."

Choking sounds came from his throat. Within seconds Teresa had reduced erudite Samuel Cole to a bumbling, inexperienced boy. He wanted to ask her how many penises she had seen, but he didn't want to talk.

Pulling back, he tested how far he had to go before thrusting into her newly opened flesh. Tucking her curves neatly into his own contours, he set a slow, steady rhythm.

Love flowed in Teresa like warm honey, the pleasure pure and explosive. She alternated trailing her fingers up and down her lover's back with tunneling them through the hair on his chest. She loved his body; she loved him!

The tempo changed, slowing, then quickening, then slowing down again. Raw sensuousness carried her to heights of passion she could never have imagined. The comforting weight bearing down on her, the hardness sliding in and out of her body, and the combined scent of their bodies and sexual desire hurtled Teresa to a place where she'd never been before.

She couldn't control her outcry of erotic pleasure or disguise her body's reaction to Samuel's hardness, which seemingly had swelled to even larger proportions. Anchoring her arms under his shoulders, she surrendered, shaking and weeping uncontrollably with the joy that hurtled her beyond herself and reality.

Pulling out before he ejaculated, Samuel reversed their position, and they lay together, limbs entwined, motionless, and waiting for their pulses to resume a normal rhythm.

Teresa, her cheek resting over his heart, fell asleep.

However, sleep wasn't as kind to Samuel. A heaviness settled in the pit of his stomach as if he'd swallowed a stone. It wasn't the first time he'd slept with a woman since he'd married M.J., but it *was* the first time he hadn't used a condom!

"Wake up, *Chica*."

Teresa rolled over onto her belly. "Go away."

Leaning over, Samuel kissed her shoulder. "You can either stay here or get up and go shopping with me in St. Thomas."

Turning over quickly, she stared up at him. He was naked! It was torture for her not to look below his waist. She sat up, and the sheet covering her breasts slipped to her belly.

"When are we leaving?"

Samuel stared at Teresa, complete surprise on his face. The full impact of her beauty made his heart slam against his ribs. The bright sunlight coming in through the window bathed her nude body in gold: hair, face, and breasts. Something in her eyes, darkening to a lush, verdant green, invited him to postpone his trip and spend the day in bed with her. He knew it would be days before they would make love again, because he wanted to wait for her tender flesh to heal.

When he'd awakened earlier and left the bed to use the bathroom the bloodstained sheet was blatant evidence that he'd taken her innocence. He was her boss, she his employee, he was over thirty, she nineteen, and they'd become lovers.

Smiling, Samuel scooped her off the bed. "Now. Come, let's take a shower together."

Holding on to his neck, Teresa rested her head on his shoulder. "I've never taken a shower with anyone."

"Then we must make certain to make your first time a memorable one."

Lifting her head, she gave him a direct stare. "Like last night?"

Samuel's gaze caressed the white-gold waves falling around her delicate jaw, the full lush mouth that was made for kissing, and the glowing green eyes that changed color depending on her mood.

"Last night was very, very special. I'll never forget it."

"Neither will I," she concurred.

For Teresa, sharing a shower with Samuel was like making love again. He soaped her body, his fingers skimming the area between her legs, then handed her the soap so she would do the same with him.

"Where do I begin?"

Samuel turned, presenting her with his back. "Start with the back, then work your away around to the front."

"But you started with my front," she argued softly.

Moving closer, he pulled her against him. "That's because your front is so delectable. He cupped a firm breast. "You have perfect breasts." His hand moved between her legs. "And the sweetest little pussy." His hand inched around her hips. "And your ass isn't doing too badly either."

Heat singed Teresa's face. "Samuel!"

He lifted his eyebrows. "What?"

"How can you say such things?"

"What things?"

Rising on tiptoe, she whispered, "Pussy."

Grinning, Samuel shook his head. She was so sexy, yet so innocent. "I could've said twat."

"Samuel!"

"Wash my back, *Chica*, before the water is completely cold."

She complied, soaping a cloth and drawing it over his shoulders, down his straight spine, and over his buttocks. Samuel Cole was beautifully proportioned for a man: broad shoulders, slim waist, hips, and long, powerfully built legs. Moving around him, she soaped his neck, chest, belly, then moved down to his legs and feet.

"You missed a spot, Teresa."

She stared up at Samuel staring down at her. She'd deliberately ignored *that* part of his body that had given her so much gratification.

"You can wash it yourself."

"No. I want you to wash it."

Teresa backed away from him. She'd avoided looking at his penis, but now he wanted her to touch it. "I can't, Samuel."

Taking her hand, he guided it to his belly. "Start with the pubic hair, then gently lift the testicles and soap them like this."

She followed his instructions, her eyes widening when his penis moved under her fingers. Her mouth formed a perfect O as she watched it grow bigger.

Samuel let go of her hand and cradled her face. Water darkened her hair to a tawny gold and spiked her lashes. "See the control you have over me? One look, a mere touch, and I get hard."

"Has it always been that way, *Papi*?"

"Lately it has," he answered truthfully.

"I'm glad."

"So am I."

Taking the cloth from Teresa, Samuel finished washing himself, watching her as she stared at his erection. It wasn't until he stepped out of the shower to dry himself that it finally went down.

* * *

Teresa stood beside Samuel as he examined a tray filled with pearls strung on silk cords. There were tiny knots between each pearl and some graduated in size, while others were perfectly matched. The colors ranged from alabaster to pink, gold, to South Sea gray and Tahitian black.

"Which ones do you like?" Samuel asked, staring at her profile.

"They're all beautiful."

He angled his head and lifted an eyebrow. "Do you have a preference?"

She liked the gold-hued, but liked the pink better. "The pink."

Samuel frowned at the jeweler hovering over them like a vulture perched on a branch waiting for carrion. The man with the thick Dutch accent was an expert gemologist. He could closely identify the carat weight, color, and clarity of any gem without his loupe.

Grinning, he picked a strand of perfectly matched pink-hued pearls off the velvet tray. "Your lady has good taste and a good eye," he said to Samuel.

Something told Hans Vanderpool that the stunning blond-haired woman with Samuel Cole wasn't his wife, but his mistress. But who was he to be judgmental? The American had already selected an exquisitely carved Italian-made cameo gold bracelet with a variety of colored stones, a pair of tiny diamond earrings, and a small crucifix and chain. These were no doubt for his wife and children.

Samuel took the strand from Mr. Vanderpool and looped it around Teresa's neck. His gaze met hers in the mirror the jeweler had placed on the counter in front of her. The pink baubles against her tawny skin took on a deeper rosy hue as if warmed by her body's heat.

"How large are they?" Samuel asked.

"Eleven millimeters."

"All of them?"

"Yes, sir."

Samuel nodded. "Where are your clasps?"

Smiling and stroking his goatee, Hans mumbled a silent prayer. Even if he did not make another sale, he would count the day as a very profitable one. Mr. Cole hadn't bothered to ask the price for the pearls.

"Would you like a simple gold one or one with stones?"

Samuel removed the pearls from Teresa's neck, handing them to Hans. They were still warm from her body. His hands rested casually on her shoulders, causing a slight shiver to shudder through her.

"What type of stones?"

"Rubies, pearls, sapphires, emeralds, and diamonds."

"Show me them all."

Teresa suffered Samuel's closeness as he bent over her shoulder looking at clasps for the pearl necklace. She felt intoxicated by his clean and masculine scent. She wanted him, oh how she wanted him, but knew that wasn't possible for several more days. They would share a bed, but not their bodies until the tenderness between her legs was gone. Eyes wide, she watched Samuel point to an elaborate gold knot encrusted with brilliant blue-white diamonds.

"I want this one. Now if you can find a pair of matching earrings we can conclude our business."

Samuel said it with a quiet finality; it was a tone of authority that was familiar to anyone who'd done business with the owner of ColeDiz International, Ltd.

Hans searched the showcase for a pair of pearl earrings, and when he found them he handed them, the string of pearls, and the clasp to a younger version of himself. He said something in Dutch, and the young boy who appeared to be about sixteen sat down at a table in a corner of the small shop and positioned a loupe over one eye.

Taking Teresa's hand, Samuel gently squeezed her fingers. "Why don't you pick out something for your mother while I settle the bill with Mr. VanderPool?"

"I . . . I didn't bring any money," she whispered.

Samuel frowned at her. "Don't embarrass me, *Chica*. Pick out something. And make certain it's nice."

She didn't know why, but she despised the woman who claimed Samuel as her husband and was also the mother of his children. Not only was she incredibly beautiful, but she was also a Diaz, heir to El Supremo Cigars. Her father died and left her millions, whereas if Ramon Maldonado died he'd leave his family *nada*! They didn't own the house they lived in.

Ramon fled Cuba with his young wife after word got to the local police that he was involved in a secret organization opposed to the ruling government. He'd escaped with only the clothes on his back and enough money to pay the passage for two to the United States.

Ramon and Silvia made it to West Palm Beach where they worked clearing land for the planting of fruit trees, cooked and cleaned houses for those too lazy to do it themselves. Their life improved once they were hired to work in a local cotton mill. Silvia hemmed towels, sheets, and pillowcases, while Ramon worked in the shipping department. The work was tedious, but together they earned enough to pay rent, put food on the table, and clothe their children.

She forgot about Marguerite and her life of privilege when she spied a pair of cameo earrings suspended from gold wires. They were perfect for Silvia Maldonado.

Teresa turned and found Samuel staring at her. They shared a smile. She beckoned to him. "I found what I want." If her father worked all of his life he'd never be able to give his wife something so exquisite.

Samuel directed his gaze where Teresa pointed. The earrings were ovals encircled with sparkling diamonds on a delicate gold braid. He motioned to Hans to remove the earrings from the case.

Teresa felt her eyes welling with tears. "I'm going outside," she whispered.

Samuel gave her a quizzical look. "Are you all right?"

She nodded. "I have something in my eye." Walking out of the shop and into the bright sunlight, she gave in to her emotions and cried. When Samuel joined her, she was back in control.

Holding his purchases in one hand, he reached for hers. "Are you hungry?" They'd left San Juan without eating because they hadn't wanted to miss the boat.

Leaning into him, Teresa pressed her face to his chest. "I'm starved."

Lowering his head, Samuel dropped a kiss on her fragrant hair. "Me too."

Samuel and Teresa returned to Puerto Rico exhausted and tanned. Both fell asleep during the short drive from the harbor to their hotel. They shared a shower, this one very different from their first one.

Teresa did not remember Samuel blotting the moisture from her body or carrying her to his bed, because she had fallen asleep before her head touched his pillow.

"Ask him how many acres were lost," Samuel said to Teresa.

She translated, then listened to Rodolfo Hernandez's response. "At least two hundred," she said.

Samuel's eyes narrowed under the shade of his Panama hat as he peered out at what had been a thriving coffee plantation. Heavy rainfall had caused mud slides, sending plants, trees, and houses sliding down the mountain into the valleys.

"Can you plant somewhere else?" he asked Rodolfo.

"There is some land in the Yauco region that is good for coffee," Teresa said. "He says Yauco is southwest of here, not far from Lares." She stopped, listening to Rodolfo, who tended to speak very fast. "The mountain location is ideal because the temperate climate offers a longer maturation period."

"What's the time frame?"

"October to February."

Samuel nodded, smiling. October was toward the end of the hurricane season. "Good. What else?"

"The clay-based soil is good for growing coffee. We employ a system of picking only ripe beans, which requires multiple passes through the coffee trees."

Samuel nodded again. "What's your time frame for processing?"

"Once the beans are picked, they are drum-washed for forty-eight hours. But then we run on a husk-until-shipment basis. The beans are de-husked only after an order has been placed. We do this to guarantee maximum freshness."

Closing his eyes, Samuel quickly figured the yield. He opened his eyes and stared at the tall, brown-skinned man with coal-black hair and eyes. "I want you to negotiate purchasing the land in Lares. And I don't want maximum production to exceed one thousand hundred-pound bags for the next three years."

Rodolfo's eyes bulged from their sockets. "That's a lot less than what we would've harvested if not for the hurricane."

Crossing his arms over his chest, Samuel smiled at Teresa. "Tell him that I'm basing my decision on supply and demand. A coffee of this qual-ity will bring a higher price if we don't flood the market. It's not Jamaica Blue Mountain, which is the world's best coffee, but very close to it."

"What about the workers?"

"What about them?" Samuel asked. "Right now none of them are working. Rehire those whom you believe are the best, and give the others two weeks' pay."

Rodolfo took off his battered straw hat, holding it over his heart. "These are poor peasants, Mr. Cole. If you give them an extra week's pay I'm certain God will bless you abundantly."

Shifting slightly, so Rodolfo couldn't see his expression, Samuel ex-haled. He couldn't believe his agent was trying to fleece him. He turned back, his expression impassive. "Miss Maldonado, please tell Senor Hernandez that I agree to paying the laid-off workers three weeks' pay. But if I find out that they did not get what they're supposed to get, then I'm coming back and blowing his brains out. Tell him, Teresa," he urged when she looked at him if as if he'd lost his mind.

"Samuel, no," she whispered.

"Tell him, or I will, Miss Maldonado." The threat was issued between clenched teeth.

Teresa laced her fingers together to hide their trembling. She cleared her throat and repeated what Samuel told her to say. She felt sorry for the agent, who stared down at the toes of his muddy boots.

"Let him know we're ready to go back to San Juan."

Samuel stared out the car window rather than look at the young woman sitting beside him in a pair of trousers, work boots, and an over-size shirt. They were halfway to San Juan, and he still couldn't bring him-self to talk to her. He had to wait until his temper cooled. Closing his eyes, he succumbed to the rolling motion. He forgot why he'd come to Puerto Rico, but not the woman whom he'd given a part of himself that he'd withheld from everyone—including his wife.

* * *

Samuel lounged in the chair, lids lowered, as he watched Teresa pace back and forth. "Sit down."

She stopped, hands on hips, glaring at him. "Oh. The master speaks."

"Stop it, Teresa!"

"Stop what, Samuel?"

"Being cynical with me."

She threw up a hand. "How do you expect me to be? It's been more than two hours since you've said anything to me."

Pushing off the chair, he closed the distance between them. "If I'd said anything it would've been to fire you." He stood over her like an avenging angel. "You challenged me in front of someone whom I pay a salary."

"He couldn't understand me."

"Oh, couldn't he, Teresa? Did you see his face when I said I'd personally put a bullet through his skull? He reacted even before you translated. He may feel uncomfortable speaking the language, but the man understands English.

"I will not tolerate anyone cheating me, *Chica*. I'd rather give away every penny I have than have someone run a con on me. That's the reason why Everett's in Costa Rica." Samuel ran the back of his hand over her cheek. "I'll forgive you this time, but the—"

Rising on tiptoe, Teresa pressed her lips to his, stopping his threat. Her tongue curled around his, diffusing his anger. "I'm sorry, Samuel. There won't be a next time."

Bending slightly, Samuel picked her up. "Promise?"

She nodded. "*Promesa*."

He kissed the end of her nose. "This is our last night in Puerto Rico. What do you want to do?"

Teresa rested her head on his shoulder. "Stay here."

"Don't you want to eat something?"

"Yes," she crooned. "We can order something and eat in the courtyard. Then we can come back and . . ."

"And do what, *Chica*?"

She blushed. "You know, Samuel."

"No, I don't," he countered, teasing her. "Tell me what it is you want to do."

"Have sex," Teresa whispered.

"Have sex or make love?"

"Make love."

Samuel lifted his eyebrows. "Are you sure you're okay?"

"Very sure."

He gave her a direct stare. "From now on I'm going to use a condom with you. I don't want to get you pregnant."

"Condom?" she asked, pretending ignorance.

Teresa knew about condoms, sperm, semen, ejaculation, conception, and contraception. She suspected Samuel would use condoms when sleeping with her, but she was ready for him.

"It's a sheath that covers the penis made from the lining of sheep intestines. It stops semen from getting into the vagina, thereby preventing pregnancy."

Tilting her head back, she smiled up at Samuel. "Will you show me how you put it on?"

"Once you learn, you can put it on all the time." He kissed her again. "Even though I like seeing you in trousers, I think you better change. And I'd like you to wear these."

Samuel grasped her hand, leading her over to the table. Reaching inside a large straw bag filled with souvenirs, he took out two of the jewelry purchases he'd made in St. Thomas and handed them to her.

Teresa bit down on her lower lip. "What are you giving me?"

"Open them and find out."

Her hands shook uncontrollably as she opened the top on the flat rectangular box first. "*Madre de Dios!*" Samuel had had her select her own gift. He'd given her the spectacular strand of pearls and matching earrings. Anchoring her arms under his shoulders, she kissed him.

Samuel lifted her off her feet, returning the kiss with a passion he hadn't thought possible. He'd weakened, succumbing to her sensual spell.

27

Lying is an occupation used by all who mean to rise.

—Laetitia Pilkington

Samuel stepped into the entryway and was met with the sound of piano playing. He placed his luggage on a low bench before moving quietly into the living room. A tender smile softened his face. M.J. sat at the piano, her fingers moving fluidly over the keys. The sapphire and diamond hair clip he'd given her for their first anniversary sparkled under the light of a massive overhead chandelier.

On the floor in front of the piano lay Nancy, sucking her thumb, and Martin, who lay on his back staring up at the massive chandelier suspended from the thirty-foot ceiling. Martin saw him, his large eyes widening in shock. Samuel placed a finger over his mouth, motioning for him not to say anything. Winking at his son, he crept silently toward M.J., sweeping her off the piano bench.

M.J. let out a shriek, startling Nancy, who scrambled off the rug. "Sammy!"

"Daddy!" Nancy squealed, lifting her arms for him to pick her up.

Smiling broadly, Samuel kissed his wife. Setting her on her feet, he picked up Nancy, tossing her high in the air. She squealed and giggled uncontrollably. He beckoned Martin to come closer. Bending slightly, he scooped him up with his free arm.

He pressed a kiss to Martin's forehead, then repeated the gesture with Nancy. Two sets of jet-black eyes stared at him. "Have you been behaving?"

"Yes, Daddy," the children chorused.

Looking over their head, Samuel met M.J.'s amused gaze. Whenever he went away he missed her, but missed his children more. A clock on a fireplace mantel chimed the half hour. It was 9:30.

"You cupcakes are up past your bedtime."

"Mother said we could stay up to listen to her play piano," Martin said, as he looked at M.J. to confirm their staying up beyond eight.

Nancy clapped her hands above her head. "Yes, she did."

Catching Nancy's tiny earlobe between his lips, Samuel tugged at it. "When did you become such a chatterbox?"

"She should be talking, Samuel. After all, she's two."

Nancy held up two fingers. "I two, Daddy."

He lifted his eyebrows, feigning surprise. "Wow. You're really a big girl. Can you tell me how old your brother is?"

Leaning forward, Nancy pointed to Martin. "Marwin is four." She put up four fingers.

Martin put both arms around his father's neck. "She can't say Martin," he whispered close to Samuel's ear.

Samuel winked at his son. "That's okay," he whispered back. "She's still a baby."

M.J. crossed her arms under her breasts, wondering how Samuel was going to react when she told him what she'd suspected for some time. She was pregnant again.

"Please take them upstairs, Samuel. They're going to have to take a bath before getting into bed."

"I'll take care of them, M.J."

"Are you sure?"

Samuel nodded. "Yes."

She smiled. "If that's the case, then I'm going to bed."

He watched M.J. as she made her way toward the staircase, his gaze lingering on her slender figure. She'd become the perfect wife *and* the perfect mother. Shifting his children to a more comfortable position, he climbed the staircase to the second story.

Samuel washed Nancy and assisted her in brushing her teeth before he slipped a nightgown over her head. She was asleep before her head touched the pillow in her crib. He stood, staring down at her delicate features. She was no longer wearing diapers. It was time he bought her a bed. He dimmed a lamp, closed the bedroom door slightly, and walked down the hall to Martin's room.

His son had undressed himself and stood on a stool at the basin brushing his teeth. A smile tilted the corners of Samuel's mouth upward when he saw him fill a cup with water and rinse his mouth, followed by a loud cough.

Samuel filled the tub with water, testing the temperature. He anchored his arms under the boy's shoulders and lowered him into the water.

"Do you want me to wash you, or can you wash yourself?"

Martin's large dark eyes crinkled as he smiled. "Mother lets me wash myself."

Samuel nodded, backing up and sitting on a padded stool several feet from the claw-foot tub. "I'm going to sit here and supervise you. Don't forget your neck or the back of your ears."

Martin rolled his eyes upward. "You sound like Mother."

"That's because mothers and fathers aren't that different."

"Why do you go away and Mother stays home?"

The child's question caught Samuel off guard. Had Martin overheard them arguing about his business trips? "I go away because I have to make money to take care of you, Nancy, and your mother. It also takes a lot of money to keep this house nice."

"When can I go away with you, Daddy?"

Leaning forward, he smiled at Martin staring up at him with an expectant look on his face. "You really want to travel with me?"

"Yes."

A feeling of pride filled Samuel's chest. His relationship with his son was so different from the one he'd had with his father. He never had to raise his voice or his hand to him. And he prayed he never would.

"When you're thirteen I'll take you with me."

Martin nodded and rubbed his chest with a soap-filled cloth. He washed his body the way his mother had taught him. Rising to his feet, he extended his arms for his father to help him from the bathtub.

Ten minutes later he lay in bed, smiling up at Samuel. "Good night, Daddy."

Leaning over, Samuel kissed him on both cheeks. "Good night, son." Reaching over he turned off the bedside lamp, plunging the room into darkness.

He used one of the guest bedrooms to shower, because if M.J. was asleep, then he didn't want to wake her. There was something to be said for building a house with four-bedroom suites, each with an adjoining bath, sitting, and dressing room.

Samuel hadn't lied to his son. His expenses for maintaining this house was twice what it'd been for the one in Palm Grove Oval. Electric expenses had tripled, and instead of paying Bessie to clean the house M.J. had added the services of a full-time cook, a laundress, and a landscaping crew for her many gardens. He had to leave the country to oversee his investments. If not, then he would be left penniless.

Securing a towel around his hips, he walked out of the bedroom and into his own. M.J. was in bed, a mound of pillows supporting her back. He smiled. She'd waited up for him.

Sweeping back the sheet, she smiled. "Come, *mi amor.*"

Samuel undid the towel, left it on the floor next to the bed, and slipped in beside her. Wrapping his arms around his wife, he pulled her to lie atop him. Her sweet scent wafted in his nostrils as he nuzzled her neck.

"I've missed you."

She kissed his throat. "Not as much as I've missed you." Resting her chin on his breastbone, she stared down at him. "I have something to tell you."

There was something in her voice that made Samuel's heart race. "What is it?"

"We're going to have another baby."

He froze and nothing moved. Not even his eyes. "Are you sure?"

She nodded. "Yes. The doctor called and told me this afternoon."

"When are you due?"

"The middle of February."

Closing his eyes, he kissed her hair. Something unspoken told him that M.J. had to know she was pregnant before he left for Puerto Rico. The time he found her throwing up she'd blamed it on something she'd eaten when she knew it was morning sickness.

"How are you feeling?"

"Okay."

"Just okay, baby?"

"Not really. The doctor cautioned me about heavy lifting."

"What else, M.J.?"

She closed her eyes, not wanting to see his tight expression. "We can't have sexual intercourse for at least three months."

Samuel's breathing deepened. "What's wrong, baby?" He didn't care if she could hear the fear in his voice.

"Nothing, Sammy."

Reversing their position, he supported his weight on his arms. "You can't lift, we can't make love, and you tell me there's nothing wrong?"

M.J. knew she couldn't continue to conceal her doctor's concern for this confinement. "I've been bleeding."

"Bleeding!"

"It's more like spotting. It happens if I'm on my feet for long periods of time, or after I pick up Nancy."

"You're not to pick up anything heavier than a fork, Marguerite-Josefina. I'm going to hire someone to take care of the children when I'm not here. I'll change my hours and come home early enough to bathe the kids and put them to bed."

"No, Sammy! I will not have another woman raise my children."

Running his fingers through her loosely braided hair, Samuel kissed the end of her nose. "She's not going to raise them. She's just going to help you out."

M.J. shook her head. "No, Samuel. I will not have a strange woman telling my children what they can and cannot do."

Samuel brushed a kiss over her mouth. "Please be reasonable, M.J. Do you want this baby?"

"Of course I do."

"Then let me help you out."

"No strange woman, Samuel."

"How about my mother?"

M.J.'s eyebrows lifted. "What about her?"

"Would you agree to let her come and stay until you're stronger?"

"Of course."

"That settles it," he said, rolling off her body and reaching for the telephone on his side of the bed. Samuel watched his wife watching him as he dialed the number for Tallahassee. "Hello, Mama," he said softly into the mouthpiece when Belinda Cole answered the call. "I'm sorry to call you so late, but I have something I need to ask you."

"What is it?"

"Do you have anything planned for the next two or three months?"

There was a pause before Belinda asked, "What do you want, Samuel?"

"M.J. is expecting again, and the doctor says she has to take it easy. And that includes not lifting anything—especially Nancy. I'm going to rearrange my work schedule to spend more time at home, but when I'm not here I need someone M.J. can get along with." He ignored her when she rolled her eyes at him. "I've offered to hire someone to take care of the children, but your daughter-in-law won't have it."

"I have to agree with her, Samuel. Give me a few days to close up the house, and I'll be there probably before the end of the week."

"You don't have to come now. I'm going to take some time off and stay home. And I know you want to be in Tallahassee when Eugenia has her baby." Thomas and Eugenia were expecting their fourth child within the span of five years.

"I'm through with Genie and her folks. I haven't spent time with my granddaughters in more than a month. If they don't come by for Sunday dinner, then I never get to see them. Genie's mother hovers over them like they're hothouse flowers, so I've let them go. Tell M.J. that I'll be more than happy to come and help her out."

"Thanks, Mama. Call me when you get here, and I'll come and get you."

"There's no need to thank me, because I love spending time with my grandchildren."

Samuel smiled. "Martin and Nancy love you, too. Good night, Mama."

"Good night, Samuel."

He ended the call and smiled at M.J. "That does it. My mother's coming."

Her dimpled smile matched his as she put her arms around his neck. "Thank you, Sammy."

Pulling back, he stared down at her, sobering. "I don't want anything to happen to you. I don't know this baby you're carrying, but I'm willing to sacrifice it if it means saving your life."

"No," M.J. whispered, as tears filled her eyes. "I don't want to lose my baby."

"And I don't want to lose you."

"You won't lose me, Sammy. Remember, we promised to give each other at least seventy-five years."

He pressed his forehead to hers. "That we did."

"Our parents' marriages didn't last a long time, but we can start a new tradition with ours."

Sliding down to the mound of pillows cradling his shoulders, Samuel eased M.J. down beside him. "I'm not ashamed to say that I'm glad my father died when he did."

She gasped. "Why would you say something like that?"

"Because Charles Cole was as mean as a junkyard dog. The son of a bitch never had a kind word to say to his wife or any of his children. Only Thomas was exempt from his venom. I could count the number of times on one hand that he didn't beat me. I got used to his whippings, but it was his constant ridicule that I'd end up dirt-poor, begging for handouts that galled me."

"Is that why you work so hard? Just to make a liar out of a dead man?"

"I work hard so that my children won't have to."

"Do you think our children will appreciate how hard you've worked if they don't know what you've had to sacrifice to make life easier for them?"

Samuel held her gaze. He knew she was talking about his business trips. "It's not always going to be like this."

"But when is it going to end?"

He sucked in a lungful of air, holding it, then let it out slowly. "I don't know, darling. Just tonight Martin asked when he could travel with me."

"What did you tell him?"

"When he's thirteen." Forcing a smile, Samuel traced the curving arch of her eyebrows with a forefinger. "He's growing up quickly. Once he's in school I'm going to take him into the office with me at least one Saturday a month. It will give us time to be together, and I want him to learn the business from the inside out."

Vertical lines appeared between M.J.'s eyes. "Don't rush it, Sammy. Let him enjoy being a boy first."

"Oh, he'll be a normal boy. I plan to take him fishing, to baseball games, and teach him to drive as soon as his feet reach the pedals."

Her frown vanished. "He's going to love that."

"This is going to be a very different world for him once he becomes a man. Right now the economy can go either way. It can continue to balloon, or it's going to go bust. Seats on the New York Stock Exchange are now selling for three hundred fifteen thousand, while economists are debating whether the jobless rate is two or four million. That's bullshit when veterans who've fought for this country can't get jobs.

"Meanwhile President Hoover has promised Americans 'a chicken in every pot, and a car in every garage.' New Fords are selling for six hundred dollars. How is the average worker able to afford a car when he doesn't earn six hundred dollars a year? Prohibition has led to an increase in crime and alcoholism. Did you know that the salary for a New York City business girl is thirty-three dollars and fifty cents for a fifty-hour workweek? That breaks down to sixty-seven cents an hour. I pay my best workers in Costa Rica and Puerto Rico more than that and for a shorter workweek."

"You should open a business here in the States."

"I can't, M.J."

"Why not?"

"Not until things change. Not until there are laws to protect the rights of Negroes to live, work, and vote wherever and whenever they want, and not until someone takes up a sword to cut off the head of the most venomous reptile to ever slither across this land."

"What's that?"

Samuel gave his wife a long, penetrating look that made her shiver. "The Ku Klux Klan."

He hadn't set up a company in the States but had become an anonymous donor to the NAACP, and recently a Florida Agriculture and Mechanical University benefactor.

M.J. was grateful for who or what had prompted her husband to disclose things he'd concealed from her in the past. His willingness to talk about his business was most surprising.

"Tell me about Puerto Rico," she crooned softly.

Samuel regarded her quizzically for a moment, his breathing catching in his throat. Had M.J. suspected something? Had she known that he'd slept with Teresa?

"What about it?" he asked calmly.

"Is it as beautiful as Cuba?"

He let out his breath in a long, silent sigh. "It's beautiful, but in a different way."

Samuel told her everything he remembered about the island from Old San Juan to the tiny villages in the mountains. It was some time before he realized she'd fallen asleep in his arms.

Guilt—raw and acrid—filled his throat like bile.

Oh, sweet heaven! What had he done?

Now he knew how Adam felt when he'd sinned against God. The verse from his Bible school instruction hit him full force: *The serpent beguiled me, and I ate.* However, Teresa Maldonado wasn't the serpent.

He'd fallen prey to another one of the deadly sins: *lust.*

Teresa sat on the porch with her mother. She handed her the small box with the earrings. "Something for you, *Mami.*"

Silvia opened the box and gasped. "Teresa. Where did you get these?"

"Mr. Cole bought them for me to give to you."

"You took these from him?"

"No, *Mami.* He told me to pick out something for you, and I thought you would like these earrings. You like them, no?"

Silvia's brown eyes filled with tears. "*Sí.* I like them. But I can't wear them."

"Why not?"

"Because it would not be right."

"What's not right?" Ramon asked through the screen door.

Teresa stood up, staring at her father through the mesh. "Mr. Cole gave me the money to buy something for *Mami,* and she doesn't want to accept it."

Pushing open the door, Ramon stepped out onto the porch. "Show me." Silvia handed her husband the box with the earrings. There was enough light coming from the lamp on a table near the door to catch the sparkle of the diamonds. "I would have to work a whole year to have enough money to buy these." His green eyes shifted to his daughter. "We cannot accept these."

"Why not, Papa?"

"Because it is not . . . it is not proper."

"What's not proper is refusing a gift given in the spirit of goodwill."

"What is this goodwill?" Ramon continued. "Why would Mr. Cole want to give my wife a gift?"

"It's in appreciation for what I did for him, Papa."

Ramon and Silvia stared at Teresa as if she had two heads. "What did you do?" her mother asked in a hoarse whisper.

Pinpoints of heat seared Teresa's face. Did it show? Could her parents discern that she'd slept with a man?

"What did you do, Teresa?" Ramon said, repeating his wife's query.

Swallowing her panic, she straightened her spine. "I was Mr. Cole's interpreter, and in doing so I saved him hundreds of thousands of dollars.

He bought the earrings out of gratitude. And it would be insulting if I were to give them back to him.

"*Mami*, Papa, be reasonable," she pleaded softly. "I could possibly lose my job. And you know we need the money." Teresa saw the tension leave her father's jaw. "Papa, you say that you want to buy your own house. You can save the extra money I'm bringing home to do that." She pressed her palms together in a prayerful gesture. "Please, Papa. Don't destroy your dream with pride."

Ramon saw the tears glistening in his daughter's eyes. He took a step and hugged her. "Okay. Your mother will wear your Mr. Cole's gift, but only for special days. If she wears them to the factory, then people will think we are too prosperous."

Rising on tiptoe, Teresa kissed her father's cheek. "Thank you, Papa."

"You really like working for Mr. Cole?"

"Yes, I do."

She liked working for Samuel, *and* sleeping with him. He was generous—in and out of bed. Before he'd put her in a taxi to take her home, he'd given her a hundred dollars. He cautioned her not to put it in the bank. Samuel also told her he would give her a little something each time they got together because he enjoyed her company.

It wasn't until she walked into her bedroom and hid the money in a box where she kept her menstrual pads that shame assailed her. Samuel Cole had given her money as if she were a *puta*.

She vowed not to accept money from him again, other than her salary, unless she was Mrs. Samuel Cole.

28

Too often the art of pleasing a man goes out the window when the stork flies in.

—Joyce Brothers

ColeDiz was almost fully staffed. The only exception was Nora Harris. She was still in Arkansas with her son, whose jail sentence was commuted because the bullet lodged in his skull could not be surgically removed. The result was that he would spend the rest of his life confined to a wheelchair.

Teresa sat in the alcove manning the switchboard in Mrs. Harris's absence, but sitting closer to Samuel hadn't eased her apprehension. She'd gone back to school, which meant she saw him three days each week instead of five. Her fear was that what she'd shared with him in Puerto Rico was over because they hadn't been alone together since their return. Samuel had changed his hours, arriving late and leaving early, instructing her to see Everett if she encountered a problem.

Problema!

Samuel Cole had become a problem—her problem. But if what she suspected was true, then all of her restless nights would soon come to an end.

She checked the watch pinned to her blouse over her breast. She was told to call after five. Picking up the headset, she inserted the trunk line for outgoing calls into the switchboard. She dialed the number, listening through her earpiece for a break in the connection.

"This is Mrs. Maldonado," she whispered when the doctor answered the call.

"Yes, Mrs. Maldonado," came a drawling masculine voice. The crackling of turning papers came through the wire. "The results of your test reveal that you are pregnant. I'd like to see you in my office some time next week for a more thorough examination."

Teresa swallowed hard, fighting tears, and unaware that a low, tortured sob had escaped her constricted throat. What she'd wanted, had planned and prayed for had manifested. She was pregnant with Samuel Cole's baby. One time, and the only time he hadn't used a condom, he'd gotten her pregnant. That was the night she'd lost her virginity.

Tears blurred her vision. "I . . . I will call you and set up an appointment."

"Make certain you do, Mrs. Maldonado."

"Thank you, Dr. Baker."

She hung up before the doctor could say anything else. The import of her condition hit her full force. She was nineteen, a part-time nursing student, unmarried, and pregnant with a married man's child. She'd boasted to Liliana that she could take Samuel away from his wife, but now she wasn't so certain.

"Are you all right, Teresa?" Everett's drawling voice penetrated her fog of despair.

Swiping at the tears streaming down her face, she shook her head. "I'm fine."

Resting his hands on her desk, he leaned closer, gold eyes moving slowly over her face. "You're a terrible liar, Miss Maldonado."

Reaching into a pocket of her skirt, she withdrew a handkerchief and blotted her cheeks. "Please, go away, Mr. Kirkland."

Everett sat down on the edge of the desk. "I can't do that, Teresa."

She stared at him, seeing genuine concern in the slanting eyes the color of tortoiseshell. "I've received some news—not so good news—and it upset me."

"Would you like to go home?"

Her gaze lingered on the jet-black mustache covering a firm upper lip. Everett Kirkland was elegant—from his neatly barbered hair to the cuffs of his sharply creased slacks.

"No. I'll be all right."

He stood up. "I'm going to be working late tonight. I'm going out to pick up supper. Would you like me to bring something back for you?"

Teresa forced a smile. "No, thank you."

Everett headed for his office, stopped, then turned and retraced his steps. "Let's go, Teresa."

Surprise siphoned the blood from her face. "What?"

"Lock up everything."

Her mouth dropped open. "I can't. It's not quitting time."

"Lock up the office, Miss Maldonado. That's an order."

"But—"

"No buts," he interrupted, grinning. "We'll have dinner, and then I'll drive you home. If your folks are expecting you, then I suggest you call and let them know you'll be a little late."

"I don't have to call them," she mumbled angrily. She couldn't call them because the Maldonados didn't have a telephone.

"Suit yourself," he countered.

Teresa was certain he could hear her slamming drawers as she locked the desk and closed and locked drawers to the file cabinets. Who did he think he was anyway—the boss?

Her annoyance fled when she realized Everett Kirkland was her boss whenever Samuel was out of the office. She usually found him even-tempered, soft-spoken, and undemanding. However, today was the exception.

"Where are you going?" Teresa asked Everett when he drove past Amelia's.

"To a little place not far from here."

"Where?"

Everett gave her a quick glance before returning his attention to the road. "Relax, Teresa. I'm not abducting you," he said in Spanish.

She stared at his profile, shadowed by the brim of his hat. "I thought we were going to Amelia's."

"It's too crowded on Friday night."

"What's different about Friday nights?"

"Music."

"They have bands?"

Everett nodded, downshifting as he maneuvered around a slow-moving farm truck. "Every month they have a different band."

"Why aren't you there with your lady?" Teresa asked him in Spanish. He flashed a rare smile. "You think I'm funny?"

Everett sobered. "No, Teresa, I don't think you're funny. If you want to know if I have a special lady you can ask me."

Lifting her chin in a haughty gesture, she stared out the windshield. "You do not interest me like that."

"Why? Is it because I'm not Samuel Cole?"

Her body stiffed in shock, the shock causing words to wedge in her throat, and if the car hadn't been moving so fast, or she didn't fear for the tiny life in her womb, Teresa would've opened the door and jumped out. How did he know? Had she been that obvious in her silent adoration or had Samuel told Everett that he'd slept with her? She took a deep breath, forcing herself to relax. There was no way she could let Everett know how much his query had upset her.

"Why are you talking about Mr. Cole?"

"I just want to warn you that he will never leave his wife—not for you, not for any woman."

Her jaw dropped. "Why are you saying this to me?"

"Because I've seen the way you look at him, Teresa."

"You're crazy!"

"No, Teresa, you're the crazy one, because what you want is never going to happen. You're young, smart, and pretty. You should be going out with boys your age during your free time instead of hanging out at the office mooning over Samuel."

"I don't moon over him!"

"Stop lying, Teresa!" The three words were cold and lashing.

Tears filled her eyes for the second time within an hour. "Why are you saying these horrible things to me?"

Everett's expression was one of pained tolerance. He liked Teresa, not the way she liked Samuel, and he didn't want her to ruin her life wishing for something she would never have. There was something about her that reminded him of himself when he'd waited in Puerto Limon for Eladia. A waiting that had become infinite. And as much as he didn't want to admit it, a small part of him was still waiting for her.

"I don't want to see you ruin your life." His voice low, softer.

She flushed, but remained silent. *It's too late for that,* she mused.

"You can let me out here," Teresa told Everett.

He'd slowed his car along the dusty road where her parents' house was one among a dozen rickety structures owned by a heartless, unscrupulous man who thought nothing of evicting entire families if they were three days late paying their monthly rent. It wasn't unusual to find people standing beside their prized possessions to keep others from stealing them after the owner's goons emptied the house in preparation for a new tenant.

Everett's fingers tightened on the gearshift. "No, Teresa. I'll drive you directly to your door."

With a barely perceptible nod of her head, Teresa stared straight ahead. She'd spent the past two hours with the accountant, and for that brief time she'd forgotten about her predicament. Much to her surprise she'd found herself more comfortable with Everett than she did with Samuel. He exhibited a wry sense of humor she hadn't thought possible because he had always appeared so serious; he spoke to her in Spanish, claiming he needed the practice to keep himself fluent.

He told her about the two months he'd spent in Costa Rica interviewing countless candidates for the managerial position. He'd almost given up when an ex-foreman for the United Fruit Company applied for the position. He hadn't brought up the subject of Samuel Cole, and for that she was grateful. She'd masked her inner turmoil with a deceptive calmness she hadn't known she possessed.

"I live there," she said softly, pointing at the one-story house with peeling yellow paint. Silvia nagged Ramon constantly to buy some paint to touch up the siding, but he refused because he didn't own the property. Everett got out and pulled her gently to her feet. She thanked him for dinner, then made her way to the rear of the house.

Teresa opened the door leading into the kitchen where her family had gathered for the evening meal. "I had to work late," she announced softly, explaining her absence.

Silvia pushed back her chair. "I'll get you a plate."

"No, *Mami.* I ate at the office," she lied smoothly. "I'm going to take a bath, and then I'm going to study before going to bed." She kissed her mother, father, and then her youngest brother. "Where's Pedro?"

Ramon tore a piece off the loaf of homemade bread and dabbed the residue of gravy on his plate. "He's doing some work for Mr. Winters."

Teresa frowned at her father. "Is he going to pay him in cash, or will he take it off the rent?"

Ramon returned her frown. "Stay out of it. It's between your brother and Mr. Winters."

"But he's a thief, Papa."

"*Bastante!*"

Her temper flared. "How can it be enough when he treats us like we're dirt, Papa? Whenever he has to repair something he adds it to the rent. This is his house, not ours, so why do we have to pay for repairs?"

Ramon's eyes paled. "Go to your room!"

"I am not a child to be sent to my room!"

Ramon half rose to his feet, but Silvia's work-worn hand stopped him. "No, Ramon." She turned her dark gaze on her daughter. The two women acknowledged what would've only ended in a stalemate, resentment, and hostility.

Turning on her heel, Teresa walked out of the kitchen. She had enough on her mind without arguing with her father about their unscrupulous landlord.

She had to let Samuel Cole know that she was carrying his child.

Teresa unlocked the door and went completely still. Samuel sat at the desk in the reception area. It was apparent he was waiting for her. He rose slowly to his feet, his gaze fusing with hers.

It had been more than six weeks since their last physical encounter, and seeing him this close made her body ache. She loved him, even more now that the result of their time together grew inside her. Everything that was so magical about the enchanting island, mountains, waterfalls, the primordial beauty of El Yunque with its ageless trees, the rare flora and fauna indigenous only to Puerto Rico, would remain with her forever.

"You were waiting for me." Her question came out like a statement.

"Yes. I want to talk to you."

"And I *need* to talk to you," she countered.

Samuel, pushing his hands into the pockets of his trousers, rocked back on his heels. "We'll talk in my office."

She stored her pocketbook in the desk drawer before following Samuel. He waited for her to walk into his office, then closed the door behind them. He cupped her elbow, steering her to the small table in the corner. Pulling out a chair, he seated her.

"Thank you," she whispered, as he rounded the table and sat down. "What do you want to talk about?"

Lacing his fingers together, Samuel stared at Teresa's bowed head. The summer sun had bleached her hair white gold.

"I didn't want you to think that I've been avoiding you, but I've been involved with a family crisis."

Her head came up slowly. She hoped his family crisis was marital discord. It would make what she had to tell him a lot easier if he were fighting with his wife.

"I don't know what to think, Samuel, because I've had my own personal family crisis."

"Is it something I can help you with?"

Nervously Teresa moistened her dry lips. "Yes, you can."

He leaned closer. "What do you want?"

"You," she whispered even though there was no one in the office except the two of them. "I want you, Samuel Cole."

"Teresa, we have to talk."

"We are talking," she chided. "I want to talk about us, Samuel."

A muscle flicked angrily at his jaw. "There can't be an us. At least not right now."

"And why not?"

"Because my wife—"

"Your wife?" Teresa asked, cutting him off. "What does your wife have to do with us?"

"She's pregnant."

Teresa stared across the small distance separating her from the man with whom she'd fallen in love, tongue-tied.

Clamping a hand over her mouth, she cut off a strangled cry. *No,* her silent voice screamed.

Samuel was hypnotized by the fear in the green eyes trained on him. He wanted to look away, but couldn't. "I'm sorry, Teresa."

She lowered her hand. "You're sorry, Samuel? Are you sorry you got your wife pregnant?"

He shook his head. "Of course not. We planned for this baby."

Shock yielded to fury with his cocky explanation. "You planned to have a baby with your wife, but what about your mistress?"

Samuel could not believe what he was hearing. What mistress? Did Teresa believe she was his mistress? "What are you talking about?"

"I'm pregnant, Samuel. I'm going to have your baby."

His face became a glowering mask of rage. "What is it you want? You want money? How much do you want?"

Teresa half rose, her right hand arcing toward his face, but Samuel was quicker. He held her wrist in a punishing grip.

"Let me go!" she warned between clenched teeth.

"Sit down. Do not, and I repeat, do not attempt to hit me again."

Her eyes filled with tears. His fingers were like manacles. "Please, Samuel, you're hurting me."

Samuel released her arm as if he feared contamination. He glared at her, frowning. "You can't be pregnant. I used a condom with you."

"Not the first time."

"I pulled out."

"You didn't pull out fast enough."

Teresa felt a measure of satisfaction when Samuel's brows drew together in an agonized expression.

"What are *we* going to do?" she asked quietly.

Samuel stared at Teresa as if she were a stranger. "There can't be a *we*. Not the way you think."

"What the hell are you now? A mind reader?"

Struggling to contain his temper, Samuel closed his eyes. He could not, did not want to believe that a single reckless encounter resulted in his fathering a child out of wedlock.

He opened his eyes. "No, Teresa. I do not read minds. Are you certain you're pregnant?"

She met his tortured gaze, her bravado slipping. He was hurting. "Yes. I went to the doctor last week. He wants me to come in for a comprehensive examination as soon as I have the time."

Two deep lines of worry appeared between Samuel's eyes. Teresa's revelation made him feel old, fatigued—too old to be in the age-old dilemma of being caught in a trap of his own choosing.

"How much do you want, Teresa?"

"What do you mean?"

"How much money do you want me to give you?"

Her eyes grew wider and wilder. "You think this is about money? That I trapped you so that you could pay me off?"

Leaning back in the chair, Samuel regarded her as if she were a business adversary. And that was what she'd become. "I don't know what to think."

Rage made Teresa reckless when she said, "I told you before that I want you. I want you to leave your wife and marry me."

Samuel stared, complete surprise on his face. Then realization dawned. Teresa had manipulated him. Her seduction had begun before she'd convinced him to take her to Puerto Rico. He replayed their encounters in his head like frames of film. His eyebrows lifted when he recalled the time she'd come to his house for the Independence Day celebration and had shown him what he could have if only he was willing to take the bait.

And like a gauche, bumbling adolescent boy looking for his first piece of ass he'd fallen into her trap. Teresa Maldonado had just executed the oldest con game in the world. She'd literally caught him with his pants down.

He crossed his arms over his chest. "What you ask is impossible. I will never leave M.J. Not for you. Not for any woman on the face of this earth."

His declaration echoed Liliana's and Everett's. Hearing it from them meant nothing, but the words coming directly from Samuel made her world tilt on its axis.

"What am I going to do?" she whispered.

Samuel reached across the table and covered her hands with one of his. "I will take care of everything."

Her eyes shimmered with tears. "How?" Suddenly his face went grim, and Teresa knew exactly what he meant. "Good Catholic girls do not have abortions."

A half smile crossed his face. "I shouldn't have to remind you that good Catholic girls do not fuck married men."

"*Me cago en la madre que te pario!*"

Removing his hand, Samuel glared at her. "I could say the same thing about your bastard's mother. Fortunately my mother raised me to respect women. But if you continue to insult me I'm going to forget my home training. And if you're so intent on having this baby, then I'll give you enough money to go to Cuba to have it."

Tears overflowed, staining the front of Teresa's blouse. "I can't go to Cuba as a Maldonado."

Reaching into the pocket of his slacks, Samuel handed her his handkerchief. "Why not?"

She blotted her eyes. "If anyone discovered I was Ramon Maldonado's daughter, then I would either be killed or imprisoned. My father had to leave Cuba with the clothes on his back or he would've been shot on sight. He has been identified as an enemy of the state.

"And once my parents find out that I'm pregnant..." Her words trailed off as she broke down, sobbing.

Samuel came around the table, eased her gently to her feet, cradling her to his chest. "I'm so sorry, baby," he crooned softly. "If things were different I'd marry you tomorrow."

Teresa buried her face against his shoulder, praying for things to be different. "I love you. I will always love you."

"Shh-hhh, baby." He shook his head. She'd just cursed him, saying, "I shit on the mother who gave you birth" in a fit of rage, then within minutes confessed to loving him.

And Samuel believed she did love him because he was the first man who'd introduced her to passion. What Teresa didn't know was that there would be other men, other men who would fall in love with her beautiful face, lush body, and unabashed raw sexuality. She was a rare gift for a man willing to cherish what she was willing to offer him.

"I can set you up with your own house," he said close to her ear.

She froze. "You want me to be your mistress?"

"You're the one who used the word, not me. What I want to do is take care of my responsibility. You and your child will never want for anything whether I'm living or dead."

"And what do I do, Samuel? Wait around for you to see me when you're not too busy with your legitimate family? No. I did not make this baby alone, and I will not have it alone."

"I'm not going to divorce my wife and marry you."

Teresa pushed against him, freeing herself. Moisture spiked the lashes framing her ice-cold, pale-green eyes. "Then it looks as if both of us have a very serious problem."

Samuel's expression was a mask of stone before it softened. "No, Teresa. You're the one with the problem, and you've worked with me long enough to know I don't take kindly to threats. Piss me off and you'll find yourself out on your ass without a penny."

Teresa knew when to push and when to retreat. This was one of those times. Samuel knew she was carrying his child, and now all she had to do was wait to see what he would do. She'd considered becoming his mistress—but that was before she found out that Marguerite-Josefina was pregnant.

And what Samuel Cole did not know about Teresa Maldonado was that she was not only patient, but also very stubborn.

She'd set out to seduce Samuel, and she had.

She'd also planned for him to get her pregnant, and he had.

She also planned to get a husband, and she would.

Everett knocked on the door frame to Samuel's office five minutes after Teresa walked out. "What's going on?"

Samuel, leaning back in his chair, did not move. "What do you mean?"

"Teresa looks as if she's been crying."

Straightening to an upright position, Samuel pushed off his chair. "I need to talk to you."

"Talk to me, Cole."

He shook his head. "Not here. Let's go for a walk."

29

Though I knew that the name of wife was honorable in the world and holy in religion; yet the name of your mistress had greater charms because it was more free.

—Heloise

Everett strolled the two square blocks that encompassed West Palm Beach's Negro business district. Hands clasped behind his back, he listened to Samuel Cole unburden his soul. What he'd suspected had manifested.

He was angry, not with Samuel or Teresa, but with himself. He'd stood by and done nothing as Teresa subtly seduced her unsuspecting boss. But when he did confront her it'd been too late. She'd attempted to use the oldest trick in the world to break up a home and get a man to marry her. He hadn't minced words when he told her that Samuel would never leave M.J.

"What is she asking for?"

"Marriage."

Everett caught Samuel's arm, forcing him to stop. "That's it?"

Both men touched the brims of their hats as two well-dressed women walked by.

Samuel gave his best friend a look of disbelief. "That's it?" he repeated. "Don't forget I'm married."

Gold eyes searched the lean face of the man who'd afforded him a way of life he never would've had even if he hadn't left the insurance company what now seemed a lifetime ago.

"But I'm not, Samuel."

Eyes wide, heart pumping uncontrollably, Samuel stared at Everett in shock. "No, Everett."

"Yes, Samuel. I'll marry her, give the baby my name, and no one will be the wiser."

He swallowed to relieve his constricted throat. "You'd raise my child as your own?"

"I'd like to believe you'd do the same for me if something happened to me or my wife."

"Hell yeah," Samuel said quickly.

Everett patted his shoulder. "That does it. I'll talk to Teresa and present her with my offer."

"What if she refuses?" Samuel asked in a low voice.

"She can't afford to. She's pushing marriage because she doesn't want to bring shame on her family. Let me handle everything."

"Why are you willing to do this?"

Lowering his head, Everett flashed a rare smile. "I'm thirty-three, tired of living alone, and because our marriage will be a business arrangement there won't be any hurt feelings once we decide to go our separate ways."

"Why are you really doing this, Everett?"

He gave Samuel a long, penetrating look. "Just say it's my way of looking out for my younger brother."

Samuel felt a wave of emotion sweep over him unlike any he'd ever experienced. He extended his right hand. "Thank you."

Everett took the proffered hand before pulling Samuel close and thumping his back. "Remember, we're in this together."

Samuel smiled, returning the embrace. "Together."

"I'm going to ask one thing from you, Samuel."

"What's that?"

"Other than me and Teresa, no one will know that the child is yours."

"I give you my word that no one will ever know."

They returned to the office, Samuel taking the back staircase, while Everett walked up the front. He stepped into the reception area to find Teresa filing financial reports. Her head came up at the same time he removed his hat.

"I'd like to see you in my office," he ordered quietly.

"Now?"

"Yes."

Everett waited for her to walk into his office; he stared at Teresa's back, smiling. He could see why Samuel was taken with her. The night he'd taken her to dinner it was as if he'd seen her for the first time, wondering why he hadn't taken note of her startling beauty. It wasn't until he returned home that he realized he preferred dark-haired, dark-eyed women.

He took off his suit jacket, hung it on a wall hook, and placed his hat on the top of a bookcase. "Please sit down." She complied, sitting in an armchair. Positioning a matching chair to face her, Everett sat, looping one knee over the other.

Stroking his mustache in an unconscious gesture, Everett reached out and grasped Teresa's hands. They were ice cold. "Don't," he warned softly when she attempted to pull away. He met her startled gaze. "I know about your condition." His heart turned over when tears flooded her eyes. "I should've warned you before this happened, but I told myself it was none of my business and that Samuel knew what he was doing. You're with child and need a husband. And we both know that Samuel will not leave M.J. for you."

Ignoring the tears streaming down her face, Teresa glared at Everett. "You're right. This is none of your business."

"That's where you're so wrong, Teresa. What happens to Samuel Cole is my business, and I don't ever want you to forget that. I'm offering to marry you and give your baby my name. I will not touch you until after the baby is born. I want you to tell your family that I'll be by tomorrow afternoon to talk with them."

Ignoring her gaping mouth, he continued, "You'll probably want a wedding, so start making arrangements on what you want. "We'll go and pick out rings in a couple of hours. I'll also ask Samuel for time off for a honeymoon, so let me know where you'd like to go."

"You—you make this sound like a business arrangement," she said once she'd recovered her voice.

"It is. I'm not in love with you, and you're definitely not in love with me. So, let's try to make the best of what could possibly become an uncomfortable situation."

"Uncomfortable for who?"

"For you, Teresa. You and the child in your belly will be the losers if you reject what I'm offering you."

Tunneling her fingers through her hair, she held the heavy waves off her face. "I'm so confused."

Everett dried her tears with his handkerchief. "Let me handle everything. I'll tell your father that I've been interested in you ever since you came to work for ColeDiz, and now that I've made my feelings known I want to do the right thing and make you my wife."

Teresa's hands trembled uncontrollably. "I don't know if I can do what you propose."

"Yes, you can. We both can."

She stared at the man offering her the chance for respectability for herself and her unborn child. She couldn't have Samuel Cole, but she was being offered a second choice, the man closest to him. They'd met and discussed her like a parcel of land they wanted to purchase, then decided who would claim her.

Her eyes narrowed. "I don't understand how you'd want to claim another man's child as your own."

Everett leaned closer, his gold eyes darkening dangerously. "You are never to speak of the child as Samuel's. This baby, whether girl or boy, will be known as the son or daughter of Everett and Teresa Kirkland."

Teresa regarded Everett with impassive coldness. She hated him, hated his supercilious, patronizing manner. And if he thought she was going to submit to him once she delivered her baby, then he was crazier than the people they locked away in mental hospitals.

The accountant was offering her what Samuel couldn't and wouldn't. She would become Mrs. Everett Kirkland, but in name only.

"Okay," she said softly. "I will marry you."

Teresa sat on the porch step with Liliana, waiting for Everett to emerge from the house. She tried staring through the curtain of rain that fell sideways. She'd told her friend that Everett had come to ask her father's permission to marry her, but hadn't said a word about the baby.

"What's taking so long?" Liliana whined like a child.

Propping her elbows on her knees, Teresa shifted her gaze to the car parked in the driveway. It belonged to the man who was to become her husband once Ramon Maldonado gave his approval. But what her father didn't know was the longer he resisted, the more evident her condition would be.

She was only six weeks into her term, and her body was changing quickly. Her breasts were fuller, her appetite had increased, and she needed to marry within the next two weeks.

Liliana popped up like a jack-in-the-box when the screen door opened. Teresa was slower in rising. Everett stepped out onto the porch. A wide grin crinkled the skin around his tawny-gold eyes.

He reached for her left hand and slipped a ring with an emerald-cut diamond on her third finger. It wasn't the ring she'd picked out the day before. The one she'd selected had a much smaller stone.

Lowering his head, Everett kissed Teresa's parted lips, inhaling and swallowing her breath. "Thank you," he whispered loud enough for Liliana to overhear.

Clinging to the front of his shirt as if he were a lifeline, Teresa stared up at him. "Thank you," she repeated softly.

"Let me see your ring!" Liliana shouted before she put her hand over her mouth. Her hand came down slowly. "Oh, *mi'ja*, it is so beautiful."

Teresa hugged her friend. "Will you be my maid of honor?"

"But of course."

The two women were babbling excitedly in Spanish when the door opened again and Ramon and Silvia Maldonado joined them on the porch.

Everett had asked the elder Maldonados to set a date for the wedding before the end of September. The next day they would leave for their honeymoon. Teresa hadn't seen her parents' homeland, so she would visit Cuba for the first time, not as Teresa Maldonado, but Teresa Kirkland.

Winding an arm around his fiancée's waist, he smiled at her. "We have to go, or we're going to be late for dinner."

"Where are we going?"

"I'll tell you in the car."

Everett shook Ramon's hand, then kissed Silvia's cheek. "I'll see you tomorrow," he said in Spanish.

Liliana smiled as Everett held an umbrella over Teresa's head when he escorted her off the porch to his car. She was relieved her friend had changed her mind about seducing Samuel Cole.

Everett Kirkland would make her a much better husband.

Teresa saw the sign pointing the way to Palm Grove Oval, and knew Everett was taking her to his home. The rain had subsided to a light drizzle by the time he parked his car under a porte cochere.

"Don't move," Everett warned when her hand went to the door handle. "I'll come around and get you."

To anyone watching them, they appeared to be a normal couple, a loving couple; but appearances were deceiving because they would begin a life together living a lie.

She watched Everett unlock the front door, step into the entryway, then extend his hand for her to take it. Trustingly, she placed her hand on his, feeling its strength when his fingers tightened.

The entryway was as large as the living room in the house where she'd grown up. It gave way to an expansive living room, and beyond that a formal dining room. All of the furnishings were Spanish or Caribbean-inspired.

"Most of the furniture was shipped from Costa Rica and Jamaica."

She smiled. "I like it. Where are the bedrooms?"

"Toward the rear." Cupping her elbow, Everett led her down the hallway, stopping at each bedroom. The two smaller rooms contained only rockers and a side table with a lamp. "As you can see I don't have company."

Walking into one room, Teresa noticed the wallpaper. Figures of circus elephants and calliopes dotted a pale green background. "This was once a nursery."

Hands thrust into his pockets, Everett angled his head. "Yes. Samuel's son and daughter slept here before he built the new house."

"This was Samuel's house?" she said without turning around.

"Yes."

"And now it's yours."

"Yes, Teresa. It's mine. And once we're married it will be ours."

She closed her eyes. She was carrying Samuel Cole's baby, she was going to marry Samuel Cole's business partner, and she would also live in a house that had at one time belonged to Samuel Cole.

How many more secondhand goods would the man she'd promised to marry accept before he developed enough of a backbone to say enough is enough?

Forcing a smile she did not feel, Teresa turned and smiled at her fiancé. "It's a lovely home." And it was. It still smelled new.

"I'm glad you like it."

"May I see the kitchen?"

"Don't you want to see our bedroom?"

"I'll see it later. Right now I need to eat something or I'm going to be sick."

Taking her hand, Everett led her into the kitchen. He seated her at a table, then opened the refrigerator. "Do you like fruit?"

"Yes."

He took out a bowl of diced pineapple, mango, and guava. Teresa had rested her head on the table to stop the spinning. "Eat," he ordered, forcing her mouth open. It was only when she'd swallowed several forkfuls of fruit that the spinning stopped.

Teresa chewed and swallowed the last piece. "Thank you."

Everett did not acknowledge her gratitude as he turned and put the bowl in the sink. She stared at his tall, slender figure as he leaned into the refrigerator.

"Why did you change the ring?"

He took out a bowl of cut-up chicken. "The one you picked out was too small."

"But it was the one I wanted."

"It wasn't the one *I* wanted."

"Why didn't you say something when we were in the store?"

Everett set the bowl on a countertop. "Because I don't argue in public, Teresa. To do so indicates you haven't been properly trained."

"You train animals, not people."

"Proper rearing and good manners are essential if you want to be accepted in polite society."

Her eyes paled. "Are you afraid I'm going to embarrass you in front of these fancy people who live around here?"

"No, I'm not, Teresa. Because that is something I will not tolerate."

She stood up. "And if I do embarrass you?"

Everett stared at the woman who wore his ring, the woman he'd promised his boss he would marry to protect his reputation. He liked his women docile and obedient. Teresa Maldonado was a lot of things, but docile or obedient wasn't among them.

A hint of a smile curved the corners of his mouth upward. "I will spank you for being naughty."

She returned his smile, her breasts rising and falling, bringing his gaze to linger there. Teresa wasn't certain, but she thought she saw a spark of desire fire his eyes, but he'd shuttered his gaze so quickly she could've been mistaken.

"I'm going to see the bedroom now."

Everett watched her retreating figure. Teresa was unlike any other woman he'd ever met. *What have I gotten myself into?* he mused.

The question nagged him later that night when he went to bed—alone. It would nag at him two weeks later when he stood in the formal English garden on the Cole estate with Teresa Kirkland, accepting best wishes from their wedding guests.

Teresa concentrated on placing one silk-covered foot in front of the other as she stared through the white veil at one of the two formally dressed men standing at the altar. She pulled her mesmerizing gaze from Samuel's startled one and smiled at Everett.

Ramon Maldonado lifted the small gloved hand resting on his suit jacket, placing it in Everett Kirkland's outstretched one. He nodded to his impending son-in-law, stepped back, and sat down beside his wife, who dabbed her eyes with a lace-trimmed handkerchief.

Ramon wanted to see all of his children married, his daughter in particular, but he'd wanted her to wait until she'd graduated from nursing school. He wanted to tell everyone that his daughter would be the first Maldonado to graduate from college, but that accomplishment would have to wait.

Everett had promised him that he would see that Teresa completed her education even if she did become a mother. The accountant said he wanted to marry Teresa and father a child before he celebrated his thirty-fourth birthday. As it was, he'd thought of himself as too old for marriage and fatherhood. The younger man had also offered a dowry for the hand of his daughter. It was enough money for the Maldonados, with the sum they'd saved, to purchase a house of their own.

Teresa stared up at Everett staring down at her. She had to admit he looked incredibly handsome in his wedding finery. A mysterious light fired the deep-set gold eyes that reminded her of honey.

During the past weeks, she'd spent as much time as she could with her fiancé, hoping to know him better before she became Mrs. Everett Kirkland. Her life had changed drastically since she'd accepted his proposal and his ring: she'd submitted a letter asking for an official leave of absence from her classes for the school year, tendered her resignation with ColeDiz, moved all of her clothes and personal possessions into the house in the Palm Grove Oval, and had begun looking for furniture for one of the two empty bedrooms. She decided to wait until April to decorate the nursery. Her doctor had estimated her date of delivery any time between late-April to mid-May.

She and Everett argued the day following their engagement. Samuel and his wife had offered their home for the wedding reception, and Everett said to refuse was not only discourteous but unappreciative. As before in all of their discussions, she found herself on the losing end, and invitations were sent out informing guests that a reception at the residence of Mr. and Mrs. Samuel Cole would follow the sacrament of holy matrimony at St. Ignatius R.C. Church.

Teresa repeated her vows, secretly wishing it were Samuel she was marrying. To the world she would be known as Mrs. Teresa Kirkland, but in her heart she would always be Mrs. Teresa Cole.

Everett raised Teresa's veil and what he saw in her luminous eyes made him hopeful that maybe they could possibly become man and wife. That perhaps one day there would be enough respect *and* affection between them to present a modicum of normalcy to those outside the wall they'd erected to hide their best-kept secret.

Lowering his head, he wound an arm around her waist and gave her a chaste kiss. Just for an instant he felt her respond. "Congratulations, Mrs. Kirkland," he whispered for her ears only.

Her eyes paled, appearing colorless. "No, Everett," she whispered back, smiling for those observing the supposedly happy couple. "You're the only winner here."

What should've been one of the happiest days in his life suddenly soured for Everett. He and Teresa hadn't mentioned Samuel since the time they argued about where the reception would be held, but it was apparent she wasn't going to forgive him for overruling her.

He caught her hand as they turned to face those who'd come to witness their union. Squeezing her fingers in a deathlike grip, he forced a smile. "Not here, not today," he ground out between his teeth. "Now smile pretty for the people," he said, as if speaking to a child.

Teresa drew in a breath against the unyielding pressure on her hand, the gesture resembling a grimace. "Please."

Bending slightly, Everett swept her up in his arms and carried her out of the church and into the bright Florida sunlight. Yards and yards of ivory silk flowed over the arm of his cutaway coat and down to his pale gray dress trousers.

Samuel, holding Liliana's hand, followed the newlyweds, who were showered with handfuls of rice and orange blossoms. He waited for M.J. to emerge from the church with Martin and Nancy. He spied her with

Ramon and Silvia Maldonado. A stylish cloche in sapphire blue matched the silk dress, artfully disguising her expanding waistline. She'd followed her doctor's instruction and hadn't overtaxed herself. She and Belinda, who'd taken up residence in one of the bedroom suites, had truly become mother and daughter.

He caught M.J.'s eye, waved to her, then left to join the bride and groom for wedding pictures.

Teresa stood in the receiving line with her husband, thanking the people waiting to offer their best wishes. A large tent had been erected in the center of the boxwood English garden to protect the guests from the sun.

Most of the invited guests were friends of Samuel's and Everett's, and coworkers. Nora Harris had returned from Arkansas after burying her son. Depressed because he would have to spend the rest of his life in a wheelchair, he'd put a second bullet in his own head, this one killing him instantly. Eddie Grady had come with his wife, and Joseph Hill, the part-time bookkeeper, had brought his girlfriend.

Nora kissed Teresa's cheek, smiling. "Be happy. You've got yourself a good man."

"Thank you, Mrs. Harris."

Teresa saw her mother with M.J., the two women laughing like long-lost friends. Silvia was ecstatic that she'd found someone from her homeland with whom to communicate. They had come from different social classes, but they still were Cuban women.

The last guest moved into the tent to be seated when Teresa leaned into her husband, a fixed smile on her lush mouth. "If you ever hurt me again I swear I'll cut your heart out of your chest when you go to sleep."

Everett froze and stared at her as if she'd suddenly gone insane. His eyes widened before he looked away. What had he gotten himself into?

Samuel had spared no expense for the reception. He'd hired two bands, one playing the pieces made popular by Edward "Duke" Ellington's big band in Harlem's Cotton Club, and he'd paid the traveling expenses of Havana's top musicians to play at his best friend's wedding reception.

Teresa picked at the food on her plate, preferring instead to drink water. The heat and the spicy food had triggered an unnatural thirst. The band slowed the tempo and she found herself pulled gently from her chair. It was time she danced with her husband. The hem of her flowing dress trailed over the grass as Everett led her to an expansive slate-covered area.

The sunlight glinted off the platinum waves framing her face as she stared up at her husband. "I hope you're happy, Everett. You've saved your boss's ass."

His mouth tightening under his mustache, Everett pulled her closer, twirling her around and around. "I was only joking before when I said I would spank you, but if you push me I *will* beat the hell out of you, baby or no baby."

She gasped. "You wouldn't!"

He tightened his hold on her waist. "Test me and you'll find out."

Teresa wasn't able to form a comeback when she found herself in her father's arms. Resting her head on his shoulder as she'd done as a child, she felt safe and protected. However, that was short-lived when she detected the fragrance of the man who had forced her into a predicament from which there was no escape.

Samuel couldn't take his gaze off the face of the woman in his arms. He found her more hypnotically alluring than when they had shared a bed for a few precious moments on an enchanting island paradise.

He was drowning, in her eyes and her sensual scent. "You are a beautiful bride."

A sun-bleached eyebrow lifted. "Is that what you said to M.J. the day you married her?"

Samuel pulled her closer. "Don't, Teresa. Don't spoil your special day with bitterness."

"You think I don't have a right to be bitter? I'm carrying your child, yet I'm treated like a slave on the auction block. You've sold me because you want to protect your legitimate family and good name from scandal. Meanwhile your bastard will grow up to call another man father."

"Do you think this has been easy for me? Do you know how difficult it is for me to know that another man will claim my flesh and blood as his own? If I hadn't met M.J., there is no doubt you and I would've stood in that church and become husband and wife. You have a part of me that I've never given any woman. You are my weakness, my obsession, *Chica*. And I will never forget you or what we shared."

"What we *share*," she said softly, correcting him. "We share a child, Samuel."

"That's where you're wrong, Teresa. I've relinquished all claim to the child you carry. The only children I will acknowledge as Coles are the ones my wife gives me."

The musical piece ended, and Samuel led Teresa back to Everett. He inclined his head. "Thank you for letting me dance with *your* wife."

Teresa floundered in an agonizing maelstrom of despair and loneliness. She was in a garden with more than sixty people who were laughing, eating, dancing, and drinking, but she couldn't have felt more alone if she'd been locked in solitary confinement.

She replayed Samuel's statement over and over until she felt like screaming at the top of her lungs. She hated him, she hated Everett, and she hated the woman whose claim on Samuel was unconditional.

"I'll be right back," she said to Everett. He pulled back her chair, helping her to stand.

Pasting a smile on her face, she headed for Marguerite-Josefina Cole. She touched her arm to get her attention, and a pair of large dark eyes crinkled in a smile.

"May I have a few words with you?" she asked in Spanish.

"Of course," M.J. replied.

The two women walked a short distance. They were shielded from the others by an eight-foot hedge.

She and M.J. were physically complete opposites, yet both had won the affection of the same man. "I'm so overwhelmed with everything, and I'd like to thank you and your husband for your generosity in hosting my wedding reception."

M.J.'s dimples deepened in a warm smile. "It was nothing. Samuel and Everett are like brothers, so there isn't anything we wouldn't do for him. I wish you and Everett a long and happy life together."

"Thank you," Teresa said facetiously. "I hope we'll have half the happiness you share with Samuel."

M.J. patted Teresa's hand. "You'll have what we have and so much more."

"Like children?"

"Of course."

"Samuel told me you are now carrying your third child."

Placing a hand over her belly, M.J. nodded. "Yes, I am."

A light went out from behind Teresa's eyes as she glared at the slight swelling under the fashionable dress. "And I'm carrying his fourth."

The blood drained from M.J.'s face, leaving it a sickly yellow shade. "What are you talking about?"

Vengeance, bitter as bile, swept over Teresa. "I'm also pregnant with Samuel's baby. I only married Everett to save your husband's reputation. I love him just that much." She pressed her attack on seeing an expression of shock mar the beauty of the woman she hated for claiming what she wanted. "Samuel told me he married you for your money, but slept with me because he truly loves me."

Lifting the hem of her gown, she turned and walked away from Mrs. Samuel Cole, feeling as if she had exacted a measure of revenge on the man who'd sold her to a man wherein by law she had to submit to his will.

Her husband rose to his feet with her approach. "I have to leave now."

His brow furrowed. "But we haven't cut the cake."

She held his hand, her nails biting into the tender flesh on his palm. "I'm going to be sick, Everett. You don't want everyone to know that your bride is with child so soon after the ceremony."

As soon as the last word was out of her mouth, her eyes rolled back and she sagged weakly against him. He managed to catch her before she collapsed to the grass. Lifting her against his chest, he made his way over to Samuel.

"Please apologize to everyone for our hasty departure, but I've got to take her home."

Samuel patted Everett's shoulder. "I'll take care of everything."

M.J. had composed herself enough to confront her husband. She tapped his arm. "I need to see you in the house."

He frowned at her. "Not now, darling."

"Either it's now or everyone will hear what I have to say to you," she mumbled.

There was something in his wife's gaze and in the tone of her voice that unnerved Samuel. "All right." He excused himself and followed her into the house.

They stepped into the living room. "Talk, M.J."

Shaking her head, she headed for the staircase. "Upstairs."

Samuel had no choice but to follow her, his gaze lingering on her shapely legs in a pair of sheer black stockings. She slowly mounted the staircase, her hand gripping the banister.

Once in their bedroom, he turned and stared at her, his heart pumping uncontrollably. There was something wrong with his wife. Was it the baby?

"Sit down, darling."

M.J. shook her head. "I don't want to sit."

"Are you all right?"

A slight smile curved her mouth. "Yes."

"Then why are we here?"

Moving over to a small round table cradling a collection of egg-shaped crystals, she picked up one and launched it at his head. Samuel ducked just in time to avoid injury. It hit a wall, breaking into shards.

"Why didn't you tell me!" she screamed before she launched another missile at him.

Samuel dodged this one, too. "What the hell are you talking about?"

The paperweights kept coming. "You fucked her!"

Samuel tried to get close enough to stop the assault, but M.J.'s aim was a little too accurate. "Who are you talking about?" A table lamp crashed inches from his feet.

"Teresa Maldonado! She told me that you got her pregnant!"

Once M.J. ran out of things to throw he came toward her. "Oh my God!"

M.J., her face streaked with tears, neatly coiffed hair falling down around her shoulders, backed up until a wall stopped her retreat. "Do not blame him for what you've done. How can you do this to me, to us, to our children?"

"I didn't mean for it to happen, M.J."

She glared at the man she loved beyond description, Samuel seemingly aging before her eyes. "You promised me that you would be a faithful husband, but not only do you fuck another woman, but you also get her pregnant."

"Don't say that word!"

"What? Fuck! Why not, Samuel? But isn't that what you did? Or did you make love to her?"

"Stop it!" he shouted.

Her eyes narrowed. "I will not stop until I've had my say. You've married her off to another man. Now I want you to send them away. Somewhere where I will never see that woman or the bastard she's carrying ever again."

Samuel felt as if a hand had closed around his throat, making breathing difficult. "But where, M.J.?"

"I don't know and I don't care. Anywhere but in West Palm Beach." Cradling her belly with both hands, she moved over and sat down heavily on the bed. "I want you to move your things out of this bedroom." She turned, presenting him with her back. "Right now I can't stand to look at you."

"You don't mean that."

"Don't tell me what I mean, Samuel Cole. If I weren't carrying this baby I'd take my children and leave you. And don't you dare tell me I can't take your children away from you, because I'm certain you wouldn't want anyone to know that you've been breeding bastards. Now get the hell away from me before whatever I feel for you turns to hate." Her shoulders shook; then came the sobs, the sound reaching down deep inside her, tearing at her heart and leaving her to bleed, unchecked.

Samuel turned and walked out of the bedroom where he'd shared his life and passion with his wife. Guilt tore through his gut like a lighted fuse, a racing out-of-control fire. His wife had issued an ultimatum.

He had to send Everett and Teresa away to save his marriage.

PART 4

1929–1947

Samuel Claridge Cole

You only begin to discover the difference between what you really are, your real self, and your appearance when you get a bit older.

—Doris Lessing

30

I must be sure to do whatever seems hardest.

—Saint Bernadette

West Palm Beach, Florida—October 7, 1929

Everett knocked on the door to Samuel's office, getting his attention. His teeth shone whitely beneath his mustache. "Kirkland, here, reporting for duty."

Samuel felt his heart sink. It had taken him a week to formulate a strategy that would banish his best friend and confidant with little or no effort or fanfare. A series of telephone calls had put the plan into motion.

Forcing a smile he did not feel, he beckoned to Everett as he stood up. "Come in. How was Cuba?"

"Beautiful. It was very emotional for Teresa, meeting cousins she'd only heard about."

Samuel approached Everett, rested a hand on his shoulder, and steered him to the conference table. "I have to talk to you about something."

"Talk to me, Cole," Everett said glibly, taking a seat at the table.

Samuel sat down and stared at the gold band on Everett's left hand for several seconds. "I've decided to open an office in Miami, and I want you to head it. You will be responsible for ColeDiz holdings in Costa Rica and Mexico. I will assume total control for Jamaica and Puerto Rico."

Everett did not move, not even to blink. "Are you sure this is what you want?" A barely perceptible nod of Samuel's head followed his query.

Letting out a breath, he stared out the window. "I understand, Samuel. It will be easier on all of us if there is some distance between you and Teresa."

"It's not Teresa."

"Then who is it?" Everett asked, his gaze swinging back to Samuel.

"M.J."

"You told her?"

"No. Your wife did."

Everett's face was a glowering mask of rage. "When!"

"At your reception."

"Shit!" The expletive exploded from the accountant. "Why the hell would she do that?"

Cradling his head in his hands, Samuel closed his eyes. "I don't know."

"I'm going to . . ." His threat died on his lips when Samuel glared up at him.

"Do not," he said softly, "do or say anything to her."

A feral grin thinned Everett's mouth. "I shouldn't have to remind you that Teresa is my wife, not your whore."

Samuel stared at the man who had become closer to him than his own brothers. But at that moment he wanted to smash his face. "Tell me now, Everett, if you want to move to Miami. Otherwise pack up your things and walk the hell out of here." His voice, though quiet, held an undertone of cold contempt.

There was a pulse beat of silence before Everett said, "I'll take what you're offering."

Pushing away from the table, Samuel walked to his desk, retrieving a large envelope. He returned to Everett and extended it to him. "I'm buying back your house. There's enough in here to buy a very nice place in Miami. There's also the name of a moving company who will come and pack up your belongings. I've included the name and telephone number of the agent of the building where you'll set up your office."

Everett took the envelope. His expression mirrored complete unconcern. "You did all of this in a week?"

"I'd do it all in a second if it meant saving my marriage."

Tilting his head, Everett stared up at the ceiling. "How bad is it, Samuel?"

He knew Everett was referring to his relationship with M.J. "I'd rather face a pack of rabid dogs than deal with M.J."

"Look, man, I'm sorry."

"No, Everett, I'm sorry. This is the hardest decision I've ever had to make in my life."

There was a lengthy pause. "I understand why you have to do it."

The two men stared at each other; then Samuel pulled Everett into a strong embrace.

"Thanks, Kirkland."

Everett forced a smile. "Don't mention it, Cole."

Samuel walked down the hallway leading to his wife's bedroom. He knocked on the door, waiting for a response.

"Yes."

Pushing open the door, he walked in. M.J. sat on a tapestry-covered chair in the sitting room, reading. She'd rested her bare feet on a matching footstool.

She'd broken her promise to him and had cut her hair. It had been her way of punishing him for his infidelity.

He met her questioning gaze. It was the first time he'd entered his old bedroom since the Kirkland reception.

"It's done."

That said, he turned and walked out, closing the door softly behind him.

Pressing her head against the chair's back, M.J. found no joy in the news that she would not be reminded that her husband's mistress was carrying Martin's and Nancy's sister or brother.

A single tear slid down her cheek. A second one followed, then more. She cried silently for the end of something that would never be the same.

"Mr. Cole."

Samuel answered the intercom. "Yes, Mrs. Harris?"

"Mr. Kirkland is on the line for you."

"Please put him through. Kirkland," he said when he heard the familiar voice.

"Have you heard the news?"

"I'm listening to the radio right now. You predicted it, Everett."

"The banks are closed. You know what that means, don't you?"

Blowing out a breath, Samuel nodded even though Everett couldn't see him. "Yes. I'm all right. How about you?"

"I'm good. How much do you stand to lose?"

Samuel smiled. "Less than five thousand." That was the projected amount needed to cover business expenses for the remainder of 1929.

"I will lose half that amount," Everett said. "How's the family?"

"Everyone's good. How's Miami?"

"Hot. There's a lot of building going on, but it still looks like a swamp. Ramon and Silvia plan to move down before the end of the year."

Samuel wanted to ask about Teresa, but held his tongue. He'd convinced himself she was no longer his concern because she was another man's wife.

The two men talked for another quarter of an hour, then rang off. They'd discussed October 24, 1929, which had come to be known as

Black Thursday, a day of trading that caused panic throughout Wall Street and spread to other exchanges and markets.

ColeDiz had been spared because it was a privately held company, and systematic cash withdrawals had protected Samuel Cole's fortune. The stock market crash and bank failures had plunged the country into an economic tailspin as President Hoover sought to use the power of his office to bolster the country's financial system.

Reclining in his chair, Samuel anchored his feet on the corner of his desk as a wave of nostalgia hit him. He missed Everett, his financial genius, sharing in-depth discussions about the market, crop prices, and tariffs.

He missed his friend, and his friend's wife. What he could not afford to think of was the child whom he would never see or claim as his own.

31

The effect of the large family upon the father is only less disastrous than it is upon the mother.

—Margaret Sanger

West Palm Beach, Florida—February 27, 1930

Marguerite-Josefina Cole opened her eyes for several seconds, then closed them again. "Did you see her?"

Samuel stared at his wife's face, its pallor enhanced by the inky blackness of her hair. She'd lost a lot of blood. "Yes, I did. She's beautiful."

M.J. struggled to keep her eyes open. Her labor was long and difficult, as it'd been with her other babies. "Are you upset, Sammy?"

"About what?"

"Three babies and they all look like me."

Sitting beside the hospital bed, Samuel leaned over and kissed her parched lips. "I don't mind, darling. You're a lot prettier than I am."

She smiled. "Have you decided on a name?"

Samuel nodded. "I like Josephine. What do you like?"

"Juliana."

"Perhaps we can give her two first names. Juliana-Josephine."

"That's too long. We'll call her either Josephine or Juliana. Help me sit up, Samuel." Anchoring an arm around her back and under her knees, he lifted her, supporting her back with several pillows. "Thank you." She unbuttoned the front of her nightgown.

A white-clad nurse walked into the room, carrying a hospital gown and face mask. Mr. Cole, you're going to have to put these on before your wife can feed your daughter."

Samuel slipped into the hospital gown and fastened the ties to the mask at the back of his head. Minutes later another nurse entered the room carrying a tiny bundle. She handed the baby to M.J., then turned and left, the rubber soles on her shoes making swishing sounds on the waxed floor.

He sat down again as M.J. unwrapped the baby, counting her fingers and toes. "They're all there."

"I just wanted to make certain." She removed a full breast from her gown, putting the nipple close to the baby's mouth. Within seconds the tiny girl closed her mouth over the nipple and began nursing.

Samuel sat, transfixed by the tiny dark-haired baby girl suckling her mother's breast. He'd missed so much: sharing a bed with his wife, making love to her, and watching her body change each advancing day of her confinement.

He'd sinned and his punishment was banishment.

He had his children, but along the way he'd lost his wife.

Samuel carried M.J. up the curving staircase a week after she delivered their second daughter, Josephine Juliana Cole. A nurse followed, carrying the baby.

Martin and Nancy, holding hands, stood at the top waiting for their parents and new baby sister.

Nancy pulled away from her brother, launching herself at Samuel's leg. "Mama!"

M.J. smiled down at her. "Hi, baby." Her voice was soft, weak.

Samuel tried shaking Nancy loose. "Let me put your mother in bed. Then you can come see her."

"I want to see her now!" she screamed, tightening her hold on his trousers.

"Martin, take Nancy to your room."

Four-year-old Martin tried to pull his sister away from his father's leg, but was bitten for his efforts. "She bit me!" he wailed, staring at the deep impressions on the back of his hand.

"Nancy!" Samuel's voice boomed like thunder, startling his wife and children. It was the first time they'd heard him raise his voice.

Martin's dark eyes widened as he stared numbly at his father, while Nancy, who'd released his pants, shrank back in fear.

M.J. pushed against her husband's chest. "Put me down."

He complied, lowering her gently until her shoes touched the carpeted floor. Raising his arm, he pointed in the direction of their bedrooms. "Go to your rooms, and don't come out until I tell you."

"I don't want to. I want to see the baby," Martin demanded defiantly.

"Me too," Nancy said, as she placed her hands on her hips as she'd seen her mother do.

M.J. nodded to the nurse, holding Josephine. "Please take the baby to the last bedroom on the right and put her in the cradle." Holding out her arms to Nancy and Martin, she gave them a pleading look. "Please go to your rooms. Mother will send for you as soon as I change my clothes. Then you can see the baby."

She wanted to get off her feet and into bed before she passed out. She'd risked her health and life carrying and giving birth to Josephine. Her doctor, who'd warned her against having another child, wanted to perform a procedure that would prevent her from becoming pregnant again, but she'd refused.

After Teresa Kirkland informed her that she was carrying Samuel's baby, M.J. had sworn an oath on her dead parents' souls that Samuel Cole would never get her pregnant again.

Nancy and Martin hugged their mother. Taking his sister's hand, Martin led Nancy to her room. He stood in the doorway to his, watching his mother and father for several seconds before he walked into his bedroom and closed the door.

M.J. leaned against the wall to support her sagging body. She glared at Samuel. "Don't *ever* scream at my children again."

Taking her arm, Samuel eased her off the wall. "In case you've forgotten, they're also my children."

She shook her head slowly. "No, Samuel. You forfeited the right to be a father when you slept with *that* woman. If you want to be a father, then be one to your bastard!"

Samuel wanted to shake M.J. senseless. "You asked me to send her away, and I did. What more do you want?"

The fire in her black eyes blazed like hot coals. "I want you to leave. I don't need you. My children don't need you."

"We can continue to sleep apart, but I will not leave my home or my children."

Raising her chin in a gesture of defiance, she stared down her nose at him. "Then I'll leave."

"With what money? Remember, when the banks failed you lost all the money in your name. Which means I've been paying for everything."

M.J. felt trapped. She'd forgotten she had no funds on which to draw. "I'll sell my jewelry."

Samuel flashed a feral grin. "And who's going to buy your trinkets? Perhaps you don't venture enough beyond the walls of your palace to know that we're in the throes of an economic depression. Millions are jobless, soup kitchens have been set up in some of the larger cities to feed the hungry, and those without homes are living in tents. I suggest you scrap your grand fantasy of leaving me. If you don't want to be a wife, then be a mother."

Bending slightly, he swept M.J. up in his arms and carried her into the bedroom. The nurse stood at the cradle changing Josephine's diaper. Samuel placed his wife gently on the bed before he walked out of the bedroom.

He'd prayed she would soften her stance after having the baby, but it was apparent she hadn't. It was the first time since Teresa disclosed she was carrying his child that M.J. spoke of leaving him. And he was steadfast when he said he would never permit her to take his children from him.

He'd make her a prisoner before he'd allow that to happen.

32

Give me children, or I shall die!

—Genesis 30:1

Miami, Florida—April 25, 1930

"Mr. Kirkland."

Everett's head came up, his eyes widening when he saw the doctor standing only a few feet away. He hadn't heard the man's approach, because he had dozed off in the chair. He glanced at a wall clock. It was after three in the afternoon. He'd been in the hospital more than twenty-four hours.

He stood up, unaware of the runaway pounding of his heart. The look on the young Negro doctor's face foretold bad news. Had Teresa lost the baby? Or had she died?

"Yes, Doctor?"

"Your wife delivered a baby boy. We had to perform a procedure known as a Cesarean because the baby was breech."

"Breech?" Everett repeated as if he were drugged or intoxicated. He was so tired he couldn't think.

"He'd entered the birth canal feet first instead of headfirst."

Everett caught the doctor's arm in a punishing grip. "What aren't you telling me?"

Dr. Jimmie Jones saw fear in the gold eyes staring at him. Everett Kirkland had carried his wife into the hospital the day before after her amniotic sac ruptured. The young woman spent the next twenty-four hours laboring to birth her baby. In the end he'd opted to operate or lose mother *and* child.

"Your wife is okay, as is your son. But I'm sorry to say she will never carry another child."

Everett released the doctor's arm and sagged weakly down to the chair. "What happened?"

"We couldn't stop the bleeding. In the end we had to perform a hysterectomy."

Pressing a hand to his forehead, Everett closed his eyes. His parents had had one child, and he was just informed that he would never father a child. The Kirkland bloodline would end with him.

"Mr. Kirkland?"

He looked up again. "Yes?"

"Would you like to see your son?"

"No, Dr. Jones. I'd like to see my wife."

If the doctor was shocked by his response, he didn't show it. "You can't see your wife for a while. She's in recovery. Go home and clean yourself up. She should be awake by the time you return."

Nodding, Everett pushed to his feet and made his way slowly down the corridor and out of the hospital and into a tropical downpour. Marriage to Teresa had turned out to be more than he'd expected. He looked forward to leaving his office and going home to her delicious meals and intelligent conversation.

Her anger when she was told they were relocating to Miami was replaced with joy when her family purchased a house in a section of the city that was referred to as Little Havana because of an influx of Cuban immigrants who had come to work in the many hotels and proposed vacation retreats along Miami Beach.

Their marriage was almost normal. The exception was even though they shared a bed, he'd kept his promise not to have sex with her. He wanted to wait until after she had Samuel's baby before consummating their marriage.

The one time he walked into the bedroom and observed her very swollen body he'd imagined she was carrying his child. That was the first time in his life that he felt the pull of fatherhood.

He wanted Teresa to have another baby—his baby.

Everett returned to the Greater Miami Colored Hospital carrying a vase of flowers. He walked into the room assigned to Teresa and found her sitting up in bed breast-feeding.

Smiling, he leaned over and kissed her forehead. "Congratulations, Mrs. Kirkland."

Dark smudges under Teresa's eyes enhanced their light color. "Thank you." Her voice was hoarse from hours of screaming. "The flowers are beautiful."

"So are you," he crooned, kissing her again.

He placed the vase on a table, then stared at the baby in her arms. A down of white gold covered his tiny round head. Everett's features became more animated. "What color are his eyes?"

"Green. He looks just like his *abuleo.*"

"Better his grandfather than his father."

"What would make you say that, Everett?" Teresa asked tentatively.

She watched as he took a chair at the foot of the bed, looping one leg over the opposite knee. Strange and disquieting thoughts began crowding her mind. She'd thought things were well between them. They'd stopping arguing, and she'd begun to think of themselves as a couple—a happily married couple. "I asked you a question, and I expect an answer."

"You expect or you'd *like* an answer?"

Her forehead furrowed. She didn't want to fight with him. "I'd like an answer, Everett."

"If you're going to have only one child, then better it look like your father than your ex-lover."

"What are you talking about?"

"You don't know?"

"Know what, Everett?" Her query held a thread of panic. "What aren't you telling me?"

A warning voice whispered in Teresa's head that something was wrong. It couldn't be her son because she'd checked to see that he was born with two ears, and ten fingers and toes. Her beautiful little baby boy was perfect. She glanced down when the sucking on her breast stopped. Her son had fallen asleep.

"You will never carry another baby," Everett said in a voice so low she had to strain her ears to hear what he'd said. "You were hemorrhaging, so in order to save your life the doctor removed your uterus."

Teresa wanted to laugh because the precious gift cradled to her breast was Samuel's, and laugh at Everett for being a fool. He'd married her to save Samuel Cole's reputation, but had been cheated out of siring his own children because his wife had been rendered barren. She grimaced as pain ripped through her lower belly when she shifted on the bed, in an attempt to find a more comfortable position.

She forced her lips to part in what could pass for a smile. "I think we're blessed, Everett."

"For what?"

"At least we have a son."

Everett wanted to tell her that the child wasn't his. He'd tried to convince himself that the child she carried was his, but failed miserably.

"You're right," he said unconvincingly. *You have a son, Teresa,* he added silently. "What would you like to name him?"

Her green eyes met his gold ones. "Do you like Joshua?"

"That's my middle name."

She smiled. "I know. I like it because it's strong and masculine."

"Do you want to give him a middle name?"

"No. Joshua is enough."

"Joshua Kirkland." There was a lethal calmness in Everett's eyes. "Let's hope he'll grow up to be worthy to carry the name of my father and grandfather."

If Everett had sought to hurt Teresa, then he was successful. She turned her face, closed her eyes, and feigned sleep. The child in her arms would be known as a Kirkland, but in reality he would never become Everett's son.

Joshua was hers, hers *and* Samuel's.

33

But who has ever known another's heartbreak—all he can know is his own.

—Sara Teasdale

West Palm Beach, Florida—March 5, 1932

Four-year-old Nancy and Josephine, a month shy of her second birthday, lay on their backs, staring up at the kite rising and falling in the wind.

"Higher, Daddy," Nancy shouted.

Samuel smiled at his daughters reclining on the grass. "It's high enough, cupcakes."

"Higher, higher," Josephine shrieked excitedly.

Samuel unwound the last of the string from the wooden dowel. "That's it, girls. It can't go any higher."

They'd waited days for enough wind to go kite sailing. Earlier that morning the weather forecast had predicted high winds from a storm coming off the Atlantic.

"Samuel!"

He turned around to find M.J. a few feet away, hands folded on her hips. The wind whipped her dress around her legs. Hemlines had dropped along with the onset of hard times.

"What's the matter?"

"Where's Martin?"

"I don't know. He was here with us, then said he was going back to the house."

Lines of concern formed between her eyes. "He's not in the house."

"Then look again, M.J. He has to be somewhere."

"Samuel . . ."

The look on his wife's face made Samuel's heart lurch. Did she know something he didn't? Nothing had changed between them. They were married, but in name only. He let go of the kite and it sailed high in the air, floating away as the two girls jumped up squealing uncontrollably.

"What's the matter, M.J.?"

Eyes wide, she pressed a hand to her chest. "Do you think someone took him like the Lindbergh baby?"

The query was barely out of her mouth when Samuel reached down and grabbed his daughters, carrying them under his arms as if they were footballs. He started racing toward the house, leaving M.J. to follow them.

Lifting the skirt of her dress, she raced after her husband and children. The news of the kidnapping of the son of famed transatlantic aviator Charles A. Lindbergh had captured the country's attention as the most intensive manhunt in American history was mounted to search for the twenty-month-old boy. President Hoover had issued an order for all federal agencies to assist in the search. More than 100,000 officers and civilian volunteers searched the entire eastern seaboard, stopping cars and questioning passengers.

Martin wasn't the son of a celebrity, but the fact remained he was the son of a wealthy man. Samuel Cole hadn't lost his fortune as so many others had during the market crash and bank failure. He'd adjusted his lifestyle, employing only essential help.

Samuel reached the house first, setting his daughters on their feet; they hadn't stopped giggling during the frantic sprint. "Stay here and don't move," he ordered M.J.

Racing to the staircase, he took the stairs two at a time. He flung open doors, searching bedrooms, dressing rooms, and bathrooms. Retracing his steps, he bounded down the stairs and began on the first story.

Samuel could not fathom losing one of his children. He walked into the kitchen, his face covered with sweat. "Have you seen Martin?" he asked Bessie.

She shook her head. "No, sir. Not since breakfast."

His steps slowed as he looked into the downstairs bathroom, pantry. Samuel's hands were shaking when he opened the door to the room where his mother slept whenever she came for a visit. M.J. had given her one of the bedroom suites, but Belinda said climbing the staircase aggravated her arthritic knee.

Sprawled across the bed, facedown, was his son. Walking on trembling knees, he sat on the side the mattress and buried his face in his hands. His son was safe!

Once his respiration slowed to a normal rate, Samuel reached over and placed a hand on Martin's head. He pulled it away. The boy was burning up!

Gathering him off the bed, he walked back to where he'd left M.J. and their daughters. Tears of relief sparkled in her eyes when she saw them.

"Oh, Samuel," she sobbed. "He's okay."

"He has a fever."

M.J. noticed the bright spots of color on her son's cheeks for the first time. "*Dios mio!*" she gasped, crossing her chest.

"Call the doctor, M.J. Tell him it's an emergency."

"What's wrong with Martin, Daddy?" Nancy asked.

"I don't know, baby girl. But I want you and your sister to stay away from him until the doctor comes."

Josephine stomped her foot. "I baby girl!"

Shaking his head while rolling his eyes, Samuel turned and headed for the staircase. His daughters were so competitive that whenever he attempted to referee their squabbles they turned on him.

M.J. sat next to Samuel on a padded bench in the hallway outside their son's room. She laced her fingers through his and rested her hand on his shoulder. He stiffened slightly, then relaxed.

She closed her eyes. He smelled so good. He felt so good. She couldn't remember the last time they'd touched, been this close. And despite all that had happened between them she knew she would never stop loving Samuel.

M.J. and Samuel came to their feet when the door opened. The elderly doctor shifted his bag from one hand to the other. His dark eyes in an equally dark face belied his seventy-plus years of living.

"Your son is going to be all right in about a week."

"What's wrong with him, Dr. Rose?" M.J. asked.

"If you'd looked under his clothes you would've seen the vesicles."

"What?" Samuel and M.J. chorused.

"Blisters. Martin has chickenpox. He probably hasn't been feeling well for a while, but once the blisters come out he'll begin to feel better. They're going to itch, so try to keep him from scratching them because they can leave scars. Give him a warm bath or shower and let him air-dry. Repeat the shower or bath several times a day during the worst outbreak. This will help dry the scabs sooner and make them fall off without having to be scratched or rubbed off."

M.J. stared at Samuel, wondering if he'd ever had chickenpox, because she hadn't. "Is there anything you can give me to put on the rash?"

"Make an oatmeal poultice. It will help speed drying up the blisters."

Samuel pulled his hand from his wife's. "What about the girls?"

"There's no doubt they've also been exposed, but they don't necessar-

ily have to come down with the disease. It's better if they do before starting school."

M.J. smiled at the elderly doctor. "May I go see my son?"

He lifted bushy white eyebrows. "Are you with child, Mrs. Cole?"

"Oh . . . no," she stammered, giving Samuel a sidelong glance. She
and Samuel hadn't slept together in more than two years. "Why?"

"Chickenpox can be dangerous for a pregnant woman, especially in
her last trimester. Have either of you had the disease?"

"I have," Samuel confirmed.

"I haven't," M.J. said.

"Well, Mr. Cole, it looks as if you may have to play Florence Nightingale.
I'll check back in a couple of days."

Samuel cupped the doctor's elbow. "I'll see you out, Dr. Rose."

M.J. waited until Samuel escorted the doctor down the staircase; then
she pushed open the door to her son's room. She stood at his bedside
watching him sleep. In a moment of panic, she thought she'd lost him.
Running her fingers through her short hair, she mumbled a prayer of
thanksgiving.

She still hadn't moved when Samuel stood in the doorway holding
Nancy and Josephine. Although slender, he possessed tremendous upper
body strength.

"The girls wanted to see Martin."

Nancy placed a finger over her lips. "Shhh-hh, Daddy. Don't wake him
up."

Josephine repeated the gesture. "Yeah," she whispered.

Samuel and M.J. shared a smile, one reserved for lovers.

M.J. closed the distance between them, holding out her arms for
Josephine. "I think it's time for you to take a nap."

"Do I have to take a nap, Mother?" Nancy asked.

"Yes, you do. In fact, all of us are going to take a nap."

Nancy smiled up at her father. "Even you, Daddy?"

He pressed a kiss to her forehead. "Yes, cupcake."

M.J. waited until later that night to seek out her husband. She found
him in his library. He'd fallen asleep on a leather chaise. She sat on the
edge, shaking him gently. He came awake immediately.

"Is Martin all right?"

"Yes, Samuel."

Light from a floor lamp displayed what she'd ignored for too long. At
thirty-four, Samuel Cole's hair was more than salt-and-pepper; he would
be completely gray by thirty-five. His face was as lean as it'd been eight
years before. There were new lines around his eyes, lines she attributed
to pain and hopefully remorse.

"Do you want something?" His voice was filled with neutral tones.

"Yes. I'd like you to consider sending Martin to a private school."

"Why?"

"I'm afraid of what happened to the Lindbergh baby possibly happening to our children."

"What else do you want?"

"I want you to hire a full-time driver who can double as a bodyguard."

He lifted a black eyebrow. "What else?"

An attractive blush suffused her cheeks and she glanced away, unable to meet his direct stare. "I'd like you to move back into the bedroom."

"Why, M.J.?"

"Because I've missed you."

"It took you two years to come to that conclusion?"

"Samuel, don't make this harder on me than it actually is."

"You, Marguerite-Josefina? Why is it always you?"

"It wasn't me who sinned with another man, Samuel."

"I suppose I should be grateful for that, because none of our children look like me."

"*Jodete y aprieta el culo!*"

He stared at her, complete surprise on his face. "I hope you don't use those words in front of the children."

She leaned closer. "Never."

Samuel stared at the too-perfect face, a face he'd found hypnotic when he first glimpsed it, and a face that a Cuban artist had immortalized for perpetuity.

He wanted to scoop her up in his arms, take her upstairs, and take her without tenderness and foreplay, ram into her celibate flesh until she gasped for breath, then pull out, leaving her unfulfilled. As unfulfilled as he'd been for the past two years.

But he wasn't going to fall into her arms and into her bed because she asked. He'd let one woman lead him by the gonads, and he vowed it would not happen again.

"I can't fuck myself," he whispered, translating her slur, "nor will I fuck you, M.J. Not now. Not when you deem it." Samuel ignored her soft gasp. "If or when I move back into *our* bedroom it will be when both of us want it. You'll know and I'll know when the time is right.

"Now as to your request to enroll our children in private school and hire a bodyguard, I'll let you know at the end of the month." Rising on an elbow, he pressed his mouth to hers. "Good night."

Stunned by his rejection, M.J. watched her husband turn over and present her with his back. "I hate you, Samuel!"

"No, you don't," he mumbled, smiling.

"I do hate you," she sobbed.

Shifting, Samuel moved off the chaise, eased her down to the Persian rug, and covered her body with his. Unshed tears turned her eyes into pools of gleaming onyx. They widened as a smile softened his features. She'd felt his growing erection.

Gasping, he closed his eyes. "I'm surprised it still works."

M.J. buried her face against his throat. "What have I done to you?"

"Nothing, baby. It's what I've done to you."

They lay together on the floor, offering each other silent absolution. Samuel got up, pulling M.J. with him. They made their way through the quiet house, up the staircase, down the wide hallway, and into their bedroom.

No words were spoken as they undressed and climbed into bed together; they did not make love; that would come later—once they learned to trust again.

34

Most rich people are the poorest people I know.

—Elsa Maxwell

West Palm Beach, Florida, October 9, 1933

"Did you say something, baby?"

"Sammy! You haven't heard a word I've been saying?"

Samuel pulled his stunned gaze away from the figures on the financial statements Everett had mailed him. He hadn't been listening to what M.J. was saying about the aborted coup in Havana because he had to make a monumental decision as to whether to curtail coffee production in Costa Rica and Mexico. A worldwide depression had taken its toll on everyone—rich and poor alike.

The United States had elected a new president, Franklin Delano Roosevelt, who in his inaugural address denounced the nation's financial leaders, saying, "These *money-changers* should be driven from the temple and never again be allowed to misuse other people's money."

The day he made his speech, more than thirteen million Americans were jobless, and in the final years of the Hoover administration scores of banks had failed, factories had closed, and farmers were evicted from their lands. Entire families were living in tarpaper shacks and competing with stray animals for scraps of food.

Although he eschewed politics and politicians alike, Samuel was impressed with the New Deal, the president's economic plan of recovery for the country. Roosevelt had closed the nation's banks for a seven-day holiday to allow for passage of emergency legislation by Congress and new regulations by the Treasury Department. He took the United States off the gold standard, passed a farm-relief bill to aid struggling farmers, and signed into law the National Industrial Recovery Act, which gave the government control over industry in an effort to bring the nation out of the Depression.

And despite the promulgation of the NRA, CCC, National Labor Board regulations, Samuel knew it would take years before the United States would regain its economic stability.

"I'm sorry," he apologized. "My mind is somewhere else."

M.J. folded the newspaper she'd been reading. "I said it's good we canceled our trip to Cuba. Government troops killed more than a hundred people in Havana who'd used the National Hotel to stage a coup. In Ivonne's last letter she wrote that she hardly goes to Havana anymore, because of the violence. Ever since President Machado declared a state of war everything has been crazy."

"But he's no longer the president."

She nodded. "True. But how long do you think de Cespedes will remain in power without the backing of the United States?"

"I don't know, M.J. You know I don't follow politics."

Her delicate jaw hardened. "Well, I do. And trust me, Samuel, when I predict that Cubans are going to trade one dictator for another if they support army chief of staff Fulgencio Batista to lead the country."

Samuel half listened to his wife rail about Cuban politics. A knot formed in his throat when he realized what he had to do. He was spending more money than he was bringing in, and if he continued at the current rate he would be penniless by the end of the decade.

"I have to go to Miami," he said after M.J. paused.

M.J. stared across the space separating her from her husband. It had taken him six months to move his possessions back into their bedroom, and during this time there were nights when they shared a bed, and others when they didn't. The night all of his clothes filled the closets was the first night he asked if he could make love to her.

Their coming together was tentative, as if they had to learn each other's body all over again, and when it ended she felt free, freer than she'd ever been in her life. Samuel hadn't used a condom, and she hadn't asked that he do so, because she wanted another child, a child that would represent a new start and the beginning of the rest of their lives together.

Teresa Kirkland's name was uttered once—when Samuel told her that his former secretary and her husband had relocated to Miami. She did not want to know when Teresa delivered, or the sex of the baby.

And M.J. was mature enough to know that her husband wasn't the first and wouldn't be the last man to father a child out of wedlock; the affair would've become more palatable if Teresa hadn't taunted her. Under another set of circumstances she would've ripped every blond strand out of Teresa's head. She'd fought and won too hard-earned a victory to marry Samuel Cole just to give him up without a fight—whether verbal or physical.

"Why?"

Samuel registered the tremor in the single word. "I'm closing the Miami office."

"Why?" she repeated.

"I can't afford to keep it open. I'm losing too much money."

M.J. blinked once. "What's going to happen to Everett?" She always liked the quiet, elegant accountant.

Sighing audibly, Samuel closed his eyes. And when he opened them his gaze was steady, resolute. "I'm going to have to let him go. I plan to give him a generous severance payout."

M.J. left her chair and sat on Samuel's lap. She wrapped her arms around his neck. "What is he going to do?"

Burying his face against his wife's neck, Samuel shook his head. "I don't know, darling. His house is paid for, so he doesn't have to concern himself with losing it. Don't forget that he's an accountant. He's a whiz when it comes to money and numbers. I'll give him enough that will hopefully tide him over until we can pull out of this stinking depression."

"When are you leaving?"

"Wednesday."

Pulling back, M.J. stared at Samuel. There was something lurking behind the deep-set dark eyes that frightened her. He'd been thinking about going to Miami for some time, and she wondered whether he was going to fire Everett or see Teresa.

"What did she have?"

Samuel knew exactly whom M.J. was referring to. There would've been a time in his past when he would've feigned ignorance, but that was over. He was older, he'd changed, and now that he was thirty-five his focus was no longer amassing a fortune or building an empire. It was now his wife and children.

"A boy, M.J.," he said in a quiet voice.

M.J. cursed herself for asking, but knew she could not spend the rest of her life wondering and imagining if every child she saw was her husband's, the brother or sister of her own children.

A wry smile parted her lips. "Now you have two sons and two daughters."

Samuel's impassive expression did not change. "He's not my son, M.J."

Her arching eyebrows lifted. "If he's not yours, then whose is he?"

"Everett's. He's a Kirkland, not a Cole."

"I don't want our children to know about him, Samuel. Promise me you'll never tell them about him."

Pulling her closer, Samuel kissed her hair. "I promise."

Samuel walked into the small Miami-based office of ColeDiz International, Ltd. There was no one sitting in the reception area, so he headed for the back office.

He removed his hat, before loosening the top button on his shirt. The heat inside the office was stifling. Where, he thought, were the fans?

The door to Everett's office was partially opened and he could hear moans coming from the other side. Grasping the knob he opened the door, and what he saw rendered him motionless and mute. Everett sat on the edge of his desk, trousers around his ankles while a woman knelt in front of him with his penis in her mouth. Both were so involved in the act that neither had noticed he was there. Backpedaling, Samuel closed the door and returned to the reception area to wait.

The telephone in the reception rang three times before the young woman came to answer it. Her eyes were as round as saucers once she recognized who sat in the waiting area.

"Excuse me," she said, reaching for the telephone. She mumbled a greeting into the receiver, her hand shaking noticeably.

Not waiting to be announced, Samuel got up and retraced his steps. Everett stood with his back to the door as he belted his trousers.

"I hope it was good, Everett."

The accountant froze, then turned slowly to see his boss standing in the doorway. As accustomed, he was impeccably attired. Samuel wore a tailored navy blue pin-striped single-breasted blazer, gray flannels, white shirt, and navy-and-white-striped tie.

Recovering quickly, Everett came around the desk, smiling. "Come in, Samuel, and close the door. I wasn't expecting you."

Rage glinted in Samuel's eyes. He did not move. "From what I just witnessed I doubt whether you were expecting anyone. I'm the last one to lecture another man about fidelity, but I can say I never shit where I had to eat."

Everett recoiled as if he'd been slapped. "Just why are you here, if not to spy on me?"

"That's where you're wrong, Everett. I'm here to close this office, and give you a severance package I feel is commensurate with your loyalty and years of service to ColeDiz."

"You can't!"

Taking half a dozen steps, Samuel walked into the office. It was his turn to gasp. Everett looked like he had when he'd first encountered him in Puerto Limon. He was emaciated, and the smell of alcohol was redolent in the small, sweltering space.

"What the hell have you done to yourself?"

Swaying to keep his balance, Everett groped for his chair and sat down heavily. "What I've done," he slurred with a lopsided grin pulling down one side of his mouth. "It's what you've done, King Cole. I save your precious reputation when I offer to marry your mistress and make her respectable, and the bitch pays me back by denying me my conjugal rights. So don't stand there and act so fuckin' pompous because I found someone willing to take care of my needs. The only time I can get some at home is when I beat the bitch into submission."

Samuel launched himself at Everett, his hands going around the throat of the man he'd come to love like a brother. His eyes literally bulged from their sockets.

"You beat her!" he bellowed, tightening his grip. Everett's head flopped as if he were a rag doll. "Where the hell is she?"

Gurgling sounds came from the accountant's throat as he clawed at the fingers choking off precious life-sustaining air. As quickly as the attack had begun it was over. His eyes filled, tears rolling down his face as he struggled to breathe.

"Where is she?" Samuel repeated.

Holding his bruised throat, Everett mumbled a silent prayer that his life had been spared. "She left me five months ago. She's staying with her parents."

Samuel hadn't realized he was sprawled over the desk until a stack of folders fell to the floor. He stood up, his chest rising and falling heavily. His body was soaked with sweat. He wasn't sure whether it was from the suffocating temperature or rage.

"And the boy?"

Everett's red-rimmed eyes closed briefly. "She took him with her."

"I'll be right back." Samuel walked out of the office to the front. The receptionist stared straight ahead. There was something about her that reminded him of Daisy. "Dial this number for me," he ordered without preamble. The woman followed his instructions, then handed him the telephone.

"This is Samuel Cole. I need you to bring a couple of men over to the ColeDiz office. I want you to pack up everything and ship it to my office in West Palm Beach. Yes, today. I'll wait here for you."

He handed the receptionist the telephone, then reached into the breast pocket of his jacket, withdrawing two envelopes. "This is for you, Miss Nelson. Your services will no longer be needed. Good luck in finding employment elsewhere." She hesitated, then took the envelope. Samuel glared at her from under lowered eyebrows. "You may go—*now*."

She retrieved her handbag from a file drawer and walked out, Samuel closing and locking the door behind her. His temper had cooled considerably when he reentered Everett's office.

He extended the remaining envelope. "This is for you." Everett stared at it, his arms crossed over his chest. "There's a West African proverb that says, 'God gives nothing to those who keep their arms crossed.' Take it, Everett. There's enough in this envelope for you to take care of your family until things change."

Everett grunted. "When are they going to change? Spare me the bullshit, Samuel, no one knows when anything is going to change." His demeanor changed, softening. "I don't need money. I want to work. Please let me come back to the West Palm office. Teresa can stay here with her family."

Samuel wanted to grant his request because he and Everett worked well together, but he had no way of knowing whether Teresa would reconcile with her husband. His reconciliation with M.J. was still too tenuous to leave anything to chance.

"I can't, Everett. Please take it."

A swollen silence ensued as both men relived the good and not-so-good times they'd shared. The seconds ticked off to minutes before Everett finally accepted the envelope. He reached for his jacket slung over the back of a chair, slipped his arms into it, then giving Samuel Cole one last, lingering look, walked out of the office for the last time.

Samuel was rooted to the spot until he heard the resounding slam of the front door. Then he sat down on a worn leather chair and waited for the movers.

35

Only colored women of the South know the extreme in suffering and humiliation . . .

> —from a letter signed "A Southern Colored Woman,"
> in *The Crisis,* 1919

West Palm Beach, Florida—October 17, 1946

"I don't believe it. The son of a bitch cheated the hangman when he swallowed a cyanide capsule."

Samuel did not glance up from the letter his secretary had just transcribed and typed for his signature. "Who cheated the hangman?" he asked his son.

"Hermann Goering."

"Who?"

"Hitler's number-two goon. The Nuremberg Tribunal said the Nazi bastard was a 'leading war aggressor and a creator of the oppressive program against Jews.' "

Samuel scrawled his signature, then blotted the ink. "How many did they hang?"

"Nine. The reporter who wrote the article said a few begged for forgiveness, while others were defiant. One bastard named Streicher shouted 'Heil Hitler' as the noose was tightened around his neck."

His head came up, and he stared at his son. Twenty-one-year-old Martin Diaz Cole, a recent college graduate, was now a ColeDiz International, Ltd., employee.

"They should've doused them with kerosene, then roasted them up like pigs on a spit."

Martin grimaced, dimples creasing his brown cheeks. "Damn, Dad. That sounds a bit heinous, even for you."

"The only difference between a Nazi and a Klansman is that one wears a hood and the other a swastika." He capped his fountain pen. "I hope you don't use that language in front of your mother."

Martin stared at his father, trying not to laugh. "I'm absolving myself of any blame for bad language."

"Why?"

"Because I learned it from you."

Samuel put down the pen and studied his firstborn. Martin's genes had compromised: he'd inherited his mother's dimples and delicate features. Martin's curly hair, height, and coloring had come from his father.

"I paid for four years of college so that you could get a degree in business, not profanity."

Martin glanced at the watch strapped to his wrist. "I suppose that's a not-so-subtle hint for me to leave."

Leaning back in his chair, Samuel ran a hand over his cropped steel-gray hair. "Please don't let me chase you."

"It's time I leave anyway. I have to go home and pick up my luggage."

"What time is your flight?"

"Two."

"Do you have the blueprints for the villas?"

"Don't worry so much, Dad. I have everything." Saluting, Martin stood up and walked out of his father's office. He was going to Costa Rica to oversee the construction of a vacation retreat.

It had taken a world depression and a second world war within a span of twenty years for Samuel Cole's dream to come full circle. He'd built an empire, a legacy, for his children, grandchildren, and hopefully his great-grandchildren.

The company's profits dropped dramatically between 1933 and 1938, resulting in a drastic decrease in coffee production. Samuel abandoned the Costa Rican coffee plantation and focused on those in Mexico, Puerto Rico, and Jamaica.

A year before Martin graduated from college ColeDiz underwent restructuring. Samuel moved the office into a new high-rise office building, employed an in-house attorney versed in international tariffs and maritime law, increased his clerical staff, hired a chief accountant, two accounting clerks, an executive secretary, and two part-time typists.

Martin worked with him during the summer and school holidays, and had accompanied him when he visited his Caribbean holdings. His son took to business like a duck to water, exhibiting negotiating skills that made Samuel feel like a neophyte.

Like a phoenix rising from the ashes, ColeDiz made a comeback with

Roosevelt's New Deal and an increase in the manufacture of armaments for the war in Europe.

Crossing his arms behind his head, Samuel smiled. Life was good. Martin had become an integral part of the company, Nancy was engaged to a fellow college student, Josephine was a freshman at Spelman College in Atlanta, Georgia, and nine-year-old David had been labeled a music prodigy.

Samuel's smile widened when he thought about his youngest son, who was the complete opposite of his older brother and sisters. He was content to spend hours by himself practicing the piano, making up lyrics for songs, and would at a moment's notice break into song.

Samuel doubted whether David would ever become involved with the family business, but M.J. belayed his doubts when she said all of their children had inherited the Cole gene for competitiveness, so there was hope for their youngest child.

A soft buzz, followed by the voice of his secretary, shattered the peaceful silence. "Samuel, are you expecting a Mrs. Kirkland? Because I don't have her down in your calendar."

Samuel sat up; his breath solidified in his throat as he mentally replayed Charlotte Rowland's query. She must have gotten the name wrong. He pressed a button on the intercom and picked up the telephone receiver.

"Did you say Mrs. Kirkland?"

"Yes. She's been waiting almost an hour. I didn't want to disturb you while you were meeting with Martin."

There was a long, brittle silence as Samuel stared at a wall covered with a soft wheat-colored fabric. He knew one Mrs. Kirkland, and that was Teresa. What, he wondered, was she doing in West Palm Beach, and why had she come to see him after so many years? Had something happened to Everett? Her son?

Not once, since she'd become Mrs. Everett Kirkland, had he thought of her child as his. That pain was too much for him to bear. It was cowardly, but easier to claim that he'd fathered four and not five children.

"Is she alone?" he asked after what seemed an interminable pause.

"Yes, she is."

Samuel knew he wasn't prepared to see Teresa again after so many years, but to come face-to-face with the son he'd denied and abandoned to the responsibility of another was a weighted guilt he would carry to his grave.

He knew he couldn't send Teresa away without finding out why she'd come to see him. "Give me a minute, then send her in."

Samuel hung up the phone and reached for the jacket to his suit he'd left on one of the chairs next to his desk. Slipping his arms into the sleeves, he then tightened and straightened his tie. He was standing behind his desk, ready for Teresa Kirkland, when the door to his office opened.

He'd believed he was ready until he saw her.

If he'd changed in seventeen years, so had she. When they'd parted she was a girl, but there was no girl left in the fashionably dressed woman staring back at him.

Forcing his legs to move, Samuel moved from behind the desk, his gaze meeting and fusing with hers. The closer he came, the more obvious the changes. There was a minute scar on her left cheekbone that hadn't been there before, and something told him the slashes around her mouth were not the result of smiling.

She tilted her head to look up at him, giving him a glimpse of the silver hair she'd pinned up under a wide natural straw hat. A slight smile softened his mouth when he recognized the haunting, sensual fragrance wafting from her body. It was Chanel No. 5. He'd bought it for her the day they'd gone shopping in St. Thomas. She also wore his other gift: the pearl necklace and earrings.

A short, black hip-length jacket, buttoned to the neck, flared out at the hips to accommodate the fullness of a matching skirt. Wrist-length black leather gloves and high-heel, ankle-strap shoes pulled her winning look together.

Her pale green gaze was steady before she glanced away. "I'm sorry about not calling for an appointment, but I felt if I had I wouldn't have been granted access."

Cupping her elbow, Samuel escorted her across the expansive office to an area where he held small, impromptu meetings. The action gave him the time he needed to get used to seeing her again. He'd forgotten how well spoken she'd been, and still was.

"If you'd called, I would've seen you," he said, seating her on a love seat.

A pale eyebrow lifted slightly. "Thank you. I know you're busy, and because I don't have an appointment, I'm going to make this visit very brief."

He sat down opposite her, crossing one leg over the other knee. "What can I do for you?"

Teresa was stunned by Samuel's cool appraisal, his impersonality. He appeared totally in control of his emotions, whereas her heart was pumping so hard her chest hurt. However, she had to admit Samuel Cole had matured exquisitely. There was no excess fat on his lean face. The new lines around his eyes added character rather than age. And the hair that had begun graying in his twenties was now a gleaming silver gray. He was impeccably groomed, as she'd expected him to be.

"I need your influence on behalf of *my* son." She was hard-pressed not to laugh when his jaw tightened when she referred to *their son* as *my son.*

Samuel was momentarily speechless in his surprise. It had taken Teresa seventeen years to contact him, and it was not for herself but her son. But the son she spoke of was also his son.

"What do you want from me?"

The pulse in Teresa's throat beat erratically at the threatening quality in his deep, drawling voice. The tense lines in her face relaxed as she called on the waning strength it took for her to travel from Miami to West Palm Beach to reunite with the man responsible for making her a mother.

"I want you to help him get into West Point."

Samuel blinked once. "The military academy in New York?"

"Yes."

"How can I help him?"

"Use your political influence. He needs letters of recommendation from elected officials."

"I have no such influence."

Her nerves tensed immediately. "You have it, Samuel, even if you've chosen not to exploit it." Opening her purse, she withdrew an envelope. "Take it."

He obeyed like an obedient child. "What's in here?"

"My son's name, address, telephone, his school principal, and a listing of his grades and test scores. I've never asked anything from you in seventeen years. The least you can do is grant me this one request."

She stood up and walked out of the office, leaving Samuel staring at the space where she'd been.

It was a full five minutes before he opened the envelope and read the contents. His eyes widened as he stared at the grades Joshua Kirkland had earned.

The boy was brilliant!

Samuel sat, losing track of time as he relived the seconds, minutes, hours, and days he'd spent with a little slip of a girl on a beautiful, seemingly magical, island what now seemed so long ago.

Hot tears burned his eyes when he realized that even though he loved his wife, he still loved Teresa. She'd had his child, but what she did not know was that he'd kept a small piece of her inside him, a small piece he would treasure forever.

36

How easy for man to break what never was bound—our song together.
                                                                —Anonymous

Two days following Teresa Kirkland's startling appearance, Samuel entered his office and saw a large box sitting in a corner. He read the note taped to a side: *This was delivered last night—Charlotte.*

He stared at the mailing label. It was from Teresa. Lines creased his forehead and he wondered what it was that she'd sent him.

The full impact of her visit did not sink in until later that night. Everything about her washed over him in vivid clarity as he recalled the exact color of her eyes—a frosty, cold green, the determined set of a mouth that was no longer lush and smiling, and the stiffness in her spine when she'd sat on the edge of the love seat. She hadn't even bothered to remove her gloves.

Reaching for a letter opener, he slid it along a flap on the box. He went completely still when he saw the contents. The carton was filled with letters, hundreds of them bundled with narrow red ribbons.

Samuel picked up a stack, staring at Teresa's small, slanting writing. The envelopes were addressed to him at his home. Untying the bundle, he realized none were sealed. He removed the first letter, his gaze racing over the fading blue ink. It was a handwritten birth announcement. He felt his knees buckle, and had to sit down before he fell.

* * *

Samuel couldn't read any more—at least not now. Teresa had poured out her heart to him on paper, yet could not summon the nerve to mail her letters.

Would he have answered her? Would he have gone to her when she pleaded for him to help her?

Samuel knew the answers to those questions as soon as they were formed in his head.

Yes, he would have.

He'd given her to his friend to protect, and he had beaten her. It was good he didn't know Everett's whereabouts, because he knew without a doubt that he would hurt the man—severely.

37

Men are beasts and even beasts don't behave like them.

—Brigette Bardot

Samuel forced himself to put one foot in front of the other as he climbed the winding staircase like someone in a trance. His mind was reeling from the cruelty and physical abuse Teresa had suffered from the man he'd trusted to take care of her. If he'd known Everett was going to treat her as he had, then he never would have sanctioned their marriage.

He hadn't lied to Teresa when he told her he would never leave M.J., but he would have provided handsomely for her and their child. He didn't know whether he would've continued to sleep with her, but knew without a doubt he'd do everything within his power to keep her safe and content.

The house was quiet with Martin in Costa Rica and his daughters away at college. He walked past his youngest son's room. There were times when he forgot there was still a child in the house.

David was born the year he turned thirty-nine. After he and M.J. "reconciled" he hadn't used any form of contraception with her. And when the years passed without M.J. conceiving, both of them thought their family complete with a son and two daughters.

Once her pregnancy was confirmed, M.J. doubted whether she would be strong enough to survive another. She'd spent the entire confinement in bed, and after she delivered her fourth child, a boy, the doctor confirmed her uncertainty with a hysterectomy. And like their other chil-

dren, David was more Diaz than Cole, and Samuel wondered whether
Joshua Kirkland was a Cole or a Maldonado.

He entered his bedroom suite, and went through the motions he'd
done countless times, undressing and showering before climbing into
bed next to M.J.

Her warmth and scent washed over him as she pressed her breasts
against his back. "I thought you were coming home early tonight." Her
voice was low, husky. There was no doubt she'd fallen asleep waiting for
him.

Samuel closed his eyes. "Why did you think that?"

"It was you who said we were going to take David to that new restaurant everyone's bragging about."

"Damn it! I forgot. Why didn't you call and remind me?" He'd been so
engrossed in Teresa's letters that he'd lost track of time.

He had instructed his secretary to cancel all of his meetings for the
rest of the week, then locked the door to his office and sat down to read
as many of the letters as he could before his eyes began burning.

Her letter of May 18, 1933, confirmed what Everett had told him the
day he'd come to Miami to close the office, that she had left her husband
after he spanked Joshua because the child had touched his watch. She'd
left Everett, but come back to him later that year when he promised
never to hit her or the child again.

M.J. draped an arm over his waist. "I figured you had become involved
in something that you couldn't get out of."

He covered the hand resting on his belly. "You shouldn't have made
that decision, baby. You know when I promise my children something,
they take precedence over everything else. Was David disappointed?"

"If he was, then he didn't show it. You know nothing bothers him too
much. Most of the time he acts as if he's in another world. I'm beginning
to worry about him."

"Why, M.J.?"

"Because he spends hours playing the piano."

"It's all your fault."

She stiffed. "Why my fault, Sammy?"

"You were the one who wanted to expose *your children* to music. And
now that you have one who's just as obsessed as you are, you think there's
something wrong with him. Leave the boy alone, M.J."

"Oh, now they are my children?"

He smiled. "They were always your children, Mrs. Cole. You've reminded me of that fact more times than I've been able to count these
past twenty-two years."

She pressed a kiss on his shoulder before rising slightly to kiss the back
of his neck. Her kisses and mouth became bolder as she moved over him
and gently pushed him onto his back.

Bracing her hands against his shoulders, she charted a path with her mouth from his throat and through the crisp hair on his chest. At forty-eight Samuel Cole still had a body that was as firm and solid as their son's.

Wrapping his arms around her body, Samuel reversed their positions and worshipped his wife's body with his mouth and hands. He cradled her face, moaning softly when her hand closed around his erection and guided his hardness into her warm, pulsing flesh. Moaning in unison, they found the tempo that bound their bodies and hearts together.

For a few exquisite moments Samuel was able to dismiss the pain, horror, and disappointment poured out on paper by a woman who'd set aside her pride and come to him not for herself, but for her son.

Samuel wanted to stop reading, put the letters back into the carton, seal it, and mail it back to Teresa, but he couldn't. Like an addictive drug, they'd pulled him in and refused to let him go.

One day blurred into the next as he cloistered himself behind the closed door. The decades passed by with the hours . . . 1930, 1931, 1932, 1933 . . .

There were only two letters in the bundle that began in the year 1946.

April 25, 1946
Dear Samuel,

Joshua turned 16 today. He did a lot of growing this past year. He is now six-one and weighs close to 170 pounds. He's very quiet and seldom smiles. Girls come by constantly to ask for him, but he tells me to send them away because they interfere with his studies. There was a girl he seemed to like a lot, but that was more than a year ago—before we moved in with Mama and Papa.

I know I told you in a prior letter that we moved in with my parents after Everett sold the cramped little place he bought after you fired him. It was only today that I found out why he walked out on us. Joshua confessed to me that he told Everett, "Do not sleep here tonight, because if you do, then you'll wake up in hell." Everett believed him, because he got up one day, put on his clothes, and that was the last time I saw him. But before he walked out he told Joshua, "I only stayed because of the money, because why else would I marry a whore?" My son was able to do what I had been unable to do for so many years—stop the physical abuse with one threat.

I had to convince Joshua that I had gone back to Everett because I believed a boy needed a man in his life, even one as cruel as Everett Kirkland. But now I know better. I should have and could have raised my son by myself. Divorced women and widows do it all the time, but I was too much of a coward to want to do it alone.

Joshua, who has always believed Everett was his father, wanted to know everything. I told him everything. He knows you are his father.

I have enclosed a photograph of him for you to see what a fine young man he has become.

I was surprised when he asked me what I wanted. And again I was forthcoming when I told him, "What I want I can't have. What I wanted I could never have."

Teresa

Samuel stared at the photograph of a tall, slender boy with hair so light in color that it appeared silver. He'd stared directly at the person who had taken the picture, with no expression on his face. Samuel couldn't discern the color of his eyes, but probably they were the same color as Teresa's. He looked like his mother.

Samuel sat motionless, staring at the face of a boy he'd come to know in name only. And knowing his name had allowed him to remain detached. It did not permit him to feel anything for a human he'd helped create through the most intimate act known to a man and woman.

Samuel was angry, angry with Teresa for thrusting the stranger into his life now that he had a face to go along with the name. A muscle twitched nervously at his jaw when he picked up the remaining envelope.

May 18, 1946

Samuel,

Joshua has decided where he wants to go to college: the United States Military Academy at West Point. If he is able to gain entrance, then there is no tuition cost.

I know he is concerned about money, but I told him that I have saved some money, and with what I earn working at the hospital I will be able to cover the costs for tuition and books at Florida A&T.

What he doesn't know and I will never tell him is that his mother had become a thief when she pilfered money from Everett's pocket whenever he drank so much that he didn't know what day it was or if it was day or night. I don't know if it is illegal for a wife to take money from her husband when he doesn't give her any, so maybe I am a thief, but no one judges me more severely than I do myself.

I am going to find out what it takes to get Joshua into West Point. My son has never asked for anything, so I will do whatever it takes to grant his wish.

Teresa

Samuel was relieved and saddened that there were no more letters. It had been a way of spending time with Teresa that was guilt-free. He could see her, touch her, and smell her without her being there.

He knew she wanted him as much as he wanted her, and would always want her, but not enough to risk losing his wife.

Martin's direct flight from San Jose, Costa Rica, landed at the West Palm Beach Airport several hours after the sun had set. He took a taxi directly to the office instead of going home. He wanted to leave the blueprints and the construction reports for his father, and he also wanted to pick up his car.

He took the elevator to the floor housing ColeDiz, walked the length of the carpeted hallway, and unlocked the door that led directly to Samuel's private office. He was shocked to discover that his father hadn't gone home. Samuel lay on a leather sofa, an arm over his face.

"Dad?"

Samuel lowered his arm, swung his legs over the side of the sofa, and stared at his son as if he were an apparition. "You're back."

"You sound disappointed," Martin teased, grinning.

"No. Not at all."

Martin's gaze swung to the stack of letters on his father's desk. "What are those?"

Massaging his temples with his fingertips, Samuel shook his head. "It's a long story."

"How long will it take to tell?"

"All night."

Martin placed the cardboard tube containing the plans and a leather-bound report on a credenza. "Does Mother know where you are?"

Samuel nodded, then rolled his head on his shoulders. "I called her a little while ago to let her know I was working late." He had to catch up with the reports he'd neglected when the carton filled with Teresa's letters was delivered. It had taken him four days to read everything she'd written.

Martin placed an arm around his father's broad shoulders. "Let's go over to Roadie's where we can talk and eat."

Samuel waited until Martin had eaten most of his dinner of oxtail stew, rice, and buttered lima beans before he revealed what had remained a best-kept secret for seventeen years.

Martin's black eyes flashed outrage. "You cheated on my mother," he said through clenched teeth.

Not able to meet his son's gaze, Samuel stared over his shoulder. "I'm ashamed to say I did."

"How many times? With how many women?"

"Martin, don't," he pleaded softly.

"Don't what, Dad? Don't make you feel guilty? What about my mother?"

"No, Martin. Your mother had her way of punishing me for my indiscretion."

"You call getting another woman pregnant an indiscretion?" He pounded the table with his fist, rattling dishes and cutlery. "I have another brother, Father!"

Samuel knew Martin was close to losing control of his quick temper. Whenever he referred to him as Father it usually foretold a hostile encounter.

"Yes, Martin. You have another brother. One I've never met. One I saw today for the first time in a photograph. A sixteen-year-old boy who wants to go to West Point, a boy whose mother thinks I have the political influence to grant him his wish."

"What's his name?"

"Joshua Kirkland."

"Where does he live?"

"Miami."

Martin ran a hand over his face. "You're going to help him, Dad." He lowered his hand, glaring at Samuel. "You owe him that much."

Pushing back his chair, Samuel stood up, put his hand in his pocket, and left a bill on the table. "I'm tired, Martin. I'm going home to my wife. Are you going to drive me home, or should I call a taxi to take me back to the office so I can pick up my car?"

Martin came to his feet. His father had dismissed him. "I'll drive you home."

38

The Lord makes poor and makes rich; he brings low, he also exalts.

—1 Samuel 11:6

Miami, Florida—April 15, 1947

It had taken Martin Diaz Cole six months and three attempts to garner the nerve to contact his half brother. He'd arranged to meet Joshua Kirkland following his Jamaican vacation. Instead of flying into West Palm Beach, he had changed his ticket for Miami.

He'd spent more than an hour waiting in a hotel lobby filled with players from the Homestead Grays and the Philadelphia Stars. They had gathered around a radio to witness history in the making. Jackie Robinson, the first Negro to integrate major league baseball, was scheduled to play his first game for the Brooklyn Dodgers at New York's Ebbetts Field in Brooklyn, New York. A rousing cheer went up when Jackie Robinson's name came through the speakers.

All the excitement paled when Martin rose to his feet on shaky legs when he spied a tall, blond boy walking across the lobby. Staring numbly, he watched Joshua Kirkland make his way toward him. There was something about him that reminded him of their father.

Martin's relationship with Samuel had changed. The easygoing camaraderie and an openness that made them more like friends than father and son were missing, and in their place was a repressed hostility.

His enmity wasn't the result of his father's adultery—that was between husband and wife—but Samuel's decision to deny the existence of a son who had as much right to the Cole legacy as Nancy, Josephine, and David.

He studied his brother intently. Joshua's hair appeared silver against his bronzed face. He had the slimness of a boy who had yet to put on the muscle of an adult male. A knowing smile creased the dimples in Martin's cheeks. Joshua had inherited Samuel's walk.

A shiver shook Martin as he noticed his younger half brother's eyes. The light green eyes were cold, icy, and he wondered whether he'd made a mistake to contact him. He'd come this far, and knew he had to see it through or live the rest of his life plagued by questions that would haunt him to his grave.

He extended his right hand. "Hello. I'm Martin."

Joshua hesitated, staring at the large, groomed hand that belonged to the tall, well-dressed man who claimed they were brothers. He shook it with a barely perceptible nod of his head.

"Joshua."

He has Dad's hands, Martin mused. Those who weren't familiar with Samuel Cole would never connect him with Joshua Kirkland, but Martin, although the similarities were subtle, knew the boy was undoubtedly his father's son.

"Would you like to go somewhere and talk, or stay here?"

"Here is okay."

Martin gestured to two facing chairs separated by a small round table. "We can sit over there." He waited for Joshua to sit, then sat down opposite him. He smiled when he and Joshua crossed a leg over the other knee as if they'd pantomimed the motion. Despite their obvious physical differences, there was no doubt both inherited traits particular to Samuel Cole.

"How are you?" Martin asked, hoping to put his brother at ease when he stared directly at him, his cold gaze straining what was already an uncomfortable situation.

"Well."

Martin frowned. It was the second one-word answer Joshua had delivered in a deep, emotionless tone.

"You don't talk much, do you?"

A pale eyebrow lifted slightly. "I only speak when I have something to say, not just to hear the sound of my own voice."

Bristling from the reprimand, Martin lowered his leg, clasping and unclasped his hands together between his knees. "I don't know about you, but I am just as uncomfortable as you are."

"I'm not uncomfortable."

"What are you?"

"Curious as to why you'd want to meet me."

Martin's frown deepened to an angry scowl. "We are brothers, Joshua."

"So you say," he said in a voice that was as flat as his expression.

"What the hell are you so angry about? What went on between our parents has nothing to do with us."

"You're wrong, Martin. It has everything to do with us. You're Samuel Cole's legitimate son and heir. I'm his bastard."

Joshua's statement as to their existence was so matter-of-fact that Martin almost laughed. "You are still his flesh and blood."

A feral grin pulled a corner of Joshua's firm mouth up. "Why isn't he here saying this? Did the cowardly son of a bitch send you to extend the olive branch? Well, you can tell him that I won't genuflect to his heir apparent because of my West Point acceptance. Tell him I would've made it without his interference."

Martin reacted as if Joshua had struck him across the face. Never had he seen such bitterness in someone so young. Had his mother spewed her venom, fueling her son's hatred for his biological father?

Struggling to control his temper, and not wanting to lash out at the brother who, up until six months ago, he hadn't known existed, Martin sat back and folded his arms over his chest.

"Samuel doesn't know I'm meeting with you."

The light green eyes darkened with an unnamed emotion. "So why did *you* contact me?"

"I'm not certain."

Joshua stood up in one, smooth motion. "If that's the case, then I'm leaving. I have to study for a calculus final."

"Sit down!" Joshua had popped up and now down again like a jack-in-the-box with Martin's unexpected outburst. "Please," he added softly. The command and the teenager's obedience had established Martin's position as Joshua's brother, his older brother.

An uncomfortable silence followed Martin's outburst. The seconds ticked off as the two older sons of Samuel Cole regarded each other with cold stares.

Joshua broke the silence. "How long have you known about me?"

Martin told Joshua how he'd come to know of his existence. "I was so angry with Dad that I wanted to hit him. All I could think of was what he had done to my mother. What she must have gone through once she discovered her husband had fathered a child out of wedlock.

"Then I thought of your mother, her pain, the shame of having to marry a man she hated so she wouldn't be branded with the scarlet letter." Leaning forward on the chair, he rested a hand over Joshua's. "Then I thought of you, what you had to go through with Everett Kirkland, what your mother had to put up with for so many years. There are no winners, Joshua. Everyone involved with what has become a dirty little secret was a loser."

Joshua shook off the hand covering his. "That's where you're wrong, Martin. The men won and the women lost. My mother was forced to marry a man she hated, a man who forced himself on her because he felt it was his right to rape her. Everett Kirkland was a selfish, manipulative, stingy son of a bitch—"

"You may not look like Dad, but there is no doubt you're his boy," Martin said, interrupting Joshua.

Joshua's eyes widened. "What are you talking about?"

"You cuss like a Cole."

A hint of a smile crinkled the teenager's eyes before he lowered his head. "I'm sorry."

"Never apologize for your feelings or beliefs," Martin chastised quietly.

Joshua's head came up. "What about your father, Martin? Will he ever apologize to my mother for selling her into bondage? Has he apologized to your mother for being an adulterer? Has he apologized to his legitimate children that they have a half brother who might mess up their perfect little world if or when he decides he wants his rightful share of their inheritance? I thought not," he continued when Martin's expression did not change. "Well, you don't ever have to worry about me telling anyone about the Coles' dirty little secret. I'd die before I acknowledge that the blood of Samuel Cole runs in my veins."

"You're angry, Joshua, and you have a right to your anger. When Samuel told me about you I'm ashamed to admit that I'd grown up believing my father was the perfect husband and the perfect father.

"I stopped speaking to him. I went into the office, did my work, and related to him like any other ColeDiz International employee. Whenever we sat down to dinner together I had to pretend all was well between us so my mother wouldn't suspect something was wrong."

For a long moment, Joshua looked back at Martin. "Your mother doesn't know you know?"

"No."

"Are you going to tell her?"

"I don't know. Are you going to tell your mother about me?"

Joshua lifted his eyebrows. "I don't know."

"Tell her, Joshua, that you met me. Tell her that I'm going to be the older brother who will be there for you."

Joshua shook his head. "You can't absolve Samuel of his guilt or what should have been his responsibility by being *here* for me."

"This has nothing to do with Samuel. This is between us. And it will remain between us."

Joshua stared down at the toes of his shoes, then Martin's. The difference was startling. His older brother wore a fashionable lightweight suit and highly polished leather shoes; his own shabby attire was a pair of faded cotton slacks, a white shirt, open at the throat, and a seersucker jacket, one Everett Kirkland had left behind in his haste to leave. They were as different as night and day in so many ways: appearance and temperament. And the most obvious difference was money.

His head came up and he gave his brother a long, penetrating look. "What do you want from me, Martin?"

The tense lines in Martin's face vanished when he smiled. "I want you to give me the opportunity to become a brother to you, and I want you to learn to trust me enough to come to me if you want or need anything. And I'd like for us to get together again before you leave for college."

Joshua's impassive expression did not change. "What you're asking isn't unreasonable."

Martin wanted to reach over and shake his brother until he showed some emotion. What type of childhood, he wondered, had he had that would not permit a teenage boy to laugh or smile? What horrors had he endured at the hands of his stepfather? How many times had he witnessed Everett Kirkland hitting his mother?

A loud roar erupted in the lobby as the ballplayers slapped one another on the back. Jackie Robinson had gotten his first major league hit. It was official; it was history; it was a momentous day.

The brothers looked at each other and smiled. It was a great day for Jackie Robinson, but a sad one for most of the older players in the Negro Leagues who'd spent all of their lives waiting for their chance to play in the majors.

Joshua stood up, Martin following. "I have to leave now." He extended his hand. "Thank you."

Ignoring the proffered hand, Martin wrapped his arms around Joshua's shoulders, kissing him on each cheek. "Take care of yourself," he said in Spanish. "And don't forget to call me."

"I'll call," Joshua replied in the same language.

Releasing him, Martin reached into the breast pocket of his jacket, withdrew an envelope, and pushed it into Joshua's jacket pocket. "It's a little something for your birthday and graduation."

He didn't give the teenager the opportunity to protest or refuse when he turned, wending his way through the throng in the hotel lobby and disappeared out a rear door where a driver waited to drive him to Miami Airport.

Joshua, tormented by confusing emotions, left the hotel. He would celebrate his seventeenth birthday in another week, he'd received his acceptance letter from West Point, and he met his brother for the first time.

He'd agreed to meet Martin Cole because he wanted answers. He hadn't gotten the answers because he hadn't asked the questions, but he felt something for Martin he did not want to feel: kinship.

39

That's all there is; there isn't any more.

—Ethel Barrymore

West Palm Beach, Florida—April 25, 1947

Martin stood in the doorway to Samuel's office. His father sat in his chair, his back to the door. "Dad?"

Samuel swiveled in the chair. A melancholy frown flitted over his face before he concealed it with a tentative smile. "Yes, Martin?"

"May I come in?"

"Why are you asking permission to enter my office?"

Martin walked in, closing the door. "I know things haven't been well between us for some time—"

"That was your choice," Samuel said heatedly, interrupting him.

"I didn't come here to argue with you."

"Why have you come, son?"

Sitting down on the chair he'd occupied countless times, Martin crossed one leg over the other. "I want to talk to you about Joshua."

Samuel's expression stilled, grew serious. "What about him?"

"Do you know what today is?"

"Yes, I do. It's Joshua's birthday."

"Good for you," Martin said facetiously.

"What the hell are you trying to say?"

"I met your other son. On my way back from Jamaica I stopped in

Miami and we got together." Martin ignored his father's audible gasp. "He's an incredible young man, Dad."

Samuel wanted to tell Martin that Teresa, at nineteen, was incredible. "I'm glad to hear that."

"I think it's time you tell Nancy, Josephine, and David that they have a half brother."

Samuel felt the muscles in his stomach tighten. "No."

Martin leaned closer. "You have to, Dad."

"No, I don't!"

"Yes, you do!" Martin had raised his normally soft voice. "It would go better if you tell them rather than have a stranger uncover the truth. You've hidden Joshua for seventeen years. It's time for the truth to be told."

Samuel glared at his firstborn. It was the first time he'd challenged him, and he intuitively knew it wouldn't be the last. "I can't do it."

Martin rested a hand on his father's shoulder. "Yes, you can, Dad. Either you tell them or I will."

He shook off the hand. "This is none of your business."

"You think it isn't? I have a brother, someone whom I share blood with, and you tell me that it's none of my business? He is as much my business as David and my sisters. Mother wants us home in time for dinner because the girls are only going to be here for the weekend. This will be your chance to put your past to rest."

Martin gave his father a lingering glare before standing and walking out of the office.

M.J. smiled across the length of the table at Samuel. It wasn't often that they had all of their children together nowadays. Martin spent several days each month traveling for ColeDiz, Nancy would complete her senior year at Howard University, and Josephine her freshman year at Spelman College.

M.J. had taken special care preparing her children's favorite dishes. It had been a while since she'd enjoyed cooking in her remodeled kitchen.

Samuel cleared his voice, getting everyone's attention. "I'd like to say something before dessert is served." He met Martin's unwavering black eyes. "Today marks the birthday of someone I've denied for more than seventeen years."

"No, Samuel," M.J. sobbed softly.

Everyone seated at the table turned to look at her, everyone but Martin.

"M.J., I have to," Samuel said almost pleadingly. "I have another son."

Nancy froze. "What are you talking about, Daddy?"

"I had an affair with—"

"You had an affair!" Josephine screamed. "You cheated on Mother with another woman?" Her dark eyes shimmered with tears.

Samuel sat up straighter, as if gathering courage to tell his family what had been kept secret for a long time. "Yes. I'm ashamed to say I did cheat on your mother."

"Was she your mistress, Daddy?" Nancy asked.

"No, she wasn't. We spent less than a week together."

"I don't care if you spent an hour together," Nancy screamed. "The fact remains you have a bastard!"

Josephine slammed her hand on the table, rattling silver and china. "He will never be my brother."

"Nor mine," Nancy said, pushing away from the table.

M.J. could not stop her tears. They flowed down her cheeks unchecked.

David got up and went to his mother. "Don't cry, Mama. Please, don't cry."

His sisters joined him, as they attempted to comfort M.J. They pulled her from her chair and led her out of the dining room, leaving Samuel and Martin staring at each other.

Samuel slumped in his chair, seemingly aging twenty years. He stared down at the heirloom tablecloth M.J. had brought with her from Cuba. "I just divided my family tonight. My wife and my children hate me."

Crossing his arms over his chest, Martin shook his head. "You're wrong, Dad. You divided your family the first time you slept with Teresa Maldonado. Nothing can change what you did to my mother or to Joshua's mother. And nothing will change the fact that Joshua Kirkland is family."

Samuel looked up, his eyes filled with bitterness. "He will never become a part of *this* family."

"That is your choice, Dad. But for now he is the Coles' best-kept secret."

Pushing back from the table, Martin walked out of the dining room and out of the house. He needed to be alone to sort out what he would have to do to heal the wounds and bring everyone together as one family—regardless of whether they were Cole or Kirkland.